D0914715

THE HOUSE AT SUNSET

By Norah Lofts

THE HOUSE AT SUNSET

NORAH LOFTS

ÆONIAN
PRESS

Aeonian Press Inc.
Box 1200
Mattituck, NY 11952

Republished 1978 by special arrangement

*Library of Congress Catalog Card Number 62–17018
Copyright © 1962 by Norah Lofts
All Rights Reserved
Printed in the United States of America*

The House at Sunset

By Norah Lofts

NORAH LOFTS lives with her husband and son in a centuries-old house on a quiet street in Bury St. Edmunds, the county town of West Suffolk, a place that American visitors think of as "typically English." Nearby is the ruin of a great 11th-Century abbey—where the barons first resolved to force King John to sign the Magna Carta. The town's 18th-Century Angel Inn was mentioned in Dickens' *Pickwick Papers.* It is easy to see why Norah Lofts, living in a town with this kind of lore, writes so beautifully of the past.

FELICITY HATTON'S TALE

At the age of seven I was a skilful pickpocket. I could also sew neatly, write a tolerable hand, make a curtsey and a correct introduction, dance a little, and play simple tunes on the harpsichord. I saw nothing incongruous in being equally at ease in the reeking streets about Aldermanbury Postern and in a drawing room in St. Albans Street, nothing strange in one day running barefoot and the next mincing along in silk hose and satin slippers. All the seven crowded years of my life had been spent in violent oscillation between one extreme of fortune and the other, each change governed by Father's luck at the card table.

When I was seven Father was thirty-eight and had been playing cards for twenty-one years, ever since, as a boy of seventeen, he had been sent up from the country to collect payment from a Smithfield butcher for some bullocks destined for the Christmas market. He'd got into a card game at a tavern and lost all the money, slept out that night in an alley, got up in the morning and sold his topcoat, hat, waistcoat, and shirt, and, with the proceeds in his hand, rushed back to join the game. It took him, he'd say, laughing, three days to get back the sum of money he had been sent to collect, and when he had it he sent it to his father with a message to say that he had found his vocation and would not be returning to Suffolk. "Not that they'd have missed me; I was one of eight," he said.

He was a man of imperturbable good humour, for all that he had the reddish hair which is supposed to denote hasty temper; I can truly say that I never saw him put out. He'd come home and say to Mother, "Annabel, we're ruined," or, "Annabel, we're rich," and a deaf person in the room would never have known whether he was announcing good news or disaster. He had two advantages over Mother and me; when our fortunes were at low ebb and we lived in squalor he could always get away, to Whaddon's where he played most often, or to Mariana's in Soho Square, or to one of the private houses he frequented; and his good clothes were never sold or pawned; they and his gold watch and his silver-knobbed cane were part of his stock in trade, without which he would not have been welcome at any of his haunts. His clothes and his unassailable jauntiness enabled him to remain detached from his background, when it was bad. He could emerge from our one wretched room in a filthy, mouldering rookery of a house as neat and clean and self-possessed as a tomcat. And he could pass along streets and through alleys where any other man thus attired would have been jeered at and spattered with filth; everyone seemed to know him by the name of "Gentleman Johnny"—his name in fact was Christopher—and his word about the merits of a race horse or a prize fighter was eagerly sought and much valued.

I realise now that my mother must have been deeply, irrevocably in love with him, for she accepted all the ups and downs, the changes, the shocks, the humiliations without complaint. Yet she was a woman of character, fiercely respectable. I was always a little, more than a little, frightened of her. In fact, though it sounds a shameful thing to say, one of the comforts of our days of poverty for me was that sooner or later she was obliged to look for work and thus divert her attention from the job of bringing me up properly. This bringing-up, concentrated as it had to be into the periods when Father was doing well, could become very tedious.

Mother herself had been properly brought up; she was an orphan with a small but sufficient income of her own when she married Father; that had long since gone the way of everything that Christopher Hatton ever got his hands on. In our bad days Mother made a little money by plying one of her two self-taught skills; she was good at dressing hair, either on the head or made into wigs, and she could wash and iron the most delicate fabrics. Sometimes she could get a job where both her arts were employed at one of the theatres; she would also build for herself a clientele of ladies—not of the first rank —who employed no body maid or regular hairdresser and merely wished to look fine occasionally. She was hampered, of course, because as soon as she had a number of regular or semi-regular customers, Father's luck would swing round and off we'd go into that other world where she could have her own hair dressed, her own muslins washed by hired hands should she so choose. And then all her energy and purpose went into making up time lost in my education.

We had no friends. There was never time. Often enough, in the comfortable, even luxurious lodgings in which our affluent periods were spent, we would strike up an acquaintance with people who lived in other parts of the same house, or next door, or on the opposite side of the road. There would be tea-drinkings, musical evenings, outings to the theatre, drives into the country. But all such friendships died young; the morning would come when Father would say, "Annabel, we're ruined." On those occasions Mother allowed herself a momentary relaxation from strict truthfulness; to anyone likely to be interested in our whereabouts she would say that we were returning to the country. Then would begin the tramping round, the frantic search for that rare thing, a really cheap lodging-house with no prostitutes in it. Mother detested prostitutes and could detect one at a distance of fifty yards. To do her justice she had an equally keen eye for what she called "a decent poor woman," and there was usually such a one somewhere handy, and to her charge I would be committed when the time came for Mother to begin looking for work. I knew the rules governing my behaviour in Houndsditch as well as those that must be observed in Bloomsbury Square; they were different, but equally strict. In Houndsditch—or Moorfields, or Aldermanbury, or once, when we had to go across the river, in a dreadful place called Pickled Herring Street—I was to keep myself to myself. I was not to play with other children in the gutter, not to look at, leave alone speak to, any man, not to enter anyone else's room, except the "decent poor woman's," if there was one.

The rules were impossible to keep. Quite apart from the fact that the life in the streets exerted an irresistible fascination over me, I was young and pliable, bound to become part of my background. Father had his "Gentleman Johnny" immunity and Mother always somehow managed to establish herself as a superior being; somebody would be scalded, or fall downstairs, or be taken by premature labour, and there'd be Missus 'Atton, cool, sensible, and resourceful, knowing exactly what to do and doing it, quite kindly but making everyone else feel a fool. I was just a little girl, remarkably small for my age, with a mop of peculiar-coloured hair; and had I tried to obey the rules, especially the one about keeping myself to myself, my life would not have been worth living.

Real knowledge drifts into the mind imperceptibly. It may be possible to say that on a certain day in March in a certain year you mastered the multiplication rule in arithmetic or how to stitch a buttonhole, but who could say that on such and such a date he acquired worldly wisdom? Somewhere, at some time before I had my fifth birthday, I had learned that in every slum street there are two gangs, that each is headed by a boy whose leadership is as plainly marked as though he wore a label round his neck, and that of the two leaders the one who is physically smaller is the one most to be feared. Any newcomer to the area is well advised to join up with this boy as soon as possible.

Once I had learned this, and applied what I learned, life in the slum streets became easy, even enjoyable. All the gangs to which, for brief periods, I belonged until I was almost seven, were made up of very young children, for the offspring of the poor begin work early, and our activities were confined to noisy play and pretty harmless mischief and begging. Then, when I was six and a half, after a period of prolonged prosperity, we moved into a house in a cul-de-sac called Tun's Yard at the back of the market in Covent Garden, and there I fell in with a boy named Fingers.

Even to me he was something new in that he had no home at all and never had had, he said; he also said that he had never known either of his parents. He claimed that he had been born in the market, on a sack, and left there like an unwanted kitten. I said, "Somebody must have fed you or you'd have died." And he said somebody did, he could remember—and it was the first thing he did remember—gnawing a raw turnip. There must have been an element of truth in this, though I do not believe that a newborn baby could eat raw turnip, but it was a fact that even when our gang had been lucky and made a haul and Fingers could have bought meat pies, or pigs' trotters, or oysters or eels, he would set off in search of a raw turnip. He had no idea of his own age; to me he seemed tall, almost grown-up, and his gang was not organised for play or mischief; they were all professional pickpockets. Within a week or two I was also a pickpocket, and a valued member of the gang.

We operated wherever there was a crowd; failing to find a crowd, we made one. Two of the boys would start a fight, or turn cartwheels, or chant some insulting rhyming lines about some important person, or do a caricature act of a mad parson preaching—anything that would make people stop and stare and forget to guard their pockets. Then another couple of us —or three if the crowd warranted it—would feign an interest in whatever was happening and close in. There was something comic in hearing a man say, "Damn you, boy, you trod on my toe!" when he might in justice have complained, "You took my purse!"

My particular value lay in my small size—at seven I was no bigger than a child of five—and in the fact that however poorly I might be dressed, I was clean and mended; I didn't look like a street child. I was, at that time, pretty, and I could lisp at will. Once when I was caught in the very act I escaped without arousing the least suspicion. My victim that day was plainly a cautious man, mindful of all contingencies, and his watch was fastened in some way to the inside of his pocket, so that instead of sliding out under my feather-like touch it jerked his waistcoat. He looked down and there was I with my hand on his fob. There was no time to think, so it must have been instinct which made me refrain from withdrawing my hand, to look up at him and smile and say, "Pwetty!"

"So are you, my little dear," he said.

I made my bob. "Thank you, sir."

"Where's your mother?" he asked.

I chose a respectable-looking matron on the fringe of the crowd.

"Over there. Good-bye."

"You stay close to her," he called after me.

Another thing which made me popular with the gang was the fact that I was never over-anxious for my full share of any loot. Whatever I took home must be explained, so usually I contented myself with what would buy me my fill of gingerbread or meat pies. Once, when things were very bad at home, I did go back with a shilling which I said I had found in the street; and as I grew older and was less supervised by decent poor women I often took home foodstuff, always with some specious story. "There was a man selling herrings and his basket broke. I helped to pick them up and he gave me four for my pains." "The woman at the bakehouse asked me to carry a cake for her and gave me these buns." In the same way I never used, in Mother's hearing, any of the words or expressions or even the pronunciations which I picked up from my associates; I grew up to be what might be called bilingual, my one tongue the Cockney thieves' talk, my other the affected speech of the well-brought-up little Miss.

So I lived my double life, and the only sign that there was anything peculiar about me lay in the behaviour of those other well-brought-up little misses with whom, in our prosperous days, I came into contact. Washed, combed, bemuslined and beribboned, and on my very best behaviour, I would be sent, from time to time, to various dancing classes, and even twice to small girls' schools. It was always the same; the other children, with their unblunted senses, could always sniff out the intruder. In return I despised them, wondering just how long they'd last in Pickled Herring Street.

I grew up to be a facile liar, but until the day of my eleventh birthday, which was in May 1736, all my lies had been expedient rather than deliberately contrived. On that day we were about as low as a family could fall; Father had had no luck for weeks on end and Mother was reduced to doing plain heavy washing as opposed to the daintier work she preferred. We were living in one small room, owed a week's rent, and were to be turned out on Saturday unless we paid up. Also, on this day Father decided, and Mother agreed with him, that his last good shirt was past further wear.

Mother said, "Well, there's no help for it; the time has come." She took a pair of scissors, made a little slit in her bodice, and took out a ring.

"My grandmother Allison gave it to me on her deathbed," she said. "It was always too small for me, so I hid it away."

I was sent to pawn it. Mother was explicit in her instructions; it was a gold ring, set with an emerald, and I was not to accept less than a pound for it. I was to put it on my middle finger and keep my hand clenched.

There is no knowing what it is that makes certain things of

importance to certain people. There is that instant sense of belonging. I've felt it once or twice in my life since then, and know what a powerful emotion it is. April and May that year had been unusually sunny and my hands were tanned light brown; they were bony and unbeautiful, but the ring, sliding onto my middle finger, worked a miracle. It belonged there, and so far as I had any say in the matter, there it was going to stay.

I ran off in search of Fingers, whom I found in the third place I looked, a yard off the Haymarket where he often slept. I simply told him that I must have a pound, reminding him of the numerous occasions when I had taken far less than my cut. He agreed that so much and more was owing to me, but said he was "skint," if we wanted money immediately we must do a job, and since there were only the two of us we'd better play the old lark of his having a fit—his fits were very convincing.

During the last two low ebbs of our fortunes I had found myself less and less inclined to enjoy the process of picking pockets; I'd lost my sense of immunity and with it the zest which made stealing seem like part of a game. However, on this day, all went well, except that some would-be kindly woman threw a bucket of water over Fingers in an effort to bring him round. We collected two watches—one with several heavy seals on its fob, and a bracelet, and Fingers went off alone, as always, to dispose of the loot. None of us ever knew the name or address of Fingers' fence. I waited where he had told me to and after a long time he came panting back and gave me a sovereign. It was then quite late in the day, but not quite late enough for my purpose, so we went and ate our fill of pigs' trotters and then drank coffee at a stall and parted. When I was almost home I began to rub my eyes hard to redden them, and scrubbed my nose until it swelled.

Father and Mother were both waiting for me, agitated and impatient. I said that I had been all over London, into every pawnshop, every gold- and silversmith's, and everywhere been told the same thing—the ring was valueless; the setting wasn't gold but some cleverly made base substitute, and the green stone was nothing but green glass. Nobody, I said, would advance me twopence on it.

Father might be a reckless gambler, but so far as I know he was perfectly honest, while Mother was the soul of honour; it occurred to neither of them to suspect me. Father immediately began to fret about his shirtless state, while Mother was simply puzzled; why, she demanded to know, hadn't a setting of base metal tarnished in all this time, and if the stone were glass, why hadn't it chipped. "My grandmother Allison was a woman for whom the very best was just good enough. Why should she cherish, and leave to me, her favourite grandchild, a trinket of no value?"

"Sentiment," Father said. "All women are prone to it." That was as near as a man of his nature could ever come to rebuking her for having kept the ring hidden through so many crises.

I gave the bad news time to sink in and then said:

"But I got the money."

"What money?"

"The pound you needed."

"In the name of goodness, how?"

"A gentleman gave it to me. I was crying and he stopped and asked why and I told him." I managed to snuffle a little. "He said," I glanced at Father, "that he'd just won a good sum on a cockfight and wouldn't miss a pound."

"I've done the same many a time when my luck was in," Father said. "Once in Drury Lane there was an old crone . . ."

"Where *was* this?" Mother demanded, cutting short Father's tale.

"Outside St. Anne's Church—I'd just been turned away from the shop in Leicester Street." I thought that it happening outside a church might cast an air of respectability over the tale. Mother was far from satisfied, however; had I ever

seen the man before, should I know him again, what else was
said, were names exchanged? On and on she went. I stuck to
my simple story; I was crying from disappointment, the man
asked me what ailed me, and I told him and he said that was
easily remedied and gave me the money.

"Were many people about?"

"Oh, scores. Coming out of the church; I think there'd been
a service."

That seemed to satisfy her a little. I knew quite well what
was in her mind and was not surprised when, a few days later,
she gave me an admonitory talk about the dangers which lay
in wait for girls who were out alone and insufficiently careful.
Poor dear, she was miserably embarrassed, torn between her
natural reticence in such matters and what she felt it her duty
to tell me. Had we been on really easy terms with one another,
I would have said, "Don't distress yourself, I know it all." As
it was I kept silent and she blundered on, blushing, almost
apologising for human beings being what they were; and it
says a good deal for her own fundamental innocence that she
should have imagined that I could possibly have reached the
age of eleven, living in the circumstances, and retained any
innocence at all. It was nothing extraordinary, in our slum
streets, to see a couple copulating in a doorway, and within
five minutes' walk of where Mother sat, blushing and euphe-
mising, I could have pointed her out a girl familiarly known
as Poll Knock-on-the-wall-for-threepence.

Yet, for all this, my knowledge remained a thing of eye and
ear and mind, in no way concerned with any experience: I
ran around with Fingers and the rest of them, and we all used
foul words and filthy expressions, and enjoyed lewd jokes, but
there was no sexual traffic within the gang at all. There may
have been an unwritten rule about it, since any personal at-
tachments would have led to quarrels and lack of loyalty, but
I think it was also accounted for by the fact that a constant
low diet, a daily preoccupation with the filling of one's belly

and the finding of somewhere snug for the night, absorbed too much energy. Also, of course, I and the two or three other girls who drifted in and out of the gang were treated and looked upon as though we were boys. Fingers, Jimmy, and the rest, when they thought about sex at all, thought in terms of good fat whores, gaudily dressed and highly scented.

Mother ended her talk by saying that crying in the open street showed a lack of that self-control which was a mark of good breeding. She saw nothing humourous in this at all, nothing incongruous. I did, for in order to avoid looking at her I was staring at my own bare feet. At the end of the talk I ventured to ask:

"What about the ring?"

"It failed me in my hour of need," she said with sudden bitterness. "It's of no use to me."

"It's still pretty," I said.

"If you admire it, you can keep it," she said.

After that, during our bad times I wore it by day slung on a bit of string around my neck, and on my finger at night; in our good times I wore it openly, and even once persuaded Mother to make me a velvet dress which exactly matched the emerald colour.

II

Two more years went by, with their fluctuating fortunes. Mother began to be concerned about my future, and the ominous name of Miss Bellsize was mentioned with increasing frequency. Mother was determined that I should grow up with some recognised trade at my finger tips; she greatly regretted, she said, that she herself had been reared in idleness and had nothing to fall back upon in bad times. Her work in the theatres and amongst the middling sort of ladies kept her abreast of the fashion changes, and dresses, she said, were becoming more and more elaborate, with more material, more stitching, and more decoration every day. Therefore, she argued, a properly trained dressmaker need never lack a job. I was to be apprenticed to Miss Bellsize, a woman who, probably without knowing it, Mother envied more than any other.

I hated plain sewing with all my heart, and embroidery only slightly less; for me one of the penances of our prosperous periods was that Mother had more time to devote to teaching me stitches. Forced to sit and sew, I did it quite well, partly to avoid Mother's displeasure, partly because something in me detested a sloppy job. Faced, however, with the prospect of becoming a sempstress, I plucked up courage to tell Mother that I disliked needlework.

"What is the alternative?" she asked.

To confide a secret ambition to anyone is difficult, to do so to an unsympathetic listener is deeply embarrassing, as well, but I managed to mumble out that I should like to be an actress. Mother was shocked.

"God forbid!" she said. "There may be an exception or two, but in the main actresses are little better than women of the streets. Even those who most convincingly portray great ladies on the stage, off it are creatures of coarse manners and loose morals."

"I might prove to be one of the exceptions."

"That we shall never know, for I do not intend to put it to the test. You can rid your head of that notion at once."

"I'd sooner cook than sew."

"Any woman can cook, given stuff to cook with. Four pounds a year and live in, on the run from morning to night and your hands ruined. You'd never attain to independence that way. Miss Bellsize asks five pounds as premium—that will show you her standard—and when next I have that sum in hand I shall approach her. Then, when you have learned all she can teach you, and your father's luck is in, I shall persuade him to set you up in a modest establishment of your own. I shall solicit custom for you from amongst *my* customers."

Her usual expression was calm and somewhat sombre, but as she voiced this plan it lightened; she was seeing herself at some future time, powdering some lady's hair and telling her that her daughter had a dressmaking business of her own, had been trained by Miss Bellsize, and only needed a chance to show what she could do. The rock of respectability solid underfoot at last, immune from the precedence of King, Queen, Knave. . . .

Twice in the year between my twelfth and thirteenth birthdays I escaped Miss Bellsize by a hairsbreadth; the first time Father stood up for me; "We've been in the doldrums long enough; let the child enjoy herself for a bit," he said.

"I'm agreeable to that," Mother said, "so long as you give me the five pounds to put away safe."

He did that willingly enough; but his luck ran out more briskly and suddenly than usual that time, and he had to have the five pounds back in a hurry. He even had to pawn his watch, giving it to me with the words:

"And don't come back telling me this is worth nothing. Tompion made it and the name is writ inside."

The next time Mother had the premium in hand I was suffering from my annual nettle rash and was such a sight that anyone would have thought me poxed.

So I was thirteen and still unapprenticed, and we were back in Tun's Yard and it was June. . . .

It had been one of those blazing hot days, so pleasant in open green places, so trying in the stinking streets of the slums. In the morning I had collected from a house in Bridge Street a great bundle of muslin caps, aprons, fichus, and wrappers, and Mother and I had spent the day washing them, and drying them, a few at a time, on a line rigged up outside our one window. At five o'clock we had eaten our dinner and Father, looking as though he had a thousand pounds a year, had set out for Whaddon's; Mother had ironed for an hour and then made herself tidy and gone off to dress several heads for a ball. I finished the ironing, laying each piece neatly in a piece of linen which we used as cover for our laundry work.

For the last few months I had helped Mother much more, and more willingly than in the past. It was a frail hope, but it was a hope, that I might make myself so useful to her that she would forget about Miss Bellsize. Also the streets had lost their fascination for me. It had been a blow to me to learn, when we returned this time to Tun's Yard, that Fingers had been taken in the act of stealing and hanged at Tyburn. He'd died, they said, as a good thief should, defiant to the last and cracking jokes, but that was small comfort to me. I'd find myself thinking about him whenever my mind was disengaged, how he'd never had anything, no home, no parents, no name even; how he'd always been cheerful in a queer bitter way, and resourceful; and how, on the day when I needed the pound, he'd worked to help me to get it. I'd twist the ring on my finger and think—In a way Fingers gave me this! Another boy, Jimmy, second in importance to Fingers in the gang, had simply disappeared; a girl named Emma, about a year older than I, was now an established prostitute. Our group was dispersed and had become part of the past over which, always, a curious glamour falls. I could remember so many times when, once again thrust forth from decent society, I had gone into the alleys in search of my friends and been welcomed and called "Flick." It seemed to me, looking back, that those had been happy times, and such days mainly sunny. That, I knew, was sheer nonsense, but the knowing did nothing to lighten my mood. The lengthening bones of the body experience what are called growing pains, and the mind, with its lengthening vistas, knows them too.

On this evening, by the time I had finished ironing I was exhausted and sweaty. I went downstairs to the yard and fetched up a bucket of water, stripped myself, and washed. We had, this time, so far skirted the edge of utter destitution and I still had two dresses. One was clean, and I put it on, relishing the coolness of its touch against my newly washed skin. I combed my damp hair. In the streets, as well as being called "Flick" I was known as "Ginger," which, because ginger is a hot-tasting substance, suggests flaming red hair. Actually in me Father's bright chestnut and Mother's pale, biscuit-coloured hair had combined and mine was almost apricot-coloured. I was no longer pretty; prettiness had gone with my childhood. For one thing I was far too thin and my face had developed a funny shape, too wide at the top, too small at the bottom; it was rather like a cat's, an alley cat's, wary and distrustful, up to a point fierce and beyond that timid.

When I was ready I knotted the four corners of the linen together, leaving room for my arm to slip through, and set off. As I neared the river the air freshened, as though the water, winding its way through the massed and crowded city, brought with it a cool green breath from the countryside. I could have followed the river all the way to my destination, but it was already a little late in the day to be delivering laundry, so I took one of two short cuts which I knew. The last of these was a little unpaved lane that ran between high walls that bounded gardens; I was halfway along it when a lout came running from the opposite end and as he passed me made a grab at my bundle. He took it in so fierce a hold, without slackening his pace, that he almost ripped my arm off. I was swung round, so that my back struck the wall and I was left staring at the way I had come while he went galloping off, carrying the washing that had taken Mother and me so long to do, and the loss of which meant no money this evening, and no custom in future, even if the lady to whom it belonged didn't turn nasty and demand compensation. I set off after him. I was very fleet of foot in those days and I caught him before he reached the end of the lane. Within a second he knew that he had no tame little laundress on his hands; he was obliged to drop the bundle, which broke open and spilled its contents into the thick dust. I clawed and bit and kicked and pummelled, beside myself with fury, and then with fear. I was no match for him, really; he was taller and heavier. Soon he had me pinned against the wall, holding the upper parts of my arms and banging me against it so that it was only by keeping my head bent forward that I could prevent myself being knocked senseless. Then help arrived; mincing into the lane swinging a gold-headed cane came an elegant young gentleman, who chivalrously, not waiting to inquire into the rights or wrongs of the case, came to the support of the losing side. He gave the boy two hearty blows across the shoulders with the cane and the boy let go of me and ran away, trampling the muslin further into the dust as he went.

"What a to-do," my rescuer said. "Are you injured?"

"Thanks to you, no, sir." My words jerked out, for I had been knocked breathless.

"I'm glad that I chanced to take the short cut. You look very shaken."

"I'm all right," I said. "And I'm very grateful to you. Extremely grateful, sir."

"It was nothing. Or should I say it was a pleasure. One wonders what the world is coming to, everywhere infested by young ruffians."

I bent down and began to collect the ruined washing. The young gentleman watched me. In the scuffle my upper lip had been slightly split, and since all the articles must be washed again I used one of the caps to dab at my mouth.

"My house is nearby. If you'd like to come with me I will have my housekeeper make you a dish of tea—if you like tea."

I liked tea very much, and it was one of the luxuries which must be done without in our bad times. And the invitation sounded quite regular; in good households the housekeepers and upper servants drank what was called the second brew—

that was the infusion made from tea leaves used once by their employers. The question of time no longer mattered, since I should be unable to deliver the laundry this evening, and I could well imagine myself being taken to some large airy kitchen and given a comforting cup of tea. So I made my bob and said:

"That is very kind of you, sir."

I gathered the last article and tied the bundle tightly, slung it on my arm, and walked along beside him. I thought I might even gain a new customer, so as we walked I spoke about how well Mother and I washed delicate things, how clever she was with shirt ruffles. He said lightly that I was very serious for one so young, and I told him that I was thirteen.

At the upper end of the lane he opened a gate; it was wrought iron, very graceful, three lilies in each half of it. Inside there was a small but elegantly laid out garden, with a green lawn and rose trees in full blow, crimson, scarlet, pink, white, and yellow, every rose swooning openhearted in the warm evening air. Tall glass doors at the back of the house were open, and he led me into a library.

I was a little conscious of the incongruity between myself in my print dress, clutching a bundle of washing, and the elegance of my surroundings, but I was not actually ill-at-ease, for sometimes, on the crest of the wave, we had lived in rooms much like this, and also I did not expect to stay in this room very long. He'd ring the bell and his footman would lead me away to the housekeeper's room.

He laid his cane and his hat on a chair by the door and said to me, "Sit down," indicating a sofa which stood in front of the empty summer fireplace. Then he opened the door which led to the inner part of the house and, tossing over his shoulder the remark that he would be gone only a minute, was gone. I dabbed at my mouth with the cap which I had kept out of the bundle and cautiously investigated my other injuries; my back, under the thin frock, felt raw, my shins were scraped, and th' bruises were beginning to show on the upper parts of my arms. Still, all things considered, I had got off lightly, and I had saved the washing. I looked round at the books, wondering how anyone could have had time to read them all, and at one or two busts which stood about, so very eyeless as busts always are. It was, I decided, a mistake for sculptors to scoop out the pupil of the eye. . . .

Then the door opened, and there was my friend. He had discarded his wig and wore a yellow silk robe, patterned with blue dragons. He carried, with the awkwardness of one not accustomed to the task, a silver salver upon which stood a bottle and two glasses.

"I had forgotten," he said, "this is my day to wait upon myself. So no tea! But a glass of cool wine, straight from the cellar, will, I trust, be equally refreshing and acceptable."

I began, at that moment, to feel that something was wrong. It was a little like waking in the night and feeling the first, dull, faraway throb which heralded a toothache. Any kindly gentleman might offer a laundress a cup of his housekeeper's tea; finding his kitchen unoccupied, he might well say—There is the tea caddy and there the kettle, make yourself tea. But only an eccentric would go into his cellar and bring up a bottle of wine to share with a laundress; an eccentric, or . . .

I said, "You are indeed very civil, sir, but I do not drink wine. I promised my mother never to drink it until I was twenty-one."

He looked at me, amused and insolent.

"Not, I imagine, a promise very difficult to keep, since opportunities for temptation must be few."

I disliked his look and the remark; so, as he set down the salver I said:

"I think I had better go now," and leaned to retrieve the bundle of washing which I had laid in an unobtrusive place at the end of the sofa. The next thing I knew he was on top of me, behaving like someone gone crazy. Even then I was a little slow to realise exactly what was happening to me: when I did so I was more frightened than I had been when wrestling with the lout, more frightened than I had ever been in my life before. And then, just as suddenly, not frightened at all, quite calm, in control of my thoughts. I went limp and quiescent, and then brought up my knee and struck him, with all my strength, in a part at that moment more than ordinarily vulnerable. Then I rolled off the sofa, picked myself up, and fled, leaving the bundle on the floor and my fine gentleman doubled over and groaning with pain.

I ran straight home, not bothering yet to think what I was going to tell my parents because I did not expect to find either of them in the room when I arrived. I just ran for cover, as thoughtlessly as an animal makes for its hole. I wasn't even aware that I was crying as I ran.

Father was at home. His good jacket hung over the back of a chair, and he was carefully arranging his breeches on the seat. He wore, as always in the house, an old frayed shirt, a pair of shabby breeches. He turned as I entered and said:

"Good God, child! What happened to you?"

To Mother I should simply have said that I had lost the washing, making it sound as though the boy had run off with it. I was upset, but not so completely distraught as to blurt out to her something which would, I knew, shock her profoundly. Father I judged less easily shockable, so I told him the whole tale. Telling him I found not in the least embarrassing; indeed it was comforting. I'd stopped crying before I reached the end of my tale, and managed a halfhearted grin when I told him exactly how I had escaped. He gave no answering sign of amusement.

"He didn't hurt you then?"

"Oh no."

"You're sure?"

"Quite sure. This," I touched my split lip, "and these," I indicated my bruises, "the boy did."

Father was thoughtful for a second.

"I'd sooner your mother didn't hear about this," he said.

"I don't think I could have told her. Only that I'd lost the washing. I meant to tidy myself and mend my bodice. . . . Father, why are you home so early?"

To my amazement he said, "I won thirty pounds in two hours, and I was hungry."

"You could have eaten at Whaddon's."

"I know. But you couldn't, or your mother. We had a poor dinner today, and I thought that for once I'd come home while I had something in my pocket, and you could go out and buy something good for supper."

I stared at him, struck speechless; never once before had I known him regard luck at the beginning of an evening as anything but an excuse to go on playing, for higher stakes. I said, when I could speak, and without the slightest wish to be ironical:

"Father, are *you* feeling quite well?"

"Except for hunger, yes. Can you run to the cookshop or must I dress again?"

"I'll go," I said gladly. My troubles were forgotten; even the loss of the laundry seemed a slight thing set against the miracle of Father having come home, voluntarily, with thirty pounds.

He gave me some money, and then, just as I reached the door, asked:

"Would you recognise that place again?"

"In Puddle Lane? Oh yes. I noticed the pattern of the gate. It was three lilies on each side. Pretty."

"And the man? What was he like?"

"Young. He had red cheeks and a chin with a deep dimple, almost black eyes. He had a pigtail wig. Oh, and he wore a ring, black with a head on it in white, a dog's, or a fox's. It was on his little finger and the finger was crooked, like this. . . ." I showed him with my own.

"I see," Father said. "Run along now."

Mother came home, dead-beat from long standing at the end of a long day, and was happily amazed to find food on the table and Father home so early and in luck. I did not feel it incumbent upon me to destroy the happy atmosphere of our home by mention of the lost laundry; that could wait until tomorrow. Afterwards I was glad that I waited.

I told her next day, showing her my bruises and the place on my back scraped raw from contact with the wall; she was grieved, but not angry. She used almost the same words that the young man had spoken in the lane, about not knowing what the world was coming to when a girl wasn't safe in the streets with a bundle of washing. She said that we must go together to the house where the muslins belonged and explain.

"Mrs. Frisby would be within her rights to demand I make good the loss, I suppose. But I hope she'll be understanding. Or if not, let's hope your father is lucky again."

He'd gone from the house when we got back from Bridge Street—where, incidentally, Mrs. Frisby had been anything but understanding. That evening Mother and I supped on the leftovers from the night before, and when Mother went to pull up the chair, she had to lift aside Father's old shabby breeches. Something clinked and she gave them a little shake and then felt in the pocket, withdrawing her hand full of money. She gave a funny, short laugh.

"They say," she said, "that with patience you can tame a lion. Here I've been for seventeen years and two months, telling him over and over that we should be all right if only, when he won, he'd put a little aside. How much did he say he'd won yesterday?"

"Thirty pounds."

She put the coins on the table, felt in the pocket again, and then counted.

"He's left twenty. Well, wonders will never cease. Maybe at last he's come to his senses."

The find quite banished the shadow which Mrs. Frisby's behaviour had cast, and for the second time running we went to bed happy.

We woke to find that Father had not come home. There was nothing unusual about that; he'd been known to sit at the tables for thirty-six hours at a stretch.

It was another hot day, and when he didn't come in for dinner Mother looked at the freshly laundered shirt she had ready and said:

"I should have thought he would have wanted a change of linen at least."

He hadn't come home when we went to bed, and he wasn't there in the morning.

Mother said, "You must manage the washing on your own. I'm going to Whaddon's and to Mariana's and anywhere else I can think of. I've never done such a thing before, but then he's never been away so long."

I looked at her, *really* looked at her, for perhaps the first time. There was a good deal of grey in her fair hair, a good many lines of strain and fatigue in her face; her clothes were tidy, but poor. She bore, I realised, an almost family resemblance to all the "decent poor women" to whose care I had long ago been entrusted. I couldn't imagine her walking up the steps, going into the pillared portico at Whaddon's.

"He won't like it," I said.

"Nor do I like being left from Wednesday mid-day to Friday morning, without a word. But I think he's ill. He's a fool and a shuffler where money is concerned, but he's never before given me a moment's anxiety on any other score. He *must* be ill."

Neat, respectable, firm in her conviction that she was doing her duty, she set out; and a full five hours later, baffled and distraught, she returned.

"At Whaddon's they said Mariana's, and there they said Whaddon's or Mr. Allenby's new house at Piccadilly. There they denied all knowledge but said try Lady Payne's. I've been to seven places, all places where he was known, and nobody has seen him since Wednesday dinnertime. He was well then and ate pigeon pie at Cathcart's chophouse in Southampton Street. And after that . . . nothing. . . ." She worked her hands together. "I don't know where else to try, all that part of his life was strange to me. I think I shall go mad!"

I said the only comforting thing I could think of.

"I expect the game moved on to some place in the country and Father went with it."

"That has happened a hundred times, and he never once failed to let me know. Over everything but money he was a most considerate man. . . . Money . . ." She repeated the word as though it revealed something. "Twenty pounds he left behind; he'd never done that before. This was planned. He *knew!*"

She sat down by the table, put her arms on it and her head on her arms, and began to cry. Through the crying she talked, wildly, incoherently, saying terrible things. She voiced the darkest, most inmost dread of her heart—that Father had gone to another woman. Bound to happen, she said, he being so handsome and gay and she herself so beaten down and mostly too busy to make herself look well. And she'd known all along, for seventeen years and two months, that really he'd only married her for her money; her grandmother Allison had warned her at the time. "But I loved him. And I've borne the dragging down, and the work and the shame, *because* I loved him. And to what end? Twenty pounds in the pocket of his ragged breeches and not even a word of good-bye."

It went on and on. When a strong stone building cracks and falls there is more disturbance than when a hut of wattle and daub collapses; Mother had always been strong, when she broke it was shocking to see.

There was nothing that I could do except offer to run out and buy some tea and brew her a dish. So I did that, and then she added to the shocks I had already sustained by saying: "Brandy would hearten me better."

I took a jug and a shilling and ran to the nearest place, and walked carefully back. At first the brandy seemed to do anything but hearten her; she cried more bitterly and talked more wildly, but presently she calmed down; her cheeks took on a pink tinge and her eyes a faraway look.

"We must just manage as best we can," she said, her voice a little thick-sounding. "Thank God he left the money; I can pay Miss Bellsize a premium and fit you out properly. You'll never own your own business, though, for he won't be coming home any more and saying—We're rich."

"I don't want to learn dressmaking. I'd rather stay with you and do washing."

Then, abruptly, she became angry in a way I had never seen in her before. The pink in her cheeks turned to scarlet, she spoke loudly and banged her hand on the table; I was to do as she said; she had enough trouble without my turning awkward; as for my helping her that was utter nonsense, it was a hand-to-mouth existence with no future to it. Besides, once I was safely established, she intended to give up the room and find herself a living-in job as housekeeper. And I needn't think that now that Father, who had always spoiled me, had run off I was going to defy her . . .

In the middle of this tirade she rose, went unsteadily to the bed, and lay down and was asleep in a minute.

I lay for a long time wakeful, feeling that at one stroke I had lost both my parents. . . .

In fact Father, or rather Father's image, came back at the end of the week, and in horrid guise. On the Wednesday of his disappearance he must have spent some time in identifying the owner of the house with the lily-patterned gate, and, that done, had traced him to a club in St. James's Square, where, in the presence of three other gentlemen, he had struck him on the cheek and called him a raper of children. This was calling-out talk, and at seven o'clock that evening Father and my would-be seducer had met in a field behind Piccadilly and Father had been shot through the heart.

The news took so long to reach us because, as Mother said, the greater part of Father's life had been apart from ours; none of his associates knew his address, or that he was married. It was not until the gentleman who had acted as his second, chanced to go into Whaddon's and heard that a Mrs. Hatton of Tun's Yard had been there in search of her husband that contact could be established. By that time Father had been buried. Duelling, common as it was, was always done in hole-and-corner fashion, with the wounded and the dead removed as quickly as possible from the scene. There'd been enough money in Father's pocket to pay for the burial; his watch and his cane his friend had sent, with the news of the death, to the only place with which Father had ever mentioned his connection—a place called Mortiboys, in Suffolk.

Once we knew the truth, Mother and I had an emotion in common—remorse. She could cry and rebuke herself loudly for suspecting him of infidelity while all the time the poor man was dead; but I dared not cry and rebuke myself for having been the cause of his death, plainly as I recognised the fact. If I hadn't come home and blurted out my tale, if I hadn't described so exactly both the gate and the man, Father would have been alive still. I'd described everything as well as I could because I had some vague idea that Father might be going to get the laundry bundle sent back to us; I understood all practical things, like earning money and doing work, but I didn't understand about a gentleman's honour, which is still of first-rate importance even when the gentleman is a broken-down gambler with one suit of clothes, his wife a washerwoman, and his daughter running about the streets with bundles of laundry.

Mother had two ways of escape—she could cry as she talked, and she could drink brandy. I had none and my natural grief combined with a sense of guilt cast me into profound melancholy. I had no appetite, could not sleep at night, shrank from going outside our room, and fell into such a state of misery and lethargy that when Mother revived her plan for apprenticing me to Miss Bellsize I put up no resistance at all. My body chose that moment to turn traitor, too, pushing me across the line that divides childhood from womanhood: Felicity Hatton seemed to disappear, leaving a lump of misery in her place. And about what happened to that substitute I cared nothing.

Four years' apprenticeship for a premium of five pounds, Miss Bellsize to provide board and lodging, Mother to fit me out with four gowns, two of woollen, two of print, and everything else that was necessary in the way of shoes and shifts and handkerchiefs.

I went to the house in Carlisle Street on the first day of August in the year 1738, and I had been there a full two months before I woke up to the full horror of my situation.

Miss Bellsize's establishment consisted of six apprentices, two girls who had completed their indentures, and a much older woman who was as skilful a cutter as Miss Bellsize herself. In the kitchen there was a cook and a housemaid and small Negro boy who wore around his neck a silver collar engraved with his name, "Guinea," and Miss Bellsize's name and address. We were spared that indignity, but we were equally enslaved.

To this day I wonder how many women, when a new dress comes home and they shake it out and view it with delight or carping criticism, spare a thought for the hours of labour, the aching eyes and backs and shoulders that have gone into its making. We never worked less than fourteen hours a day, and when trade was brisk sixteen and eighteen were not uncommon. I've seen girls fall asleep over their work, or drop senseless from exhaustion. The room in which we worked was at the very top of the house and well lighted by a great glass dome in the centre; in August it was too hot for comfort, later in the year too cold. It was always completely lacking in fresh air, as was the basement in which we ate and slept.

There were at that time many dressmaking establishments in London which were nothing more or less than houses of assignation. Miss Bellsize's was not one of those; there was on the ground floor an ornate parlour and to the rear of it a mirror-lined fitting room, and some customers came to the house, making a morning's outing of a fitting, drinking tea and eating ratafia biscuits. Others preferred to be waited upon in their own homes, and when Miss Bellsize visited them she was followed by Guinea, who carried a length of silk or velvet or muslin, or a half-completed garment, wrapped in linen and balanced upon his head. Miss Bellsize liked to provide her own material because thus she pocketed the profit that should have been the mercer's; she never, of course, expressed this preference outright, that would have been to forget her place; what she did was to criticise, often by no more than the lift of an eyebrow, the pursing of her mouth, material which ladies had procured for themselves or had sent to them as presents.

Why money mattered to her so much that in the pursuit of it she was prepared to sacrifice every human feeling, I never knew. She had no family, no friends. She could have done half the business that she did and still been prosperous, and not made her employees' lives so wretched; but she always behaved as though each order were her first, and the only one she could hope for in a year.

She was very clever, capable of making a waist seem half

its size by the insertion of a panel of contrasting colour in the skirt, or of making a flat bosom look seductive by a puckering of lace. It always seemed to us that her most brilliant inspirations came when a gown was half done, so that it had to be unpicked, slashed about with the scissors, and stitched all over again. What did half a million extra stitches matter? It was we who did the work.

Even for girls who had once liked sewing it was a wretched life. There were so many parents who, like my mother, wanted their daughters to have steady work of some superficially refined kind, that people like Miss Bellsize could afford to be strict to the point of brutality. It would all have been more understandable had we been pauper children, apprenticed to her by the parish, but Miss Bellsize scorned such, they would lower the tone of her establishment. I worked alongside the daughters of a scrivener's clerk, a barber-surgeon, a master baker, a yeoman farmer, and a ship's master. They all grumbled, and wept, they all suffered genuine hardships, but they all considered themselves privileged.

Miss Bellsize did her best to make me feel privileged; she told me that she had taken me to oblige my mother, a woman of whom many ladies spoke well and who had been sadly bereaved; and in taking me she had ignored her waiting list upon which there were twenty names at least. She hoped I was suitably grateful. . . .

For the first two months I stayed sunk in my dull apathy, myself alive but dead. I suppose I did my work, otherwise there would have been trouble, but I didn't notice much, and hardly spoke. The effort to speak seemed not worth making. I kept on seeing myself rashly accepting that offer of a dish of tea, and Father lying dead as a result. It is possible to weep inwardly, and I did it, even as I sewed.

On Sundays we did not sew. We had time, between breakfast and morning service, to attend to our affairs, washing and mending, and then, neatly dressed, impeccably behaved, we all went to St. Anne's. Miss Bellsize was a staunch church-woman. After that we had an early dinner and then set to to clean the house. Everything was put into such a state of cleanliness and polish that for the rest of the week a mere flick of a duster sufficed to keep it in trim. This routine was varied by a free Sunday afternoon and evening until eight o'clock for two of us in turn; this worked out at one free day in a month, and we were allowed to use it to visit our families, if they were within reasonable distance, or to attend the Female Apprentices' Sunday Refuge, a charitable institution started by some ladies who had been shocked to see girls, apprenticed to places less strict than Miss Bellsize's, wandering the streets and mis-behaving during their leisure time. I attended this refuge two or three times towards the end of my stay with Miss Bellsize; up to a point it was well run; the ladies provided tea and cakes and a number of games suitable for children of the ages eight to eleven. Mostly the time was spent in gossip and in the comparing of conditions. It surprised me to learn that we at Miss Bellsize's were regarded as highly enviable. Many of those who frequented the refuge were pauper girls who had been apprenticed by the Poor Law Authorities and had no parents to care what happened to them. Much of what did happen was quite shocking.

Not that—at the moment—it seemed much of an advantage to have a parent. When I went home for my free day in October I was still in my dazed state, too lethargic to talk much. Mother was sunk in a melancholy from which she emerged only towards the end of my visit when she consumed sixpennorth's worth of brandy. She then reverted to her talk about finding herself a living-in job, spoke of wearing a black stuff gown, carrying a bunch of keys, and being able to order underservants about. In November when I made my visit this dream seemed no nearer to fulfilment, and by this time I had recovered, was myself again and able to take notice. There were changes both in Mother and in the room; she was

thinner and not so neat as I remembered; she had, in ways not
to be accounted for by any list of details, lost her "decent poor
woman" look; and the room, hitherto well kept, despite its
poverty, was now neither clean nor tidy. She reported that
she had been busy, and certainly there was food on the table
and brandy in the jug. This time when her melancholy lifted
she became garrulous in a peculiar way, telling me about a
number of situations for which she had applied, none of which
was suitable for a respectable woman. If she was to be believed every man who wished to employ a housekeeper had
designs upon the poor creature's virtue; or, in the cases when
the employer himself was guiltless of such designs, there was
a steward, or a butler, "with a nasty leering look. I knew what
that meant!"

Faced with such a tale of disappointment upon disappointment I produced my own, seemingly small, grievance with
some timidity.

"I don't like the work, or the way we live. I don't want to
stay with Miss Bellsize," I said.

Mother gave me her attention long enough to ask what was
wrong, and, put into words, it didn't sound much; the over-
long hours, the wretched food, the fierce discipline, the way
all but a few of the people in the house were continually spy-
ing and carrying tales. "I can't bear it," I said.

"You must. A little hardship now—and it will lessen as you
accustom yourself to it—will save you years of misery later
on. Look at me. Had I had some proper training in my youth,
I should not now be traipsing round and being insulted at
every turn." She told a few more stories of the insults she
had endured. Then she said, "In any case there is no help for
it; your premium is paid and there are penalties for the breaking of indentures. I can't afford to pay fines, or to buy you
out." She looked at me and added, "The food can't be so bad,
you're fatter than you were when you lived here."

That was true. Had anyone ever had the temerity to accuse

Miss Bellsize of underfeeding her apprentices, she could in all justice have pointed out that every one of us weighed more and bulked larger than we had done when we arrived. This was due in part to the complete lack of exercise, and in part to the kind of food we were given; porridge, bread, dumplings, fat-and-lean pork, so fat that the lean was a mere pink thread in the lardy whiteness, thick pea soup served with a full inch of liquid mutton fat floating on top, and potatoes of a kind which even in our poorest days Mother seemed not to have discovered: they came from Ireland and were called "horse potatoes"; they were very large and completely without flavour.

On this diet—varied about once a fortnight by a dish of very salt stockfish—we all grew fat; we also grew oddly alike to look at; our hair lost its original colour and texture and became lank and greasy and dull; we all had red irritable eyelids and red sore patches at the corners of our mouths, between our fingers and toes. We were so perpetually on the verge of hunger that Miss Bellsize's greatest weapon in keeping us in order was the forfeiting of a meal. Faulty work, or even a sullen look, would evoke the dreaded words, "No breakfast tomorrow." The situation was aggravated by the fact that Miss Bellsize did not stint herself on food; the three senior members of the staff ate with her, and often, as we passed the kitchen door, we could smell the good things cooking.

I said to Mother on that November Sunday:

"If you find the post you're looking for, I could come back here and take over the washing."

"It isn't the washing that pays the rent of this room, it's the hairdressing," she said.

"Then I could learn the hairdressing."

"It would mean going into places where you would be exposed to temptation. And so would your living here. I shall get a job; there must be some decent people about, and I couldn't leave you here by yourself. Besides Miss Bellsize would know and make trouble. An indenture is a legal thing, you can't just break it at will. You must go back and resign yourself to what doesn't exactly please your fancy. You should be grateful."

I went back, meditating the possibility of running away. How would Miss Bellsize ever find me if I didn't go back to Tun's Yard? On the other hand, if I didn't go there, where should I go? Only a short time before I should have thrown myself gladly upon the charity of the streets, but I'd learned that for me they were no longer safe.

During the next few days, cunningly making it sound like a general, impersonal discussion, I talked about apprenticeship with a girl who most often worked alongside me. She was a year my senior in age and in apprenticeship; her name was Emily and she was the daughter of the yeoman farmer.

"They're always caught," she said, referring to runaway apprentices; "otherwise we'd all run, wouldn't we, and then where would people in business be? They put it in the papers and on bills on the walls, saying 'Lost' and giving a list of everything you're wearing, and telling what you look like. So then everybody is on the lookout for you and when you're caught you're whipped and whoever apprenticed you must pay the premium all over again. I don't know what your father paid for you, but I know mine paid eight pounds."

"My father's dead," I said. And for a moment I realised that I *had* been privileged. Five pounds against eight!

"I was just wondering," I said, anxious to allay all suspicion. "Those girls at the Refuge . . . you were telling me about who were so sorely beaten, for just nothing at all except their mistress' whim. I wondered why they didn't run away."

"We aren't beaten," Emily said. "We're very lucky in some ways."

(This is a philosophy which, all my life, I have found difficult to accept. You sprain your ankle and a friend says, "You should be thankful you didn't break your leg." Where's the sense in that? Why be thankful? If you carried that to its logical conclusion we should all go about in a state of perpetual thanksgiving that we weren't black slaves in the Sugar Islands, or squint-eyed or harelipped.)

In the next month, December, nobody had a free Sunday at all; instead we all had Christmas Day; Emily and another girl, the baker's daughter, who lived at a distance, were given two days.

I went home for Christmas, and it was upon this supposedly merry day that I first suspected that something was really wrong with Mother. Always before, even in our worst times, she had managed something special to mark the season, a green bough over the door, a real candle instead of a rush dip, something, no matter how humble and cheap, that was tasty to eat. This year there was nothing—not even an apology for the nothingness. Her one, most incongruous, recognition of the fact that it *was* Christmas, lay in a heap in one corner, a lot of soiled linen.

"There was no point in washing yesterday, nobody would have welcomed back their stuff on Christmas morning," Mother said.

Her hair had whitened rapidly since the summer, and it seemed to have grown shorter, too, so that, being difficult to confine, it hung straggling about her face. It struck me that it would be an exceptionally trusting woman who would employ, to dress her hair, one whose own looked so unkempt. I asked about the hairdressing.

"Oh, I gave that up; too much standing. And going out late in the evening."

"But you said it was that which paid the rent of the room."

"That was when I was spending more money on food. Nowadays I need very little. A half-quartern loaf lasts me a long time."

I then asked the question which had been bothering me ever since my arrival.

"What's for dinner?"

"Look in the larder," she said.

Our "larder" was older than I was; Mother had had it made when she first had experience of what it meant to keep house in one room more likely than not to be visited by rats. It was a stout wooden box with a hinged door in which were bored a dozen small holes for the admission of air; it had four legs which could be folded flat against its base. Wherever we went the "larder" had come with us, in prosperous times to be pushed out of sight in a cupboard, waiting for the day when it should be reinstated, outward and visible sign of Mother's difference from the sluts whose circumstances she might be compelled to share.

I went to it now, half cherishing the hope that she had after all planned to surprise me; I didn't expect *much*, knowing her poverty, half a pig's cheek perhaps, a slice of brawn; any kind of meat, in fact, except fat-and-lean pork would have been welcome, any kind of fish except salt stockfish. There was nothing in the larder except the heel of a loaf, a small piece—about two ounces—of very dried-up cheese, and the jug in which I had fetched the brandy on the night when we were told of Father's death. It was now three-quarters full of clear water, which puzzled me because we always fetched up water by the bucketful from a well in the yard.

"Don't touch that," Mother said. "It's Geneva; it's much cheaper than brandy and does me the same good."

There is this to be said for taking blows when you are young; they shape you, and harden you, they do not break you. It's like making horseshoes; if a smith took his great hammer and hit an old horseshoe the way he hits a young pliable one, hot from the forge, it would fly into fragments. I stood there by that makeshift, almost empty larder and took the blow of realising that my mother, that most resolutely respectable, self-respecting woman, had fallen prey to Madam

Geneva, the sly bitch who held thousands of poor wretches in thrall, and gained new slaves every day. Madam Geneva was the fancy word for gin, and I knew about gin—probably more than Mother did, though I had never drunk it—from hearing talk amongst Fingers and Jimmy and the rest. It was the drink of the poor, for it was very cheap, being untaxed, and it could be purchased anywhere—at shops as well as taverns. Its immediate effect, Fingers said, was a feeling of well-being, of cheerfulness; he drank it himself when he could afford to, but was careful never to drink before going out on a job because to do so would have made him over-bold, made him underestimate risks. When the effects began to wear off you became extremely melancholy and the only cure for that was more gin. In the end nothing in the world mattered except your need for gin and the necessity for satisfying that need. People would commit any crime, subject themselves to any indignity, just to get a few pence—that was all that was needed—in order to get drunk on gin. There were shops with signs, "Drunk for a penny; dead drunk for twopence," and for those who minded the implications in the second statement there was the promise of straw to lie upon while oblivion lasted.

Now I understood why Mother had given up the hairdressing, why she had completely ignored Christmas, and why a half-quartern loaf lasted her for a long time. Before long, unless something was done, she would give up the laundry work, too, and be a beggar, or even, incredible as the thought seemed, one of those old, horrible whores willing to sell themselves for a penny.

My mother!

And if you went right back to the root of the matter it was all my fault for accepting the offer of a dish of tea from a stranger.

On that dreadful Christmas Day I did what I could. I made

a little fire and toasted the bread and then the cheese, laying one on the other and making it look as tempting as I could, and I persuaded her to eat a little. Halfway through the sorry meal she began to cry and to talk about Christmas last year . . . two, five, ten years ago. Her memory was unimpaired; she could speak with equal confidence and sorrow of a Christmas in Aldermanbury Postern with pigeon pie, and of a Christmas in Downing Street with roast goose. She stopped eating, and I felt despicably gluttonous for finishing up my own portion of toasted cheese on scorched bread.

After an hour of it I was almost relieved when she fetched the jug, and drank, and presently began to speak hopefully of a job she had in mind, keeping house for an old lady, crippled with rheumatism, in Enfield. It was all nonsense, and I knew it, but it made better listening than the sad reminiscences of other Christmases.

At the end of this miserable day I went back to Carlisle Street and next morning asked, in proper fashion, through the senior apprentice, who asked one of the ex-apprentices, whether I might speak to Miss Bellsize. I was sent for at about seven o'clock in the evening.

Miss Bellsize said, "What, what is it?"

I told her, as politely and concisely as I could, that my mother was ill, that there was no one in the world to look after her except me, and that I begged leave to go and do it.

"But you are indentured to me for four years, and nobody has the power to break those indentures save a justice of the peace, who would have to be given some sound good reason. Your mother's illness would not be accepted as such reason— nor would her death."

"She needs me," I said.

"That may well be. But then, so do I. You have been here five months and are just beginning to be useful. I gave you preference over twenty other applicants, to oblige your mother.

Am I now expected to begin all over again with a girl who must be taught to whip an edge?"

"There was the premium," I ventured.

"Indeed there was; five pounds. And you have been here for five months. In how many places in London would you find board and lodging for four shillings a week, leave alone the tuition you have received? If indentures were to be broken because a parent fell ill the whole system would be made nonsense of; girls would learn all they could in a few months and then go and set up in opposition. I suggest that if your mother is seriously ill she should enter St. Thomas' Hospital."

I said, very humbly, "I felt it was my duty to ask, madam."

"In that you were right, Felicity."

I went back to my work and in the ensuing days, as subtly and secretly as I could, set about finding out how much my fellow apprentices knew about the laws governing indentures. The scrivener's daughter was the best informed. She told us—and I take credit to myself that she said it all in a joking manner—that if Miss Bellsize died, or went bankrupt, the indentures would be void, and so they would if any one of us became, through disease or affliction, incapable of benefiting through further training. She told of a known case, of an idiot boy apprenticed to a cabinetmaker and released, after a year, as unteachable.

"But it had to be properly done, even so, in front of a magistrate, because if not, anybody who gave the poor boy a job he could do, might be had up for harbouring somebody else's apprentice."

I never gave a sign that anything she or the others told me about the rules and regulations was of any importance to me, or of any interest more than the usual gossip, but I tucked away every fact in my head. I went home in January, and again in February; Mother was more emaciated, more strange in her manner. Enfeebled as she was, she still did enough washing to pay her rent and provide her with gin, and she still talked of finding a post in some pleasant place like Twickenham or Hampstead. She could have had no idea how her appearance had deteriorated.

Early in March we had an unseasonal thunderstorm. Ordinary people, during a storm, cover anything made of steel, and shroud their looking glasses; but in our high room, which with its dome seemed horribly exposed, the work went on as usual, the needles held in fingers which twitched at every lightning flash, the shears still in use. Miss Bellsize tolerated no waste of time on account of the weather's vagaries.

There came one exceptionally vivid flash, accompanied by a roll of thunder that sounded like the end of the world. Emily, sitting next to me, said, "That was a blinder!" and instantly I saw my way out. I dropped my work and clapped my hands to my eyes, saying, not loudly, but in an awed voice, "It blinded me."

The next few days brought the severest test of will power that I have ever known. I had to *be* blind, to keep my eyes set in a mild, unfocussed stare and sit for hours in a state of complete idleness. I think it would be a valuable bit of training for anyone who wished to act upon the stage, to be obliged to maintain such a pretence for a while. I managed by convincing myself that directly in front of my eyes there hung a black velvet curtain into which I stared. When anyone spoke to me, or touched me on the shoulder, I turned in the direction of the sound or the touch, slowly, taking my black curtain with me.

At this point the laws governing the indenturing—though not the treatment—of apprentices, worked to my advantage. Left to herself, Miss Bellsize would have turned me into the street, useless and unwanted as an old dog. But the cancelling of indentures required a magistrate's permission, and questions might be asked. She had a desire to stand well in the eyes of the world, and although the vast majority of people cared nothing for what happened to apprentices, there was a small and vociferous minority. So she kept me and fed me for several days, and arranged, through that same charitable organisation which ran the Female Apprentices' Refuge, that I should have the benefit of a doctor's advice. He was an elderly man, named Rayson, and not much interested in my case. He stared into my eyes, prodded around them perfunctorily, and then passed his hand swiftly in front of my face to test whether I flinched or not. I managed not to. Then he called for a candle, and I was frightened. I'd observed—without realising that I observed it—that when the candles are lighted the pupils of people's eyes contract. With blind people, who wouldn't be aware of the light, this most likely wouldn't happen. So I should be trapped. And then I remembered something else, my eyes were greenish-blue, but whenever I was tired, or angry or bothered in any way, the black centres would grow until I looked veritably sloe-eyed: I'd first noticed that long ago when, before going out to join Fingers on a job, I'd look in a scrap of looking glass to see if I was tidy. So now, while the candle was being fetched, I deliberately worked myself into a state of agitation; let the doctor prove that I was not blind, and I should be locked up here for four years and Mother would die of starvation and gin-drinking, and God knew what punishment Miss Bellsize would impose upon me for deception.

Dr. Rayson passed the candle twice before my eyes and I stared into a black curtain, with horror behind it.

He said there was nothing to be done.

Miss Bellsize was never one to waste time; within four days after that, she, and I and Mother, looking hopelessly confused, were up before Mr. Timothy Sales, justice of the peace in Bow Street, for the cancelling of the articles of indenture. I was careful to remember that I carried my black curtain with me everywhere, and avoided looking directly at anyone.

I did, however, catch a glimpse of his face, and I recognised what I called a "kind" mouth, full lips, laid on flat as though moulded from the outside, and deeply indented at the corners, the mouth of a man who would be indulgent to himself and to other people.

There I was right; for when the formalities were complete he said to Miss Bellsize:

"Madam, whatever the poor child has learned during her short apprenticeship can never be of use to her. I am sure that in the circumstances you would wish to return some part of the premium."

Miss Bellsize said, quite pleasantly:

"I have fed and housed her for eight months, and learners, you know, often make costly mistakes, Your Worship. However, the circumstances are sad and exceptional. I will return four pounds of the premium."

He thanked her very courteously, Mother wept a little, and even I said "thank you" with some semblance of warmth.

"Now let's see what we can contribute," he said, and I heard a clink of coins. "People who lack one faculty often develop exceptional skill in other directions," he went on, meaning it kindly. "The blind usually make baskets well, or knit, or make lace. Or maybe she could sell flowers. . . ."

Quite suddenly, and for no reason at all, for I had attained exactly what I had schemed for, a terrible melancholy took hold of me. Suppose it were true, suppose I were doomed to live in darkness for the rest of my days . . . and there *were* people to whom it happened. In the middle of my pretending to be blind, just for a moment I was, looking blankly into a future of lacemaking, flower-selling. . . .

Not that my own immediate future was without its problems. From Bow Street to Tun's Yard was no great distance, but Mother stopped at two taverns on the way. She said that the gin would hearten her, but all it did was to make her cry more. I had decided, for some unknown reason, to defer telling her the truth until we were at home, but by the time we arrived there she was in such a state that I found it hard to make her understand. She looked at me stupidly when I said:

"I'm not really blind, Mother. I pretended to be, in order to get away from Miss Bellsize. I wanted to come home and look after you."

"Somebody mentioned lacemaking. There was an old woman once, I'm trying to think of her name and where she lived. . . ."

"I don't need to make lace. I can help you with the washing. I'm not blind, Mother. It was all pretence. Look!" I moved unhesitatingly about the dirty cluttered room, touching things and naming them. "And what a heap of washing," I said, pausing by a pile in the corner. "Too much for you to do alone. Aren't you glad that I'm here to help you?"

There was just a glimmer of the woman she had once been in her next words.

"That was a very wicked thing to do. By rights I should send you straight back."

"I wouldn't go. Nothing would ever get me inside that door again." I paused by the larder, opened its door, and looked in; this time there was nothing at all. I wondered when, and what, she had last eaten.

"Give me some money," I said. "I'll go and buy some real food and we'll have a proper meal for once."

"Buy what you like for yourself," she said. "A bit of bread and twopennyworth of Geneva is enough for me."

The next weeks were horrible. I still have, three or four times a year, a nightmare, when I am back again with Mother in that room in Tun's Yard, cajoling, persuading, quarrelling, listening to her crying. She would wake up crying, and cry on until she had had her first drink. The curious thing was that one drink, about half a cupful of gin, would restore her, both physically and mentally. For about an hour after gulping it down she would wash, or iron, and make sensible remarks, and eat a little of whatever was handy. Then she must have a second drink, a third, a fourth, slopping it out more and more clumsily; passing through the stage of false cheerfulness when she spoke quite firmly of a new apprenticeship for me, a living-in post with a lady for herself, and on into incoherence and finally into insensibility. Often, somewhere along these stages, she would cry in a different way, wildly, and become extremely garrulous for a while, saying that she was cursed with ill luck, that Father had always been lucky until he fell in with her, saying that when she had managed to set her daughter on the way to a respectable life the poor creature must go and be struck blind.

Meanwhile I washed and ironed, ironed and washed, collected bundles and delivered them, solicited new customers, hunted up old ones. The relationship between Mother and me, never quite what it might have been, worsened.

"Who made you my keeper, I'd like to know. I drink to ease my sorrow. Is that more reprehensible than lying and cheating as *you* did? Yes, you did, Felicity, you lied and cheated to get out of earning your living decently. Your superior attitude is quite unwarranted, let me tell you."

Once, in a moment of anger, I exclaimed, "But you're killing yourself."

"Nothing will kill me. I shall live to be a hundred with the pain gnawing me away." She beat on her flat breast. "There he was, dead and buried and me cursing him for a faithless rogue. What other woman ever had such knowledge on her conscience?"

"You didn't know. You couldn't know," I said, speaking to my guilt as well as to hers. Once again I stood in that warm dusty lane; had I said, "Thank you, sir, but I must take this home and rewash it," none of this would have happened. I beat my fist on the table and said:

"It's over, it's over. It happened and we didn't know, we couldn't help it. We have our own lives to live and make the best of."

"You're heartless," she said. "All Hattons are, except your father."

April went by, and May; the weather turned warm again. The four pounds from Miss Bellsize and the two guineas and a shilling which the kind magistrate had given from his own pocket had, so far, supplemented the poor income that could be made by washing. Maddeningly, in the summer, when the stuff was more easily and quickly dried, the supply of laundry lessened because so many customers went away to their country houses, or to the seaside, or to stay with relatives. When the rent was paid, the firing which we must have in order to heat the water and the irons, and the soap was bought, we were narrowed down to the point where it became a question of how twopence should be spent, on a loaf, a meat pie, or on gin.

This is the scene that comes back to me in my nightmares. I came back with tenpence, payment for a considerable bundle of washing which I had risen early to do, and which Mother, after her first drink, had ironed carefully and well. I'd left her with another drink, or perhaps one and a half, in the jug. On my way home I bought a penny loaf, and twopennyworth of salmon, ready-cooked and cold. The woman in the shop had given me good measure and I was, to tell the truth, looking forward to my meal. I sped up the stairs. Mother was waiting for me. She was in a state which I had learned to recognise, a kind of sober interlude in the midst of drunkenness. She said:

"Did they pay you?"

"Yes. Look what I've brought."

"You didn't spend it all?"

"Of course not. Threepence."

"Give me the rest," she said, and held out her hand. I backed away.

"There's tomorrow," I said, "and we have to buy soap. . . ."

"Who did the ironing? Any slut can wash. But we won't quarrel about that. Fair is fair. You like to eat, and you're welcome. I need to drink. Give me my fivepence."

I had a sudden, terrible memory of her as she had been in the past, during the good days, gracious and dignified, during the bad ones, unyielding and respectable.

I said, "No, Mother. You come and eat, the bread is fresh and so is the salmon. The sevenpence I have left will buy soap and food for tomorrow."

She said, and it shocked me, "Damn the soap and food for tomorrow. I want that money, *now*."

"I'm not going to give it to you," I said. In my stupidity it seemed to me that I was doing the right thing; I hoped she'd sit down and eat and for once go to bed sober.

"Very well," she said. "I'm not going to take part in a vulgar brawl." She turned about and made an exit, ridiculously over-dignified. I thought—Well, nobody gives gin away; this may be the turning point; she'll come back defeated and be glad of her supper. I divided the fish scrupulously, sliced the bread neatly. I waited. Half an hour; an hour. My own appetite had fled and I looked at the food with disgust. Where was she? What was she doing? In the end I was compelled to go down and search.

I found her quite quickly; she was sitting on a stone mounting block near the opening to Sawyer's Court. All the area around Tun's Yard had once been inhabited by people of substance and a few signs of that time—the mounting blocks for example—still remained. She was helplessly drunk. How she had obtained the necessary pence I never knew, I couldn't inquire too closely into that, even in my thoughts. I could only hope that somebody—perhaps already drunk—had taken pity on her and given her the money. The alternative was too dreadful to contemplate.

She allowed me to help her home, no easy task, for although she weighed very little she seemed to have no bones; it was like dragging a November Guy along. However, I managed, and laid her on the bed where she seemed to fall asleep. I lay awake for a long time, alone with my miserable and hopeless thoughts. When at last I slept I did so heavily, and woke to find the light bright in the room, Mother beside me awake and sober, and a good deal of blood on the pillow.

I began to fuss about, blaming myself for not noticing whatever injury she had sustained the night before.

"It's from within me," she said. "I'm going to die, Felicity."

She spoke in her old placid manner, just as in former days she might have announced that she was going to the baker's. I had no doubt that she was speaking the truth; quite apart from the evidence on the pillow, she looked like a dying woman, had indeed looked so for some time, emaciated to the bone, and her skin the colour of cold porridge.

Something in me accepted the fact that she was dying, and that there was here no reason for small, personal grief; only a great dull ache in the mind that life, for so many people, should be hard and unhappy, and for all, so brief. For a whole year she had dragged about with her incurable wound, thinking of nothing but its easement, and that easement in itself a disease. Death would be a release for her. For me . . . ?

I put the thought away and spoke cheerfully and falsely:

"That is no way to talk," I said. I offered to make her a basin of bread and milk, to fetch a doctor. . . .

She said, in the voice of authority which had governed my childhood:

"Listen to me. There is no time to waste. Lift me a little."

I put my pillow and a hastily rolled bundle of washing behind her. Even as I did it she was talking, still with authority, but rapidly, like someone with little time to spare.

She said that she had never thought me suited to the role of poor relation, "But if you could deceive everybody by pretending that you were blind, you could feign gratitude and meekness just as easily."

She said that at the bottom of Father's old valise—which, like our larder, had accompanied us everywhere—there were papers, proof of her marriage to Father, proof of my legitimacy. These I must take and go to a house called Mortiboys, in Suffolk, somewhere near a town named Baildon. There I should find my father's family and they would take care of me.

As she spoke she choked, and with her skeleton hand pressed the sheet to her mouth; it came away stained.

I said, "I'm going to fetch a doctor." I thought of the ring on my finger which she said was an emerald; I'd pawn it and pay a doctor; though even as I planned this a voice in my mind asked where was the use. If she were mended up this time, she'd begin to drink again as soon as she could move.

"Don't do that. I want to die. I've been wanting to die for a whole year. I tried to make you safe and set you so you could earn a respectable livelihood, but that chance you threw away. . . ." She choked again. "Promise me to go to the Hattons; I can't die easy, leaving you here; you're too young, it wouldn't be right."

I said, "I promise, I promise." All the last year was wiped away, my brief and never too secure ascendancy was ended. This was the Mother whose standard of respectability I had never once openly affronted.

"You promise," she said, and slightly moved her hand as though to take hold of me. Instead I reached out and took her hand in mine; hers was icy cold. She said, "You'll be . . ." and instead of finishing the sentence turned her head into the pillow; her eyelids fluttered and then closed; her breathing made a harsh rattling noise and then stopped.

I sold the green ring so that she might have a proper funeral. I knew that it made no difference; but I had seen pauper funerals in my time and knew their horror. They do nothing to hide the stark fact that an interment is a shovelling away of what, left lying around, would soon become offensive to the community. A proper funeral has at least a kind of sombre dignity, and Mother, being what she was, would, I thought, be glad not to be tumbled by callous hands into a common grave.

I finished and delivered what washing was still in hand, collecting in all eighteenpence; the contents of our room I sold for three shillings. Then, wearing one of my print dresses, clean and well starched, and carrying the papers and the rest of my wardrobe tied into a bundle in Mother's shawl, I went along to *The Angel* in the Strand, a place used by many coaches. Coach fare for the whole distance would, I knew, be beyond my means; what I needed was information as to which way to take, and a short ride through the crowded streets between city and country. I finally bought a seat as far as Ware, where I alighted and began to walk, hoping for lifts as I went. I was singularly lucky, perhaps because I looked harmless and a little pitiable, a servant girl on her way to a new place. At one point I was even given a ride in a gig which carried me twelve miles at a spanking pace and set me down at Newmarket. I made my final stage of the journey in a goods wagon which lumbered to a standstill in the yard of an inn called the *Hawk in Hand* in Baildon, at about seven o'clock on a beautiful summer evening.

III

My friend the carter said, "Wait here, I'll go and ask do anybody know the whereabouts of this place. Mortiboys, you call it?"

"And the people are named Hatton."

He went into the inn and presently came out with another man; they both carried tankards.

I then had my first experience of the difference between life in London, where everyone is too busy with his own affairs to bother much about his neighbour's, and the country, where other people's business is almost the sole source of entertainment. The man from the inn looked me over, slowly and thoroughly, and then asked:

"You going to work over at Mortiboys?"

I didn't blame him; I knew what I looked like; yet I replied in a stiff, distant voice.

"My relatives live there. My name is Felicity Hatton."

His face took on an inward-looking expression, the face of someone doing sums in his head. Once or twice he gave himself the wrong answer to his problem, and knew it and repudiated it. Finally he said, in a tentative way:

"All I can think on is Chris Hatton. You wouldn't by any chance be his little mawther?"

The word was new to me and I didn't know that in Suffolk it has an almost affectionate connotation, in that you speak of a good mawther, a poor mawther, a little mawther, or even a silly one, but never of a bad one. In my ears on this evening the word had an over-familiar, almost a contemptuous sound, so I said even more stiffly:

"Mr. Christopher Hatton was my father."

He said, "Oh," drawing the word out long and thin. "They expecting you at Mortiboys?"

I would have given anything to be able to say "Yes" but had the sense to realise that if I were expected I should have been met.

"No," I said.

"Well, thass none of my business"—I was to learn that in Suffolk this confession is an invariable prelude to a piece of busybodying—"but I hope you ain't counting on a welcome.

The owd gentleman is a rare one to bear a grudge. That'd be about a year ago now, I had a chap here, come all the way from London to bring Master Chris's few things home, and he towd me what the owd gentleman did with 'em. Chucked 'em into the horse pond." I expect my face showed how I felt about that, for he said quickly, "Sorry, miss, maybe I shouldn't hev spoke of it. But I don't like to think of you walking all that way just to get the door slammed in your face. Be dark by the time you got there too."

I had never until that moment doubted my welcome, or even thought of the Hattons as a number of individual people. All I knew was that Father had been an outcast from his tribe and that Mother's last order to me had been to return to it and be safe.

I stood there, with less than a shilling in my pocket, and I was alone in the world. No, not quite. The carter, draining his tankard, said:

"I can't make head nor tail of this, but I go on to Colchester tomorrow and back to London that way. You can ride along if you want to."

"I don't know," the man from the inn said. "Maybe she'd do better to go to the Old Vine."

"What's the Old Vine?" I asked, fearing that it was some fancy name for a Poor Farm.

"Thass a house where Mr. Rupert Hatton . . . now, less see . . ." Once again he made a mental calculation, this time a brief one. "He's your father's cousin, though a good bit older. He hev some peculiar ways but he's reckoned openhanded. Anyway, the least he'd do for you'd be to give you a meal and a bed for the night and hev you drove out to Mortiboys in the morning."

"You do that," the carter said, "and if you want to get back to London, I shall set off well by seven."

I thanked him, and then asked the other man how I went to the Old Vine. He told me. "And to Mortiboys?" I asked, for I had not yet made up my mind. Both places lay in the same direction.

Somewhat as an afterthought the man from the inn asked if I was hungry or thirsty; I was both, but I had my dignity to consider, so, thanking him and the carter once more, I left the inn yard and, following directions, emerged onto the emptiness of the Market Square, dominated by an immense stone gateway, and on through a broken-down arch and into what the man who had directed me had called Southgate Street. The Old Vine, he said, was the fourth or fifth house along, on the left, and unmistakable, built of red brick, with two gables and with a garden all ablow with roses in front of it.

As I walked some of the things Mother had said, not much noticed at the time, came back to me. "All Hattons are heartless, except your father." "I never thought you fitted for the role of poor relation." "You could feign gratitude and meekness." I saw now how sinister these words actually were, and began to wish that I had never left London. Before I was into Southgate Street I had decided not to go on to Mortiboys; an old man who could, in a few minutes, receive news of his son's death and turn and throw that same son's cherished silver-knobbed cane and watch into a horse pond wasn't likely to welcome his granddaughter; the man at the inn had showed perspicacity there; and of the Hatton at Old Vine he had said, "He hev some peculiar ways," and who knew what form they might take? By the time that I drew level with the Old Vine, walking on the opposite side of the road, the better to see it, I had just about decided that my best plan was to take advantage of the kindly carter's offer and go back to London.

Then I saw the house. The last slanting rays of the declining sun caught the panes of some of its windows, and woke the secret colours hidden in the depths of the red bricks of which it was built, so that some looked rose-coloured and some orangy-pink and some almost purple, and all at once sharply real and completely unreal, the way things are in

dreams. The two gables and the massed solidity of its chim-
neys were outlined against the pale sky; and in front of it
hundreds of roses, widehearted after the warmth of the day,
spilled fragrance into the evening air.

Except that what I felt was more violent, it was exactly like
the moment when I first saw the green ring; the same feeling
of completion, of belonging; the same desire to possess; and,
deep inside me, where reason and sense no longer operated,
the same certainty that with cunning and a little luck, I might
indeed possess.

Absurd on the face of it, standing there, fourteen years old,
in a print dress and clumped shoes, and all I owned tied up in
a bundle, but the feeling was powerful enough, and lasted just
long enough to carry me across the road, up the short path
between the roses, and to the door, where I rang the bell.

A manservant of a type with which I was familiar opened
the door. Men, if they are strong and able-bodied, are inwardly
shamed by performing tasks which call for neither strength
nor skill; they feel, wittingly or not, emasculated, so they make
up for it by adopting supercilious manners. They also steal
and cheat and are shameless about soliciting tips because they
are all aiming at buying their freedom; as soon as they have
enough saved they buy taverns or apartment houses or
brothels.

Before this one's look of surprised disapproval had time to
discourage me, before he could tell me to go to the back door,
I said:

"I am Miss Felicity Hatton. I should like to speak to Mr.
Hatton."

I realised that he was staring at my bundle, that symbol
of humble status. I thrust it forward, saying, "Yes, you may
take this."

He was not to know that I, free, because desperate, was
wreaking upon him some slight vengeance for insults endured
under many a doorway. He was so unmanned that he took the

bundle, rather as though it had been a dead cat. Holding it in one hand and the door in the other, he said:

"If you would wait here, please. Miss Hatton, Miss Felicity Hatton, you said?"

He left me. The hall was wide and high and richly furnished. At its far end a very beautiful staircase went up gently to a half landing, and there turned, its upper half invisible. Despite my bold face I was too nervous to sit down on any of the settles, stools, or chairs, and walked about, held my face over a great bowl of red roses on a table, looked briefly in a gilt-framed glass, and away again because the sight was so discouraging, paused by the figure of a naked black girl holding a seven-branched candlestick in her hand, and then, near the foot of the stairs, found a little picture. Myself as a child! The girl in the picture had hair of a deeper chestnut—my father's colour, in fact—and her clothes were outlandish, but apart from these small differences she had exactly the face, pretty and innocent, which had served me so well in my pickpocketing days. I wondered what had happened to *her* prettiness. Mine had disappeared into a hunted, hungry alley-cat look; but that was due to the life I had led. The girl in the picture, full-fed, had, I supposed, grown plump, puddingy.

The servant came back. He had recovered. He said:

"Mr. Hatton will receive you. Will you come this way?"

We went to the right, along a short passage. He opened a door and said, with an underlying irony:

"Miss Felicity Hatton."

The room was so brightly lighted as to be dazzling; dozens of candles. And two men, standing together; one quite young, the other old. "Your father's cousin, but a good bit older," the man at the inn had said, so I took three steps towards the older man, and then with a flicker of gratitude towards my mother, made, for all my skimpy print skirt and clumped shoes, an absolutely perfect curtsey.

The younger man turned away, saying petulantly, "My

God!" and threw himself into a chair. The older one looked at me, and away, and at me again, and said:

"Felicity Hatton? You claim some kinship with me? I can't for the life of me see how." He spoke fast, in a snatchy, peevish way. That and something indefinable about the way he held himself gave an impression of crippledom, invalidism. "How do you come to be called Hatton?"

"I was born in wedlock, the daughter of Christopher Hatton and Annabel, his wife. I have proof of that."

"Oh yes, of course, Chris. I was forgetting him. That's feasible. And now I come to look I think I perceive a likeness. Andrew, my dear boy, come here. Does this face remind you of something, of someone?"

The younger man rose and came with a slow, posturing step near to where I stood.

"A vague resemblance to the girl in a ruff, but these features are far coarser."

He regarded me with a distaste which even my shabbiness and travel-stained appearance did not justify. I did not know then that there are some men to whom all women are hateful, or that Andrew Sawston would have looked at me with equal distaste had I been clad in satin. I felt anger begin to coil in me like a spring which tightens to a certain point and then must be released. I was hungry and thirsty, tired and disappointed, all states which make for touchy temper. Rupert Hatton said, in a judicious, impersonal way:

"Slightly coarser—but then poor Chris probably married his washerwoman. He was fastidious about his linen and how else could he be sure of a clean shirt twice a day?"

It was all the more hurtful for being so very near the truth. I gave my rage full rein, forgetting everything else.

"Let me tell you . . ." I began, using the voice which had on occasion made itself heard from one end to another of Horsemonger Lane, and I told him exactly how respectable and admirable my mother had been, in terms which, if she could have heard them, would have shocked her past bearing. I railed at all Hattons—save only my father—quoting what the man at the inn had said about the old man at Mortiboys throwing the cane and the watch in the horse pond. I said that even when we were most down on our luck, if a kinsman had arrived hungry and homeless we'd have given him some sort of hospitality. . . . And so on and on, using the worst words I had learned in the London streets, and stopping only when I realised that both my listeners were leaning together for support, helpless, drunk with laughter. That put the finishing touch to my rage, I said:

"Oh, go on, f—— yourselves!" and swung round and made for the door.

Rupert Hatton, gasping from laughter, cried:

"Andrew, stop her! Stop her! This, you must admit, is absolutely unique. A treasure."

The young man seemed to slide towards me over the polished floor. I said:

"You lay a finger on me and you'll be sorry," and I reached out for the doorknob. If it had turned in the ordinary way, from left to right, the whole of my life might have been different; but it was one of those contrary ones which turned the other way, and while I fumbled with it Rupert Hatton, with the presence of mind which never deserted him, had pulled the bell rope. When I did get the door open I found myself face to face with the manservant, and from behind me Rupert Hatton said in his rapid, peevish-sounding voice:

"Oh, Plant, my cousin, Miss Felicity Hatton, has come to stay. I think the Yellow Room. And supper as soon as possible; she has had a long journey."

I stood there for a second rather like one of those entertainers whom you sometimes see in public places balancing on the tip of a sword held by another person and juggling with plates. Out into the road, with my justifiable grudge, a night under a hedge, and back to London and the washing in the morning; or the Yellow Room and chance what might happen. . . . I took the chance.

It was at the supper table on that first evening that I realised that my first fleeting impression of Rupert Hatton as a cripple, or an invalid, had been right. His left hand was useless and was always pushed into the pocket of his breeches; his left leg dragged a little. The leg didn't matter; the hand did, because he had been a violinist. He had suffered an apoplectic fit when he was twenty-five, which is an early age to have a stroke, and his career was finished.

I did not, of course, learn all this in one day, or even in one month. On that first evening I saw that any food which had to be cut, was cut for him by someone else; he then took his fork in his right hand and delicately picked up the pieces.

The food that evening was delicious; the room assigned me was beautiful and luxurious in the extreme; and Rupert Hatton set himself out to be charming, as though anxious to make amends for a bad beginning. I was deceived, having yet to learn that his moods were as unreliable as the wind, everything about him, in fact, so contrary and perverse that one might at times, with some justification question his sanity. Over supper that evening, however, he behaved in exactly the way in which, had I ever allowed my mind to run ahead and visualise my reception into the family, I should have imagined it. He asked me many questions about my former life and I answered with some reservations; I was frank about our spells of poverty, but did not mention my apprenticeship in case he should wonder how I had freed myself; I told him that Mother had died of a broken heart, not of gin-drinking: I was also careful to let him know that there had been prosperous times as well, that I had had some schooling, attended a dancing class, and taken lessons on the harpsichord. He'd listened to everything I said with interest and attention, but at the mention of music the interest sharpened.

"How well do you play?"

"Badly, I suspect; it is more than a year since I saw the instrument."

"You must try again," he said. "We have a small, somewhat amateur orchestra here. If you have any talent at all you will be useful."

Andrew, who had maintained a sulky silence all this time, broke it to say:

"Thomas won't like it; he detests anyone else to touch his harpsichord."

"Thomas must lump it then. I'd gained the impression—how, I don't know—that the harpsichord belonged to me."

I saw their eyes meet across the table; my cousin's stare was cool, almost without expression; Andrew's was defiant, and then reproachful, almost womanishly so; he looked down at his plate and I thought for a moment that he was going to cry. Rupert Hatton then turned to me and said:

"I have taken a liking to you, Felicity, and when I like anyone all that I have is theirs. But I will be frank and tell you that there is another reason for my opening my home to you—it will irk my uncle Barnabas, who happens to be your grandfather, and a carping, self-righteous old prig. He would have given you a cold and grudging welcome and treated you as a charity child, as indeed he treats his own unfortunate womenfolk. I shall dress you in silk and load you with jewels and flaunt you in the neighbourhood."

I disliked the tone of this speech, so I said:

"Like a French poodle!"

He laughed. I stopped eating and gripped my hands together.

"I don't think I'm truly welcome here, either. And if I'm not I'd better leave tomorrow when I can be sure of a ride. Later on I might not be so lucky."

"You take offence much too easily. Look . . ." He reached into his breeches pocket and brought out four guineas.

"Tuck those away in a safe place, then, any time that you wish to return to London, you can engage a seat on a coach and will have lost nothing." Without allowing me time to thank him, he went on, addressing the young man, "Cheer up, Andrew, this is not a complete invasion of the monstrous army of women, merely one rather exotic specimen. . . ."

It is a little difficult to be truly sorry for anyone who is rich if you yourself are poor; the mind will try to slip away from under the burden of sympathy and think—But with all that money . . . When, in course of time, I had pieced together my cousin Rupert's story I could see that it *was* a tragic one. He'd always, from earliest youth, been devoted to the violin, and was reckoned to have phenomenal talent. His father had died when he was young—nine years old, I think—and his mother, left very well off, had indulged his every whim. When he was twelve he had gone and put himself under the tutelage of a famous violinist named Danielli who had used him hard and made him practise many, many hours each day, and who had also—I wonder was jealousy at work here—held him back from performing in public, promising that every month of waiting was improving his performance and would increase the impact his playing would make when finally he did appear before the world. When he was allowed to emerge he became famous almost overnight, and in the summer of 1695 was invited to play in the Gallery of Mirrors at Versailles before the King, Louis XIV, and all the French court. Halfway through the performance he collapsed and was carried out senseless; and when he recovered consciousness it was to face the knowledge that he would never again hold a violin.

A sad, a terrible story; but as I say, the mind will slip away, insisting that it would all have been worse had it happened to a poor man. We know that he had his comfortable, even luxurious home to return to, a doting mother to console him: he could afford to indulge his understandable melancholy, to remain withindoors, shunning all company. Later, when his mind had healed, he could afford to indulge his whims. He travelled a good deal, bringing back from far places beautiful things with which to adorn his house; the Nubian girl holding the candlestick had once stood in a palace in Florence, the rugs on the floor of the music room had been wall hangings in a house in Ispahan: he owned the first pianoforte in Baildon, possibly in all Suffolk. I gathered that he had been much sought after as a husband; I, at least, understood why he had never married; marriage, no matter how coldly undertaken, involves some permanence, some intimacy, and imposes its own limitations in a country where monogamy is the rule. Rupert could never have had four or five wives at the same time and played one off against the other, in the way that he did his favourites, over whom he had complete power.

I may wrong him, but at times I suspected that a lust for power over other people may have lain at the root of his determination to play the violin better than anyone else; to sway people, to hold them, to affect their emotions, that is the aim or at least one of the aims of the musical performer, just as it is of the stage player. Cut off by his infirmity from the kind of power he had briefly enjoyed, he had taken to substitutes.

His favourites fell roughly into two classes; there were the poor "pretty" boys of humble status whom he had noticed because of their looks, whom he installed in his home, and spoiled and teased and with whom he quarrelled. They had one thing in common, an insatiable greed; whatever he gave them they always wanted more, and many of them sooner or later stole from him. The other kind were young men from the solid, wealthy but dull families in the neighbourhood who for some reason found themselves at odds with their background. Any discontented young man whose father had refused to send him on the Grand Tour and thought him better employed riding his own acres and learning to carry his port wine, could come to the Old Vine, eat a meal prepared by Rupert's Neapolitan, Georgio, listen to music, or to Rupert's talk of his travels, and go away feeling sophisticated.

None of them showed any interest in me. The pretty boys were averse to women; the local young men were often in temporary revolt against females, their mothers, their sisters, the young women whom their parents wished them to marry. Any girl with an ordinary past would have been lonely, out of place and embarrassed several times every day, but I flourished. Long ago I'd learned to dispense with female friendship; I was a natural liar and not above making mischief if the opportunity offered, and I had known enough hardship to make luxury delightful to me.

I had had the chance to leave Rupert and the Old Vine. Within a fortnight of my arrival my grandfather came to offer me a home. In appearance he was my father, grown old, grim, and purposeful. He stormed at Rupert for taking me, unsuitably dressed, to a Musical Evening in the Baildon Assembly Rooms and letting everyone know my identity without informing him. Rupert said:

"But I feared for her. You might have thrown *her* into the horse pond."

My grandfather told me to collect my clothes and go home with him. Something in me, inherited from my mother, something that craved security, respectability, urged me to go with him, strict and parsimonious as I knew him to be; something else, more powerful, drove me to say that I preferred to stay where I was. Then my grandfather turned on Rupert and said:

"You're a moral leper and you contaminate everything you touch. You make me ashamed of my name."

Rupert said, "Dear me, you do sound cross!" and gave his most affected laugh.

My grandfather became incoherent with anger, and only the words "you cursed Sodomite" emerged with any clarity. And just then they meant nothing to me, for neither as little miss, nor as a child of the gutter, had I learned the names of the cities of the plain, or what they meant in terms of abuse.

In actual truth I never believed Rupert to be a pervert, for even an unorthodox attachment demands some human feeling, some affection, some warmth; and any kind of physical traffic would have committed him and lessened his power if only for a short time.

So, in this curious, unreal atmosphere I spent the next two years, very comfortably and happily. And then I was sixteen and a lot of things happened all at once.

Rupert found a new friend, neither a pretty boy nor a discontented son of a neighbour. William Talbot must have been nearing fifty and his skin, even his eyeballs, were yellow from some disease that he had picked up during his wanderings. As Rupert was to the local young men, so William Talbot was to Rupert; he'd lived in India, in the East Indies, and in the Caribbean Islands. He could talk entertainingly—even to me—for hours on end; he had beautiful manners; he was musical, well read, self-assured. He never for a moment felt that he was dependent upon Rupert, therefore he was never grateful, or sycophantic, nor did he ever show sycophancy's other ugly face, insolence. Rupert met him, invited him to stay, and he came. The moment Rupert was bored with him—or, even more important, the moment he was bored with Rupert—he'd be on his way. . . . That was implicit in everything he ever said or did. He was a match for Rupert, who never before in all his life had met his match. Upon everyone else—myself included—Rupert had played, as once he had played upon the strings of his violin. Now he had found somebody upon whose heart and mind and greed he couldn't play at all, and he was completely subject.

One day I heard Rupert say, "But, William, you must realise, all that I have is yours."

I thought to myself—And that means the house, the Old Vine.

That was a blow. Always, at the back of my mind, there had been the hope that he would leave me his house. I was his kinswoman, and somehow I had survived a whole series of favourites. Rupert was not entirely without a sense of values and he must see, I had thought, that no pretty boy was fit to be left in charge of his beautiful house. William Talbot was. He constituted a real threat.

I began to wonder about Rupert's age and discovered that he must be nearing seventy. It was hard to believe. It was as though his stroke, falling so early, had aged him in a flash but at the same time rendered him immune to the ordinary creeping damage of the years. His tempers, his violent enthusiasms and prejudices were all things of youth. But he was already older than many men live to be.

It was at this time that George Turnbull first came to the house. He was the nephew of Rupert's attorney and had recently come to help his uncle, who was old and who suffered from a weak chest. George was a big, rawboned young man whose clothes always seemed a little too small for him. He wasn't handsome, but he was young, and ordinary, and to me, who knew only posturing young fools and two aging men, he seemed attractive. Rupert said he was brilliantly clever and had handled a tricky bit of business in a manner quite impossible to old Mr. Turnbull, and he somehow contrived that after his first visit George always had some say in his affairs. Occasionally he asked him to supper. George was always civil to me—unlike the pretty boys—but no more. It was on those occasions that I greatly regretted not being pretty.

Someone had opened a coffee house on the Market Square at Baildon, and one morning, when I was shopping at the stalls, George Turnbull emerged from it and, coming face to face with me, greeted me with seeming pleasure. He asked after Rupert's health, and added, "No need to inquire after your health, Miss Felicity. You look blooming." It was the first time anyone had ever paid me anything approaching a compliment, and to my mortification a slow hot blush ran from my neck to my hair.

"I have managed to persuade my uncle that time spent in the coffee house is not wasted," George said. "A good deal of business goes on there and many a man will approach an attorney in such a place who would shrink from coming to the office. From the window I sometimes see you. You often walk in that direction." He nodded towards the opening of a narrow lane which ran off from one corner of the market.

The infuriating blush which had almost receded, swamped my face again. I had a perfectly good reason for walking in Pound Lane, and it was nothing to be ashamed of. But it was secret.

He said, with unusual awkwardness, "I'm sorry. I wasn't intending to betray curiosity. Only interest."

I regained my self-possession.

"If what I plan when I stand in Pound Lane ever comes to anything you'll know about it," I said.

So would everyone else, for what I planned was to open a tea parlour which would serve women in the way the coffee house and inns served their menfolk. I'd hit on the idea when I first began to think seriously about what might happen to me after Rupert's death. Pound Lane, so near the market, would be the ideal spot, and one small house, with a big bow window, would be the ideal house. No great amount of capital was needed, a quarter's rent in advance, a few dainty cups and pots, some tea and some fuel. I already had five pounds saved, gained a mite at a time by shrewd marketing, by saying that I had had three teeth pulled when in truth I had only had one extracted, by saying that I had had two pairs of shoes made when in fact I had had one. The most usual source of revenue for women—the false dressmaker's bill—was not available to me because Rupert delighted in ordering my clothes himself. He loved subtle colours and fine textures.

"I wonder what you plan," George Turnbull said. "I have

plans of my own. I'd like to tell you them, one day, Miss Felicity."

I felt singularly honoured, as well as vastly surprised.

"I'd like to hear them," I said. His, no doubt, would be glowing and ambitious, not just a poor second best, a bowing to necessity, like mine.

"Will you be visiting the market on Saturday morning?"

"I market almost every Wednesday and Saturday," I said.

"Then shall we go and see the display of Dutch tulips in the Botanical Gardens? I hear it promises to be extraordinarily fine this year."

It was the first time that I had ever heard the Botanical Gardens spoken of as anything but a joke. There'd once been an Abbey in Baildon; the Great Gate on Market Square was part of it, and beyond the gate there had been ruins and rough ground, used by the townspeople for grazing geese and goats and donkeys. Some time before I came to Baildon Lord Bowdegrave, who already owned great estates, discovered that this wilderness was in fact his property. The story ran that a secretary, told to clear out a cupboard, had come across an old parchment that was a deed of gift, signed by Henry the Eighth. Lord Bowdegrave, like a child with fifty toys who takes a disproportionate joy from a whistle made out of a hazel bough, pounced on his new property, and said he would make it into a miniature Kew Gardens. He was building an orangery in which tropical plants and trees would be housed; and there were already beds of flowers, a rose pergola, and some unusual shrubs which people might view upon payment of twopence.

Few people, and none of them Baildon natives, ever went there. Poor people had other uses for their pence, and resented the loss of their common rights; well-to-do people had gardens of their own and thought the charge of twopence a ridiculous example of a rich man's penny-pinching. So, on the Saturday, and on several subsequent occasions, George and I had it to ourselves, except for the workmen who were busy with the orangery, and it was easy enough to avoid them.

We used to sit on a piece of ruined wall and talk. That was all. In a curious kind of way he was to me a replacement of my old friend, Fingers. There'd been nobody else in my life to whom I could tell things, and I deeply appreciated being able to talk freely again. At the same time I was miserably aware that something was wrong. Just because I wasn't pretty, or skilled in the way some quite plain-faced women are in making themselves seem pretty, it was possible for me, a young female, to meet George, a young male, in a secluded and rather romantic spot and merely *talk*. I valued this friendship and at the same time resented it; I suppose there is no more deadly insult that one sex can offer the other than friendship.

Maybe I was, in my own way, as awkward and perverse as Rupert. I'd spend hours on an evening before I was to meet George, trying out new ways of doing my hair, colouring my cheeks and lips, making myself more attractive; then in the morning I'd feel silly and despise such cheap wiles. It was a friendship, no more.

He told me his secret ambition, which was to own land. He heartily detested his lawyer's trade. "Being at the beck and call of any low fellow with a grievance and seven and sixpence to spend," as he called it. I in turn told him about my aim to have a tea shop. He found that amusing. Surely, he said, my cousin Rupert would provide for me.

"I doubt it," I said. "That would be the ordinary way to behave and Rupert never behaves in the ordinary way."

"What exactly is the relationship between you? The word cousin is loosely used."

"He is my father's cousin."

"And this William Talbot. What relation is he?"

"None at all. He's just a friend. But a very special one, and I'm afraid that Rupert will leave him everything."

I even confided to George my feeling about the house. I said I wouldn't mind if I were left the house and just enough money to enable me to live in it.

"I'd sack that dirty Georgio and that supercilious Plant and just have a nice maid in a mob-cap," I said. "And I'd get rid of all the instruments from the music room, except the piano. And I'd buy a good horse to ride and have a big dog to go on walks with and a small dog to cuddle."

"You have it all cut and dried," he said. "Is that all?"

I wanted to say—And I'd ask you to marry me, even if you didn't think I was pretty enough to love—I'd be very kind and generous to you, and there'd be children. . . . But that was the kind of thing no girl could ever say. I could only say:

"Oh, I daresay I should think of other things as I went along."

After a talk like that I'd go home raging angry; because if George felt for me one thousandth part of what I felt for him he could never have sat and discussed my future like that. Not with the trees breaking into leaf and blossom overhead and the cuckoo calling and calling. . . . Oh, that was a miserable spring for me.

Since William Talbot's arrival there had been a great peace in the house and perhaps that is why when he and Rupert did have a falling out, Rupert took it so hardly. It all began in the most stupid way. In the middle of May there came a spell of glorious hot weather; and one day we were all sitting in the garden and William said something about being a sun worshipper and not intending to spend another winter in England.

Rupert said, "What did you say?" and when William repeated his words, proceeded to lash himself into a fury. The truth was that he loved emotional scenes and he hadn't had one since the last of the pretty boys, so he made the most of his chance. He said some ridiculous things and William was justified in saying:

"Really, Rupert, you must be beside yourself," and in getting up and walking away. Rupert grabbed his stick and set off after him, and when he had taken about four steps he seemed to lose balance; he swayed about a bit, making a funny noise, and then fell down.

William turned back, I ran for Plant, and between them they carried him to bed. Dr. Cornwell came. It was another stroke, very slight. As soon as he was bled he regained consciousness and lay in his bed looking very pale and reproachful. William, awkward and remorseful, hovered round apologising without fully realising what he had done wrong. Rupert very plaintively and sweetly forgave him. Except for the stroke, which though slight was real enough, it was the kind of scene which had played at the Old Vine many times before. William simply hadn't known his part in the play, that was all.

Then, very dramatically, Rupert sent for old Mr. Turnbull. He didn't say so, but it was obvious that he was going to make a new will, or alter an old one.

When next George and I met there was in his manner a difference of which I was instantly aware; it was warmer, far more confident, and, beyond all, sympathetic—almost as though, since our last meeting, I had suffered a bereavement. The day was warm and sunny, but it had rained overnight and he insisted upon taking off his coat and spreading it over the stone before I sat down. Twice he called me by name, omitting the "Miss." He said:

"Oh, by the way, I have a piece of information for you. I thought you'd be interested. The little house in Pound Lane is let on a lease that has three years to run but . . ." He added something about the age of the tenant; I didn't listen because something had flashed, like a firework inside my head. His pitying manner, and now this! He had seen Rupert's will.

I said, "Rupert has left everything to William Talbot, hasn't he?"

George put his bony hand on mine and closed his fingers in a warm, comforting grasp.

"Felicity," he said, "you must never even *think* that I would betray a client's confidence. Not that I could, in this case. My uncle made your cousin's will—if indeed a will was made."

"We know it was. And we know what was in it. And you're sorry for me. That is why you've been treating me for the last five minutes as though I were an invalid." I did indeed feel weak and sick. Not about the money; the house.

He kept his hand over mine.

"You've completely misunderstood me. Now, before another word is said, Felicity, tell me this. Have I ever, in any way whatsoever, made any reference to your prospects, or lack of them?"

"Rupert quarrelled with William; he was ill; they made it up in just the kind of way that Rupert delights in. Your uncle came to the house. And now you're sorry for me, and you've set yourself out to get information about the house I want for a tea parlour. I can add all these things together and give myself an answer."

"Quite the wrong one. You're absolutely and entirely wrong. Come now, can't you think of another reason, a much better and more personal reason for my offering you that discouraging piece of information?"

"*Discouraging?* I thought you meant it consolingly. Telling me that in three years I might hope . . ."

"To have a tea parlour?" He lifted my hand and turned it over so that it was cupped in his own. "Are you deliberately making it hard for me? Don't, please. I'm not very skilled at this kind of thing."

I looked at him. His eyes were fixed on my face in a very intent and pleading gaze. I thought . . . and then—No, it can't be . . .

"I've so little to offer at the moment," he said, "but in three years—which you would have to wait for that little house. Felicity, in my awkward way I'm trying to tell you that I love you and want you to marry me."

I almost died. All the bright garden went into a whirling blur through which I was falling, falling. I think I should have fallen, but George put his arm around me and pulled me close. He kissed me, clumsily, and I kissed him back.

We spent the next precious ten minutes explaining ourselves to one another. He said that he'd been in love with me since our first meeting, but that I had always seemed so cool and self-possessed, and never gave him an opening to show his feelings. And I told him that I had been afraid to do so because I knew I wasn't pretty and thought that he could never regard me as more than an acquaintance. He said that he thought I was beautiful; and when he said that I *felt* beautiful; I would be so, too, now that I was free of the fear of making a fool of myself; I could try more attractive ways of doing my hair; I'd colour my face, smile with more confidence. It was like being re-born.

We laughed as we talked, laughed over our own hesitations and foolish fears. Then, suddenly, George became immensely grave and said:

"It isn't going to be easy, though, even now." He explained that his uncle had said, time and again, that any professional man who married young was a fool.

"Then we must wait," I said. I would have been quite happy to wait for years now that I knew myself loved and desired. "We're young," I said.

"Why should we waste our best years?"

"What else can we do? Unless you can persuade your uncle to change his views."

"He has *never* changed his view on any subject! And to mention the matter even would give him the idea that I was frivolous. There *is* a way out, but"—he looked at his watch—

"there is no time now to go into that. When can we meet again? Can you ever get away in the evening?"

"I can get away at any time. Nobody cares what I do."

"Don't!" he said. "That sounds so forlorn. From now on remember that *I* care."

In all my sixteen years I'd never felt so cherished, so precious and important as I did when he said that.

When we met next time and he said that he had thought it all out and had come to the conclusion that the best thing for us to do was to have a Fleet marriage, I agreed. I would have agreed to anything he suggested. He asked, "Do you know what that is?"

"The only Fleet I know of is a debtors' gaol in London," I said.

"That's it. Clergymen, like other people, run into debt and are thrown into the Fleet, and are hard put to it to find money for food and what small comforts a bribed gaoler can provide. So they ply their trade and are always ready to marry people without fuss about licence or banns."

"Are they legal, such marriages?"

"Oh yes. That we know from the recurrent attempts to have them made illegal. A clergyman, however heavily in debt, is still in orders. And they keep a register."

"That's all right then. The only thing is, if I say I want to go to London, my cousin Rupert will wonder why. He doesn't *care* what I do, but he is as curious as the cat in the adage. If he had the slightest suspicion he'd tell your uncle from sheer malice."

"Yes," George said, "I've thought of that too. But there's no need for you to be there, Felicity."

"No need? At my own wedding!"

"It could be done by proxy. Nobody would know us by sight. All that really matters is the entry in the register."

Suddenly, and completely against my will, I found myself

crying. I'd never been an easy crier and these tears were indicative of my new, pliable state. I've often heard women claim that by weeping they get their own way. It isn't true. A weeping woman gets exactly as much as the man who makes her weep was willing in the first place to concede, no more, no less. And all that she might have gained by *not* weeping is thrown away.

In the silly state I was in I just thought—How squalid this all is. A parson who can't pay his bills, secrecy as though what we did was a crime, no wedding dress, no bells, no good wishes, and I not even there. So I cried, and George held me and made soothing sounds and dabbed my face with his handkerchief and I ended as weeping women always end, soft and grateful and complaisant. False to myself.

At the same time I could see the advantages. Once the thing was done, however shadily, it was done. Old Mr. Turnbull could go on dragging George around—as he did—to various houses where there were families of girls, younger than me, and it wouldn't matter. However pretty they might be, however well-provided for, they couldn't hope in years to come to have George, because there'd be some written words that made him mine. It wasn't that I didn't trust him, or that I doubted his love. I just wanted to be sure.

"Can *you* go to London without arousing curiosity?" I asked.

"I am obliged to go. I have an examination to pass. That is why I have tried to persuade you—perhaps too hastily. Such an opportunity may not come again, but if you have doubts . . ."

I hastened to deny that I had doubts, hastened to repudiate my tears. He took heart and said that all that he needed now was money for the clergyman. His uncle fed, clothed, and taught him, but did not consider that he needed money for his pocket.

"An outside coach fare to London and a shilling a day for

my keep when there is as much as I can hope for from him," George said.

So I sent him off to London with all my savings, five pounds, five shillings, and a sixpence.

"And pick a decent woman to stand proxy for me," I said. Poll Knock-on-the-wall-for-threepence flashed before my mind's eye.

He said decent women were unlikely to lend themselves to such a purpose but he would try to find one not too hardened.

The coaches for London left the *Abbot's Head* at eight o'clock in the morning, and on the Monday when George was due to leave I woke early and determined to go and see his departure. I could stand in the deep shadow of the old Abbey gateway and watch, unseen, and still be back in good time for breakfast, which on sunny summer mornings Rupert and William and I took on the terrace outside the music-room window. I rose and made a careful toilet, and then, still too early, and feeling restless, occupied myself by making my bed.

The Abbey gateway lay in shadow, the *Abbot's Head* on the opposite side of the Market Square was bright with sunshine, so I had a clear good view of George as he climbed to the outside seat of the coach. He wore his best suit, which was like all his clothes, a little too small for him, and carried a small hand valise. I reminded myself that Rupert, not easily impressed, thought highly of George's ability; he would pass this examination easily and soon be independent of his uncle. All would be well. The future stretched ahead of me, as full of shimmering promise as the sunny dew-drenched morning.

The coach set off at a spanking pace and I turned and walked without hurrying, back to the Old Vine.

It was only a quarter past eight, but Rupert and William were already on the terrace with the breakfast before them.

Rupert wore his most unpleasant expression.

"Where have you been?"

"For a walk," I said. It was unusual, but no sin; nevertheless my face turned hot.

"Where?"

"As far as the South Gate."

"That's a lie to begin with; five minutes there and back. It's a good half hour since I went to your room and found it empty and your bed not slept in. Try again! *Where have you been?*"

"I told you. For a walk."

He lost his temper completely and began to splutter out incoherent words of abuse and accusation. I wasn't to think, he said, that he'd been blind to my "frimmicking" of late, curling my hair and painting my face and "other bitchy tricks."

William said, "Rupert! You do yourself no good. Excitement is bad for you. And there's no harm in taking a walk."

Rupert said venomously, "That's right. Take her part. You're all alike!" And then suddenly he wasn't saying words any more, just making noises like those he had made during his last quarrel with William in the garden. The look of anger on his face slid into one of terror, astonishment, blankness. Then he slumped forward.

At the same moment Plant came to the end of the terrace and said:

"The carriage is ready when you . . . Oh God!"

There'd never been any fondness between Rupert and me and his death brought me no real grief. Remorse, yes. All through that hot sombre day I kept telling myself that it wasn't my fault that Rupert, too, had wakened early that morning and decided to drive down to Bywater in search of coolness, sent a servant along to rouse me and William, and ordered the carriage and an early breakfast. It wasn't my fault. Nevertheless the fact remained that by leaving the house and then not giving a frank explanation of my errand, I had made him lose his temper. And after all he had taken me in, fed, clothed, housed me; but for him I should never have known George. . . . I owed Rupert an immense debt and I had repaid him ill.

When the will was read I suffered one last, greatly inflamed feeling of remorse and then forgot Rupert entirely. He had left all that he owned to me, except for a legacy of five thousand pounds to his friend William Talbot, "to enable him to return to Jamaica and enjoy the sun." But what mattered to me at that moment was the fact that the will was written in George's hand.

So he had known, and that knowledge had governed the change in his attitude towards me.

It took me less than a moment to look back and see that at heart I had always known. George had fooled me but largely because I had wished to be fooled. The truth had confronted me every time I looked in the glass and seen my alley-cat's face. Beautiful, he'd said. Yes, had I been pitted by smallpox, disfigured by a birthmark, I should have been beautiful to him, once that will was made.

It was rather like those fairy tales where a person is granted his wish and then finds himself worse off than before. I now had what I had longed for, the beautiful house and enough wealth to maintain it, but I had at the same time such a deadly humiliation of spirit, such a loss of self-esteem as would last for a lifetime.

Almost as hurtful was the certainty that if I saw him again, accused him of deception and upbraided him, he'd talk me round. I myself had given him some power over me, so that with him I was weak, yielding, self-deluding; typically female, in fact.

I reverted, promptly, to my true character, to the hard resourcefulness bred in me by my childhood's circumstance. Nobody, I told myself fiercely, not even Miss Bellsize, had ever finally got the better of Felicity Hatton. I could outwit George Turnbull.

I could see by the way people looked at me that they thought me a trifle demented by grief; and demented people are not closely questioned, since they are prone to give silly answers, nor are they lightly crossed lest they grow worse. Besides, I was now an heiress.

My first apparently witless question was to Mr. Turnbull and concerned the writing of the will. He said that he had jotted down particulars and then allowed George to make a fair copy which was brought back and signed and witnessed. "He writes a better hand than I do, these days," Mr. Turnbull said, with some regret. After that I busied myself getting people to make their mark or sign their names against a statement so obvious as to be ridiculous. So when George came home with his paper evidence that I was his legal wife, I had evidence to the contrary. A number of people, his own uncle among them, had testified that Felicity Hatton had been in Baildon on what lawyers call the relevant dates. I kept the original paper and sent a copy to await his return. He understood.

He was crafty, too. Within twenty-four hours he sent me back the money I had lent him—I wonder how he'd managed to scratch it together—with a laconic message, he had been unable to do my errand, he said.

Maybe that was true, maybe not. Some years later George married a rich man's only child and the thought occurred to me that he might—this well-thought-of, up-and-coming young Mr. Turnbull—be a bigamist, actually married to someone like Poll Knock-on-the-wall. The thought amused me. But then, once I had recovered from my girlish green-sick love, a great many things did amuse me.

INTERLUDE

To those rustic philosophers who liked to look for motives and explanations Miss Felicity Hatton's behaviour appeared explicable enough, unnatural though it seemed. Rupert Hatton had brought her up, they said, forgetting that she was fourteen when she arrived in Baildon, and he'd always been odd and his ways were womanish, so it followed that she should be odd and act like a man and never wear a dress, always a severely tailored jacket and plain full skirt such as other women wore only for riding. Even her hair, her one beauty, being naturally curly and glossy, though of a colour never seen on a human head, she wore brushed straight back and tied in a queue and when she wore a hat it was a man's, made in a small size to fit her. When she drove in her gig, behind a shiny horse named George Brown, and had a rug across her knees, she could easily be mistaken for a boy whose face had lost its childish look and not yet acquired manliness. She had a foible about the name George. She called her hunter George Rider, her great hound George Rumbelow, her lap dog George Yapp. Once, early on, she had a little black boy, also named George. Somebody ventured to ask her the reason for her partiality to that name and she said that it was the name of young Mr. Turnbull, the attorney to whom she owed a great deal. It was typical of her unreasonableness that, this being so, she never employed him as her man of business.

She got rid of the black boy when she began making a fuss about the way some people—Rennett the tailor amongst them

—treated their apprentices. She went to the mayor and asked him couldn't the council pass a bye-law about ill-done-by boys, especially when they came from the Poor Farm which was under council jurisdiction. The mayor, a retired man and thus not concerned with keeping a rich woman's custom, said that any criticism of the Poor Law Authorities came ill from someone who kept a slave. She retorted that George was not a slave; he was a free Briton, born in Deptford, and he earned his keep and twelve pounds a year which she'd wager was more than the mayor paid any servant of his. The mayor knew his Bible and threw a quotation at her, about avoiding not only evil but the appearance of evil. A few days later the black boy, with twenty guineas in his pocket, went on the coach to London, and cried all the way to Colchester, saying he would never again have so easy a place or so kind a mistress.

Despite her strange, unfeminine ways a great many young men and even more ambitious mammas showed interest in a young lady so richly left. Somebody once said, maliciously, that Felicity Hatton collected proposals just as her cousin Rupert had collected objects of art and her old grandfather at Mortiboys, acres. Unlike most malicious statements, this was true. In the library at the Old Vine there was a small leather-bound book which had no title on its binding, but had a heading on the first page, "Proposals made to Felicity Hatton." The earliest entry read "George Turnbull. May 1741" and might have been considered a refutal of the idea that all men were after her money, for it was not until June of that year that she became a woman of property. There followed a long list of names, all dated, most of them in the seventeen-forties and early fifties, thinning out towards the end of that decade. The last entry was made when she was thirty-seven. The name of the man she married when she was thirty-eight was not in the little book; and that was as it should be, for the proposal was not made to, but by, her.

She'd always been charitable in an odd, unpredictable fashion. There had been a time when she kept open house at the Old Vine for apprentices, male and female on alternate Sundays. The amount of meat consumed on these occasions was out of all proportion to the number of children fed. The visits, never very popular with the employers, came to an end for the boys when, one Sunday, crammed with meat, they divided into two gangs and fought a pitched battle on the Market Square; and for girls when a little milliner's apprentice turned up one Sunday suffering from what she called nettle rash, which proved to be measles, and infected all but two of the other girls. Miss Hatton argued stoutly that boys had always fought and always would, and that there was no greater risk of catching measles in her house than in church; but the outings had always been regarded as subversive to discipline, and for once all the employers were of one mind, and those to whom Miss Hatton's custom meant little or nothing stiffened the others. Henceforward she fed the meat-starved child that she saw in every apprentice by means of parcels, delivered every Wednesday morning—sheer waste in the case of Swift the saddler's boys, who ate at their master's table and fared well, but greatly welcomed in several other places.

She had a name for being generous to beggars, knife sharpeners, and such; and once when young Christopher Hatton, who had inherited Mortiboys and with it the Hatton passion for gambling, was neck over ears in debt, she set him clear. Rumour said to the tune of four thousand pounds, but such stories were always exaggerated, and who could know, for sure? What was known was that in return for the money she extracted a promise that he would never play again, a promise he kept for a little less than a fortnight. Up to that time the singularly handsome, unbelievably stupid young man had been regarded as likely to inherit all she had. After the breach people wondered. There were no other young Hattons, even on the distaff side, for old Barnabas' strict ways had condemned his daughters to spinsterhood. And as the years crept by it became less and less likely that Miss Hatton would marry and provide herself with an heir, the Old Vine with another doting owner.

Then, one winter's day in 1763, a man arrived in Southgate Street and went from house to house offering to do any kind of job in return for a few pence, or a meal. He was a tall thin fellow, with black hair cropped close and a wild look in his eyes; he coughed more frequently and more hoarsely than the ordinary cold-afflicted person in that season, and his left arm ended in a stump. Most people turned him away at once, without bothering to ask what a maimed man could do in the way of work. He came to the back door of the Old Vine—whence no one was turned away without reference to the mistress—in a flurry of snow.

Felicity, fetched into the back lobby, regarded him critically and said:

"What could you do?"

"There's progress!" he said. "At least you asked before saying 'no.' Thanks for that, ma'am. Do? I can do most things; saw logs or split them, mend harness, sharpen knives and scissors, tinker a kettle, cane a chair, patch bellows. . . ." He broke off to cough, turning his head away, and then facing her again, his eyes light against the darkness of his weathered skin. He lacked entirely the whining, cringing manner of the ordinary back-door suppliant, and as he listed what he could do his voice had a cheerful, almost a mocking ring. She found herself looking at him more closely, and approving of what she saw. He wore an ancient buff leather jerkin, and around his neck, neatly tied and tucked, a scarf of scarlet and yellow; he looked clean, and his lined brown cheeks were well shaven. A man—she thought—to whom a handicap had been a challenge, so that over keeping himself neat, as over the mastering of various skills, he must always do as well as a man with two hands. A man who, for all his poverty, gave an impression of owning himself.

A whim seized her; and she was accustomed to giving her whims rein, untroubled by thoughts which ruled other people's behaviour—What will the servants say? How would it look? "Come in," she said. "I've no doubt I can find you a job. You're welcome to a meal, anyway."

She led him into the library where a great fire burned, and there she pulled the bell and said to the mob-capped maid who had replaced the supercilious Plant, "I have a guest for dinner."

When she turned back to her guest she found that he had moved to the great bay of the window and stood looking out at the thickening snow. He seemed so self-possessed, so much at ease that one would have thought it was usual for him to be invited into fine rooms in large houses and treated as a guest. Even the carpenter's bag of woven straw which he carried in his hand did not seem wholly incongruous. With an almost animal sensitivity he became aware of her gaze.

"It's beginning to lie," he remarked, nodding towards the snow. "What's the date today?"

"The sixteenth of December."

"Five white weeks, then."

"How do you know?"

"You develop a nose for weather, when you live with it."

He slipped the bag from his arm and set it on the floor.

"It's a fine house you have here." He looked around the room. "So many books! A man could read his life away and not get through them all."

"Can you read?"

He laughed. "A milestone. A poster offering a reward for a stolen horse. Once I read almost a whole book—in Leicester Infirmary. *Robinson Crusoe* it was called. A good story; but I was better and came away before I reached the end."

"Was that when . . . ?" She looked at the handless arm.

"Oh no. That was only a year or two back when I broke my leg. My hand I lost when I was about fourteen. A farm dog bit me and the bite didn't heal. My father was alive then and he dealt with it. He sharpened up his knife and poured a pint of rum into me and . . ." He gestured with his right hand. "Before that I used to play the fiddle." A look of concern touched his face. "I'm sorry, ma'am; no talk for lady's ears— but then, I'm not used to ladies' company. I had no meaning to horrify you."

"It isn't that. It's just that it seems so strange because you're the second person . . ." She told him, with brevity, Rupert's story.

He said, "That's the way it is when anyone's born with a knack. I used to think myself that one bright morning God Almighty had got up and said to Himself—All that round world needs is somebody to play the fiddle. Let Rancon Follett be! Then a little yellow dog, doing its duty, as a dog should, if a bit over-anxious, put a stop to such nonsense, and I've no doubt in the long run I've been happier without my high-flown notions. And the world seems to have done well enough without R. Follett's fiddling."

"You were lucky. My cousin was twenty-five when his blow fell. It wasn't so easy for him to adjust himself and be cheerful."

"Cheerful." He repeated the word as though he had never heard it before. "It depends. I'm only cheerful when I can keep on the move. That time I mentioned, in Leicester Infirmary, the same thing to look at every day, the same people, the feeling of being shut in. . . . Oh, even with *Robinson Crusoe* to help, I almost went mad. I wasn't cheerful then."

"You mean you *like* the life you live?"

"I live the only way I can. The way we've lived, father and son, since time out of mind."

"Suppose . . ." She paused; began again. "Suppose one day one of those posters you spoke of offered an enormous reward, five hundred pounds, say, and you found, or did, whatever was necessary to gain that reward. What would you do then?"

"Just what I'm doing now. With one difference. No, two. On a bad day, when nobody wanted a job done, I'd have supper, nonetheless. And I could take roads in Wales, and Cornwall, and far north in Scotland that no man like me can make a living on; the people are too far scattered, and too poor, and too self-sufficient. But I could go . . ." He lifted his head slightly, as though facing the wind in an unknown place. And he said, "There's an idle fancy, if you like. Five hundred pounds. The top price I ever saw on a poster was one hundred and that was for a murderer."

She said, "But what are you looking for?"

"For? Nothing. I look *at*. At whatever there is round the next bend of the road, over the brow of the next hill, past the next clump of trees."

"And you never find, round the bend, or over the hill, or past the trees, the place where you would, if you could, settle down, make your own, belong to and have belong to you?"

He said, "No. I've no craving for belongings. I carry a few tools because without them I'd be useless, and at the end of a good day I lay in a bit of food." His eyes narrowed as he smiled. "I will own that over that book, I was tempted. I did wonder whether the chap ever got off the island, and if he did what happened to the blackamoor and the goats. And no-body'd have noticed, nobody cared about the two or three books that some old parson had left for the benefit of the sick who could read. But I thought to myself—It'll be that much more to carry; so I left it."

"You're a strange man."

"Maybe. I'm the way I am."

The mob-capped maid said that dinner was on the table.

She remembered Rupert and was prepared to cut this man's meat for him; but he was adept. Holding the fork between his stump and his body, he held the meat firmly while he cut it, and then, transferring the fork to his right hand, ate quickly but with a kind of deliberate delicacy.

She spoke again about his attitude towards owning things.

"When you are old, infirm, what then?"

"I shall lie down and die."

"Easily said."

"Easily done. A man knows when he's finished. At least, he does if he's lived in tune with his nature. I go by my father. *He* played the fiddle, not very well, to my mind, but he could juggle too. He carried six pewter plates in his pack and he could keep them all in the air—it looked as easy as kiss my hand. But there came a day—Lincoln Fair, it was—when one plate and then another got off kilter. Nobody else noticed, but he did. So he packed up and we moved off, and a mile or so out of town he said to me, 'Boy, I'm done for. We'll find a place to lay down.' We turned off, into a wood, beeches, the leaves thick, and he said, 'This'll do.' And he laid down. And he died. He *knew*. When my time comes I shall know. That may sound daft to you, ma'am, but I know by how I felt when my leg broke. If I'd felt done for I'd never have let them carry me into that infirmary. I didn't feel done for. I knew I'd be mended and have years yet on the road."

She thought a little and then said:

"It all seems so pointless, just walking about, going nowhere."

He said gently, "Tell me, ma'am, what sort of life would seem to you to be *not* pointless. I mean I might sit at a loom all my days, and the stuff I wove would in the end wear into holes; I might guide a plough and as soon as I died the weeds might creep over the furrows. Or suppose that dog hadn't bitten me. . . . I'd have played tunes that pleased people for five minutes; even if a few had carried the memory till they died, what difference? Isn't it all, whatever you do, and wherever you go, as you say, pointless?"

It was a question for which even the cynicism of Rupert

and his friends had not prepared her, because, in his heart, though he no longer spoke of it, Rupert had believed that it had mattered whether or not he played the violin; and his possessions mattered too. So had hers; the owning, the flaunting, the unstated dictate—I can do as I please because I am Felicity Hatton, possessor of this, and this. . . . And now suddenly, in a few words, a back-door beggar made nonsense of it all. For a moment she felt despondency like a sickness; no point to possessions, or to self-assertion, or to revenge, all the things which had mattered for so many years; and no point to the future, to the strange and desperate thing she had been planning now for a year or more. Ever since . . .

She remembered the moment with clarity; the twilight of an autumn day, a bronze-red sunset in the sky, the leaves of the trees already thinning, tawny and scarlet and sharp yellow, a faint smell of frost in the air. She was riding home from a day's fox-hunting, and as always, as soon as her house was visible, she looked towards it. My house. And then suddenly, as though she had been speared, came the thought, with its thrust of pain—I shall grow old and die. Whose house, then?

The question went with her into the house, and up the stairs. On the half landing the answer came, simple and clear, bringing, like most simple-seeming things, its own complications. If she had a child of her body without a husband, it would be a bastard, mocked at, eyed askance. If she married it meant the end of all independence, of all ownership. There was no third way, and, unable to accept either alternative, she had done nothing, fretting away another fourteen months, hating her birthday. Thirty-eight now; and many women were past childbearing at forty.

And now, perhaps, perhaps, a third way was opening. She probed deeper. Suppose, she asked, some unlooked-for freak of chance put him in possession of property. Wouldn't he then feel a wish to settle down and dwell in his own place? He shook his head. No property could be worth the tedium of staying in one place all the time.

"How do you know?" she asked shrewdly. "You might feel differently if the chance ever offered."

"But it has," he said, with the same narrow-eyed smile. "Twice."

"In what circumstances?"

The smile disappeared and he gave her a look which made her feel that she had pushed her questioning a little too far.

"This is not idle curiosity," she said. "I have a reason for asking."

"Once was in York, a little girl on a runaway horse—the sort of horse no child should be let to ride. I was handy and stopped it. The girl was the apple of her father's eye, a spoilt brat, couldn't be content with a pony. The father was a leather merchant, well-to-do; he wanted to make me his partner or some such thing. He meant it too. His idea of gratitude was to nail me down in York for the rest of my days."

"And the other?"

"Of that let's just say that loneliness is a thing some women dread more than anything else—and some farms are lonely places." He smiled again.

"Was she old? Ill-favoured?"

"She was as bonny as a hedge rose."

"So you're still unmarried?"

"We don't marry, ma'am. My mother hooked onto my father and stayed with him about eighteen months. I was born on the bare earth, in Epping Forest. She went off with a horse dealer at Barnet Fair. My father reared me." Anticipating her next question by a fraction of a second, he went on, "If ever I find a woman to my taste, and willing to walk the road with me, I may have a son of my own. And I'll teach him to play the fiddle and read the mileposts and how to hole up out of the wind and all the other things I know."

"How old are you?"

His eyes took on an inward-looking look.

"I reckon thirty-three, or four, could be five."

"Then you've plenty of time."

"Oh yes. Plenty of time. And if it never comes about I shan't fret. What comes, comes, like the weather." He laid down his fork, though there was still food on the plate.

"I've had my fill," he said. "And very good it was. Now what would you like me to do in payment?"

She pushed her plate aside and put her elbows on the table, and, resting her chin on her linked fingers, said:

"Just listen to me, and don't laugh."

HATTON FOLLETT'S TALE

I always thought that my sister Annabella was very beautiful, and I was not alone in that; but there were others to whom her looks made no appeal. One of these, rather unfortunately, was the great-aunt—we always called her Aunt Dorothea—who brought us up. Aunt Dorothea was an extremely conventional woman and her ideas on the subject of beauty were conventional; she deplored the fact that Annabella grew tall, and thin and pale, and that nothing, not even crude bear's grease, could persuade her hair to grow long. In 1782, when Annabella first emerged as a young lady, accepted beauties had masses of hair to be curled and frizzed and tormented and reared into fantastic shapes, topped by even more fantastic decorations; Annabella had short, close curls, like the fleece of a young lamb, and almost silver-gilt in colour. Except for our height we had nothing in common in the way of looks; people said that I was a typical Hatton, with craggy features and reddish hair. Strangers found it difficult to believe that we were twins, always thinking that I was much older than I was, Annabella much younger. Our attitude towards one another bore out this erroneous judgement. I always, from my earliest days, considered it my duty to look after Annabella, and she, with the exception of a few wayward and defiant occasions, always looked on me as an elder, indulgent and protective.

We were parentless almost from birth. Our mother died less than three weeks after we were born, and our father had vanished months earlier. About him and his marriage to our mother there was some mystery. Aunt Dorothea once incorporated into some rebuke to us the remark that, fond as she'd been of our mother, she must admit that she'd been very eccentric; and another time, scolding Annabella, she said it was bad for girls to be headstrong or to give way to impulse—"as your mother did, marrying a vagabond."

Mother had chosen Aunt Dorothea to bring us up, and an attorney with the apt name of Steward to see to our affairs, and in both cases she had chosen well. Aunt Dorothea was the youngest of my strict old grandfather's daughters and until she came to the Old Vine to rule she had had a dull, repressed life. She was therefore much disposed to enjoy herself, and on the whole she was a remarkably lenient guardian. She liked me better than she liked Annabella, I think because I listened to her orders and tried to obey them. Annabella was very seldom directly disobedient, but she was both absent-minded and forgetful, not quite of this world. In moments of annoyance Aunt Dorothea would call her silly and simple-minded, but that was an exaggeration.

When I went to school and heard other boys speak of their sisters I realised that I had been singularly blessed in having for my childhood's companion a girl who was tireless, physically fearless, indifferent to the state of her clothes, and inventive about games.

Aunt Dorothea taught us to read and write and count a little, and when we were eight a young curate from St. Mary's Church came to the house four mornings a week to give us two hours' tuition and to have what Aunt Dorothea called "a good square meal." At the age of twelve I went to Harrow. I think mother's cousin, Chris Hatton, who had inherited Mortiboys, chose my school; he'd been happy there himself, though he'd learned very little, being incorrigibly stupid. Life itself couldn't teach Cousin Chris anything.

I was very much attached to my home and expected to be miserably homesick; actually, after about three weeks I settled down and was happy. It was pleasing to discover that I was regarded as a clever boy. It had never occurred to me, nor, I think, to our tutor, that at home all our lessons had ambled along at Annabella's slow pace. Also, perhaps surprisingly, considering my upbringing, I much enjoyed the company of other boys, beings for whom I felt no responsibility, and with whom I could share coarse jokes, quarrel wholeheartedly, and even exchange buffets occasionally. I was indeed so happy, that though most of my contemporaries—some heirs to great estates, some with their way to make in the Navy or the Army, or in the worlds of scholarship or politics, or mere fashion, left school at seventeen, I was prepared to drift on, fortunate, unambitious, moderate fellow, with no pressure either from without or within, who would eventually go back to Baildon, inherit his comfortable competence, collect books, listen to music, shoot pheasants at Mortiboys, Ockley, and Abbas, entertain and be entertained, marry some girl who took his fancy, and try to give his children as happy and secure a life as he himself had known.

II

Annabella and I had our seventeenth birthday in November 1781, and Aunt Dorothea had long ago decided that Annabella should make her first "appearance" at the Easter Ball in the Assembly Rooms in 1782. Our town had—and still has to a large degree—its own self-contained society. A few very rich or very aristocratic families in Suffolk owned houses in London and launched their nubile daughters there; but for our kind of people, Hattons, Whymarks, Fennels, Shelmadines, and a dozen more, London was practically a foreign place, not, mark you, in any way enviable, in fact inferior, for, as Lady Fennel once said, "You never know whom you may meet in

London." In Baildon you *knew*. Back to Adam practically. And that fact lent pungency to the dispute which arose between Aunt Dorothea and Annabella.

Aunt Dorothea. "Everybody knows that your mother was eccentric and they're going to say, like mother, like daughter, and avoid you."

Annabella. "Everybody knows what my hair is like. If I wear a wig I shall be a laughingstock."

Aunt Dorothea. "A wig would make you look like everybody else."

Annabella. "But I don't want to look like anybody else."

Over the wearing of the wig Annabella had her way, but in all else, flat-heeled shoes to make her seem shorter and a complicated arrangement of frills and ruffles on the bodice of her gown to give her more figure, she accepted Aunt Dorothea's dictates. I thought that she was by far the most beautiful girl at the ball, and when I was not being forced to be "dutiful" to some poor creatures, doubly unlucky, first in lacking partners and then in being trodden upon by me, I stood in corners or at the foot of the staircase in our wonderful new Adam ballroom, and watched Annabella with pride. She looked especially well after supper when so many pink cheeks were flushed and all the elaborate work of Mrs. Bolt, the hairdresser, was falling into disarray. Then she looked like a water lily.

She had no lack of partners, despite Aunt Dorothea's doubts, and I was glad for them both. When at the end of the evening we drove home I had only one small regret and that was that Annabella had danced twice with Richard Shelmadine, a young man whom I heartily disliked, with, perhaps, insufficient reason. Many other men in our neighbourhood gambled, ran into debt, got girls into trouble; and though I was, by nature, steady and maybe a trifle smug, it was not that he was a spendthrift, a gambler, and a lecher that I held against him. It went deeper. There was something almost inhuman about him. He was witty, but his remarks were always barbed; he was handsome, but his looks were marred by a sneering, saturnine expression. He was often at Mortiboys and my Cousin Chris, and other people, too, blamed old Sir Charles Shelmadine for his son's behaviour, saying that he was over-strict, Puritanical, and two hundred years behind the times. He was all those things; but for the last three years he had been paying three shillings a week to one of his tenant's daughters upon whom Richard had fathered a bastard child, and in the previous December he had paid all Richard's debts, he said for the last time, making it a condition that he should stay at Clevely, incur no more debts, never gamble again, and settle down. That meant, eventually, marriage. Please God, I thought, not Annabella. On two occasions I'd seen him behave very brutally to a horse that was doing its best, which may not sound much, but it is in small things that a man shows himself.

But in June, back at school, I received one of Annabella's rather childish letters, saying that she and Richard were engaged and were to be married at Christmas, when I could give her away. "Everybody," she wrote, "even his grumpy old father, is very pleased and I am so happy I can't tell you. If you think it is sudden, it isn't, I fell in love with him at Mortiboys when I was forteen and I was always afriad he would marry somebody else before I was old enough so I never said anything."

I remember standing there in the big classroom and thinking how terrible it would be to see Annabella married to a man to whom I would not lend my horse; and how things were better in the old days when marriages were arranged for girls. How could anyone who couldn't spell "fourteen" or "afraid" be expected to show sense and judgement when it came to making the most important decision of a lifetime?

I fretted about it all day—incidentally earning myself a massive punishment for absent-mindedness—and in the evening I wrote her a letter, completely frank and honest, telling her what I disliked about Richard Shelmadine, imploring her not to be in a haste to marry. I couldn't carry it down to the post stop until next day, and by that time I had thought better of it. After all, she hadn't said that she was *contemplating* marrying, she had said that she was engaged to marry, so whatever I said would serve only to alienate her. I tore up my letter, excusing myself to myself with the thought that in a few weeks I should be home and able to *talk* to her. Two or three days later I had a letter from Aunt Dorothea. Jubilant. Almost every other word underlined. "Dear Annabella is *radiant* with happiness. It does one's *heart* good just to *see* her. And they make such a *handsome* pair. We know that Richard has been a little *wild* in the past but is so much *better* for a young man to have his fling and then settle down. . . ."

Of course she was pleased. Under her veneer of convention she had about as much worldly wisdom as a hen. The girl in her charge had scored a triumph, which she shared; engaged within three months of her first ball, to the son of a near neighbour, heir to an estate and a title. All absolutely in order.

Would this term never end?

When at last, on a Friday, in blazing high summer weather I reached the Old Vine it was to learn that Annabella had gone to Mortiboys to stay with Cousin Chris and the nice, sensible woman whom he had married. She was the only child of a well-to-do yeoman farmer, and ill-disposed people hinted that Chris had married her for her money. That was not true, for he was the least calculating of men and the least imaginative; it would never occur to him that he might one day need more money than he had. They had a baby of about eighteen months old.

"The invitation included you and you can go when you like," Aunt Dorothea said. "Annabella was eager to go at once. It's nearer Clevely, for one thing, and of course she can talk more freely to Clara, who is nearer her own age."

I said sourly, "I hope Cousin Clara will enlighten Annabella to the disadvantages of being married to a gambler."

"But, Hatton, dear, Richard no *longer* gambles. He's really *quite* reformed."

"Even so, I think it was all done in too much of a hurry. And I don't think he's the man for Annabella."

"But it's a most suitable match. What have you against it? Against Richard?"

"Annabella needs to be taken care of. She's very young and . . ." I couldn't lay my tongue to the right word; "simple" was one which Aunt Dorothea had sometimes used and which I had then resented; "silly" sounded unkind and was not really accurate. Before I could think of "immature," which was perhaps as near as I should get, Aunt Dorothea had cut in.

"Girls grow up far more quickly than boys, Hatton. And at the risk of making you *angry*, I'm going to say this. You are unlikely to take kindly, at first, to any man, whoever he was, who married Annabella. You're *twins*, you've always been exceptionally *close*, and you must beware of jealousy making you prejudiced."

I thought about that for a few seconds. Then I said:

"I'm not jealous of Richard. I'd simply prefer her to marry somebody kind and steady who'd be likely to make her happy."

"But you silly boy, she *is* happy. She is *alight* with happiness."

"Is he likely to be at Mortiboys over the week-end?"

"He was going to stay from Saturday till Monday."

That decided me to go on Monday; and by making that decision I missed being on the spot when the gaming session which is still spoken of with awe and wonder took place under Cousin Chris's roof.

Monday was a glorious sunny day; I was back in my own well-known, well-loved countryside, with my own good horse, George Rufus, between my knees. And I was going to see

Annabella. I should have been absolutely happy but for the thought of Richard Shelmadine.

I reminded myself that I must be careful in what I said; I mustn't sound dictatorial. I remembered one of the few occasions when Annabella had defied me. That was at Mortiboys. I had forbidden her to ride, and when that failed, forcibly restrained her from riding, a horse known to be dangerous. She'd kicked and screamed as I held her, and then cried and sulked, saying, "Just because you're stronger than me . . ." In the evening she'd lured the horse with an apple to the fence of the pasture, climbed the fence, and thrown herself on his back, and, clinging to his mane, ridden three times round and then slipped down, saying, "You see, he wasn't dangerous at all!" I'd suffered agonies, standing there so helpless, only able to pray—Oh God, don't let her be hurt. Afterwards I had to go into the house and change my clothes; it wasn't all sweat I was wet with either.

My best move, I thought, was to try to persuade her that a summer wedding was much prettier and more comfortable than a winter one. I had a reasonless feeling that if only the decisive moment could be deferred something might happen to change things.

Thinking these thoughts, I rode between the fields of ripening wheat and barley, between the road verges gay with poppy, bugloss, scabious, and wild clover in which the bees were busy, and I had just crossed the old stone bridge known as Abbot's Bridge when I saw a woman, riding very swiftly, towards me. Annabella.

I waved and called. She came on, slowing down a little as we drew close, but not stopping.

"Turn round," she said. "Oh, Hatton, I am so glad to see you. You can help."

I swung George Rufus round and fell in beside her. She certainly looked "alight" with something, not, I thought, pure happiness.

"What's the matter?"

"I'll tell you as we go. Come along. I've got to get to Mr. Steward's as soon as possible."

"Whatever for?"

"I'll tell you," she said. And she did.

On the previous evening—Sunday—Cousin Chris, his friend Nick Helmar, Richard Shelmadine, Sir Edward Follesmark, and some other men whose names meant nothing to me had settled down to play cards at seven o'clock. They'd played right through the night. Cousin Chris, in a final burst of recklessness, had staked Mortiboys, the place where his fathers had lived for more than three hundred years, and lost it to Nick Helmar. Richard Shelmadine had also lost and now owed two thousand pounds. He had in fact lost rather more, but Sir Edward, with his usual good nature, had told him to forget what was due to him.

"So Mr. Steward will simply have to advance me some of my money."

"He can't. We can't touch our *real* money until we are twenty-one."

"You can't. Mine is different. Mine is mine when I marry. Aunt Dorothea said so. And now we shan't wait until Christmas; we can be married in three weeks. Surely Mr. Steward could let me have two thousand pounds just three weeks early. You see, Richard is not supposed to play at all, and if his horrid old father gets to hear of this there's no knowing what might happen. The dreadful man who won his money is *waiting* for it. Did you know that what you lost at cards had to be paid at once?"

"Yes," I said. "And so did he, when he sat down to play. . . ."

She gave me a sidelong look.

"Well . . . anyway, if Mr. Steward is obliging there's no harm done."

I said, "How can you say that? It's mad. Two thousand

pounds is a lot of money. And all gone for nothing. He'd promised his father not to play, too."

"If you're going to be like that, don't come with me. I was counting on you to help to persuade Mr. Steward. You don't know what being in love is. If it was fifty thousand pounds and I could get it I'd be happy and proud to give it to him."

"No proper man would take it."

She then tried, by urging on her horse, to get ahead of me, but I kept up and we pounded into St. Mary's Square, where Mr. Steward had his home and his office, neck by neck.

As we reined in she said, "If you speak against me now, Hatton, I shall hate you for the rest of my life."

"I could bear that a lot better than the knowledge that you'd impoverished yourself for the sake of a rogue."

She wouldn't even wait while I looped the horses' reins to the railings.

Actually there was no need for me to speak at all. Mr. Steward did that—or rather, not Mr. Steward, but our mother, who had been dead for more than seventeen years. The vague, unreal person who'd been eccentric, called all dogs and horses George, made a strange marriage, been fond of Aunt Dorothea and loved the Old Vine, suddenly emerged on this summer morning, a woman of wisdom and foresight. Obviously she had looked at her girl child and thought—Nobody is going to marry her for her money! Nobody shall fritter away her inheritance. Annabella's share was all in a settlement. The interest, four hundred and fifty pounds a year, did pass to her upon her marriage, or upon her becoming twenty-one. Aunt Dorothea had been right there. But neither Mr. Steward nor anyone else in the world could give her two thousand pounds to give to Richard Shelmadine.

Mr. Steward explained it all, clearly and concisely, and I sat there thinking—Dear ghost of a mother, in my most need, here you are, an ally.

"Now if it had been you," said Mr. Steward, addressing me,

"the circumstances would be different. When you are of age you inherit outright, and upon such a prospect it is possible, within limits, to raise money."

Instantly Annabella said, "Then you do it, Hatton, please. I'll pay you back. In three weeks I shall be married and you can have the whole of my money until you're paid back. Hatton, please, please."

She was always pale, but as Mr. Steward had explained, her pallor had changed quality, turned greyish, and she looked wild and distraught. For me it was an awful moment. I loved her, I'd have given her, for herself, every farthing I had in the world, but for Richard Shelmadine. . . .

This time it was Mr. Steward who saved me. He said smoothly:

"But if I understood you aright, you need this money immediately."

"Now," Annabella said. "This morning."

"Then I fear that your brother, however willing, cannot help. To arrange for the sale of a reversionary interest in his estate might very well take . . . shall we say six months?"

She said, "Have I *any* money at all?"

"Your allowance of fifteen pounds for the next quarter is due on the first of September. You can have it now if you wish."

I said, "Annabella, what use is fifteen pounds?"

"He spoke of going to London. He can't go home, surely even you can see that. Fifteen pounds would be better than nothing."

I thought—Let him go to London, let him be out of the way, with his good looks and his spurious charm. That'll give me a chance to talk sense into her.

"Can I have my next quarter's allowance too, please?"

Mine, thanks to Cousin Chris, who said that schoolboys needed money to spend on food, was twenty pounds.

Mr. Steward unlocked his iron-doored cupboard, took out a

padlocked box, unlocked that, and counted out the money, giving us each our own.

Outside, Annabella went and leant against her horse in an attitude of despair.

"I promised. I said don't worry. I said it would be all right. Whatever will he say?"

"He should be damned grateful. You won't have a penny till Christmas and I shall go back to school and starve. Anyway," I said, with what I thought was cunning, "there's no need for you to face him or to explain anything. Come back home. He's no good, Annabella. He broke his word to his father, didn't he, and that just shows . . ."

She had her not-listening look, the faraway, remote look which had upon occasions so much exasperated Aunt Dorothea.

"There's no *need* for him to go to London. He can come to the Old Vine. In three weeks we can be married. His old father can stamp and rage and so can the man he owes the money to. *We* don't care. The Old Vine is my home as much as it is yours, and I shall have my money coming in. I'll go and tell him." In a flash she was round by my horse. "I'll take George Rufus; he's fresher and quicker."

I said, "Annabella, I'm sure you're making a mistake. Come home and let's talk this over quietly."

"While Richard goes, without a penny to London? You must be crazy."

I stopped to throw twopence to a little ragged boy who had taken upon himself to see that two firmly tethered horses didn't run away, and by the time I was in my saddle Annabella was almost out of sight.

I could have gone home then; but I bore in mind that Annabella was carrying unwelcome news to a bad man and I feared for her; so I set the slower horse's head towards Mortiboys.

Mortiboys was a beautiful house. I'd never envied it because my heart was set on the Old Vine, but I could admire it, and as I neared it that day I thought how dreadful Cousin Chris must be feeling. I was as uneasy at the thought of meeting him as I would have been had he suffered a bereavement, or an amputation. I need not have worried.

I've often thought of that moment since. It set me a standard of behaviour which I have tried to match. There is a kind of courage which though it may be rooted in stupidity and lack of perception is none the less admirable, and that Cousin Chris had in full measure. He had issued an invitation and here I was in answer to it, and he greeted me as though nothing had happened. Mumbling, he made me welcome; mumbling, he said that this was the last time he'd have the pleasure of entertaining me under this roof; not a sign of regret, not a glimmer of self-pity.

I said I was sorry to hear of his ill-luck, and that I hadn't come to stay after all. Where was Annabella?

"Mumble Clevely mumble Richard, I believe." I gathered that he was sorry for Richard, his father being a devil when roused, but at least he couldn't mumble rip so much with mumble there.

He, Chris Hatton, ruined completely, was sorry for Richard!

On my way out I saw Cousin Clara and to her I gulped out some clumsy words of sympathy. She said, with bitter calm:

"At least we still have a roof over our heads. Green Farm is mine. Even madmen can't dispose of their wives' freehold property. And thank God, I can still run a dairy."

I rode on to Clevely. Sir Charles, a landlord of the old-fashioned kind, had just come back from seeing the harvest started in one of his great open fields. He said he hadn't seen Richard since Saturday. He had obviously heard nothing about the card playing and I didn't mention it. I said that

I thought my sister had come to Clevely with Richard. He rang bells and shouted and eventually a frightened servant said yes, Master Richard had come in, soon after mid-day, thrown some clothes into a valise, and gone off again. But he'd been alone; there was no young lady with him. No young lady had been seen at all.

Anxious to put a good face on things, I said that perhaps I had been mistaken, Annabella might have gone home; but Sir Charles flew into a purple-faced rage.

"Then where's he gone? I'll tell you. Back to his London doxies. I've known all along it was too good to last. A sweet little girl, your sister, and I said to him, 'You're luckier than you deserve,' I said, 'and you make her shed a single tear and I'll cut you off *without* a shilling.' And I meant it."

I left him still fuming and shouting. On the tiring horse I rode slowly back to Baildon, happy and relieved. Richard Shelmadine had run off to London—the best place for him, and Annabella would no doubt grieve for a while. However, she was young, and pride would come to her aid.

But when I got back to the Old Vine Annabella wasn't there. I could only think that she had gone with Richard, or had followed him, to London. With exactly fifteen pounds— unless she had handed it over.

In a hasty, brutal manner that I regretted even as I used it, I told Aunt Dorothea as much as I knew or guessed, and she, like a gallant old hunter that will take the last fence even if it kills him, rose to the occasion.

"Nobody must *know*. That is what matters most. Her whole reputation, her *future* is at stake. Bures. Bures. We have connections there. From Mortiboys Annabella went direct to Bures. That is what we must say. For the moment. And we must bear in mind that it is quite possible that they have gone to London and will be married there."

"God forbid," I said.

"God forbid that she has gone chasing after Richard, un-chaperoned, to London, and for some reason is *not* married. Hatton, that would be fatal. We should never hold up our heads again. The scandal, unthinkable."

"I'm going to London, now, this afternoon. I can get as far as Newmarket."

"To Bures, Hatton. Bear in mind how servants talk. Anna-bella has gone to Bures and you are going there too. Now let me think. In London . . . Where do you begin to look? Rich-ard, we presume had nothing, Annabella you say had fifteen pounds. He'll go to try his luck most probably. Now let me think. My brother—your grandfather, Hatton—lived in Lon-don by gambling and I remember hearing my father, in temper, rail against two places especially. One was called Watton's, or Whaddon's, and the other was just a woman's name. I shall think of it presently. Have you any money?"

"I have the twenty pounds Mr. Steward advanced to me."

"It won't be enough. I have a little saved." She went up-stairs and came down with a netted purse, well filled.

"I have remembered the other name. It was Mariana's and I think it was in Soho Square."

In London I was wretched. Most of the time I was racked with anxiety about Annabella, and if that anxiety lifted for a moment I was conscious of being a stranger, a boy up from the country, incorrectly dressed for the places I must enter, and insufficiently knowledgeable about the ways of the world. However, I set out on my search in a methodical and pertina-cious fashion. I went first to Mariana's, which was at once flashy and luxurious. Richard hadn't been seen there for al-most a year; but he was known. I left the first of many half crowns there with a menial in return for a promise that should Richard appear some effort would be made to find out where he was living. There also I ascertained that the other place known to Aunt Dorothea was named Whaddon's. I went directly there and was told that I had missed him by about an hour. It wasn't a place where, as in an inn, one could stand or sit about and wait, so after a while I plucked up courage and asked could the porter suggest any place where Mr. Shelmadine was likely to be at the moment. He named several, Mariana's among them.

And so I went on for a whole week, picking up a clue here and there. At most places somebody kindly or officious would name another place where Richard might be found, and off I'd go like a hound. In addition I harried a number of clergymen, asking about marriages by licence or the publication of banns.

I worked unavailingly for a fortnight. I'd laid out quite a bit of money in bribes and was now so well known in several places that when I went in I had no need even to frame my question; doormen and waiters would just shake their heads and say, "No news, sir." One of the places where Richard had been seen—and it must have been soon after his arrival in London—was a chophouse, not far from Whaddon's. I'd eaten my supper there on the first night I was in London, and found the food good and reasonable in price. So I often went there, asked my question, received a negative answer, and then ate a modest meal.

On the fifteenth evening of my hunt I followed this procedure, and when I sat down at the table noticed a man nearby looking at me with interest. To begin with, asking the same question in the same places had made me feel self-conscious and conspicuous, but now I was hardened to being looked at with amusement and curiosity, and I was on this occasion too much depressed to care. I'd failed. And that very afternoon I'd had a crushing disappointment. I'd arranged with Aunt Dorothea that if she had anything to report she would let me know. I'd taken a lodging at the *Saracen's Head* in the Strand, which was where the Baildon coach stopped, and every afternoon I looked for a letter. That day there had been one, and in the two seconds before breaking the seal I'd thought— She's home! The letter, however, was one of Aunt Dorothea's rambling, underlined epistles, all about how Sir Charles was going around saying that Richard had committed the final enormity of jilting a sweet young girl, and her own careful subterfuges to conceal the truth. So I sat there in dull misery, and if a man wanted to stare, let him.

Presently, though, he rose and came to my table and cleared his throat and said, "Excuse me, sir. I couldn't help but over- hear. You were inquiring for Mr. Richard Shelmadine."

I said, "Yes, I am. Do you know where he is?"

"Alas, no. But I'd like to have a word with him myself." His clothes, his manner, his voice all bespoke the decent tradesman in a good way of business. "I'm a tailor," he said. "Mifflin's the name."

I told him to take a seat, and he thanked me and began to tell his tale. For years he'd made Richard's clothes, been paid a little now and again, but always been owed a substantial sum. Then in December of last year Sir Charles had cleared the debt, and with the money sent a letter saying he would pay no more and anybody who gave his son a pennyworth of credit was a fool.

"Up to a fortnight ago, sir, I thought I'd lost his custom. That's often the way, pay up and go elsewhere; for some rea- son tailors' bills always leave a grudge. However, a fortnight ago, in he came and said he needed a new suit, which was true enough. In a way he's a *good* customer, pay or no pay, because clothes look well on him and I get the credit and a new custo- mer now and then, so I took the risk. He wanted the clothes in a hurry, and he gave me the address and swore he'd pay on delivery; but when my man took the parcel Mr. Shelmadine wasn't there; there was only a lady who said she didn't know where he was, and she wouldn't take the clothes. So there I am with . . ."

"What address did he give?" I was already on my feet.

"It's in Charles Street. A couple called Petter have an apartment house . . ."

I said, "Thank you, thank you," threw some money on the table, and ran.

The street was respectable-looking, the house well kept. The door was opened to me by a hard-faced woman in a dress of stiff black silk and a gold chain about her neck. I gasped out breathlessly:

"Is Miss Follett living here?"

"I don't take single ladies. This is a respectable house."

I said, "I'm sorry. I meant Mrs. Shelmadine, of course. I'm her brother."

She gave me a very peculiar look indeed.

"You'd better come in."

"Is she *here?*" I asked, almost crying.

"Yes," she said, "she's here."

I seemed to go blind and deaf and senseless. I can't remember going into the house, or into the parlour, but there I was, sitting in a chair, and Mrs. Petter was talking.

". . . for the best, I hope you'll understand. If I'd turned her out, the state she was in, and so pretty, *anything* could have happened."

"Let me see her."

"I'll fetch her. There's money still owing, you know."

She went away and I took my handkerchief and wiped my sweating face and neck and hands. Then there was Annabella. She said:

"Hatton," and ran to me and began to cry.

I just stood and held her and said, "It's all right now, darling. Everything will be all right, now I've found you," and things of that sort, over and over again. She'd always been very fraily built; now it was like holding a starved stray kitten, and every sob seemed to shake her so violently that it was as though somebody were giving her a terrible thrashing from inside. Finally I gave her a tiny shake and said:

"Annabella, you must stop. I've found you, and whatever it was, it's over now."

"Yes. It's over."

I gave her another little pat and then held her at arm's length. She looked ghastly; thin and pale, her eyes sunk back into her head, her crisp shining hair gone dull and limp. She was wearing the lightweight riding skirt and jacket of pale green trimmed with white braid in which she had left Baildon fifteen days before, and it looked as though she had never taken it off in all that time. The skirt was pinned up, and she wore a coarse sacking apron. Her sleeves were pushed above the elbow, and at the end of her thin white arms her hands hung, red and swollen.

I said, "Darling, what have they been doing to you?"

"Nobody did anything. I did it to myself. Richard didn't want me to come. I insisted. I thought that after . . . after . . . But it didn't work. It was worse. And then we quarrelled and he just went away and didn't come back."

"You're not married?"

"No. That's what we quarrelled about. I thought that after we'd lived together, he would. But he said . . . he said I'd asked for it. And that was true. He never did want to marry me, it was only the money."

"Well, there's no real harm done, then," I said in my innocence. "Everything will be all right now. I've come to take you home."

"I can't go home. Everybody laughing and pointing."

"Aunt Dorothea is busily spreading the story that *you* broke off the engagement because of Richard's gambling. You're supposed to be at Bures, getting over the shock. Sir Charles is going round saying 'jilted'—that's the kind of word he would use—but nobody will take much notice of him. You just come home and carry it off like a girl of spirit; show everybody how little he mattered to you."

She said, "I haven't got any spirit left, Hatton."

"You'll see. You'll feel better with a good meal inside you. I'll just pay this old dragon and get out of this place."

"She meant well, really."

I pulled the bell, and Mrs. Petter, who couldn't have been far away, came in.

"There was five guineas owing—that was a week for one and five days for the other, I don't charge for what wasn't eaten—when the tailor's man came and I learned the truth. After that I won't charge for because though she's not very handy, she did her best. And so did I! You may think putting her to work in the kitchen was a bit hard, but what else could I do, the state she was in. I couldn't put her out in the street, could I?"

I said, "I'm very much obliged to you, Mrs. Petter. By keeping my sister here you enabled me to find her." I put five guineas on the table and added a sixth. "For your trouble," I said. "Come along, Annabella."

Mrs. Petter said, "She can't go out in the street like that, can she, sir?"

I noticed, for the first time, that Mrs. Petter addressed herself to me, speaking of Annabella as though she were an idiot, or a child. I looked at Annabella and saw, with a pang of something like fear, that she had made no move even to pull down her sleeves or remove her apron.

"Petter's very good at cleaning and pressing," Mrs. Petter said. "He could have those clothes as good as new in about an hour. And if she liked she could have a bath meantime; and a wash and a vinegar rinse'd do her hair no harm."

"Would you like to do that, Annabella?"

"Oh yes, Hatton. If you say so."

"All right then. And I'll go and send Aunt Dorothea word by postboy and tell her we start for home tomorrow." That reminded me of something else. "What happened to George Rufus?"

"Richard sold him. He sold them both, the first day. I *told* him that at the Old Vine we never sold horses to people we didn't know, but he didn't take any notice."

To my heaped-up hatred of Richard Shelmadine I added a handful more. George Rufus was my horse, a good horse, and I was attached to him.

"Can you remember where he sold him, or to whom?"

"It was a livery stable," Annabella said vaguely. "Not far from here. In a lane."

"That might be Hawkins'," Mrs. Petter said helpfully. "The lane's just at the back of this street, running down to the Haymarket."

"I'll be back in an hour," I said.

"Come along, then." Mrs. Petter took Annabella by the arm. "We've got a lot to do." Annabella went like a somnambulist being led back to bed.

George Rufus was at Hawkins'. In a fortnight he'd lost flesh and gloss, but he was still the best horse in that stable and the man Hawkins was not disposed to part with him easily. We haggled for a bit, then I remembered something.

"That horse was stolen," I said. "The man who sold him to you had no more right to sell him than he had to sell you. And I can prove it. I will, too, unless you take the fair price I'm offering." He gave in, and I clapped down an extra two shillings so that George could have a good fill of oats and a currying before I called for him next day. Then I went into a coffee house and scribbled a message to Aunt Dorothea, dispatched it, and went back for Annabella.

Finding her, knowing that the worst hadn't happened and that she hadn't married that rogue, recovering George Rufus, and having good news to send home, as well as all the hurrying I'd done, had thrown me into a state of high spirits. Here we were, Annabella and I together again, and in London, which now took on the aspect of a vast pleasure ground. I took her back to the inn where I was staying, engaged a room for her, and ordered the best meal available at that hour. She ate very little, and that without interest. I asked if she would like to go to bed.

"No. I can't sleep. Things go round and round in my head."

"Then shall we go to Vauxhall Gardens?"

I'd been there, on my hunt, and thought it would be delightful to go now, with Annabella beside me.

"Oh no. We went there. You go, Hatton. It's pretty."

"I want to do something with you. Shall we go to a play?"

"If you like."

At that season fashionable people had deserted London for Bath or Brighthelmstone, and many places of entertainment were closed and being refurbished; the few still open were not employing their most famous actors and actresses. The play we found was an old one, and none the worse for that. It was called Mr. Thinkwell's Solution, and it was at once comic and pathetic. You laughed, and then felt ashamed of your laughter, Mr. Thinkwell was such a dear little man, so shamelessly exploited. Whenever I laughed I was doubly ashamed, for Annabella sat beside me staring at the lighted stage as though she were looking into the black depths of a cave. Presently I ceased to laugh. When I did that I began to hear a curious echo in the names mentioned in the play. Mr. Thinkwell lived in a town called Maildon; his married daughter lived at Blaxham, his brother at Tevely, and so on. It sounded to me as though the man who wrote the play knew our neighbourhood and had used our place names, lightly disguised. When we went out I looked on the play bill to see the playwright's name. It was Oliver Stanton. I'd never heard of a family of that name in Baildon. Perhaps he had been a visitor at some time.

For the greater part of our journey home, which took two

days, Annabella remained silent and withdrawn. A mile or so out of Baildon she asked in a small, miserable voice:

"Must we tell Aunt Dorothea the truth?"

"I don't see why. We can say that you followed Richard to London to give him the fifteen pounds. So far as I could make out you weren't seen to leave Clevely together."

"No. I waited in the lane."

"Then we tell her that you failed to find him, had your pocket picked, and your landlady made you stay to work off what you owed. That is near enough to the truth and will account for the state of your hands. But to bear out that story, you must perk up and not go about looking as though the end of the world had come."

"It was the end of my world."

"Don't be silly. You're still the sweetest, the prettiest . . ."

"Oh don't, Hatton. I know what I am; useless and unwanted without ready money in my hand."

III

We slid back into place without much stir. Most people at heart are more interested in other people's money than their feelings and all our circle was still agog with Cousin Chris's loss and his moving out to a humble farm, and in Sir Charles's firm refusal to pay his son's last debt. People thought that Annabella had been right to break the engagement. Aunt Dorothea insisted that we should act merrily. She gave a supper party at the Old Vine. Cousin Chris, with remarkable hardihood, had a "farewell" party at Mortiboys and there was a twenty-first birthday celebration at Ockley. Annabella, who had never been a chatterer or a giggler, seemed little changed to the casual eye; but I knew that her composure was forced and that nothing but pride kept her going.

The night of the Ockley party was exceptionally warm for September, warmer than any night in June that year. It was late when we got back to the Old Vine, but when Annabella said:

"It's too hot to sleep. Come in the garden, Hatton," I saw nothing strange in the suggestion. It was moonlight. We went to the very end of the garden and sat down on the stone seat by the sundial.

After a minute or two she said, with more urgency and vigour in her voice than she had used since the catastrophe:

"Hatton, have you any money at all?"

"Yes. I went and dunned Mr. Steward. He spat blood, but he advanced me twelve pounds."

"Then will you do something for me? Hatton, it is a most loathsome errand and I hate to ask you; but in a way it is for all our sakes. I'd go myself, but I know what *that* would lead to."

"Out with it. What do you want me to do?"

"Go to Mrs. Bolt's for me."

"The hairdresser?"

"Yes. She . . . she does another thing beside. I would go myself, but she remembers and holds it against you and is insolent in a sly way. And you have to give her presents. She made Mary Felton give her a garnet brooch."

I thought her wits had gone astray. She spoke in a reasonable way, but it didn't make sense.

"What *are* you talking about?"

"It's all so horrible! Hatton, I think I'm going to have a baby. Mrs. Bolt makes pills. . . ."

It was my turn to be struck simple-minded. I waited so long without speaking that she said:

"Please, Hatton. It's our only hope. Not just me. Aunt Dorothea, it'd kill her."

I said, "I think it would. Yes, yes, of course I'll go."

"Oh, thank you. Thank you. You see, I've been thinking it

over. That isn't an errand most boys would do for their sisters, so even if she does recognise *you* I don't think she'd connect it with *me*."

"I'll make damned certain she doesn't. I'll tell her . . . Annabella, is it *safe?*"

"Mary Felton took them. She was sick. I don't mind being sick."

"I'll go tomorrow."

"Hatton, if you do this for me I'll be grateful all the rest of my life. You see, it's different for men. She'd never dream of blackmailing you. If you'll just do this for me I'll never ask you to do anything for me ever, ever again."

I set off on foot, feeling that I should be less conspicuous that way, and to the North Gate was quite a walk from the Old Vine. Part of the time I diverted my thoughts by imagining a scene in which, suddenly, without a word, I walked up to Richard Shelmadine and slapped his face hard, twice, once on each side, so that his teeth rattled. And then I thought about Annabella's words—"It's different for men"—such true words. Here was I, free to walk up to Mrs. Bolt and say, "I've got a girl into trouble," and nobody would think a whit the worse of me. In fact rather the reverse. Whereas a girl, like poor Mary Felton, who had nobody to trust with her errand, would be subtly blackmailed, probably as long as she lived. It didn't seem fair. . . .

There were several new houses just beyond the North Gate, and I asked a man which was Mrs. Bolt's. I had an uneasy feeling that he guessed my errand, which was nonsense; Mrs. Bolt in her capacity as hairdresser must have many callers. When I saw the woman I understood what Annabella had meant by "insolent in a sly way." The stony-eyed, hard-faced bitch knew her power.

"Started young, haven't you?" she said. Since I was so tall, and looked so much older than my age, I took that to mean that she did know me by sight so I took greater pains with my story than I should otherwise have done. The girl, I said, lived in Harrow and I was going back there on Thursday and had promised to take the pills with me.

She took three sovereigns and gave me some pills in a cone of paper.

"And understand this, young sir. If aught goes wrong, you're to blame, not me. I make herbal pills, like my mother and my granny did. Young ladies take them to make their cheeks pink, young gentlemen take them to cure their spots. Understand?"

"Why should anything go wrong?"

"It's tampering. What goes up must come down, but nine months is the rule, ain't it? Doing a nine-month job in a week or ten days must be a bit risky, it stands to reason."

"She . . . the girl wouldn't *die*, would she?" I asked, feeling quite as sick as Mary Felton ever had.

"Women take a lot of killing. Still set on your sweetheart, eh? Most that come here only think about getting outa the mess even if killing is the cure. But she'll be all right. I take it she's young."

"A year younger than I am."

"Every year they start younger. What it'll come to . . . ? Well, if you're fond of her and the pills work, next time you . . ." She added some words of such gross obscenity that I cannot bear, even now, to recall them. (Not when I am awake, that is. Sometimes in an evil dream the words are shouted at me by one of the gargoyles on St. Mary's Church and, oddly enough, always their effect is aphrodisiac.)

There were ten pills, one to be taken night and morning for five days; they took a week or ten days to work. I looked ahead and saw myself leaving for school on the morning of the fourth day, not knowing, dependent on the post, going to bed with the thought that something might go wrong, getting up in the morning wondering. I knew I couldn't bear it. I handed the pills to Annabella and sat down straightway and wrote a letter to my master, informing him that I should not be returning to school.

In any case, what with one thing and another, I no longer felt like a schoolboy. I felt ninety years old.

When Annabella began to be sick past the point where concealment was possible, Aunt Dorothea sought for explanations; some fish on the turn, some over-fat pork, a copper pan not properly cleaned. But these were all evasions and at heart she must have known because we, too, had eaten the fish, the pork, whatever was cooked in the copper pan. I'm *sure* she knew, because on a day when Annabella had been most horribly sick and then fainted and had to be carried back to her bed, I said, in a panic:

"I'll fetch Dr. Cornwell," Aunt Dorothea said in a voice that I had never heard her use before to anyone:

"No, Hatton. Wait!"

She went into the bedroom and in less than ten minutes came out again, her normally rosy face the colour of suet and gone loose on its bones so that everything sagged. She looked at me with eyes like a beaten dog's and said, "Oh, what are we going to do now?"

I said, "Stop her taking any more of those horrible pills. And then we must make the best of it." I was better prepared than she was, poor old dear, for I'd had time to think. Ever since I'd brought the pills back from Mrs. Bolt I'd been turning over in my mind what we should do if they failed to work. I now said with misplaced lightness:

"All the best families have a bastard."

"And the worst," Aunt Dorothea said. "Not people like us. Look round the people we know, Hatton. There isn't an illegitimate child, nor has been. We should be ostracised. And all the blame would fall on me. People will say I wasn't careful enough. Everybody said I spoilt you both and that ill

would come of it. Oh dear, oh dear, whatever are we going to
do?"

My thoughts were selfish. I didn't know many babies, but I
liked those I knew. Cousin Chris's boy Barney was about eighteen months old and a most taking little fellow. I looked ahead
and saw Annabella, Aunt Dorothea, and me, with the baby
living at the Old Vine, happily enough. It'd be a good-looking
child, and the moment I saw any one of its father's nasty
characteristics showing I'd clout it, boy or girl, good and hard.
Not being very socially minded, I could bear the idea of being
ostracised. Aunt Dorothea, however, as the first shock passed,
grew more and more frantic. She wept and shivered and
seemed about to have a fit. I had to fetch her some brandy.

"I cannot, I will not face it," she said. "It reflects on me,
and so unjustly. I've devoted myself to you both and I *have*
taken proper care of Annabella."

"No mother could have done more," I agreed.

"But nobody will believe that. They'll blame me. I can't
bear it."

She began to talk wildly of throwing herself from the Abbot's Bridge.

I said, "Now that is nonsense, Aunt Dorothea. What we
could do is move right away and pretend that Annabella is
married and widowed."

"There's always someone who knows, it doesn't matter how
far . . ." She broke off, was silent for a few seconds, and then
said, in a much more controlled way, "The obvious thing,
and I wonder I didn't think of it before, is to find someone to
marry Annabella."

"Oh no!"

"Oh yes! We've said that she was in Bures. Now we say
that there she met someone whom she'd known for quite a
time—it mustn't seem too sudden. She can be married within
a month and the baby will be a seven-months child, there's
nothing so unusual about that."

Not treating this too seriously, and trying to cheer her up, I said:

"All we have to do is to find a likely man."

She said gravely, "That will be a little difficult, but not impossible. I shall go to Bures tomorrow and take Cousin Caroline into my confidence and ask for her help."

"Oh, come," I said, "you don't mean that. You can't just marry Annabella off like that. She wouldn't be happy."

"Annabella," Aunt Dorothea said with amazing harshness, "has lost all right to expect happiness. She has acted with selfishness and lack of consideration for other people and wrecked her life. She should be grateful if we manage to salvage a little."

To my everlasting astonishment Annabella fell in with this fantastic plan. She lay in her bed, looking like death, and said, "Yes, Aunt Dorothea," and, "If you can arrange it, Aunt Dorothea." And Aunt Dorothea said, "My cousin Caroline at Bures has a connection, a younger son with no money who wanted to be an artist. He could get no commissions and had to take up some other employ. A wife with an income of her own is just what he needs."

I said, "You talk as though this were the Middle Ages! And what kind of man would he be who would marry a girl he knew nothing of just for her four hundred a year?"

"No worse than most," Aunt Dorothea snapped.

I tried another tack.

"How can you trust them not to talk?"

"Cousin Caroline is one of the family; and she has daughters; it will be in her own interest to keep silent. When one female in a family does . . . what Annabella has done, it reflects on all."

"How can you trust the man—if you find him—not to hold the circumstances against Annabella? I think this whole scheme is quite insane."

"The man, naturally, will not have that respect for Annabella that a man should have, but if Annabella is a good and dutiful wife he will become fond of her, in time."

This conversation took place in Annabella's presence, and once again she was being discussed as though she were a child or an imbecile, without will of its own. I was astounded by Aunt Dorothea's attitude; I'd always known her gentle, kindly, rather simple.

I said, "I still think my plan is best. We could go . . . we could even go to America, or Jamaica."

"And what have I done, to be uprooted at my time of life? Besides, think of the time it would take to make arrangements. We couldn't just walk away and leave the house. And wherever we went, even to the ends of the earth, the poor child will still be born out of wedlock. *My* plan is best, my plan is the only one. I shall go to Bures in the morning."

"I think this is something Annabella should decide. It's *her* life, after all."

I turned to the bed.

"I'll do whatever you say," she said. "Everything I've done so far has been wrong."

"Atwood, Francis Atwood," Aunt Dorothea said. "That was the name. My cousin Caroline's husband's sister married the elder boy. She's Lady Atwood now!" Abruptly she began to cry. "You had every chance, you wicked, wicked girl," she said, quite ferociously, turning to the bed and without knowing it voicing all her own grudge against life. "Looks, and money, loving relatives behind you, and what must you do? Throw it all away . . ."

I took her by the arm and said:

"Aunt Dorothea, you are beside yourself. Come and lie down."

"What good will that do? Who wouldn't be beside herself, faced with such disgrace? And so unfair!"

I got her out of the room. I said:

"I have an even better idea. Annabella will have a cough and Dr. Cornwell will advise her to winter in Italy."

"What then? What of the poor baby? It's part of the family. My way it will be born in wedlock and have a father. I'm going to order the carriage for half past eight tomorrow morning."

"All right. And as soon as you've gone I shall hire the town crier to go calling that Annabella Follett is pregnant."

She looked at me with such horror, such terror and loathing as I had thought only existed in nightmares.

She said, "They were right. . . . People laughed and said it was superstition, but those who knew . . . they said it was the Devil who came in a snowstorm and could do more with one hand than any man could do with two, and bewitched your mother and then vanished. . . . Nothing else could account for it."

She flung away from me and went into her bedroom and, for the first time to my knowledge, locked the door.

In the night Mrs. Bolt's nostrums did their work and within ten days Annabella was downstairs again, pale and thin, as might be expected after such a prolonged stomach upset, but safe. So there we were, three people who had each had a private taste of Hell, and outwardly none the worse. Things were sadly different, though.

Aunt Dorothea seemed to be able to forgive me my moment's defiance; she never forgave Annabella and never missed a chance of making a slighting, spiteful, and derogatory remark. Annabella's behaviour was little help. Long periods of melancholy brooding were broken by spells of almost crazy lightheartedness. Aunt Dorothea, who regarded marriage as the ultimate goal of a woman's existence, refused to abandon her efforts on Annabella's behalf, though privately holding the view that Annabella did not deserve to find a husband. Invitations were punctiliously accepted, as punctiliously returned.

Annabella was capable of attending one party in such a state of gloomy indifference as repelled everyone who ventured near her, and at the next displaying such frenzied hilarity that everyone was shocked. She struck up a great friendship with Mrs. Helmar, about whose free-and-easy behaviour there was already a good deal of talk, and Aunt Dorothea spent a lot of time pointing out that between what was permissible to a young matron and to an unmarried girl there was a great gulf fixed, and a girl crossed it to her everlasting peril.

"Nobody wants to marry me anyway," Annabella said. "I'm too tall, too thin, and my hair isn't right, so I might as well enjoy myself in my own way." She talked a great deal about Celia Fiennes, an unfeminine young woman who had ridden all over England alone, noting down what she saw. The moment she was of age and could please herself, Annabella was going to do the same, but not in England only. She would ride across Europe, go to Jerusalem, to Baghdad, to India. . . .

Time seemed to go fast; we were eighteen, nineteen, twenty. Aunt Dorothea became rheumaticky, which did not sweeten her temper.

"I'm concerned for *you*," she said to me. "A pretty situation it will be here when you want to take a wife."

"I've not even seen any woman I wish to marry," I said, intending to console her.

"Nor will you, while you have eyes for nobody but your crazy sister."

"Annabella isn't crazy. You mustn't say that."

"Tell me a better word and I'll use it," she said.

There were times when, after a stormy session, ending with tears from Aunt Dorothea or Annabella or both, I thought of running away myself, but I had no stomach for it. I loved my home; I loved every room in my house, every step in my own stairway, every bush and plant that blossomed in my garden; I even loved the way the light fell at various seasons upon certain places. On a winter's afternoon, just before sunset on a clear day, a ray of light would come in at the library window and touch, for a brief moment, the backs of the books on a certain shelf . . . it had done so last year, it would do so next year at the same time, it was doing it at this moment . . . nothing significant about it, except a sense of continuity, of being fixed, of having one's own place. And the same was true of the way the early sun came into my bedroom on a summer's morning and the scent of lilac, or roses, drifted in at the window.

And being so innately settled myself, I wanted those I loved to be settled too. Every time Annabella said, "I must get away," "I can't live forever in this climate of disapproval," "What is there for me in Baildon?" and that kind of thing, I had a pang in my heart.

When Tom Mallow loomed up, in the autumn of 1785, just before our twenty-first birthday, nobody could have been more pleased than I.

From the worldly point of view—Aunt Dorothea's—he was not a match for anyone. He was forty years old, ugly, aggressive in manner, and deadly poor. He'd been in the Navy and still called himself captain, though he had been dismissed—according to Cousin Chris, the first person in our circle to befriend him—either for disobeying an order or for interpreting it so ill that disaster followed. (The story, told in Chris's mumbling way, was completely confused.) He'd come to Suffolk, bought a tumble-down house called Nudd's Hall, which had become separated from its land and stood like a whale stranded in a small pool, and there he lived on thirty pounds a year and what he could make from rearing pigs and chickens. His father—though he disowned Tom—was a baronet and an admiral, and Tom, though so poor, rode to hounds and had the clothes and address necessary to a gentleman, so he was accepted, with reservations, in our circle. Aunt Dorothea succinctly summed the situation up when she said:

"Four years ago I should have thought him utterly presumptuous; now I think Annabella is fortunate to get a man at all."

I liked him—which proved that Aunt Dorothea had been wrong in accusing me of being jealous of Richard. I admired his indomitable cheerfulness in the face of misfortune. When some pigs he had been fattening for market contracted some mysterious disease and died he reported the disaster by saying, "I thought they were damned quiet, so I went in and there they were, lying about like a lot of bloody corpses! Well, that's what they were, of course. And I thought to myself—This would happen to me! If I could choose I'd have those words on my tombstone. Come to think of it, they could go on *all* tombstones, couldn't they?" I liked him for his unconcealed liking for Annabella, coming as it did at a moment when her self-esteem was in need of such a prop; and I liked the way he handled her moodiness, not unsympathetically, not over-indulgently. She would, I thought, be safe with him.

She and I privately mentioned the possibility of her marrying him quite early, almost as soon as he had shown signs of a partiality for her company. She said, without any great enthusiasm, that he was the only man she had seen lately whom she could bear to marry. "And if I stay in these parts I must marry someone."

"I wouldn't call that a good reason for marriage," I said, hoping with all my heart that she was actually more enthusiastic than she sounded, and just evincing a maidenly coyness. I wanted her to stay in the neighbourhood of Baildon, I wanted her married and settled down, but above all I wanted her to be happy. She replied, as she so often did, to what I was thinking rather than to my spoken words.

"I'm not in love with him. I shall never be in love with anyone again, thank God."

Yet when, in the weeks immediately preceding our twenty-first birthday, his attentions seemed to be slackening off, when he danced with her only once at the Michaelmas Ball, rode straight past the house without calling on two successive market days, and then replied to our invitation to our coming-of-age party with a brief note saying that he was unable to come, her chagrin was obvious, though she did her best to conceal it. She bought herself a new horse, immensely tall and strong, young and quite insufficiently broken, and spent hours patiently schooling him. She began to plan herself a fantastic riding habit, the jacket composed largely of pockets of various sizes. She intended to leave Baildon just before Christmas, thus avoiding any more festivities where she would be regarded as an old maid.

For what happened next I hold myself solely to blame. I rode out to Tom's place, endeavouring to make the visit seem casual by saying that I was on my way to Cousin Chris's, and thought I'd look in on him, not having seen him lately.

Nudd's Hall was a sizable house in a state of advanced delapidation, unused except for two rooms, Tom's bedchamber and a kitchen which also served as a living room. It was indescribably cluttered and yet comfortable, and there, by a blazing fire, he made me sit down, and heated some ale by the simple expedient of plunging a red-hot poker into it, and presently, in what I considered a bluff, manly way, he explained his position. He was frank about his feelings for Annabella, "head over heels in love with her" was his expression; but it was impossible for him to marry her because he had no money and no prospects of having any. I muttered that Annabella was not penniless and he said that that simply made matters worse.

"A man should be master in his own house, otherwise there's no peace; and how can he be that when he knows and she knows that he's nothing but a bloody parasite?"

It was strong October ale we were drinking, and we drank a lot of it; by the end of the session we were neither of us quite sober. All things considered, I suppose his demands were modest; he needed, he said, four thousand pounds to set him up.

With that sum he could buy back the acres which had originally belonged to the house, he could repair the house, and the
farm buildings, and stock the latter properly. He would have
money in the bank to enable him to hold his own until his
new fields and animals began to show a profit. . . .

To me it was as delightful as it had been in the past when I
planned a "surprise" for Annabella for a Christmas or birthday
morning. There was the same element of secrecy; for no one
was to know, we agreed, that I had lent Tom the money; let
everyone, Annabella included, think that he had come in for a
legacy. (That would change Aunt Dorothea's tune, I thought
with some spite.)

Feeling like God, I pulled out my watch and said, "Go into
Baildon now, and ask her to marry you, Tom. I'm supposed
to be at Green Farm. I shall get home this afternoon and have
a most stupendous surprise!"

I left him delving into a drawer to find himself a clean shirt
while a pan of water for shaving heated on the fire.

I rode on to Green Farm feeling like a man who has just
bought himself out of the Army; for all along I had known
that I should never be able to bring myself to let Annabella
ride off alone; in the end I should have been compelled to go
with her, and I didn't want to go visiting strange places. I
wanted to stay in Baildon, at the Old Vine, and presently find
myself a pretty cheerful girl and marry her and have a family.

Tom had said all the right, manly things about the money
being a loan; but I didn't intend it that way. I didn't want
him to set out on marriage with a debt round his neck. The
four thousand pounds would be a free gift . . . no, not that,
either, an investment. An investment in the thing that mattered most in the world to me, Annabella's happiness.

Nudd's Hall, made weatherproof, made comfortable, became a second home to me. In the bedroom known as "Hatton's room" I kept spare clothes in the closet, an extra shaving

set on the stand, so that I could stay at any time without pre-meditation. Some of the happiest days of my life were spent there, seeing Annabella, busy with her own household, busy in reclaiming the neglected garden, busy being the young hostess, firmly entrenched at last; seeing Tom, cheerful in adversity, become exuberant in comparative affluence.

I was busy too. Almost against my will, for I was by nature idle, easily content, unambitious, a little out of place perhaps in the pushful modern age in which I lived. I knew that I had depleted my estate by four thousand pounds and felt vaguely that I ought to make some effort to replenish it by that amount. I sold some not very remunerative stock and invested the money in a newly founded hat factory out at Steeple Strawless where the raw material—rabbit fur—was to be had cheaply and in abundance. The two young men to whom the place belonged promised, within two years, a return of twenty per cent on the money.

And then I had my wonderful idea about building a Corn Exchange in Baildon. Dimly aware that I was old-fashioned, it pleased me to associate myself with something so extremely timely. Great changes were afoot just then. In all our district only Clevely, under Sir Charles Shelmadine's benevolent autocracy, still held to the open-field system. Everywhere else farms were individual and enclosed. And no longer were bullocks killed off and their meat salted down, as soon as the summer pastures failed; they were brought in and stall-fed on the new crop, turnips. This had two results: cattle markets increased beyond belief and were held all through the year, and the "muck" from the stall-fed beasts, spread on the fields, led to corn yields heavy beyond imagination.

In the year 1783 the Baildon Town Council had made a separate market place for cattle, and it happened that adjoining the new market I owned a huddle of ancient, low-rented houses with very long back gardens. Just at a time when the farmers and corn merchants were crying out for a place in which to do their buying and selling. I decided to give all my Saltgate tenants notice, raze the houses to the ground, and build a spacious hall with a glass roof. It would cost me—I reckoned—fifteen hundred pounds; I should charge every farmer and corn chandler a shilling for entry on Wednesday, the corn market day, and on other days of the week I should let the hall for a guinea a session for all the various public and private functions for which the mediaeval Guildhall was too small, the Assembly Rooms too grand. I visualised it as a plain, utilitarian building in which the Yeomanry could drill in bad weather, prize fights could be held, the Baildon Traders' Musical Society could hold their biannual concerts, the Maypole Dance could be held should May Day be, as it so often was, inclement, and any hospitable person with a small house could hire it for a wedding or christening party. It seemed to me that by building this Corn Exchange I should be doing my town as well as myself a service.

I thought myself extremely fortunate to meet, at Mortiboys, a man named Selby who was an architect and an artist. He specialised in the modernisation of old houses. Lady Fennel had engaged him to give Ockley Manor a new front and Mrs. Helmar had asked him to come and look at Mortiboys and see what could be made of it. Actually Nick Helmar was against any innovation—he was right there, and I think it was with some notion of "making up" to Charles Selby that Mrs. Helmar introduced us.

I was clay in his hands, chiefly because he was so full of praise for my house, and for Baildon as a whole. When he said, "But you can't spoil the town by building something not fit to set beside the Abbey Gate, the Guildhall, the Assembly Rooms or the Old Vine or a dozen other superb buildings," I knew that he was right. "A grey brick cow shed," he called my proposed building. And then we were off.

In his youth, in order to get to Italy, he had gone as "bear-leader" to a rich young man making the Grand Tour. He'd

visited a place called Paestum where there was a temple to
Poseidon with which he had fallen in love.

Sketching as he talked, he said, "It'll be a bit like hitching a
blood horse to a plough, but a beautiful thing is a beautiful
thing, whatever use it is put to," and there before my eyes
was the six-pillared front, the flight of steps. My imagination
took fire.

"And over here," I said, pointing to the top of the pillars,
"the heads of farm animals, and sheaves of corn. And some
words. 'The earth is the Lord's and the fulness thereof.' How
would that be?"

"Highly suitable," he said, drawing away. The lines flowed
into one another. In the centre a woman's figure, well curved,
lightly clad, her lap piled high with fruit and flowers. "Ceres,"
he said, "the Mother of all living. And that must be in marble,
carved by Jeremy Thrush. The pillars must be of Bath stone."

Now and again I'd wake in the night and sweat a little,
thinking that my Corn Exchange would cost me five or six
thousand pounds if things went on this way; and that no matter how beautiful it was my originally planned charges
couldn't be increased so that even if I lived to be a hundred
I could never hope to see my money back. And then Charles
would come along and say, "Look at the house you live in,
Hatton. Those old people built things to last forever, and that
is the only way *to* build," and within minutes we'd be planning
some new extravagance.

Another year went quickly by.

It is difficult to say when exactly I became aware that all
was not well between Annabella and Tom. I discounted the
first few times when I heard sharp words exchanged and saw
angry looks. Married people couldn't be expected always to
agree. I certainly did not, as Aunt Dorothea and later Tom

accused me, automatically agree with Annabella in everything. Nobody knew better than I how headstrong and exasperating she could be. I should say that in the beginning my sympathies were rather with Tom, for I judged him to be the one who was in love and therefore in danger of being put upon, and liable to be hurt.

He never complained; for one thing he was not the complaining kind, nor was he very articulate about any but everyday matters, but now and again from the expression on his face, from a word let slip, I gathered that he had come to realise that Annabella was less in love with him than he would have liked. Probably he hesitated to admit that even to himself; he said that he did not "understand" her. Once he said to me, "What goes on in that pretty little head? That's what I often ask myself. What goes on?"

"The usual mysterious female thoughts, I expect," I said.

"Mysterious all right. But one way and another I've known a lot of women in my time, Hatton, and sooner or later you know where you are with them. Not with her, though, not with her."

His puzzled sense of something lacking in their relationship had two results—an abject desire to please, which merely increased Annabella's innate capriciousness, and an almost demented jealousy which extended to every person, every thing for which Annabella showed any fondness; he was jealous of her horse, her dogs, her friends, and finally of me. Often of course the two things came into head-on conflict and one could watch him, poor fellow, desperately trying to be friendly and civil to someone like Mrs. Helmar while privately wishing her in Hell.

"She's a bad lot, Hatton; anybody can see that with half an eye. And what the devil *can* they have in common? Sweet pretty girl like Annabella and a painted hussy like that one?"

One thing they had in common was being married to one man and in love with another; youth, too, and an impatience with the rules of correct behaviour as understood in the set wherein they moved. On Annabella's side there was defiance too; Aunt Dorothea had disapproved of that friendship, and by disapproving fostered it; now Tom was making the same mistake. I hinted as much to him and with an unusual surliness he said:

"Why don't you speak to her about it, then? When you get to rock bottom you're the only person for whose opinion she gives a tinker's curse."

"But I don't particularly disapprove. A young woman needs a friend of her own age and sex; and Mrs. Helmar was very kind to Annabella when . . ."

"When what?"

"When she wasn't very happy. My aunt and Annabella didn't get on very well, you know."

On most Wednesdays Tom drove in to market in his high new yellow-wheeled gig, and more often than not Annabella came with him and spent the day with me. Tom set her down at the Old Vine and then drove on into the town and called for her at about four o'clock. There came a day, in mid-September 1786. Annabella and I had had a happy day; she had bought the stuff for two new warm gowns and then walked with me to the site of the Corn Exchange, where the walls were now almost six feet high. At four o'clock, according to our custom, we were in the hall, with Annabella's parcels piled on the window seat, watching through the window for Tom to arrive. He was about twenty minutes late.

When he came I carried out the parcels and went to stow them in the gig's boot while Annabella put her foot on the step and accepted Tom's extended left hand to help her climb in.

I heard her say:

"You've been drinking again. Move over. I'll drive."

Once or twice in the past I'd suspected Tom of being a little drunk on Wednesday afternoons—but no more than what was called in Suffolk "market merry." I happened to know that things on his farm hadn't been going particularly well; he still insisted upon regarding the money I had given him as a loan, and found it necessary to give me, from time to time, an elaborate account of his affairs as an explanation of his inability to repay me, and I could well understand the temptation it was to a man whose marriage was slightly unsatisfactory and whose business was not thriving to take the one extra drink that would induce a cheerful state of mind.

He said, "Get in," in a quiet, almost sinister voice. The quietness informed me that he wanted me not to hear, the sinister note warned me that it mattered to him that I shouldn't hear, so I pretended deafness and went on stowing parcels.

Annabella said:

"Leave go my hand!" and then, very sharply, "Hatton!"

I moved round to her side of the gig just in time to see Tom give his hand a great jerk. The force of it lifted her off her feet so that for half a second she hung suspended like a doll being carried by a child, and then dropped on her knees on the floor of the gig. With his right hand he slapped the reins across the horse's back and it shot forward. With a flurry of skirts and petticoat as Annabella righted herself, and a spurt of dust from the wheels, the gig tore off along the road.

I had a momentary impulse to go and get my horse and ride after them; but there was nothing I could do; being followed would merely make Tom drive more recklessly. So I stayed where I was, trying to convince myself that almost any man would in the circumstances have acted much the same. But I was worried and early next morning got up and went to the haberdasher's and bought three yards of satin ribbon. I'd take it out to Nudd's Hall and say that Annabella had left it on the window seat. When I got back home and went into the yard for my horse, Annabella was just dismounting. She had said that she had left a parcel on the window seat.

"What was in it?" I asked.

"Three yards of blue satin ribbon, I *said*."

"Here it is." I held out my purchase.

We thought that was rather extraordinary; people tell peculiar stories about twins sharing thoughts and emotions, even illnesses, but it had never happened to us before. We laughed and exclaimed and it was easy enough for me to say:

"Tom wasn't all that drunk, was he?"

"He didn't turn us over. But he was drunk enough to be unpleasant. I shall never ride with him again."

"Oh come!" I said. She turned her blindest, blankest stare on me.

"I shall never ride with him again," she repeated. "He has turned the gig over once. In fact I'm going to Jackson's this morning and order myself a phaeton. George Burke will pull it for me, won't you, my love?" She turned to the tall horse and pulled his nose against her face. I understood for a moment why Tom called Burke "an ungainly, ill-broken brute." (In point of fact George Burke justified Annabella's faith in him and took kindly to the phaeton, which was a very odd-looking rig, because, he being so tall, it had to be made with the most sharply angled shafts ever seen on any vehicle.)

Life went on. My Corn Exchange grew, gulping down money. Charles Selby came and went. He was very busy. The modernisation of Ockley had brought him several commissions from people who thought that they couldn't do better than copy Lady Fennel. Mrs. Helmar still wanted Mortiboys to be transmogrified, but Nick still refused to give the word. During this period, on one of his visits to me, Charles suggested that I install one of the new water closets, and found a place for it, on the half landing of the stairs. Aunt Dorothea protested that indoor privies were the most insanitary things ever invented and ignored the existence of ours, hobbling out in all weathers to the old one in the passage opposite the woodshed.

Her rheumatism worsened rapidly, and in November of that year Dr. Cornwell suggested that she might obtain some relief from taking the waters at Bath. She said she'd think about it "after Christmas" and she would have put it off until after Easter had I not taken matters into my own hands and escorted her there during a fine spell in January. I left her, comfortably installed in an hotel and within six weeks she reported that she had derived considerable benefit; she had also made a friend, a lady of about her own age, similarly afflicted, and equally convinced that they would live more cheaply and more comfortably in a small house of their own. "You know, Hatton dear," she wrote, "that I never *intended* to stay at the Old Vine once you and Annabella were able to look after yourselves. Bath *suits* me and Lady Frances is an *ideal* companion. We have found the perfect little house and Lady Frances' old nursemaid is anxious to come and look after us both. . . ."

My duty was clear. It was also, at that moment, a little painful, but I did it. Lady Frances, Aunt Dorothea's ideal companion, proved to have no resources at all. I bought the little house, and the annuity which would keep two elderly and one middle-aged females in comfort for so long as Aunt Dorothea lived. And once again I felt like God. Except in the night when I'd wake and think about the hat factory which so far showed no sign of making a profit, of that vampire Corn Exchange which so far had never had a chance to show any, and of a Joint Stock Company in which I had—on another get-rich-quick impulse, invested three thousand pounds, and lost it. Then I felt like a fool. . . .

So we came to June 1787; one of those very rare summer evenings when the sunny rose-scented day melts imperceptibly into the star-spangled night. In my garden, that day, the strawberries had come to perfection and after supper I had carried a great basketful up to my Corn Exchange where the men were working late. The exterior was complete; my peristyle, with the heads of farm animals, the threshing flail, the milk yoke, the plough, the harrow and the scythe and sickle, and the flower-and-fruit-bearing Ceres had been put in place two days before, and now the men were working on the inside, determined to have it all ready by the first of September. Stripped to the waist in the warm summer weather, they worked, glazed with the sweat of labour, and I had ordered in a cask of beer and carried along my basket of strawberries to refresh them.

It was nine o'clock when I set out for home. I had one of those curiously elated feelings which I was to learn boded no good. Down the ages, ever since the Tower of Babel, there has been a kind of obscure curse on men who build ambitiously for anything but domestic purposes. I didn't know that at the time; like all of them I was elated . . . look what I have made! Children, all of us, rearing our pitiable little sand castles in the path of the incoming tide.

Ahead of me as I walked home a purple cloud began to muster in the sky. It would rain tomorrow. But rain, all through these last weeks, an enemy because it stopped work, could not hurt me now. A good rain, I thought complacently, would refresh the garden, swell the crops. I hoped Tom would have a better harvest this year.

And then, as I neared home, I saw against the purple back cloth, made, by some trick of the light, very small and clear, I saw a woman's shape outlined. It made me think of Annabella. But why? Annabella never walked anywhere; she certainly never shuffled along wearily in the summer dust as this woman was doing. Annabella rode proudly, or drove dashingly in her phaeton.

But it was Annabella.

Her face was very pale, caked in places with dust that had stuck to the sweat-dampened skin, her eyes were feverishly bright and over-wide. I saw that as I ran to meet her, blurting out questions. I took her hands, which were as cold and limp as a corpse's. She said:

"It's all right, Hatton, now I'm here. I've got here, after all."

She was wearing a white muslin dress, crumpled and soiled and torn, bits of leaf and some wild-rose petals clung to her curls.

I went on gulping out questions. What had happened, why was she walking, why was she here at all?

"Let's get indoors," she said, and with a final burst of speed moved towards the house. I had my hand on the door handle when she shied off, like a nervous horse. "Tom isn't here, is he?"

"Not to my knowledge. I've been out almost two hours."

"Look, then."

I opened the door and looked; the hall was empty. She shot past me and ran up the stairs, calling breathlessly:

"I'm going to my own room. If he's here, get rid of him."

I went along to the library. It was empty. I rang the bell and Polly came. Without waiting for my question she said:

"Oh, sir. Time you was out Captain Mallow come, hunting Miss Annabella. He wouldn't take our word for her not being here, went all over the house, he did, into the garden, everywhere, looking and looking."

"But he's gone now?"

"Yes. He went off, cursing."

I went up. Annabella had locked her door and only opened it when I assured her that I was alone.

"Now," I said, "tell me what happened."

"Tom's gone mad. He locked me up. *He* locked *me* up!" She broke into laughter, shrill, high-pitched, very unpleasant to hear. Then, just as suddenly, she stopped laughing and said plaintively, "That was yesterday at six o'clock. I haven't had anything to eat or drink all day."

I said, rather shortly, partly because I was worried, partly because I wanted to hear what she had to say:

"Then you'd better come down and have something."

She said, "Oh, Hatton, don't be angry. Honestly it wasn't my fault. I thought everything would be all right if I could get home."

"It will be. It is. Come down and eat and tell me all about it."

"Lock all the doors, then."

"Tom's been here. He won't come back tonight. Why are you so frightened?"

She said, "He tried to strangle me. Look!"

The white dress had a fichu at the neck. She loosened it. The light was dying fast, but I could just see against the whiteness of her throat some dark blotches—too low down near the collarbone, I thought, to be proof of attempted strangulation. I realised in an instant what had happened. Exasperated by something or other, he had taken her by the shoulders and shaken her, and his thumbs had left those marks.

"What had *you* done?"

"Nothing. Nothing at all. We were to go to Mortiboys and in the end he said he wouldn't, so I said I'd go by myself. He ordered me not to and I said I *would*. He just leaped at me and tried to strangle me."

"Shook you," I said. "Tom's much too fond of you to want to hurt you."

"But he did, Hatton. He shook me senseless, dragged me upstairs, and locked me in. 'I'll show you,' he kept shouting. I tell you, he's mad."

"This was yesterday evening. What then?"

"I pulled the chest in front of the door, so he couldn't get in. He laughed and said I should come out when I was hungry. And then today, when he was hay-making, I climbed out of the window and down by the honeysuckle and came home, through Layer Wood and the fields. I'm never going back,

Hatton, never. Nobody can make me. You don't know what I've been through these last few months." She began to cry. "I swore I'd never cry again, but I can't help it, I can't help it." Crying, she revealed in little broken sentences a state of affairs far more innately shocking than the single and perhaps understandable assault of the previous evening. Tom had shot her dog. "He said it was by accident, but it wasn't. He did it deliberately, just to hurt me." He had said that if George Burke could pull the phaeton he could pull a tumbril. "Burke didn't understand, and Tom beat him and beat him. . . ." And then there'd been Phoebe Tunstall.

"Hatton, I daresay you'll think I was wrong, but you've never been married, so you can't *know*. It's awful to talk about. And that *was* my fault. I told you once that Tom was the one person I could *bear* to marry. I honestly did think so and I did my best. But it wasn't enough, it wasn't the same; so I thought that if Phoebe could do . . . could make him satisfied, I could bear it. But she got so arrogant; the way she behaved to me, everybody would have known. . . ."

Fold by fold the whole sorry story was spread before my eyes.

Tom arrived next morning while I was at breakfast. He looked so wild and wretched that I said instantly:

"She's here, safe and sound." He sat down and put his head in his hands and for a moment I thought he was crying. Then he began to talk, describing in detail his misery since five o'clock the previous afternoon, when he found her room empty and the window open. He'd ridden straight to Mortiboys, then to Green Farm, then to my house; finally it had occurred to him that she might have taken the way across the fields and through the woods, and he'd walked about, calling and swinging a lantern. Of the quarrel he gave much the same account as Annabella had done, but he said one thing which momentarily puzzled me. "I made sure she'd gone to Mortiboys. Your friend Selby is there again." I didn't interrupt him then, but when he had finished I said:

"What has Selby to do with it?"

"You know as well as I do. She's in love with him."

"What arrant nonsense," I said hotly. "My God, how little you know my sister. What she wants she goes straight for, and if she were in love with Charles—or anybody else—she wouldn't have stayed with you for five minutes." I was as sure of that as I was of anything in the world. I had another reason for discounting the story too. In a moment of confidence Charles had betrayed to me the fact that he was hopelessly in love with Caroline Helmar.

Tom said sulkily, "You don't know her either. Or else you're deliberately blind. You think she's perfect. You're very largely to blame for her being so hard to handle."

"You find her hard because you go about it the wrong way. You were pretty rough the other evening."

"She defied me."

"Who wouldn't, when you get a bee in your bonnet and go issuing arbitrary orders? I may as well tell you, here and now, that unless you get rid of your daft ideas about her and Charles Selby and give me your word never to mishandle her again, I shan't even try to persuade her to go back with you."

I could see anger and doubt and a kind of hope war in his face.

"Is it so daft? I've only your word for that. And you don't know everything. I go by what I see; if that damned smooth fellow is anywhere around, she's different. She seems to . . . come to life. Laughing, talking, on with the best dress."

"He has exactly the same effect on me," I said. "For one thing he's very witty and amusing; for another he comes to us straight from London and we try not to appear too rustic. If you're honest with yourself you'd admit that you are inclined to be jealous and since you couldn't find anyone else to fix on you chose him."

After a moment he said:

"I *am* jealous. Any man in my shoes would be, Hatton. There are things . . . but there, you've never been married, you wouldn't understand. There are times when a man needs to feel . . . something more than just to be *tolerated*. Oh, to hell with this. I'll admit I was wrong. I'll forgive her and try to make a fresh start."

It was because I felt sorry for him that I said:

"Isn't it rather a case of asking her to forgive you?"

He said, quite meekly, "I will, Hatton. I'll apologise and ask her to forgive me. Will you fetch her?"

She was unwilling to see him, but I persuaded her, assuring her that he was genuinely sorry. I left them in the room together and went out onto the terrace, far away not to be able to hear the actual words that were spoken, near enough to distinguish the two voices. There were the alternating tones for a while and then a crash, followed by a cry, quickly cut off. I ran to the open window and into the room. I had to dodge past the table at which, when Tom arrived, I had been breakfasting. It lay on its side. Beyond it there was Tom, backing away towards the door and dragging Annabella with him. He had one hand clenched in her hair, the other clapped over her mouth. She was clutching at everything she passed, her frail little hands gaining a moment's purchase on the edge of a table, the back of a chair, and then being torn by sheer force away.

I shouted at him. I yelled, "Let her go! Stop it, Tom. Stop!" But I doubt if he heard me. He looked quite crazy. Even the whites of his eyes were red and his lips were drawn back over his teeth, like a snarling dog's. As soon as I reached him I laid hold of the arm the hand of which was holding Annabella's hair. The arm seemed to be made of iron, and I realised that by pulling on it I merely increased her pain. So I did the only thing left to me. I went round behind him and gave him a short chopping blow on the back of the neck, the kind of blow with which merciful people dispatch rabbits.

I thought I had killed him. His hands dropped. Annabella went reeling backwards, and he went sideways, like a crab, staggering until brought up short by the wall. I said:

"Go and lock yourself in." I looked at her as I spoke and saw a thin thread of blood running down from the edge of her hair. "It'll be all right," I said. She put her hand to her head and brought it away, looking with a kind of stunned horror at the blood. Then she turned and went away and I gave my attention to Tom. All over his red face there were white patches, like thumb prints which, as I looked, widened and ran into one another. I felt no compunction at all; if ever a blow were justified mine was; but I wanted him out of my house, so I took him by the arm and pulled him towards a chair and set him down. Then I opened the cupboard and poured some brandy and held it towards him, saying, "Here, drink this and pull yourself together."

He had difficulty in drinking; his hand shook, so did his head. I didn't feel disposed to help him, and eventually he managed. Presently he said, in a wooden way like somebody speaking in a foreign tongue:

"She . . . wouldn't . . . come . . . home."

"That didn't give you the right to assault her."

He turned his head, cautiously, left, right, left again.

"Man . . . can't . . . assault . . . own wife," he said.

I said, "Don't talk rot. Drink up and get out."

He took another swig, and the white patches began to contract.

"I shall go when I'm ready. I've got something to say to you first."

"I've no wish to hear any more from you. I just want you out of my house."

"My God! Who d'you think you are?"

"I know. I'm your wife's brother. And so long as I'm alive

you'll never get near enough to lay a finger on her again."

"And I'm her legal husband. Get that into your thick Suffolk head. I've got rights. She's my *wife!* You've no more right to stand between us than anybody else."

"I've got the right to see that you don't ill-use her. So far as I'm concerned you've forfeited any rights you ever had. If you can't be alone with her for five minutes without . . . I was more or less on your side, but not any more. I've done with you!"

"You may have done with me, you arrogant young whelp, but I haven't finished with you. Not by a long way. I'm warning you. Unless you hand her over you're going to be very sorry."

I said, "I wish you wouldn't talk about Annabella as though she were a handkerchief. She isn't mine to hand over, or yours to claim. She is mine to protect, and I shall do that. Now, I've had enough of this for one day. Please leave my house."

He'd got to his feet and stood looking at me with fury. For a moment I thought he was going to attack me, and wondered what chance I should stand; not much. My one blow had taken him unawares, and been lucky; but he was very massive, very angry. I remembered the hardness of that muscular arm. I moved towards the bell rope, hoping that my handy man was in the yard, within call. Maybe Tom thought of that, too, for he restrained himself and said, quite calmly:

"Look, I'm giving you one last chance. Unless you fetch her down and hand her over, you're outside the law, harbouring another man's wife. And you do yourself no good. I shall get her back if it takes every penny I have, and an act of Parliament to do it."

I said, "All right. Go ahead. Nothing in this world will make me hand Annabella over to somebody capable of using her as you did this morning."

"You'll learn," he said, and turned and walked out of the room.

I ran straight up to Annabella, who was bathing her head in a bowl of reddened water. She was shaken, but not, thank God, tearful.

"You see," she said, "he is mad. I can't live with him any more. But I can't stay here, either. Tom would make trouble for you." She held a towel against her damp, discoloured curls. "Did he use the word 'harbouring' to you, Hatton?"

"As a matter of fact, he did. But he's talking wildly. Nobody who knew the whole story could possibly expect you to go back, or me to let you."

"I don't know. Men make the laws, for men, don't they? Honestly, Hatton, I think if you could lend me a little money I'd better go right away."

"But where could you go?"

"Anywhere where he couldn't find me." She sat down on the edge of the bed. "Oh, I wish to God I'd gone away in the first place. I knew in my heart that was what I should do. I was free, I'd got my own money, my own horse. Now I have nothing at all. But you'll help me, won't you?"

I said, "I think the first thing to do is for me to consult with Mr. Steward and learn just how we stand."

Mr. Steward, his face inscrutable, listened to my story. "I'd like to know where I stand," I ended. "What exactly could my brother-in-law *do*?"

"I can't give you a full or comprehensive answer, offhand, but I can tell you roughly. Captain Mallow has several ways open to him. He might, for instance, apply to the Ecclesiastical Courts for a restitution of conjugal rights—which would most certainly be granted. He could take an action on tort against you for harbouring his wife. Against that your only sound defence would be that you did it on humanitarian grounds—a defence successfully proffered in the case of Williamson vs. Johnson, in which it was claimed that the wife was in danger of life and limb."

Greatly relieved, I said, "That's it! Why, only this morning . . ."

"This morning, if I heard aright, Captain Mallow exerted no more than a permissible amount of force in his endeavour to compel his wife to return to her home. In the case I mentioned the husband had actually discharged his shotgun, with intent to kill. From treatment that might lead to death or permanent injury anyone is entitled, indeed morally obliged, to protect any woman; but a shaking, a pulling by the hair. . . . Mr. Follett, if such trivial acts entitled wives to leave their husbands, half the women in England would be living under roofs other than their own."

"Trivial!"

"Don't misunderstand me. I had no wish to sound callous. In the eyes of the law such injuries would be regarded as trivial. After all, a man's right to beat his wife as a corrective has never been questioned. And in a beating injuries more grave than a few bruises and a torn scalp are frequently sustained."

I'd always got on well with Mr. Steward; he was not a person to inspire much positive feeling, but I'd liked him rather than not. Now I found his cool appraisal of the situation quite appalling. And what he went on to say was even worse.

"I imagine that Captain Mallow's first act will be to send you a properly phrased demand to cease harbouring his wife. Should you receive such a demand, you would be well advised to think seriously before ignoring it. If the case came into court you would have the expense of defending yourself, and you could have small hope of success. The court would then make an order for the wife's return, and if you disobeyed you would be in contempt of court, the penalty for which can be very heavy. If you were sentenced to a term of imprisonment you would be of little use to Mrs. Mallow, who would then be compelled to return to her husband, to whose original grievance would be added the bitterness which any litigation invariably leaves."

I felt a bit hollow in my stomach; but I braced myself. He was always inclined to take a gloomy view, I reminded myself. He was old, over-cautious, dried up. Never once had he referred to Annabella as "your sister," always as Tom's wife; that showed whose side he was on.

Because I wanted to be back at the house as soon as possible I had ridden to Mr. Steward's office. When I had left him, and remounted, I toyed for a moment with the idea of riding to Colchester or Bury St. Edmunds in search of other, more heartening advice. Then I remembered that almost within arm's reach there was another lawyer whose response to my tale I might at least test without further loss of time.

Mr. Turnbull was as old as, if not older than, Mr. Steward and he had been in Baildon longer, but he was less desiccated in appearance, less judicial in manner. He had married an heiress and was well to do; unkind gossip said that his wife was a shrew, and that he had only continued the practice of his profession in order to have an excuse to get away from her. . . .

He received me with understandable surprise, but genially; and when I had explained my situation he delighted me by taking an exactly opposite view from Mr. Steward's. He agreed that Tom had the law on his side:

"But the law as written and the law as applied are two very different things. It is still law, you know, that a theft of over five shillings is a capital offence, but how often does a thief hang for stealing small sums?" He talked in this strain for some time and still further encouraged me by making a sensible and practical suggestion.

"Get the doctor to your sister without delay. A wound that has received medical attention sounds more serious, and doctors make good witnesses, in my experience. Not that I think it will come to that."

He came with me to the door and there dropped the attorney and became the country gentleman with an eye for a horse's points. He praised George Rufus and then asked, with a twinkle:

"And what do you call *him*? George Numskull?"

"Why no. He's far from stupid. He's George Rufus because of his colour. It was a whim of my mother's to call all horses and dogs . . ."

"I know," he said.

As I mounted I caught a glance of the brass plate by the door and realised that Mr. Turnbull's name was George. I thought nothing of it. If anyone had called a horse or a dog by my name I should have been flattered rather than otherwise.

I do not believe that—as has been sometimes suggested—Mr. Turnbull was my secret enemy. I think he gave me sound and considered advice, and that it differed from Mr. Steward's because the two men differed in character. And in any case, had I not found in Mr. Turnbull the kind of attorney I needed, and received from him the only advice which I was prepared to take, I should have gone elsewhere. I shall believe until I die that had we stood fast and fought we should have won our case on humanitarian grounds. Tom's behaviour became more and more irrational after Annabella left him; and he was drinking hard. It would have taken a judge of exceptionally stern calibre to have ordered any woman, leave alone Annabella, back into the keeping of such a man.

It is odd to reflect that it was Tom himself who made nonsense of everything. Had he pursued the legal course open to him, at once, a verdict would have been given one way or the other and Annabella would have been returned to him, or permitted to remain with me. Maybe the first lawyer he consulted was a cautious and pessimistic fellow. In any case, before trying more civilised ways of gaining his rights Tom made an absurd attempt to abduct Annabella by force.

I say "absurd" because I had imagined that he might try, and had almost dismissed my imagination as absurd; then I had taken precautions against such an act on his part, and even in the doing thought to myself—This is absurd! I'd felt ridiculous when I insisted that Annabella was not to go out except into the garden, and even more ridiculous when I ordered the front door to be kept locked and chained and the gate into the yard barred, except when someone was actually going out or coming in. It seemed the height of folly to engage another man to help Bill Cooper in the yard and garden, and to have them both sleep in the house with stout cudgels always handy. As I made each arrangement I felt like a bad actor in a cheap melodrama—and yet I made them.

I wonder how Tom felt when he planned his assault.

One evening when Annabella and I were in the garden, Polly, our maid, came running to say that a young woman and a man had come to bring some of Mrs. Mallow's clothes and things.

"You wait here," I said. "I'll see to it."

In accordance with my orders Polly had opened the front door on the chain. Outside stood a girl and a man, with a wheelbarrow, heaped high with valises, bags, and boxes.

"My mawther here," the man said, saluting me civilly, "reckoned the pore lady'd like to have some of her gear. So the Capt'n being away for the night we took the chance to fetch it over."

"Mrs. Mallow always being very kind to me, sir," the girl said.

I was profoundly touched by this evidence of fidelity—the more so because since her arrival Annabella had been rooting out and furbishing up old garments which she had left at the Old Vine, things not good enough to be taken to her new home when she married.

Opening the door wide, I said, "How very kind! Mrs. Mallow will be so pleased."

They began to load their arms with the stuff from the barrow.

"Put it down here," I said, indicating a space in the hall. "I'll fetch Mrs. Mallow so that she can thank you herself. And then you must have some refreshment. It is a long way to push a barrow."

I left them carrying in the gear and went to the garden and told Annabella. "You have one good friend at Nudd's Hall," I said.

We came into the house by the library window and so into the hall where the man and the girl were just setting down a bag which they had carried in between them. Annabella hurried forward, saying:

"Jimmy, Jenny, how extremely kind and thoughtful of you!"

The girl said, rather shyly:

"Oh, ma'am, thass nowt. Only whass yours by rights."

I turned aside towards the door that led to the kitchen. It was a swing door, padded and covered with baize, and had I once passed through I should have heard no more. My mind was busy with the idea of providing cool ale and meat pasties for these faithful, humble friends; and five shillings apiece, I thought, would not be too much.

With my hand on the door I heard the man say:

"There's suthing we ain't quite sure about, ma'am. If you'd just look in the barrer. . . ."

I let the door thud back into place and turned. Annabella mustn't go outside the door, I thought wildly. I shouted:

"Annabella, stay ind . . ." as I ran back into the hall, and saw that I was too late. She had already stepped ahead of the fellow and he was behind her. Framed in the open doorway I saw Tom's gig, the horse's head turned towards Nettleton, the horse, roughly checked, slithering to a standstill. The girl ran to take the horse's head and Tom prepared to descend.

I threw myself forward and took the man by the neck, digging my fingers into his windpipe and pressing with all my might. Like many countrymen, he was built like a bull, and he was strong enough to move forward, carrying Annabella in front of him and dragging me behind. We were almost over the doorsill when I changed my grip and put my fingers in his eyes and pulled. He made a sound, half grunt, half scream. I pressed mercilessly and he let his hands fall. Annabella slipped away and came behind me. I raised my knee into the small of the man's back, loosed my hands, and sent him flying. He and Tom, who was just charging into the house, met with a great impact and reeled together for the necessary moment in which I could slam the door, slip home the chain and then the bolt.

Annabella put her hand to her side and bowed forward as though she had a stitch.

"That was far too close to be pleasant," she said breathlessly. "You see, he is mad. He'll stop at nothing. Did you see his face when he thought he had me?"

I had seen it, crazily triumphant, gloating.

"You'll have to let me go away, Hatton. I'm frightened. He might try again and we might not be so lucky. If he brings the case and wins . . . I couldn't bear it, Hatton, I just couldn't bear it; it was bad enough before. You must give me some money and let me go. As soon as it's dark I'm going to Bywater and get across to France or somewhere where he can't find me. And then you'll be safe too. They can't say you're harbouring me if I'm not here, can they?"

I remembered what Mr. Steward had said about the possibility of my being committed to gaol for contempt of court. If I made her stay and then failed to prove my case, what then? I realised that it was a risk I dare not take. In my heart I was still certain that I was right and I was prepared to face anything that might happen to me; but Annabella must be made safe beyond all doubt.

"I think you're right," I said. "But we'll both go."

She protested at that. She knew, she said, how much I loved the house, the town, the countryside; she accused herself of ruining my life. Under that blank, cool, self-engrossed front which she had always presented to me, she had been neither unobservant nor imperceptive. In what to an unenlightened outsider might have sounded like a hysterical outbreak of self-accusation—she even went back to the precipitant ending of my schooldays—she said the whole truth about our relationship. "It was never," she said, "as though somebody else was doing something for me; it was as though I were doing it for myself."

She seemed to deplore that; but I could say, truthfully and with pleasure, "It seemed like that to me too."

And the fact was that we were really one person, split by some accident of birth into two separate people and further severed by our difference in sex, and the social pressures which had compelled us to lead two separate lives, each conscious of a lack, each seeking satisfaction in people and things fundamentally alien to us. The realisation came to us a little late, but not too late. Our pattern was set, of course; and to the end of her days Annabella would go on thinking that Richard had been her one true love; I should go on grieving over the loss of the Old Vine. But they were only symbols. Somewhere safe, somewhere in the sun we should be happy enough, like two old sailors safe home from the sea.

INTERLUDE

Having reached his decision, Hatton Follett went, almost automatically, through force of habit, to consult with Mr. Steward, who, as usual, adopted a cautious and reasonable attitude. He was convinced, he said, that by far the best plan would be for Mrs. Mallow to return to her husband and endeavour to endear herself to him. He argued that Captain Mallow's behaviour was evidence of a strong attachment.

Hatton would have none of that. Brusquely he passed on to the question of the disposal of what property he still owned in Baildon.

"But, my dear young man," the old lawyer said, "can't you see that the moment it is known that you are selling out, Captain Mallow will be on the alert? The inference is obvious. The moment your properties are advertised . . ."

"I don't want them advertised," Hatton said.

"Then how do you expect to receive that full value which is only ascertained by competitive bidding?"

"I want them sold privately."

"The Corn Hall? A house like the Old Vine? Your remaining properties on St. Mary's Hill? You ask the impossible. On the Corn Hall, as I warned you at the beginning, a loss is inevitable. Sell it or keep it, it represents a loss. Eventually—and by that I mean in a hundred and fifty years' time—it may earn its keep; no more. Now your house is a very different proposition. Properly presented in *Sexton's Advertiser*, or *Houghton's Mart*, papers to be found in every coffee house and hotel in London, it would attract a special type of client —the men returning from India, rich, rootless, and homesick and fundamentally old-fashioned. But without advertisement . . . Can you imagine anyone slipping up alongside one of the nabobs and saying, 'There's a pleasant old house in Baildon, being offered for sale on the quiet'? No, that kind of business might be done with a local cattle dealer, over a mug of ale in the *Abbot's Head* perhaps; but local cattle dealers are hard bargainers."

Inured as he considered himself to be to the idea of selling his house, Hatton flinched at the thought of its falling into the hands of a cattle dealer.

"Surely," he said, with a hint of impatience, "there must be something between the two."

"There may well be. I was merely pointing out the disadvantages of an unadvertised sale such as is needed if your purpose is not to be exposed."

"To my mind, Mr. Steward, you are over-inclined to consider the difficulties in any situation."

"I endeavour, as I have always endeavoured, to offer you impartial advice, Mr. Follett." The old lawyer spoke reproachfully, his face flushed slightly. "Had you paid me any heed you would not now be faced with the painful necessity of disposing of your properties. I advised, you may remember, against the Corn Hall undertaking, against your investment with the Marshall brothers, and above all against the harbouring of Mrs. Mallow. In these, and in several instances of minor importance, you have consistently rejected my advice. I beg you, before you take this irrevocable step, to think the matter over. Your leaving England will solve nothing; it will actually add the charge of abduction to that of harbouring another man's wife. . . ."

All the nervous disturbance of the last few weeks found vent in Hatton's voice and manner as he said:

"Oh, for God's sake, man, don't keep saying 'wife.' She's

my sister! She was my sister before she was married and she remains my sister and I have a duty towards her."

"That," said Mr. Steward, "is the kind of emotional attitude of which the law, rightly, takes no count."

Hatton rose and stamped out of the office and straight into Mr. Turnbull's, where he was received with the comforting assurances, the soothing understanding which his heart craved.

Annabella and Hatton made a hasty, furtive departure from Baildon, leaving everything in Mr. Turnbull's hands. His performance in gaining reasonable prices for what remained of Hatton's estate fell somewhat short of his promises and the Borough Council who bought the Corn Hall and the cattle dealer named Walker who purchased the Old Vine were particularly fortunate in their bargains. Fortunately for the brother and sister, living was cheap in Italy, where they eventually made their home in a small hillside villa a few miles outside Florence. They were able to live in modest comfort and still have funds to devote to an ever increasing family of stray dogs and lame or aged donkeys. The natives of the little village regarded them as highly eccentric, but eccentricity was expected of the English anyway.

They made no friends and seemed happy in one another's company. Annabella died in 1796 at the age of thirty-two, of a cold which could not be thrown off and which settled in her chest. Hatton could have returned to England then, but felt no desire to do so.

In Baildon, Job Walker, having proved to himself and to anyone else who cared to notice the fact, that he had prospered sufficiently to be able to afford a fine house, discovered that the only place within its walls where he felt really comfortable was the kitchen.

LYDIA WALKER'S TALE

I hate the railroad. Whenever I say that, people think I'm daft. They say, "I can't see as the Eastern Union Railway ever done you no harm, Lyddy. Made you rich, din't it?"

All right, it made me rich, which I don't care about all that much; there's a lot in this world besides being rich and the Old Vine is one of them. But whereas I can say, "I hate the railroad," as easy as kiss my hand, I can't say, "I loved the Old Vine." Don't ask me why. Or rather, ask me why and I'll tell you as best I can. Saying you hate a thing makes you sound kind of angry, big and strong; saying you love something sounds kind of weak and feeble. Specially when what you love is just a house. And when you live amongst people who only say *love* when they mean wanting to hop into bed with. Hate is different; you can say you hate wasps or onions or people with red hair. And I hate the railroad.

I'm a plain woman—in all senses of the word, and I'll stick to plain facts. My grandfather was a cattle dealer who'd made a mint of money and wanted to end his days in Baildon; so he bought the Old Vine, outbidding everybody else. He never set anywhere except in the kitchen, and he never used any but the back stairs; but odd times, like the Fat Stock Show or Horringer Sheep Fair, he'd have the whole place lighted up and fires going and make a real brave show. And when my father took over, he did just the same.

I was born at the Old Vine in the year 1830. I was a disappointment to my parents, because, like everybody else, they wanted a boy to carry on where they left off, and a girl couldn't very well be a cattle dealer. There'd been two boys before me, but they'd died, and there were three after me, and they died too. Father once said, "Weeds'll flourish where a set plant'll die," and I knew what he meant, though he wasn't talking to me. He didn't grudge me being alive, he was just sorry that none of his five boys had been so hardy. But then boys ain't, not to begin with. God knows why, but I've seen it over and over; there's measles and mumps and bad throats, they'll strike a family and the wenches'll come up smiling and none the worse, while the lads'll be carried off in coffins.

Almost as soon as I can remember I was living in two worlds, one that everybody knew about and one secret to me. There was the kitchen, big and cluttered up, but comfortable enough, specially in winter, where Mother was always cooking something. My father liked his fodder and so did the two drover boys who lived in the house. My mother was a country girl who'd been brought up in a clod cottage and she reckoned the Old Vine kitchen a wonderful place and she never, in all her days there, got around to believing that the rest of the house really belonged to her. When we did have a do and use the big rooms she always looked like a visitor, she even kept a special voice for such times. But I belonged there from the first time I pushed the heavy door that divided the kitchen part from the hall. I never even asked myself what there was to like about it. I don't reckon children do. They like a thing or they don't. Later on, specially when it came to parting, I did know more or less; all the rooms were the right shape and the painted panelling was always the right colour, though not the same in every room, and there was something to give a surprise almost every time. There was pictures in the plaster of the ceilings in three of the rooms, girls with not much clothing playing with lambs, boys blowing pipes, great bunches of fruit and wreaths of flowers. There was one room with a frieze, all done in plaster, harps and fiddles and pipes with ribbons. Even the floors was laid out in patterns, even the stairs.

Then there was the furniture. My grandfather bought a lot of it in a sale, soon after he took over the house. Not all what was once there, just what he reckoned would be useful and what was going cheap. And that was all the right shape, too, and pretty. There's a difference, even in chairs. Father, for instance, had his own chair in the kitchen, big and strong, and old, it'd been my grandfather's before, and they'd got a good polish on it where their backsides and hands had rubbed all the years; but it wasn't pretty. The sticks in its back were just plain and straight, the arms plain and squared off. In the other part of the house the chairs didn't have plain stick backs, they had shapes, and their legs had curves and feet like big cats' paws kind of clutching the floor.

Most little girls'll play house, given half a chance, up in an attic, under a bush, alongside a haystack; but I was a very lucky little girl with a whole proper house to play in. And play I did. Hour after hour. I wasn't alone, either. I made up friends for myself, people who came to pay me visits. They weren't nothing like the visitors who came at Christmas or Horringer Fair time, who were ordinary folks just like my father and mother, though dressed in their best for the occasion. My visitors were all people like them you'd see going into the Assembly Rooms of an evening, people fit to sit in the pretty chairs and not putting on a special voice because the ceilings had pictures and the curtains were silk.

Apart from the visitors I had two special friends who lived in my house with me. Make-up, of course, but I swear just as real to me as my mother back there in the kitchen. One I called Lizzie and one was Ethel; they were both pretty as could be, though different. Lizzie was two or three years younger than Ethel, for one thing, and not so good-tempered. I used to take cake, or tarts, and a cup of raspberry syrup or something and we'd have a feast. Of course I knew that I ate and drank everything really, but somehow, at the time, it didn't seem like that. There's a lot about children's minds that people don't understand because when they grow up they forget. I never forgot, and I reckon I should have been a good mother, given the chance. On the other hand . . . now I've thought that, I wonder; maybe a mother that has forgot is better really. I surely wouldn't have cared to have my mother know, or even guess, about Lizzie and Ethel. They wouldn't have been so much mine then.

To start with I went into the front of the house just to play. "Oh, get out from under my feet," Mother'd say, and off I'd go. Then it got so I didn't have to be told to go. Then it got to the time when Mother said, "If you want to go play in the front, take a duster and wipe the worst off." Taking care of that part of the house got to be just as good as playing at having visitors. The game just changed, that was all, I was getting the house ready for a party. Presently I was lighting real fires, and cleaning the windows and polishing the floors, as well as wiping off the dust. I still had Lizzie and Ethel for company.

I reckon I'd be about twelve when it struck me that really I didn't fit into that part of the house any better than my mother and father and their friends did when they used it. Most of all my voice wasn't right, and I didn't know the right words. Lizzie and Ethel had voices like the ladies going into the Assembly Rooms. I had a voice like a cattle dealer.

One day I said to my father, "Father, I'd like to go to school."

"Godssake," he said. "What for?"

"I'd like to read and write." I wasn't going to tell him I wanted to talk like ladies.

"And what good'd that do you?" He set to work on his dinner. "Stuff your head up with a lotta nonsense. And cost me good money."

To my astonishment Mother gave me her support.

"Fred Clopton, out Nettleton way, send all his in to Miss Brooks at the Female Academy. So did his father afore him. And what they can do, you surely can."

Fred Clopton was one of the farmers that Father had a lot of business with.

"Maybe. There's a difference though. Cloptons been at Clevely time outa mind."

"Whass that gotta do with it?"

"Jumped up, thass what. Like my owd father said when he bought this place. 'Getting on is all right, but nobody ain't gonna say I'm jumped up.' He was right. Me neither."

"I can't see sending the girl to get a bit of learning got anything to do with jumping, neither up nor down. You said yourself, a week back, could you write you'd send Toby Backhouse a letter'd make his eyes pop. Year at Miss Brooks and *she* could write you anything you wanted to say."

"Stow it," Father said.

But he must have thought it over. About ten days later he came home wearing the look we'd learned to dread. It meant bad business. Mouth pressed thin and turned down at the corners, thick black eyebrows knotted in a scowl. Prices had dropped, or beasts gone sick. Mother and I began to walk about quietly. He wasn't, on the whole, a bad-tempered man at all, but he could get upset, and when he was, everything and everybody was wrong. If we talked he said, "Shut your jaw," and if we were quiet he said, "What're you sulking about?" The food was never right at such times, either.

Mother dished up. We always had our main meal in the evening, like gentry, though we didn't call it dinner, we said supper. Father was mostly out at mid-day and when he got home, between six and seven, he was ready for his food. This day it was one of his favourites, boiled beef, onions, and carrots, with dumplings the like of which only Mother could make, squashy on the outside and brown with gravy, inside as white and light as a feather. He looked at his plate as though he'd got frog-spawn or something disgusting, managed a mouthful, stopped, tried again and then said, "Here, Nip," to the collie cattle dog which went with him everywhere and wouldn't allow even me to pat it, and set the plate on the floor. Mother looked sorrowful, as well she might; and for a while there wasn't a sound in the kitchen except the sloshing sound of Nip gobbling down Father's supper. It just so happened that both the drover boys, who ordinarily ate with us, were out on a job, bringing some steers in from Minsham. Otherwise there'd have been more noise, not talk, in the kitchen. They sloshed their food a bit worse than Nip, even.

At last Father said:

"Well, you can put all your fancy ideas about schooling out of your head, Lyddy, my girl. I been to see Miss Bloody Brooks and they don't want no cattle dealer's daughter a-mixing with their young ladies."

Mother said, "Jack Walker!" in a voice she didn't often use to him, but when she did she meant it.

"Now what? Thass the truth. You might as well know."

"You could have put it different. I'll lay she did!"

"Yes. She said she didn't hev no room—vacancy, she called it. Lyddy didn't need no room, 'cept a desk and a chair. She didn't need no bed nor no place at table, nothing 'cept a desk and a chair and if you believe them couldn't hev been fitted in someways then you're a bigger fool than I reckoned. I knew what she meant, and so do you."

"Don't take it to heart, Lyddy," Mother said.

But of course, I had already.

"Take it to heart! I should hope she got better sense. Any girl got enough to eat, a good bed to sleep in, and a new dress when she want it, got a lot to be thankful for without hankering arter airs and graces. Get on with your supper."

I knew why he'd given his to Nip. The meat was like eating an old boot, the dumpling like eating a bit of blanket. I was so disappointed. Puzzled too. If you wanted to learn to read and write and have some airs and graces, what was wrong with being a cattle dealer's daughter? One thing was, my father was honest; he didn't, as some did, feed his beasts hay all sprinkled with salt for three days and then let them drink and drink and drink so that when they went on the scales they weighed a lot more than they should. And he was particular about separating any animal that seemed sick from the rest and not putting it in the market to spread the sickness.

I looked at him across the table and managed to smile. "You tried," I said. "Thank you." I then added, and it was a lie, "I don't care."

"Thass my girl."

After a minute he said, "Ruth, got a dumpling left?"

"Plenty. I'm keeping it hot, beef and all, for the boys."

"Bugger the boys. Give us a fresh plate."

So that was all right. He'd only minded for me, really.

Two or three days after that I had a funny experience. I never told nobody so I never could try how it'd sound to anybody else. Even to me . . . well, I know it happened and at the same time I know it couldn't have.

Baildon Fat Stock Show was coming up in two-three days' time, and Mother knew by this time she could leave the getting ready of the front house to me. Such times we used two of the three big rooms on that side; the dining room, where we had a big meal and then moved off, leaving the clearing up for next day, into what we called the parlour, but was rightly the drawing room. Mother said, "How about airing out them rooms? Make good big fires." So I did.

Maybe I was getting a bit old for make-believe; maybe I was more upset by Miss Brooks not having me than I knew. Anyhow I felt a bit against Lizzie and Ethel with their sweet voices and their airs and graces. I didn't even try that morning. I went marching in, with my dry kindling and logs; cattle dealer's daughter getting the place ready for a lot of cattle

dealers to come and sit, knees wide apart, talking about the
beast that took the prize and why it should and why it
shouldn't and what it weighed and who reared it. And, back
of my mind, the knowing that I didn't fit here, and never
should now.

I was kneeling by the hearth in the drawing room, blowing
on the fire because it was slow to take hold, when I knew that
Lizzie and Ethel were there, close to me, wanting to play.

I'd brought nothing to eat or drink.

I know this didn't happen; and yet I know that it did.

I said, "You'd better go away, both of you. It's over. Miss
Brooks would have had you, she won't have me. You can read
and write, you have airs and graces. I'm no friend for you."

The thing is that I had for years and years talked to them
in my ordinary voice and they had . . . what's the word? . . .
communicated with me, not in sounds that went into my
actual ears, but in ways that went into my mind. This is difficult to explain. Lizzie, for instance, was very careful about
what she ate, she was afraid of getting fat; Ethel was always
hungry. Did I make that up? I swear that when I was twelve,
their ways of eating were as real to me as my own.

Well, to get back to this particular morning. It wasn't play,
it wasn't make-believe. As clear and as plain as I can hear St.
Mary's clock strike the hour, the half, the quarter, every day
of my life, I heard Lizzie say that her grandfather had taught
her her letters and after that she'd taught herself; and Ethel
said an old parson had given her lessons.

But I was leaning forward, blowing into the sulky smoking
fire, and maybe I was dazed and lost my senses. Mother never
bothered about me when I was in the front of the house, but
that morning I suppose she must have done because the first
thing I remember after hearing Ethel speak of an old parson,
is Mother shaking me, and the room full of smoke, and my
hands all black. And she said we must have the sweep. . . .
And I was sick, throwing up like a drunken drover, time and
time again.

So perhaps it was the smoke. The funny thing is that after that I never had the same feeling about Lizzie and Ethel being there. It was like I'd told them to be off and they'd gone. And I stopped my game of having visitors in the front of the house. I still kept it all clean and polished, but the thoughts I thought time I worked had altered. I began to think about real life, when I was grown-up and married. I made up my mind by hook or by crook to marry somebody fit to live in them big lovely rooms with me; not a sit-down-in-the-kitchen-in-your-shirt-sleeves sort of man.

And I bore in mind what Lizzie and Ethel had told me the day I got sick with smoke. Not that it was a mite of use, in a way. My grandfather was dead and when he was alive he didn't know A from a bull's foot, my father the same. And we had no doings with parsons. Father never went anywhere, Mother and me, sometimes of a Sunday evening, went to the Methody Chapel that'd been built at the end of our street. I know the minister there could read, he used to read out of the Bible, and he used to read the hymns out before we sung, so we could know the words more or less. But he was one of the busiest fellows you ever saw, having chapels scattered about for miles round. He used to ride a rat-tailed nag twelve-fourteen miles out of Baildon to take a service, leaving us to what was called "local preachers"; most of them couldn't read at all. So if he'd had any time to spare for learning people to read he'd have learned them. So grandfathers and parsons was useless to me.

Still, I was always one of them that, once a idea was in their skull, didn't give up too easy. I kept turning the matter over and over and one day when I'd got a shilling—I was lucky that way, Father'd often chuck me sixpence or a shilling when he'd had a good day—I went into a little shop at the top of Cook's Row, kept by an old chap called Rigby. He sold crockery and buckets and bushel skeps mostly, but he had a book or two, and some paper and pencils. He was one of the local preachers who *could* read.

I went along with my shilling that morning and asked him to sell me what I needed to learn myself to read and write. He laughed and said:

"Can't do that, Lyddy. Got no teachers in stock this morning."

"You got books."

"Yes, I got books. Look at this. What'd you make of that?"

It was a rag book, every page a doubled piece of cloth with a picture each side, and letters, a big red one in one corner, a little black one in the other. The first picture was a apple; the next was a boy, then a cat, then a dog, and so on.

"Well?" he said.

"I reckon these here are letters, these marks. Or is it the names?" If it was the names, if you had to get the whole "apple" sound into two little old marks it was going to be harder than I'd counted on.

"You was right first time, Lyddy. A for apple. Big A. Little A. But, you see, you could never've worked that out for your-self, could you? Thass what I meant, you gotta hev a teacher to start you off."

He fetched out another book. Worse. All lines and loops like a skipping rope when you chuck it down.

"Thass a copybook," he said. "Used for writing. And that'd be no use to you either. Fourpence each, they are. And a lotta folks'd take your eightpence, Lyddy, and let you go off. But I ain't like that. They're no manner of use to you so I 'on't sell."

"No, thass jannock," I said, using my father's old-fangled word for honest, straight-dealing.

"I tell you what I will do, though. Come in some time when I ain't busy and I'll explain a bit."

"When ain't you busy, Mr. Rigby?"

"No time arter seven. I shut shop then."

"Thass masterous kind of you, Mr. Rigby," I said. Then I remembered he was a local preacher, so I said, to please him,

"Like the Good Samaritan, Mr. Rigby. And the time is fine and dandy. I'll hev time to wash the supper dishes and then come."

I paid for the books and took them with me and went galloping home to show Mother and tell her about Mr. Rigby's kind offer. She didn't fare as pleased as I reckoned.

"That'll be black dark by seven. I shall hev to talk to your father. He 'on't like you traipsing to and fro after dark."

"I shall run. Shan't take five minutes."

"We'll see what your father say."

She brought it up at supper. Both the boys were in that night, sloshing into mutton stew. One of them was called Freddie Baker, and one was Jack Plant. I didn't like either of them much, but Jack Plant was better-looking and not quite so rough-mannered.

Father took just the view Mother'd thought he would.

"Now you waited so long you can wait till summer and the light evenings. Thass a good offer and next time we kill a pig you can take Tom Rigby a rib of pork."

"But I ain't afraid of the dark."

"Maybe not. All the same I ain't gonna hev you running about arter dark."

"Why not?"

His scowl began to show.

"Because I ain't."

Jack Plant wiped his mouth on the back of his hand and said:

"Mr. Walker."

"Now what?"

"If it'd put your mind easy I could walk along of Lyddy any time and fetch her home." He spoke a bit shyly.

Father's scowl bit deeper, not angry, thoughtful.

"I s'pose that'd be all right. Mind this though. You walk home as sober as you set out."

"You can trust me, Mr. Walker."

"I'd better."

Afterwards Father more or less apologised for not making the offer himself. "Fact is," he said, "once I git my boots off and my bum settled I don't fare like moving no more till I make for my bed."

That I could understand; Father worked as hard as anybody; four markets a week often enough, and all round the farms as well. He had a horse and gig to get to places, but he had to walk when he got there, and by night his feet had swelled up cruel.

Jack Plant, of course, walked as much or more, but I never thought of that. He was young, seventeen or eighteen, and always walked as if he had springs in his heels.

All that winter and on into the next spring I went to Mr. Rigby's twice a week. Once you'd got the alphabet off and knew that the names and the sounds of the letters weren't the same, reading wasn't at all hard to learn. Writing took longer. I had a slate and pencil that squeaked and made my teeth shudder, and he wouldn't let me do anything in the copybook until I'd got it right on the slate first.

In January I had my birthday and was thirteen. And soon after that I had to have two new dresses because there wasn't room in my old ones for my new figure. I was pleased enough to get two new dresses at once, but I wasn't much pleased with the reason. Mother said:

"Don't be so soft. It happen to every girl." And that was small comfort, because in them days I didn't want to be every girl, I reckoned I was something special.

I no longer thought of Lizzie and Ethel as if they was real; I knew that I'd more or less made them up because I was lonely; but I could call to mind that when we had our pretend parties Lizzie wouldn't eat much because she didn't want to

get fat. So I began to cut out second helpings and going to
the pantry odd times to eat a slice of cake or cold pudding;
that way I hoped not to bulge so much.

Every time I went to Mr. Rigby's Mother sent something;
a cake or some sponge fingers, or some sausages or brawn.
When I started having lessons we'd always knock off halfway
through and have a bite; but after I began to bulge I'd say
no thanks, even if his feelings was hurt. He'd been a widower
for more years than you could count and his daughters was
all married and gone, so he'd learned to cook a bit, and once
he give me some of his own oatcake, and I praised it just to
please him. So later on he'd always be coaxing me, if I
wouldn't eat a bit of whatever Mother had sent, to eat a bit
of oatcake that he'd made special for me.

Once he laughed in a funny way and said had I gone off
my food on account of being in love. I thought he'd gone daft,
me only thirteen. Being in love, for me, was something years
away in the future, but it was all as clear as daylight in my
head. I'd have mastered the reading and the writing, and
somehow—I hadn't settled how, but I'd do it somehow, I
knew—I'd know how to talk like ladies, and how to behave.
And I'd fall in love with a young gentleman and we'd live at
the Old Vine, in the best rooms, and have visitors and drink
tea and laugh without chucking our heads back and showing
all our teeth. And then one day we'd have some children. The
boys'd all go to the King Edward Grammar, and the girls'd go
to Miss Brooks' Female Academy.

That was being in love.

The evenings got light, but Jack Plant still walked with me.
I knew why; while he waited he used to go to the *Rose and
Crown* and he liked that. Father was a bit strict with the
drover boys who lived in; the outside ones was bad enough.
Drovers take to drink more than any other trade, droving being very thirsty work with cattle kicking up the dust. Still, I
will say for Jack Plant, he kept his word. He was always as

sober when he fetched me as when he left me, though I could smell the beer on his breath.

So it got to June and hot weather, and I'd got yet another new dress, the prettiest I ever had, yellow with little white roses and green leaves all over it, and white ruffles round the neck and at the elbows. When I had it Mother made one of her "when I was your age . . ." speeches. Her father had been a shepherd and she'd been one of nine children; she never had a new dress until she had the one to be married in, and that my father had bought.

"I know," I said, "I know I'm lucky." But to tell you the truth I wasn't thinking of the dress, pretty as it was; I was thinking of the reading and the writing and the time when I'd live in the house like it was meant to be lived in. . . . It all seemed specially close just then because when I looked into the future it always seemed to be fine sunny weather with long warm evenings and roses in bloom, except for just a few days round about Christmas, with snow on the ground and the sky very starry and huge fires blazing everywhere.

So this June evening Jack Plant and me set off, just as usual. Mother and me had spent the day making strawberry jam—there was a very fine strawberry bed at the Old Vine—and I carried a pot for Mr. Rigby, still warm.

He was waiting for me, with the copybook open. "Thou God seest me." I wrote it on the slate, wrong two times. A small g for God, first time, and only one e in seest, the second. Then I got it right and was let to use the pen and the copybook. When I got it right he patted me on the shoulder and said:

"Good girl. Coming on like a house afire, you are."

I liked to be praised but I did hate to be patted. The thing was, lately, every time he patted me it was a longer-lasting pat. And we weren't much of a family for patting, even dogs. My father would have jumped in the river with his boots on any day to save Nip, but he'd never *pat* him, and the only time

Mother ever laid a hand on me was to see if I was running a fever.

Still, I bore the patting, because Mr. Rigby had been so kind, teaching me to read and write and all. But he had nasty hands, dried up and all speckled brown on the backs.

Then he said, "Since you're off your food, Lyddy, and it being such a warm evening, maybe you'd like a drink. Home-made blackberry wine."

Mother made wine; cowslip, parsnip, blackberry; and black-berry was my favourite. Still, I was a bit surprised at Mr. Rigby. Mother made wine because she wasn't what I call real chapel, only a Sunday night now and then, and Father wasn't chapel at all. The real chapel people were dead against what they called "intoxicants" of any sort or kind. And if anybody was real chapel, Mr. Rigby was.

Still, there it was, in a jug, looking very tasty, and it wasn't for me to tell him, old enough to be my grandfather, what to do. He poured out two glasses. It wasn't as sweet as Mother's, but I'd got a whole glassful whereas at home I never got more than a half, so it wasn't for me to grumble. I drank it down. Mr. Rigby drank his, too, and filled his glass again. He'd have filled mine if I hadn't stopped him. The one glassful was act-ing very funny. First I felt like a blown-up bladder, all light and bouncy; then my face went hot; then my head began to go round and round. Once I looked at Mr. Rigby and there were two of him, not quite separate and side by side, but mixed up.

But I heard him say, "Now we'll do your reading," and I thought to myself—If I can read it'll be a wonder. And then there was the book with the words sort of blurred and dancing up and down, and Mr. Rigby sitting beside me, the way he always did when I read.

And then he put his arm round at the back of me and under my arm and sort of took hold of one of my bulging breasts, kneading and squeezing like milking a cow.

I was as innocent, in a way, as I had been when I was five. My father was rough-tongued enough, but clean-minded, and my mother was country and half chapel, modest past telling. I'd got no notion in my mind of what Mr. Rigby was after, but my body seemed to know and be disgusted. I sat for half a minute struck dumb and still, then I jumped up and made for the door. I'd reckoned without the blackberry wine, though. As soon as I stood up everything went into a whirl. Mr. Rigby came after me and took hold of my arm and said about meaning no harm, and not to make a fuss about nothing, and come and sit down and go on reading. I still couldn't speak, but I pushed at his hand and took another coupla steps and fell against the door, just saving myself from falling by catching onto the knob. And what with the wine and everything I forgot that in his house all the knobs worked the wrong way and turned it the right way and got no further, which give him time to say:

"And don't go telling your father, because if you do I shall tell him what you and the Plant boy get up to on the way home."

What Jack Plant and I got up to on the way home was he'd say, "Hev a nice lesson, Lyddy?" and I'd say, "Yes. How'd you do?" and he'd say, "Lost twopence" or "Won twopence," meaning at shove ha'penny that he'd been playing at the *Rose and Crown*. And sometimes he'd say where he had to go next day, mostly in connection with the weather, like, "Well, the midges is dancing, fine day tomorrow for Bures," or something like that.

So what Mr. Rigby meant, I didn't know. I was more concerned with turning the knob the way I'd just remembered it should be turned. So I got into the shop, and he followed me, still talking about not telling my father. And my head got clearer and I could just see myself saying anything to Father about my horrid great bulging breasts and Mr. Rigby going

for me as though I was a cow! I'd die of shame. I managed to
find my voice and say:

"I wouldn't tell nobody. Too disgusting." And then I was
out in the street and there was Jack Plant leaning against the
wall, whistling, though any other night I shouldn't hev been
out for a good half hour.

He looked right surprised to see me.

"You're early," he said.

"So're you."

"Oh, I'm mostly here in good time. What you done with
your books? Didn't he set you no task today?"

Only then did I realise that I'd left my books and my slate,
that generally I took home to practise with, on the table.

"That was my last lesson," I said. "Matter of fact I now
know all Mr. Rigby can teach me, Jack."

"Well," he said, "thass a lickser!" A lickser was something
out of the ordinary, enough to knock you backwards, taking
its name from the blow that gets somebody licked.

"So you and me 'on't hev no more walks, Lyddy," he said,
right sadly. I thought he was missing the chance to go to the
Rose and Crown without Father grumping.

"Father 'on't mind your going out, Jack. Twice a week all
these months and you never took a drop too much. He'll know
he can trust you."

"I weren't thinking about that. Lyddy, you don't reckon I
walked to and fro and stood there propping owd Rigby's wall
up, just to get my nose in a beer mug! God bless my soul,
I'm a free Englishman, if I want to go to the *Rose and Crown*
the Queen on her throne couldn't stop me, leave alone your
dad. No. I been coming out, night after night, simply to pleasure *you*."

"And it did pleasure me, Jack. Thank you very much."

"And now thass over. And you're only a young little maid,
but you bear this in mind, Lyddy. Here's a chap that'd walk
a hundred miles, and go hungry and thirsty and sleep on the

bare earth to pleasure you. Will you remember that, two-three years from now?"

"I'll remember."

We walked a little way and then I said:

"You could do me a favour right soon. Where are you off to tomorrow?"

"Bury market."

"They hev shops there?"

"Plenty."

"Then if I give you the money will you buy me a copybook—that is, to write in, and any sort of copybook would do. And a book called Child's Reader, part four."

It was part three that I'd left open on Mr. Rigby's table.

"Right you are. Any sort of copybook and Child's Reader, part four. I got it right? Don't owd Rigby sell them sort?"

"I don't know. I didn't want . . . to hurt his feelings, letting him know I meant to go on past where he could teach me."

When I told Father and Mother that I now knew all Mr. Rigby could teach me, Mother smiled and Father slapped his leg and said just what Jack Plant had, "Thass a lickser!"

During the next months I learned that what my make-up friend, Lizzie, had said, that her grandfather started her off and then she learned by herself, was true. It was like the first push downhill on a slide; once you started you just went on and it got easier and easier. Inside a year I could read almost anything and I could write a good clear hand.

But . . . and this is a terrible big but, and it is a thing that isn't taken into account, not even by the kind people who started up the Ragged Schools. If you learn to read and write, but belong to a family that can't, everything you learn is like a foreign language. Ordinary common people talk in a ordinary common way and if you gotta live with them you gotta talk the same. You can write different. Father was mighty glad when I could take up my pen and write a letter and maybe save him a long traipse into the country, or, if somebody had offended him, write and say just why with no chance of interruption. And in his way he was proud. But if I'd ever started to talk the way I wrote (you see, Father would have said *writ*, not *wrote*) he wouldn't hev felt at his ease with me. And after all he was my father. I ate his food, wore clothes he'd paid for. The same with my mother.

Bilingual is the word. And if, when I was fourteen, fifteen, sixteen, I'd been set down amongst people who could read and write and spoke grammatically, I'd have done the same. My mind would have shaped itself. But I was with the other sort too long and so it was natural for me to say "hev" for "have" and "writ" for "wrote" and a thousand other things of that sort.

All this time I'd still tended the front part of the house, and also the garden, what was left of it. Once upon a time it had been a big oblong garden, but my grandfather, when he bought the house, had wanted more room than there was in the yard for beasts held over from one market day to the next, or fresh ones coming in to wait till they was sold. So he'd knocked down a rare old nice brick wall and put up a fence. Father said that his father'd have turned the whole garden over to cattle but my grandmother said she didn't want beasts blaring right outside the windows. So now the garden was wide near the house, then cut off and running narrow down to a stone seat and a sundial. On the kitchen side of the wide part there was a bed of asparagus and a bed of strawberries, and room for peas and other vegetables. Father was willing to let a man put in an afternoon tending that part, and he'd spare a barrowload of muck from time to time. The rest, but for me, would've gone wild. I kept it tidy, with the grass shorn and the bushes clipped, just as I kept the front of the house tidy; all against the day when I should live there proper fashion. All the work I did there was on top of what I did to help

Mother, and the time I spent was the time most girls spend curling their hair and walking about with chaps. The hard work and careful eating had got my bulges down considerable.

So the years went by, with me dreaming my dreams. How and when they'd come true exactly, I never did think out properly. It'd take a miracle, that I knew. But I could wait.

Now and again one of Father's cronies'd bring a boy along, hoping I'd take a fancy to him. I scorned the lot. Sometimes, specially when she had one of her dizzy spells, Mother'd say, "I shan't make old bones, Lyddy, and I'd like to see you settled afore I go." But the next minute she'd say she didn't know how she'd get on without me. Truth to tell she'd still got a good many years to go, but she was heving what they called "a bad change" and often felt low.

So I got to nearly eighteen; and it is a fact that, be a girl plain or pretty, dark or fair, fat or thin, at eighteen she's as good-looking as she's ever going to be. Even at that age I was no Queen of the May, but I wasn't bad. I was tall and straight and slim, and I'd got nice eyes, greenish-brown with black lashes and arched eyebrows, a bit like Father's but not so thick, thank God, and my black hair grew in a point on my forehead.

I knew, though I never really faced up to it, that Jack Plant was soft about me. He was still living with us and more or less one of the family. Others had come and gone, but he stayed on and was Father's trusted right-hand man. His eyes used to follow me about, and more than once he'd asked me to take a walk with him, or go to Baildon Midsummer Fair, or out to a Harvest Horky. I always made some sort of excuse and he always looked as though I'd smacked his jaw. I hated being cruel to him, and that made me hate him for making me be cruel. Sometimes he got on my nerves so much I *could* hev smacked his jaw!

Then one time, when Father and him stayed away overnight in an inn at Kelvedon, they got drinking beer together and Jack plucked up courage to ask Father whether he'd hev anything against his courting me. Father came home and told Mother and me.

"I reckon he was too bashful to ask you hisself," Father said.

"'Twasn't that at all. It was nice feeling," Mother said. "The proper way is to speak to a girl's father first. Even I know that."

"Well, he spoke; and I said I'd nowt agin it, but 'twas for you to say, Lyddy. To my mind you might do a lot worse. We known him since he was a tiddler, he's clean and decent, and he know the trade. He could carry on when my feet fail me."

"And he'd eat outa your hand, Lyddy. I seen that four-five years ago."

But I didn't want anybody we'd known as a tiddler, nor somebody that'd eat outa my hand. I wanted somebody that'd be at his ease in the big rooms with the pictures on the ceiling.

"It'd be all right if I loved him. But I don't."

"Then there's no more to be said." Father was willing to end it there. But Mother wasn't.

"Being in love is one them fancy notions you picked up outa books. There's nowt to it. What a girl want is somebody that'll treat her kind and turn to and make a good living for her." That was as good as saying that she'd married Father for what he could give her, and she realised that, too late, and went off into one of her hot flushes.

"Thass all right, lass," Father said. "Nowt to blush for. That was how we fixed it, and we got along all right. I never fooled myself that on John's Eve you ever seen *my* face in the glass."

"Well, that was what I was meaning to say. No need to take me up so sharp. There's fancies that go on in silly heads and there's real life that go on to the grave. I reckon you'd best give this a bit of thought, Lyddy. 'Less you got somebody else in mind."

"I have thought about it. And I got nobody in mind."

"Them thass too choosy go right through the wood and come out t'other end with a crooked stick, or no stick at all. You don't want to go a maid to your grave, do you?"

"Better that than wed somebody I got no feeling for," I said.

"Well, maybe somebody you can fancy'll come along. But I feel sorry for Jack," Mother said.

Father said, "I reckon you'd best tell him, Lyddy. I doubt whether he'd take no from me."

And that old well-known feeling of anger with Jack came back to me. Putting me in such an awkward place! It wasn't even as though I'd done anything to encourage him. It was unfair of me; it wasn't his fault that he didn't measure up to what I wanted.

It was worse than I'd thought though. He was terrible upset. He said he'd been in love with me since I was a little girl, and he'd waited and never looked at no other wench.

"And most what I done for your Dad I was doing for you, Lyddy. Like Jacob serving his seven years for Rachel. What you got against me?"

"Nothing, Jack. Nothing at all. I just don't love you."

"Who do you love then?"

It'd sound silly to say, "The Old Vine"; so I said, "Nobody."

"Then why don't you give me a chance? Come out with me a time or two. See how we get on."

"It wouldn't be any good. Why don't you walk out with Alice Fickling?"

"Alice Fickling! What'd I want to walk out with her for? She mean nowt to me."

"Well then . . ." I left it there. I saw what I meant sink in. He went a bit white.

"So thass the way it is."

"I'm sorry, Jack, but thass the way it is."

"I shan't stay here then," he said. "So long as there was hope

I didn't mind how long I worked, or how hard. I was doing it for you. But if you got no use for me I shall make myself scarce. I shall go to Ameriky, where good cattle men are wanted."

I thought to myself that I didn't care where he went. I was a bit glad he was going to take hisself off and not sit every day looking at me with sheep's eyes across the table.

It was the Old Vine made me cruel and uncaring; and if anybody had told me then that when he went off he took with him all my hope of ever living in the house, I'd have laughed in their face. But it was true for all that. The way things worked out . . .

This is how things worked out. Jack Plant took off for America, and Father missed him sore. Drovers was ten a penny but either they didn't know the job or they didn't care, or they'd think Father was too fussy and go off and work for somebody easier-going. Father's feet began to trouble him more and more, and it got so the minute he was home, off with his boots and into a foot bath of salt water. Often his ankles were so swelled they'd hang down like half-blown bladders. In the morning they'd always be better, and Sundays, too, because he had more rest then.

One day Mother said, "I reckon you should show them feet to the doctor." Father said:

"Don't talk so daft." But she kept on saying it; and one night, when he came home swelled nearly to the knee, she said it again and Father said:

"To make you stop your jaw, Ruth, I will. Fetch him now, Lyddy."

So Dr. Cornwell came, and he scarcely looked at Father's feet at all. He held his pulse and then made him bare his chest, and laid his ear to it. And he said the swelling legs was just a symptom. It was Father's heart that was failing him and 'less he took things easy, no walking about, no cattle markets, no heaving beasts about and so forth, he'd fall dead very sudden and very soon.

When he'd gone Father said, "The one thing he didn't tell us was how we're gonna live time I take things easy."

Mother said, "We'll manage somehow. I'll bake cakes and sell 'em. That there big winder in the parlour'd make a good showing-off place. And Lyddy can find a job. She can't sew, more's the pity. But she could be a governess."

Father said, "When the time come that I hev to be kept by my womenfolk I hope I do fall dead!"

Out in the backhouse, later on, Mother said to me, sudden and vicious:

"Now you can see what you done. If you'd married Jack Plant your father could hev set back and left all to him."

There was no argument to that. And somehow just then it came to me, like a slap in the face, that I was nineteen and my miracle hadn't happened.

Father kept struggling on, very stubborn. And I don't know whether other symptoms, as the doctor called them, then began to show theirselves, or whether, being warned, we saw what we had hitherto missed. But there was shortness of breath, too, and a tinge of blue in the red of his lips. And sometimes, through being careful, he'd miss a deal and take it very much to heart and talk about being ruined.

Then, all suddenly, there was talk of the Eastern Union Railway, which had got as far as Bury, running out a line to Baildon. Men came out measuring and taking levels and presently we heard the line was coming and the station was going to be at the end of our street, just at the bottom of the hill on the Nettleton Road. The E.U.R. had bought a cornfield and a pasture there and the line was to come in at right angles to our street. It was said that they'd chose the position so that in due time they could run the line clean through to Bywater.

Naturally, by this time there'd been plenty of rumours and

contradictions of rumours about whether the line was coming at all, and where the station would be if it did; but this was true. There was a piece about it in the Baildon *Free Press* on the Friday. Father got me to read it out to him, twice. Then he said:

"Well, that put a different face on the matter. This street'll come into its own now. Everybody get off at the station got to go along this way, and no other, to get to the market. This'll be the busiest street in Baildon. And I," he said, slow and satisfied, "own this freehold, with two and a half acres of yard and garden. Read that bit agin, Lyddy. This'll be the savation of us. I can ask my own price and retire and live like a lord."

Mostly I can do whatever I set my mind to, and mostly I tried to do whatever my father wanted, but I could only get out, "All progressive-minded citizens of Baildon will be pleased to learn . . ." and there I stopped.

"Go on, girl," Father said. "Gods sake! You took ill, Lyddy?"

"You mean you'd . . . sell? Sell the Old Vine?"

"I don't aim to *give* it away," he said, joking the way he would when things went right with him. "There's no need to look so stricken, Lyddy. You'll hev a roof over your head. We'll buy a right cosy little place, somewhere where I can set in the winder and see other poor sods go to market in all weathers, and get swelled feet."

He was so pleased. He looked ten-twenty years younger. What could I say?

II

Later on, of course, I said plenty. I put up no end of a fight. Make the Old Vine into a tea shop, I said, where folks could sit and wait for trains, or come and get a bit of a meal at the end of the journey. There'd be cattle shifted by rail, I said, the yard could be used for them. Travellers aiming to catch early trains would want to get into town the day before and spend the night somewhere. We'd let off bedrooms. I'd do all the work, I said. But where was the use? It was like offering a man sixpence when he'd already been bid ten shillings. All down our street, both sides, the selling mania had got hold of folks.

Ours had always been a quiet street, a place to live in. Between what was called the South Gate and the place where the new station was planned there was about ten houses, five a side, all big and set in good gardens, and the Old Vine was the only one that had ever been used for trade of any sort. Most of the folks who lived there had no need for money, but even they sold out. The trains'd be noisy and dirty, they said, and the road always full of people, coming and going. The Batsons, with the house next door to where the station was coming, sold their house and it was pulled down and in its place up went the Station Hotel, too ugly to be believed, all little turrets and narrow windows with red and green and purple glass.

That didn't happen to the Old Vine, thank God; though what did happen was bad enough. Father sold it off piecemeal, with the same unthinking ruthlessness as in the old days he'd have sold a cow away from its calf, a calf away from its mother. Five separate shops. Holes knocked in the walls for new doors and windows, nasty new staircases, partitions of cheap pitch pine cutting my lovely big rooms into two or three, even four little boxes. And I was as helpless as men in old wars who, once they was defeated, had to stand by and see their children killed, their wives raped.

Father bought a pretty little doll's house on Market Square —the Old Market, not the Saltgate—and he kept his word and set up his big chair in the parlour window where he could see everybody go by. Most of the stuff that'd been in the big rooms at Old Vine were sold by auction and fetched a fair price. I'd asked Father if I could take what I wanted for my own bedroom and he said why not hev all nice new stuff, he could afford whatever I wanted. I said I'd rather bring the old stuff, and I filled my poky little bedroom so full that getting in and out of bed was a acrobat's job.

The move aged me—or not the move so much, as what it stood for. The end of a dream. For as long as I remember I'd always thought there was something special about me, and that something special was bound to happen to me. Now here I am, old before my time, with a thin, lined face and white in my hair and nothing to live for except to see my father and mother comfortable to the end of their days. A good daughter, they say. A cattle dealer's daughter who dreamed too long and woke up too sudden.

Father put quite a bit of the money he made into railroad stock. They pay seven and a half per cent interest now, and talk of doing better: and the stock itself has about doubled in value. You can see why people think it's queer when I say I hate the railroad.

INTERLUDE

The five shops into which the Old Vine had been made did not immediately make the huge profits anticipated by their owners. Not everyone took to railway travel with enthusiasm, and those who did were mainly of the poorer sort. The valuable "carriage trade" still patronised the older shops in the centre of the town. The Old Vine was not called upon to cater for people of fashion until the year 1854 when the railway was finally extended to reach Bywater. Then everything changed. A month by the sea in August became the fashion, and much the easiest way of reaching the coast was by rail from Baildon, and the easiest way of making the journey was to drive to Baildon overnight and stay at the Station Hotel. At the same period an interest in "antiquities" revived, so that to have spent any time in Baildon and not visited the ruins of the great Benedictine Abbey, or viewed the angel roof in St. Mary's Church, was to brand oneself as a barbarian. And to reach the Abbey one must go along Station Road. The whole area entered upon a period or prosperity.

One result was surprising, not more shops, fewer. The house almost opposite the Old Vine, where once upon a time Mrs. Clipstone's idiot boy had horrified Elizabeth Kentwoode, was taken over by Thorley's Bank and restored to dignity, a great convenience to gentlemen about to holiday in Bywater, or even farther afield via the cross-channel packet which now ran from that little port. And then, because ladies and children who had been recommended to try the sea air for some ailment real or imaginary, often needed the services of a doctor during their brief stay at the Station Hotel, young Dr. Cornwell thought it worth-while to buy the house next door to the bank and set up practice there. A third lawyer, breaking in upon the long monopoly of the two existing firms, Turnbull's and Steward's, hung out his plate in Station Road.

The other result, human nature being what it is, was not altogether surprising. Admittedly, the station had brought prosperity, but what a mundane, proletarian sound "Station Road" had to the sensitive ear. It suggested that there had been nothing there before the station came.

"Which is a false impression," Dr. Cornwell said. "My own house is certainly Elizabethan, and that part of the Old Vine which faces the street is a good deal older."

What had the street or the road been called in the old days? The old days, which in the bright dawn of this new and bustling period were beginning to assume a wistful nostalgic charm which was to increase and deepen as the years and the mechanisation went on. It had had two names; it had been known as Nettleton Road because it led to Nettleton; and it had been known as Out Southgate because it had lain outside the town boundary on the south side. Neither name pleased the new inhabitants enough to make them adopt it; neither was "romantic" enough.

The manager of Thorley's Bank was something of an antiquarian and in the end he produced a suggestion acceptable to everybody. The old stone bridge out on the Nettleton Road had been built by one of the last abbots of St. Egbert's in 1496. Doubtless he had gone out, more than once, to see his bridge building and, being a monk, vowed to poverty, he had probably walked. (When he made this statement the manager of Thorley's Bank could *see* in his mind's eye, the sandalled feet slapping the dust.) So what name more suitable, more apt, more pleasant-sounding than "Abbot's Walk"?

The name, with the Town Council's approval, was officially

adopted. It sounded better; it looked better on letters, on the
lawyer's letterheading, on Dr. Cornwell's bills. Your ordinary
East Anglian is, however, as unmalleable as the rich heavy
soil from which he springs. The name Station Road was obvious, down to earth, and it replaced only a vague direction,
"Near the Old Vine," "Out Nettleton way," "Just beyond the
Old Gate." So it had been accepted, and once accepted it was
not easily jettisoned. A good fifty years after the change you
could ask the way to Abbot's Walk and receive, first a blank
stare and then, "Oh, Station Road, you mean."

The Old Vine was not affected by the invasion of professional men. The shops there were too prosperous, and too
small. In those days of light taxation the lives of the shopkeepers in the Old Vine followed a definite pattern, interrupted
only by early death, chronic drunkenness, or some kind of
mania. They worked, they lived in cramped quarters, they
saved money; somewhere between the ages of fifty-five and
sixty they retired, either selling out or leaving the running of
the business to their sons. And they built houses on the west
side of the town, and grew roses and joined the Bowls Club.
Some became town councillors. Finally they died and the Baildon *Free Press* brought out its usual headline, "Death of
Prominent Businessman." And it was recognised that it was
a duty for other businessmen to attend the funeral. It was supposed to be a great comfort to the widow. . . .

But there were exceptions. Samuel Armstrong was one of
them. He kept a grocer's shop in what had once been the entrance hall to the house at Old Vine. He, his wife, his two
daughters, and his son lived in what had been the Great Chamber above, now divided into four portions, a kitchen-living
room and three bedrooms. In the year 1886 his son, David, was
seventeen years old.

DAVID ARMSTRONG'S TALE

It was one of Father's many kindnesses that first brought me and Miss Lydia Walker together. And if there's a God in Heaven, He must have had a good laugh over that.

We were all walking home from chapel, one cold November evening, and I heard Mother say how poorly Miss Walker looked.

"I noticed," Father said. "She looked half starved to me. More'n half, in fact."

"I was thinking more about that dirty old cape and her shoes, soles right away from the uppers. But there's nobody to blame but herself. They say she's ever so well off."

"That might be just a tale," Father said thoughtfully. "Maybe she was rich and lost it all. People do, you know. Or maybe what she had was exaggerated and she's come to the end. In any case, poor creature . . ."

I thought—Wait for it! And it came; one of Father's specials. ". . . if she's got the money and can't or won't spend it, she's as much to be pitied as if she was poor."

Mother said, "I can't see that, Samuel."

"I can," Father said, "and a man must act according to his lights. David, if it should slip my mind, remind me tomorrow. I'll send her a mite of something."

I heard Mother give a sigh. I knew there were times when she found being married to a saint very hard work. I sighed too, partly for the same reason, and partly because I knew who'd have to run round with the mite of something after the shop was shut and all the other work done. I was old enough to have noticed something else. In this world, to get money you've got to like it, think about it, care for it. Treat it like Father always did, as though it was rather mucky and fit only to be given away, and naturally it won't come to you.

We were all right; we always had enough to eat, and a fire in winter, good stout clothes and shoes; but, though we had a flourishing little business, and Father and I (and sometimes even Mother and Marty) worked like slaves all day long, we were never any better off. How could we be, when Father'd lump a pound and a half of fat bacon on the scales and charge for a pound because the customer was the wife of a ganger on the railroad who'd been off work for a month; or let some shiftless family run up a bill as long as your arm, knowing they'd never pay. I had different ideas about money. One I'd heard Father preach—he was reckoned a very powerful local preacher, though inclined to be long-winded—about not laying up for yourself treasure on earth, where the moth and the rust did corrupt. I thought to myself at the time that neither moth nor rust could do much harm to a good golden guinea.

Next day he remembered Miss Walker as soon as he started on a new side of bacon; he cut off the hock and laid it aside, and bit by bit through the day he added other small items, sugar, butter, tea, some sweet biscuits. He made them all into as neat a parcel as if for a paying customer and told me to run round with them after tea. Tea in our household was the substantial meal that we had as soon as the shop shut. Mondays was never a busy day and we'd done soon after seven; Tuesdays much the same. By Saturday we were working till half past eight or nine.

I said, "If she is starving, Father, that much isn't going to save her."

"Sufficient unto the day. Something else might turn up. There's so much misery in the world, lad, you can't look at it as a whole. You have to just do what little bit you can, as and when you can."

I'll give his due, he always practised what he preached.

I wasn't against having an errand after supper. He wasn't a severe man, but he was strict, and he never would have us what he called "running loose round the streets" at night. I was nearly eighteen, my elder sister, Marty, was sixteen, but he still treated us like children. We could go out after dark to anything connected with chapel, temperance meetings, prayer meetings, camp meetings during the summer, and of course I could go any time to do an errand or deliver groceries. Boys I'd been at school with were drinking in pubs and going with girls, and I often envied them and looked forward to the time when I should be old enough to stand up to Father and have my own way.

I always thought I'd do it when I was older; in fact I kept pushing it off into the future. It wasn't that I was scared of Father; he never had beaten me, and he certainly couldn't have started then; and I wasn't really against hurting his feelings, there were times when I'd have done that with pleasure. But he had, and I knew it, a much stronger character than mine. He was always so sure that he was *right*, and for the first twelve years of my life I'd thought he was too. That kind of thing takes a lot of breaking away from. But I meant to, one day, because with every month I lived I felt myself more and more drawn towards all the things Father disapproved of, and more and more bored with chapel, chapel people, and good deeds.

Father said that Miss Walker lived, so far as he knew, at Number 4, Market Square. It was rather a pretty little house, pressed in between two much bigger ones; it had four steps up to the door, and a railing. It looked very shabby and neglected. I pulled the bell and it felt so loose I wasn't surprised not to hear any sound from within, so after a minute I rapped sharply on the door. At once a child began to cry. Then the door was

opened by a boy I'd been at school with, though he had been
in the top class when I was in the lowest; a big, simple fellow
named Mike Saunders who was such a shocking dunce that he
only got moved up because the desks in the top class were the
only ones he could sit at.

He was angry at the bell starting the baby off and said:
"What do you . . . Why, if it ain't Dave!"

"Hullo, Mike. What you doing here?"

"I live here." He looked sheepish. "Got married back in
August."

Quick work, I thought, if that's your baby.

"Where's old Miss Walker, then? I got a parcel for her."

"She live up top. Millie and me hev the two down and the
scullery. Take a good slice out your wages, paying rent. And
then there's the baby. . . ." He looked miserable for a moment, then cheered up, and said in a lower voice:

"Dave, do us a favour. It ain't so easy to get out of a night
nowadays. Millie's always on the grizzle. D'you think you
could make out that apart from bringing that there parcel for
the old girl you come to call me out on a job? Give a bang
on the door when you come down and make out you're in a
hurry."

I said, in the same quiet way, "What do you *do* now,
Mike?"

"Carpenter. Say you got a door jammed or something. Tell
you more about it later." He then said, in an ordinary loud
voice, "Straight up the stairs. And I'll be ready right away."
He went into the room that opened off the little hallway and
I went blundering in the dark up the stairs and knocked on
the door that I could find by feeling about. Nobody came, and
I knocked again. Then a door behind me opened and there
was Miss Walker, holding a candlestick.

I'd never taken any notice of her; I don't think that she came
to chapel much, and if she did, to me she was just one of the
dowdy old women who made up most of the congregation.

And the bit I'd heard Father and Mother say about her had prepared me for some meek poor old woman, so her voice gave me a shock. It was very high-class. If I hadn't seen who was speaking I'd have thought it was Lady Fennel or Mrs. Booth-Sandell.

"Who are you and what do you want?" she asked me.

I did feel daft.

"I've brought you a few groceries, ma'am."

"I've ordered nothing."

"No. I know. But my father thought he'd make you a present."

"Indeed. How exceedingly kind. But why? Who is your father?"

"Mr. Armstrong, the grocer." The parcel in my hands suddenly seemed to weigh a ton. "Last night . . . in chapel," I said, "he got the notion that you looked hungry. He's a bit odd, he can't bear to think . . . so he sent you this, ma'am." I pushed the parcel towards her.

She said, "Your father was right. I am hungry. But not, I fear, for anything that he could provide. Kind, yes indeed, very kind, but. . . . Come in, young man."

She stepped back and I followed her. It was a small room, crowded with furniture, big things that loomed up out of the shadows; a huge fourposter bed, with curtains, great heavy chairs, not arranged for use, packed as though in a store. The room was deadly cold.

"Your father is the grocer who has the shop in the middle of the Old Vine."

"That is so. And he thought . . ."

"What he thought doesn't matter. He's one of the interlopers. Oh, I have nothing against them, please don't think that. It's just that they shouldn't be *there*. And given two-three years they won't be, none of them. None of them. Let me think, now. Armstrong's grocery. In the centre, what was the hall. You have the main staircase . . . and the big room

above. Don't you ever think, when you've finished weighing
out your lard, that you shouldn't go and walk up those stairs?
You're young, you should have some modicum of perception,
surely."

In the Bridewell Lane Board School I'd been reckoned a
very bright boy, good at reading, sums, and spelling, but I'd
never heard words like that before. And what the Hell had
weighing lard got to do with walking upstairs to your meals, or
bed, as the case might be?

I made no attempt to answer. I tried to push the parcel
at her again, but she wouldn't have it.

"No. No. That would be conniving. I never buy anything
at any of those shops."

"I know. But my father's very goodhearted, and seeing you
in chapel . . ."

"I only go there to get warm occasionally. Tell him that,
and his charitable impulses will be checked."

"And you don't want the parcel?"

"No, thank you."

"All right," I said. Already I'd had a good idea what to do
with it, and I was turning away when she raised the candle a
bit and looked at me closely.

"Your face is oddly familiar."

"You must have seen me in chapel."

"I don't mean that. You remind me of somebody. What
did you say your name was?"

"David Armstrong."

"What was your mother's maiden name?"

"My mother's what?"

"Her name before she was married."

"Plant. Mary Plant."

"That accounts for it then. Yes, that'd be it." Suddenly she
laughed, the way crazy people do, for no reason. "But I shall
do it alone now. You remember that, young man. When we're
young we always want help and support, so our plans come

to nothing. Later on we know that we can stand on our own feet and need help from nobody. And then, only then, can we achieve things."

She kindly held the candle to light me down and then went back and shut herself in. I banged on Mike Saunders' door. The baby was still wailing, but more quietly, and I could hear a woman's voice, thin and whining. Mike opened the door, this time with his coat on and a dirty old muffler round his neck.

"You never told me exactly what you wanted doing, Dave," he said in a loud voice, and winked at me.

"It's a back door, swelled in the damp, and it'll neither open nor shut."

"Right ho. Millie, I reckon I'll be a good hour. I'll hev to rehang it, see?"

"I shall go to bed, then."

He shut the door behind him. Then we were out in the Square and he blew out a great breath.

"Poooh! My God, Dave, little did I think I'd ever come to this, glad to be give the excuse to get out for a hour. Blasted baby crying all day and half the night, and Millie nag, nag, nag. Come on, we'll go to the old *Rose and Crown*, and I'll buy you a drink."

The truth was that at school I'd never been friendly with Mike Saunders; he was big and strong and older than me, so I was glad to have done him a favour and so belittled him. But for the same reason I didn't like to say to him, as I would to anybody else, "I'm not allowed in pubs." That would have set him even again. I did a bit of quick thinking; Father's cronies didn't go in pubs, and if somebody else saw me and recognised me and went and mentioned it I should say he was a liar. I should say, "You know where I was on Monday; and Miss Walker kept me talking." After all I'd had a good look round her peculiar room, so I could describe that, and tell how she'd asked after Mother's name before she was married.

So I said, "Right ho," and in we went, right into that den of iniquity, that outpost of Satan's empire.

To me it looked all right. It was warm, with a good fire, and brightly lighted. Mike pushed up to the bar, where several men stood, and came back with two big mugs, yellow with brown rims. A man by the bar said:

"Ain't seen you around lately, Mike," and Mike said:

"Been busy."

Then he went over to a sort of pew near the fire and I went gladly, being almost out of sight there. And he began to talk about the miseries of married life. The bitch, he said, went and got herself in pod, and said he was to blame. Then she told her father and he went to Platt, the builder Mike worked for, and *he* said if he didn't do the right thing by the girl he'd give him the sack. Just with summer ending and work hard to find. So they'd got married and had quarrelled ever since.

Inside myself I thought he was a fool, and serve him right. Then, when I was about halfway through my pint, I began to be grateful to him, in a sort of way, partly for treating me as though I was as old as him, and partly for bringing me into the pub. I didn't like the taste of the beer much, but I liked the feel, happy and carefree, different.

He finished his mugful, took out some money, counted it, and put it back.

"I dassent," he said.

I'd got the parcel by my side. I said:

"Look, Mike. In here there's four bobs' worth of stuff. . . ." I told him what was in it and how I came to have it. "I'll sell it to you for a bob and then I'll buy you a pint." That way I should still be eightpence to the good. "And you can say that for turning out so late, Father let you have this lot for one and fourpence. That should please her."

"Godssakes, I should think so."

"You go get the beer. I don't want to be seen more than I have to. My father's got funny ideas about beer and pubs."

"Millie the same," he said. He fetched two more mugs. I finished my first and began to feel a bit queer, still happy and carefree but rumbling in my belly, as though I might chuck up. So I let him drink my second, and he got a bit fuddled.

"You reckon Millie *see* you?"

"I didn't see her."

"Then I shan't shay it was your dad's door. You jusht brung the message, see? I shall shay it was Roper's; and he let me have the grosheries cheap and give me a pint. Not that he would, mean old shot! But Millie'd go shniffing my breath."

"Oh my Lord. So'll Father."

There was no hope, living so close as we did, of slipping off to bed. You had to go through the kitchen where we lived to get to any of the other rooms. And Father would want to know all about what Miss Walker said.

"You want to chew a clove," Mike said.

"He'd smell that too."

"Shay you had toothache."

I thought that was very smart, and I marvelled a bit that Mike had been such a dunce at school, and then caught by Millie with a trick so old even I knew about it, when he was really so smart. Then I thought I'd better be getting home. Mike didn't leave with me. He'd still got sense enough to know that it took longer than that to hang a door. So I left him.

Outside it was even colder, it met you like a smack, and before I'd got as far as the South Gate I was all of a shiver and my belly rumbling so I hoped I *would* throw up. And I did and felt better, but downhearted again, a bit trembly about the legs. However, I got home, let myself into the shop, found a clove and chewed it, and went up the stairs.

I told a long yarn about Miss Walker keeping me talking, and I described the room and the way she was huddled in a shawl with no fire. I said she was heartily pleased with the parcel and thanked Father very much, but would he excuse her for not thanking him herself because she felt ashamed to be down to taking charity.

Father said just what I hoped; poor soul, he'd have to find her a mite of something regular. Then he asked about the clove smell and I said the cold had given me a twinge of toothache, but it was better now.

And so—as it said in one of the pieces in the *Short Passages from the Classics* that we used to have for a reader at the Board School—to bed.

II

If you're strictly brought up and your father is a saint it cuts both ways when you do wrong. You get more fun out of the doing—just as that apple Adam and Eve ate tasted better, I bet, than any of the ones they'd been made welcome to; but for a time, at least, you have to deal with your conscience. I took naturally to being bad, just as Father took to being good, but all the same there were times when I'd look at him and know he was *right* really, and wonder how he ever came to have a son like me. Then I'd stiffen up and tell myself that it was *because* he was as he was that he had a son like me.

For one thing, he should have let me go to the Grammar. Some old man, dead two hundred years or more, had left some money for scholarships, so that poor boys could go to the Grammar School. Webster, his name was, and the scholarships were always called Websters. When I was at the Board School our headmaster one morning took six of us and gave us some paper and turned over a board with a lot of questions on it, mixed up questions on every subject, and told us to write the answers. He didn't say what for, or why. We did what he said, and about three weeks later he said that a boy called Barrowby and I had won Websters. I went home and told Father and he said he was glad to know that I'd minded my book and learned all I could, but about the scholarship he'd just have to see. I don't know what he saw . . . at least I do; he saw I'd be still going to school and only able to help him mornings and evenings, and not even Saturdays, because the Grammar had lessons on Saturday till mid-day; and he saw that the scholarship, though it paid the fees, didn't cover the short black gowns or the mortarboards the Grammar boys wore, or the books they used. The long and the short of it was that he couldn't afford to let me take up the scholarship, and he needed me in the shop.

"But, Davie, don't think that what you have learned is wasted. Far from it. The chapel is going to arrange Bible readings for the poor old crippled people in the workhouse, and Mr. Phipps'll be glad of your help."

So the boy who came third in the examination went off to the Grammar and had his mortarboard and gown and bag of books; and I went in the shop.

That was one thing. Then there was money. Father never could see why I needed any money. A boy with a good home, what did he need money *for*? Food, clothes, everything provided. It wasn't that he was mean, far from it. Once, when I asked him for two shillings to buy myself some fishing tackle, he said, "We'll see," and went off and bought me the best rod Pearson had in his shop. And to make up for that extravagance, next time he was due to preach at Clevely, he *walked* instead of hiring, as he usually did, a pony cart from Wrenn's livery stables.

He was daft, my father. One Saturday night, coming home from delivering a late order, he fell in with a silly old drunk named Smithers, and helped him home. Back home himself, he said to my mother:

"The Smithers'll be on short commons tomorrow. What have we got?"

Mother said, "Loin of pork."

It was already cooked, because in our house no cooking was done on Sunday. Loin of pork is made up of so many separate chops and Father took the knife and said, "There's Bill and his missus and one, two, three, four youngsters," and cut off six of the chops, leaving three for the five of us.

That was the way he was, and there was no help for it. And my mother was nothing. If he'd gone to her one day and said Jesus wanted her to cut off her right hand and give it to a hungry dog she'd have sighed, and done it. When I was a little boy I sometimes thought that she was like one of those disciples whose names don't come in for much mention. The ones who just sighed and didn't say anything that could be put down.

It was a fortnight before Father gave another thought to Miss Walker. That was partly because of the time of year, stocking up for Christmas, foresighted people already putting in their orders, and the various charity organisations that gave groceries to the poor at this season poking round trying to get the best value for their money. Armstrong's at the Old Vine was very popular at that job, and well it might be.

Father chose a Wednesday night—when we'd been run off our feet all day—to remember Miss Walker. He lumped together four or five shillings' worth of odds and ends, parcelled them up, and sent me off.

"I may be quite a time," I said. "She's a one to talk once she gets going."

"She's lonely. And maybe it's as much a charity to talk to her as it is to take her a mite of food."

So I was covered there. How to get Mike out was another matter; I couldn't very well come the same dodge again. I was nearly on his doorstep before I'd thought of a good reason to get him out.

Millie answered the door this time. You could see she'd been pretty in a pale, pinched sort of way, the way that doesn't last long even in the best circumstances. She looked slovenly and pulled-down and peevish.

"Well?"

"Mike home?"

She'd have said no, if by that time he hadn't come up behind her. I said:

"Oh, hello, Mike. Do me a bit of a favour. I'm trying to make something for my mother, for Christmas, and I can't get it fixed right. It's a workbox. I wondered if you'd mind stepping along and give me your advice, you being a carpenter and all."

"That I will, bor. Right gladly. You don't mind, do you, Millie?"

Though he'd have made three of her, and spoke as though he hated her guts, it was easy enough to see that he was more than half scared of her.

"Thass right," she said, "come in, gobble your grub, and go off to play. What about chopping that kindling?"

I said, very soothingly, "That's all right, Mrs. Saunders. I can wait. Ladies first."

"You'd best come in then," she said grudgingly.

Inside, the room was terrible. It was bigger than the kitchen where the five of us lived and Mother had to cook and everything, but there wasn't anywhere to sit that wasn't piled with clothes or something, and the table looked as though she hadn't washed up for a week. The baby stank like a ferret, or worse. Millie was no nosegay, either.

Mike went out to the back and I could hear him chopping. He came in very soon with an armful of kindling and threw it down on the hearth just anyhow.

"That do?" The baby woke and began to wail.

"Now look what you done," she said.

He said, "Come on, Dave," and we went out.

"Thass married life," he said bitterly. "Sometimes I think I'll bloody well swing for her."

"That'd be a waste. I should just give her a clip on the jaw and tell her to shut up. Why don't you?"

"If I was to lay a finger on her she'd go straight to her dad. You know who he is, don't you? Owd Strongarm Fickling, the blacksmith. He give me a proper pasting once. I was off work for two days."

Strongarm Fickling was not a man to trifle with. He was quite a character. Year after year, at the Midsummer Fair, some old broken-down prize fighter would stand up and challenge all comers, and Strongarm'd wait until he'd bashed five or six brash youngsters about, then he'd step up and lay the basher flat.

"Are you really making your mum a box, Dave?"

"No. That was just an excuse. I thought you'd like to get out and have a drink. Not the *Rose and Crown* this time. How about the *Pot of Flowers?* And, Mike, I haven't any money. But you can have this five bobs' worth of groceries for my share. That all right?"

"No. For one thing I'd be outa pocket. Millie do the shopping; she could use what you got there but she wouldn't give me eightpence for it. And I should hev to explain where I got 'em. And thass a waste. Five bobs' worth of stuff should be worth two. Lemme think. Maybe I could plant them on *my* mum. I'll try anyway. Thass only a step outa our way."

I waited outside the little house in Pound Lane and grew very impatient, he was gone so long. When he came out he said:

"Spun her a proper yarn. Towd her I'd done a bit of shopping to give Millie a surprise and Millie'd gone and got the very same goods and towd me what I could do with mine. Against Millie my mum is, always was. She give me two bob and made me stop and drink a cuppa tea."

"So we're all right, except for time."

"Well, this is a backhanded way of going about it, Dave. If

you want two bob, why'nt you just take it outa the till when your dad ain't looking?"

It'd be easy enough. Our till was just a drawer under the provision counter, and so far as I knew Father never checked it during the day. Every evening he scooped the money into a bag and carried it upstairs and put it in the cupboard. Though he was so easy to give credit if he thought anyone needed it, he hardly ever bought anything without paying for it on the nail. Sometimes, just before he took delivery of some goods, there'd be quite a bit in the box; then after goods had come in there'd be nearly nothing. I suppose he kept some sort of accounts in his head, and now and again he'd make a remark about the day's takings, "a good day," "a bad day," or, "Well, there's the rate money safe, at least," but he didn't take much interest, and would be quite easy to rob.

To rob. "Thou shalt not steal." On the other hand, to take from the till was no worse than what I had already done twice; and far simpler. I felt a bit peevish that I hadn't thought of it myself but had waited for that great dunce Mike Saunders to put it into my head. Still, I'd got another brand-new idea to offer him, presently.

The *Pot of Flowers* was a newer pub, and a good deal bigger than the *Rose and Crown*. I was still a bit shy of entering such a place, and scared of being seen, so I kept well behind Mike and took a quick look round. It being market day, the place was full, mainly with country people, nobody known to me.

Then I nearly trod on Mike's heels because he'd stopped short and half turned, and for a moment he looked trapped, the same as I might have done if I'd found Mr. Phipps in the bar collecting pennies for the Christmas Charity Fund. A girl's voice, very clear, though pitched low, called:

"Hullo, Mike! There you are, another of my old customers have followed me from the *One Bull*." Some men laughed and one said, "No wonder!"

Mike, very red in the ears, went up to the bar, to the end

where she was serving. I looked round. There were no pews in this pub, just benches set beside the wall.

Mike brought the two mugs, white with a blue rim, here, and sat down, and said sulkily:

"I din't know she'd moved. Wild horses wouldn't hev got me in here if I had."

"Why, don't you like her?"

"Don't talk daft!" He buried his nose in his mug. It dawned on me that he'd liked her too well, and would rather have had her than Millie. That made me look at the girl with more interest. I hadn't, up to then, been much for girls. I had two sisters, all the girlish company anybody could wish for, and no time for playing about. Now, having taken one look, I took another and another. She wasn't a pretty girl at all, but there was something very taking about her; she looked as though she thought a lot of herself; and she was very neat; black hair, smoothed back as though it was painted on, and pinned in a great shiny knob at the back of her head, a high-collared dress of dark violet, with no trimming at all except a row of little gold-coloured buttons all down the front. She could have been one of the female chapel members—but she wasn't.

"What's her name?"

"Lily."

There never was a girl more unsuitably named. Rose perhaps, just . . . if you thought of a dark one. But one of the old Bible names would have been better, Esther, Rebecca, Jael, Jezebel. Not Sarah; my younger sister, the one who was lame, was Sarah.

"Lily what?"

"Cattermole."

"Not one of that Steeple Strawless lot?"

He nodded, and I looked at her again with even more interest. The Cattermoles were a notorious family, poachers, horse copers, and higglers. (A higgler, in Suffolk, was the lowest kind of dealer, one who'd buy anything for twopence if he thought he could sell it for twopence ha'penny, and would steal if he couldn't buy.) It'd be almost safe to say that at any given minute there'd be one Cattermole in Ipswich gaol, one coming up before the Petty Sessions, and one waiting for the Assizes. Nothing was ever heard of their women. There was more than a streak of gypsy in the family, and gypsies tend to keep their women in the background.

Being told Lily's name, I understood her colouring and her air of being pleased with herself. Whenever there was a case involving a Cattermole, people'd crowd into court. They made such cheeky, witty answers that even the magistrates were said to smile behind their hands. And it paid; everybody said they always got off very lightly, even the ones who did go to gaol should have gone for twice as long.

Tonight, my stomach knowing what to expect, the beer settled down better. There were no rumbles, and soon I felt happy and light.

I said, "Mike. I been thinking. If we want to get out now and again, we want a good excuse. How about joining the Workmen's Institute? Would Millie let you?"

"Damn you. Don't say that."

"Well, she seemed against your coming out tonight."

"I don't wanta be reminded of that, do I?"

I hurried on. "You could say you were trying to catch up on your schooling, aiming to get on in the world. She'd be all for that, surely. There're some sums carpenters find useful, I should think."

"Thass right, now chuck at me that I were a dunce at school."

"If you're going to be like that . . ."

"Shut your jaw!" Considering that I'd got him out of that horrible room and provided the wherewithal to buy the beer, that was pretty rough, I thought. And I could sulk as well as the next. So I sat and thought that I didn't need him . . .

much. I could join the Workmen's Institute; it was a strictly
teetotal place, aimed at keeping men out of pubs and giving
the ones who'd missed school a chance to learn a little. Father would approve of that, at least I hoped and thought so.
And though I shrank, just then, from the idea of walking into
a pub and drinking by myself without Mike's support, it could
be done.

Presently, his beer finished, Mike got up and fetched some
more. Halfway through he had the grace to apologise.

"I never meant to snap at you, Dave. It's just I feel so bloody
awful. Seeing her again. I ain't been in the *One Bull* since I
knew I'd gotta marry Millie."

I said, "What I don't understand is . . ." And then I
stopped. There was one short bad word I knew for the process,
and several Biblical ones, "get with child," "have carnal knowledge of," "uncover the nakedness." They all sounded quite
daft, so I used the bad one I'd learned at Board School. "Why
you ——ed Millie at all, if you liked Lily better."

He said gloomily, "You don't understand nothing. You
ain't hardly born yet. Lily'll lead you on and then laugh. You
go off with a —— on you like a bloody post and then you meet
Millie and she's all over you like a bitch in heat. And there
you are . . . Bloody pasting from Strongarm, threat of the
sack from Platt, nailed down for the rest of your life."

"I think I should have run away."

"I never thought of it. Wish I had."

He finished his beer in silence and then said:

"You gonna be all night?"

I drank quickly and we got up to go. Lily called:

"Good night, Mike. Good night, Handsome."

I blushed a bit, but nobody saw. Outside I fumbled in my
pocket and brought out two strong peppermints. Father kept
a few sweets—acid drops, clove balls, peppermints—in glass
jars on the counter. Lots of women'd buy a ha'pennorth if

they had a child with them, and if they didn't Father loved to dip in and give the brat what he called "a sweetie."

I said, a bit nastily, "You not minding what Millie thinks, won't want one of these, will you?"

"Give it here and don't talk daft. What was you saying about the Workmen's Institute just now? I didn't listen much."

I outlined my plan again. The classes, all run by good-hearted schoolmasters who hadn't had enough teaching during the day, and by chaps who thought they were specially good at their trades—like shoemaking and such—started at seven and went on till half past nine. It wasn't like school; you went in and came out when you liked. I knew quite a lot about the Institute, though I had never been, because our Mr. Phipps, besides being superintendent of the Sunday school and chief organiser of the Christmas Charity, and the arranger for readings at the workhouse, found time to go to the Institute to teach what had been his trade before his Aunt Symonds left him enough to live on—which was tailoring. He'd once set everybody by the ears by suggesting that women should come to his classes to learn the simple things, putting on patches, turning garments inside out. But he'd had pointed out to him that it was the Work*men's* Institute, not the Work*women's*.

"What I thought was, we could go in for an hour or so, make sure we were seen, and then slope off and have a drink. It's the only way I can think of to get out for anything except chapel."

"How you stick that, you poor sod, I don't know."

"I don't see how you stick Millie, and that baby crying."

He laughed. "In the same boat, ain't we, Dave?"

I thought—Not quite, thank God!

I said, "The Institute'll start up again in January. You try to talk Millie round and I'll tackle my father."

"Here, half a minute . . . something to come, boy. Two bob and we spent eightpence."

"We'll halve it then. You tell Millie I gave you eightpence for helping me with the box. That'll put her in a good temper."

"There ain't a thing in the world'd put her in a good temper, Dave, and thass the truth. The best I can hope for is to keep her outa bad temper."

III

In the new year, that was 1887, life opened out for me. Father agreed that I should go to the Workmen's Institute, and then I told him that there I'd fallen in with an old school friend, Mike Saunders, who was married and had a baby and lived in part of old Miss Walker's house, and sometimes asked me in on the way home for a cup of cocoa, and that sounded harmless enough. Thursday was the peak of my week. I admit that I was always in deadly fear that some Thursday there'd be somebody in the *Pot of Flowers* that knew somebody, knew somebody that knew Father, or some other chapel member; and there was another fear running alongside, which was that Mr. Phipps or one of the others'd notice that I never stayed in the Institute more than an hour, sometimes less. (The truth was that in no time at all I could do in ten minutes what it took others two hours to manage. The classes were mostly made up of men of forty who'd missed the compulsory education that began in 1870 and were doing infant lessons. I suppose Mr. Phipps and the others thought it natural that I should pop in, do my bit, and be off. And Mike they must have known was unteachable, so nobody bothered about him.)

I was learning to live with danger and like it. Eightpence out of the till, two pints each for Mike and me. Then another twopence and we could have ten cigarettes. (Most grocers

stocked them, but Father refused to . . . Thou shalt not cause
thy brother to stumble!) Then one evening in the *Pot of
Flowers* I heard a man say to Lily, "Have one on me, miss,"
and she said she'd have a small port and gave him her funny
half-mocking smile. After that it was two pints apiece, or even
three for Mike and me, ten cigarettes, and a small port for
Lily.

Father never noticed. And if he had done I was ready. I
worked hard enough, I was nearly eighteen. I should have
been *paid*. If it came to the worst I was prepared to say so.

For a month or two of that new year, right into April, in
fact, he was still being sorry for Miss Walker and still sending
her bits and pieces for me to deliver either as I went to the
Institute or on my way back when I dropped into Mike's for
cocoa. I used to give them to Millie. She'd quite taken to me
by that time; she thought I was a good influence on Mike,
getting him to the Institute.

Then, in April, all the shopkeepers in the front of the Old
Vine had communications from Turnbull's the lawyer's, asking were they prepared to sell their shops, and if so at what
price, since there was "a client" anxious to purchase the whole
lot.

Father was terribly upset.

"It's the United Provision Retailers," he said. "They've been
trying to get a foot in this town for the last year. They sell
cheap muck, they give no credit, they'll undersell for a year to
ruin honest traders, and then get a monopoly. . . ."

Mother said, "You aren't bound to sell to them, are you?"

"I wouldn't sell to them, no matter what they offered. But
Robins might, or Steggles." They were the two shops next
door to us. "Or Grigg or Ashworth"; they were the two at the
outer ends. "And then where should we be?"

Mother said, "If you could get a good price, Samuel . . . and
buy another shop. A village store maybe. The country air'd
be good for Sarah."

Father said, "But I'm *against* the U.P.R. Their principle's all wrong. Cheap, nasty stuff, no credit, and flourishing like the green bay tree."

Mother sighed.

It was almost comic. Father, being a grocer, was sure the U.P.R. was the client; Robins the chemist was just as certain that it was Bloom's Cash Chemists; Ashworth the linen draper even went so far as to say that he suspected a big London firm, Harrod's, of trying to open up in country towns. And while they were all talking, saying what price they'd ask, and whether they would or would not sell, and trying to find out who the mysterious client was, the Baildon *Free Press* got wind of the affair and had a column all about progress and the improvement of trade. The Baildon *Free Press* came out on Friday, but it was Wednesday of the next week before Miss Walker got a piece of it, wrapped round a loaf or a sausage, and when she did, she went raving mad. She came down to the Old Vine and into every shop, crying and shouting. "You mustn't sell except to me. I've scrimped and saved and starved and perished all these years, getting the money together. I've almost succeeded. Four thousand pounds my father sold the house for, and put the money in the railway. But I hate the railway, so when he died I took it out and made two bad investments. But I have almost the whole four thousand saved again. Promise me, promise me, not to sell to anyone else."

She started off at Ashworth's, that being the end shop, and by the time she got to us the crowd of children that'll gather anywhere, any time, out of the blue, were giggling and mocking behind her. Father took up the first jar of sweets that came handy and threw a handful out into the road and then came in and bolted the door. All the time she was crying and shouting and Father set himself to calm her down. He even put his arm round her and set her on a chair. She was a rum-looking old girl at the best of times, with a shock of white hair and a face like an organ-grinder's monkey, and crying hadn't improved it. Father behaved as though she was the Queen of Sheba. I don't think he noticed at first what she said about having four thousand pounds; or if he did, he didn't connect it with the little parcels he'd sent her.

"Now, now," he said, "you mustn't upset yourself, Miss Walker. Nobody's sold anything yet."

"It was in the paper. I read it in the paper. You mustn't do it. Please. All these years. I've been *saving*. I've been hungry. I've been cold, I've been humiliated. . . ."

Father said, "Pop upstairs, David, and tell your mother to make a cup of tea."

Mother was already at the top of the stairs, come to see what all the row was about; and at the same minute Mr. Ashworth came in the back door, meaning to warn Father, saw it was too late, and went hopping over the fence into Robins' garden.

Miss Walker said, "It isn't tea I need, thank you. It's your assurance that you won't sell to anyone but *me*."

"But my poor dear," Father said, "your four thousand, even if you got it, wouldn't buy out five flourishing businesses. When your father sold the place he sold the *place*, and that was forty years ago. Money's lost value, and then there's the goodwill and all to think of. Come on now, calm yourself."

She said, "You're a good man, I can see. *You* wouldn't go and sell behind my back, would you?"

"I'm not anxious to sell at all. I got a good business, and a lad to follow me."

"But it isn't *right*. My own father did it, but it was a *wicked* thing to do. It was a house, a beautiful house, meant to be lived in and enjoyed. *Enjoyed*. That was what none of them understood. Look at those stairs . . . just look. Scuffed and worn. I used to polish them every week. Nobody's polished them. . . ." She cried worse than widows at a funeral.

"We have to go up and down in a hurry. Besides, my little girl is lame. Polished stairs'd be dangerous," Father said, just as though he was talking to a reasonable being, not a daft old crone.

Mother came down with the cup of tea. Miss Walker ignored it.

"This'll kill me," she said. "Not that anybody will care, or understand. All these years, all I've had to live for."

"Now, now," Father said, beginning to get into his stride. "That's no way to talk. . . ." He preached her a sermon, not half bad for one made up on the spur of the moment; all about the good she could do if she'd really got four thousand pounds, the people she could help; and about the folly of setting your heart on any earthly thing. We brought nothing into the world and we could take nothing with us, all we could do was love God, and our neighbour, and hope for Heaven when we died.

The sermon was wasted. She cried, and when she put in a word it clearly showed that she hadn't heeded a word he said. Somebody came and rattled the shop door and shouted. Father said:

"Look. Miss Walker, you go home now. David'll walk with you. I got a customer."

He went and opened the door.

"But you haven't promised me."

Father said, "I'll promise you one thing. I won't sell without letting you know."

"That's something. If I can get the others to promise the same. There must be something I can do. I shall think of something. . . ."

The customer came in, and we went out. She wouldn't go straight home, but into both the other shops, where she got short shrift.

"Everybody's against me. They always have been. From the day I wanted to go to the Female Academy. But even there I had my small triumph; years later, when a mistress left hurriedly, Miss Brook sent and asked me to teach there temporarily. But I was more gainfully employed with my private pupil."

That thought seemed to calm her. When we were opposite Thorley's Bank, I said:

"Do you use the new bank, or the old one, Miss Walker?"

"Neither. I'm capable of learning from experience. Money that is out of sight, just figures written on paper, isn't money at all. It can vanish overnight. After the debacle I put my money into cheap property, the rent from which I scrupulously saved. And recently I sold out. So when I say I have four thousand pounds I *have* four thousand pounds, I assure you." We walked a little farther. "That is what baffles me. I have *always* achieved what I set my mind to, never easily, but in the long run successfully. I *can* read and write, I *have* acquired what they call airs and graces, and I have saved four thousand pounds." Suddenly she gave a cackle of crazy laughter. "I aimed at the wrong target, of course. As the kind little grocer explained. It's not enough. I was stupid. In many ways I am a stupid woman. I might have seen that anyone who would eat out of my hand, as my mother expressed it, would have been pliable enough to adapt himself. . . . Dear me, if only one had, with youth, the wisdom one attains later, how different life would be." She walked on, snuffling a little. Presently she said, "The one who was kind said something about goodwill. What would that be?"

"Well, telling the customers that you were selling out and you hope they'd buy their stuff from the new man. That sort of thing."

"But I shouldn't *want* any customers."

"No. But my father and the others have built up the goodwill—that is, got the customers together; and they'd want something for that, whoever they sold to."

Just as we turned into Market Square she stopped dead.

"I really am an extremely foolish woman. Imagine overlooking such an asset." She seized me by the arm. "Will you beg your father not to be hasty? And ask him to tell the others.

If they'll just wait, give me a little more time. . . . . I haven't come so far to be beaten in the end. Tell them to wait. Of course, I don't expect you to act as my emissary for nothing. I shall give you a token of my goodwill. If you promise to try to persuade your father—and the others."

"I'll do my best," I said.

When we reached her house she told me to come in, but added, with one of her sudden changes of manner:

"You mustn't come upstairs today. Wait here."

Inside the room where Mike lived the baby was putting up its feeble, dogged wail. I seemed to wait there a long time before Miss Walker swooped down the stairs, pressed what I thought was sixpence into my hand, and said urgently, "Don't forget. Tell them I have another asset."

Outside, in the lingering April twilight, I saw that what she had given me was a half sovereign. As I pocketed it I recalled how on my first visit she had asked me into her room; tonight she wouldn't even have me upstairs. Allowing for the changeability of a crazy woman's mind, it was still possible to think that this was because during the interval she had turned property into ready cash, and so was on her guard.

I thought this over on the way home, and bore it in mind at supper when Father was giving it as his opinion that the poor old woman was even more deranged than we'd thought. During my absence Robins the chemist had come in and talked with Father and told him that he remembered the failure of two firms in which Miss Walker had money invested; a lot of other people had been affected by it too.

"People whose minds are unbalanced," Father said, "often get set ideas. She'd set hers on buying back what her father sold for four thousand pounds; so that's the sum she stuck at, like a stopped clock. And no doubt what she's got look like a fortune to her, because it took such a lot of scrapping together. But I don't believe she'd got anything like that much. Where'd she have got it *from?*"

"She told me . . ." I began; and then I realised that what he had just said was extremely important. So I stopped.

"Well?"

"She told me to beg you to wait, and ask the others to. She said she had another asset."

For once Mother spoke up.

"Whatever she has, Samuel, I reckon it's more than *we* have saved. And if you want to give food away you could find a more deserving case."

"You may be right. There're enough about, in all truth."

That night I lay awake for hours, going over and over everything in my head. I sat up every now and then, just to make certain that I *was* awake and not slipping off into a dream where everything seemed possible and easy. I was awake all right; and in the morning, in the bright light, surrounded by ordinary everyday things, what I'd planned in the darkness still seemed possible and easy. Turn it this way and that and not a fault could I see in it, always providing I was careful and didn't lose my head. And today was Thursday, when I'd be seeing Lily. I took that as a good omen.

Just before seven I called in on Mike, meaning to tell him that I wasn't able to go to the Institute, or afterwards to the *Pot of Flowers*. That meant that I should have Lily to myself, or at least Lily without Mike, for he'd made it plain to me that he only went to that pub to please me. I'd been glad enough for him to make the first advances; he was an old acquaintance of hers and he knew more about how to make up to a girl than I did. I shouldn't have known how to set about asking her if we could walk her home—she didn't live in, but lodged in Baker Street. Mike just said, as casual as casual, "Walk you home, Lily, if you look sharp." And she had looked sharp, she'd said to Bill Cobbold, who kept the pub, "I'll clear up here in the morning." No "if you please" or "by your leave" for Lily Cattermole. No nonsense, either.

Over a bit of old cobbled street Mike had taken hold of her arm, muttering something about it being rough walking; she'd jerked herself free and said, "If you're too drunk to walk straight, lean on David."

We often walked her home on Thursdays. I told my father that after the Institute, in addition to giving me cocoa, Mike taught me a bit of carpentering. Mike told Millie the same. Father thought we carpentered in Mike's house because his tools were there, Millie thought we did it at my house so the noise wouldn't disturb the baby. To back up my side of the story Mike once made a little hanging bookshelf which I took home and gave to Father for his Bible and hymnbook and *Life of St. Paul* and *By the Sea of Galilee*. To back up Mike's side of the story I sometimes gave him a shilling. So Father put his head on his clean pillow thinking his son had found a useful hobby—and after all Our Lord was a carpenter; and Millie put her head on her dirty pillow thinking that Mike, stupid as he was, did try to turn an extra penny. And we made use of the time thus gained to walk Lily home, straight as a wand between us.

On this Thursday, when I reached Mike's home, Millie wasn't there. She'd taken the baby round to the Forge because it had a tissicky cough and the smell of burnt horse hoof was supposed to be good for it. Mike was just finishing off a bit of bread and cheese at a table so cluttered that there was only just room for his elbows. A great mound of indescribable rubbish that took up the greater part of the table was crowned by a pretty little hat, blue straw, shaped like a bonnet with pansies all about it.

"Bought that this morning, she did," Mike said, jerking his thumb at it. "Hadta hev a new hat for Easter, and us in the —— muddle that we are."

I said nothing, thinking he was referring to the muddle in the room, into which, since I first saw it, many extra things had been brought and nothing, so far as I could see, ever taken out.

"Got notice to quit now," Mike said, wiping his mouth with the back of his hand.

"From Platt?"

"No, that frigging old bitch up there. Come down last night and give us notice, fortnight from Saturday. Going to sell the house, she say. Millie say we can go and live with her dad, but that I 'on't do. And who else is gonna take in a slut like her and a baby that stink and cry day and night? I tell you, Dave, I had about enough of this. If Millie go back home I shall take my tools and sling my bloody hook. I couldn't be worse off, could I?"

Twenty-four hours earlier this would have concerned me; he'd been my alibi for four months. Now it meant less than nothing, so I merely said that I wondered he'd stuck things so long.

"Truth was I was scared of Strongarm, and getting the sack from Platt. And you can take it from me, bor, you can get yourself in a worse mess trying to act safe than if you take the bull by the horns. The minute Millie towd me she'd got one in the copper I should've made myself scarce. Strongarm couldn't hev pasted me, nor Platt give me the sack, if I was in London."

All perfectly true. But he had no imagination, no brain; he was a dunce. Very different from me!

I told him what I had come to say—that I couldn't stay out this evening. Then I left, taking care, lest he should look out of the window, to turn towards home, and then whipping round the corner, into Looms Lane and so to the *Pot of Flowers*.

I was earlier than I'd ever been before and Lily was alone in the bar. Bill Cobbold and those who would later on be his customers were still eating their late teas.

I'd been alone with Lily just two times before this, nights

when I'd walked her home without Mike. Once when I'd got out on a Tuesday because Father had gone to a local preachers' bun fight at Nettleton, and once was a Thursday when Mike had to work late.

The first time we'd talked about our families, and ended up laughing because she hated her family for not being respectable and I hated mine for being *too* respectable.

She said, "We should've been swopped when we was babies. But I'd bet you'd have swopped back, time you was six."

"So would you. Even the way you walk wouldn't have suited my father."

"Whass wrong with the way I walk?"

"You walk in a proud way. You should walk humbly before your God. Didn't you know that?"

It wasn't only the way she walked; it was the way she could look. In the bar, if she was talking to somebody and interested, she'd just go on, no matter how men banged their mugs or said, "Hi, Lily," or, "Here, miss." She treated Bill Cobbold, who employed her, like dirt.

"I'd walk humbly before my God or anybody else that could give me reason to walk *proud*. Sort that out if you can, you being so clever. I walk like I do, and talk like I do, and act like I do because there's nothing to fall back on except pride. Drunk guzzling fools, hawking in their throats and spitting, sicking their hearts up, or undressing you with their eyes. Fine company!"

Yet, for all she was so proud, Mike claimed that they'd had many a kiss and a cuddle, and he'd once said that he reckoned she'd have married him in the end, if he hadn't got all tangled up with Millie. The time he told me that I'd looked at him and tried to see him with Lily's eyes. Big and strong; mild, rather silly blue eyes and straw-coloured hair bleached nearly white in places, and a good smooth brownish skin. There were dozens like him. Yet she'd kissed him. Like that poem we had to learn in school—Say I'm so and so and so, say that health and wealth have missed me, say I'm growing old, but add, Jenny kissed me.

I couldn't claim that she'd kissed me. But I had kissed her. That was the second time I walked her home alone. That time we'd hardly talked at all, because as soon as we were out of the *Pot of Flowers* we could hear, faint and yet clear, the music from a concert that was going on in the Assembly Rooms. I did make one remark but she said "sssh." And she walked on, listening. We walked past the Baker Street opening and into Pound Lane, which ran alongside the Assembly Rooms. One of the windows—they were all made of frosted glass so people shouldn't look in—was open, it being one of those March evenings which because of their suddenness seem hotter than a summer night. Lily put her hands on the window sill and jumped, like a cat, and stood there, looking in.

I stood on the ground and looked at her. Enough light came out of the window for me to see her side face clearly. She had a little short hooked nose, like a bird's beak; and her chin jutted out. One day, when she was old, she'd look like Punch in the Punch and Judy Shows which Father disapproved of, but which we children watched whenever we had a chance. But tonight her nose had a proud and masterful look.

The music came to a stop. She said, into the sudden silence: "There they sit, all bare-shouldered, and their jewels shine, and their fans. Oh, ain't life *unfair?*"

She was ready to jump down, but didn't quite dare. So she said, "Help me, David." And I put my hands on either side of her little waist and jumped her down. I didn't let go. I turned her about, and kissed her. And what had happened to me only in dreams before and been very pleasant, happened in real life and hurt more than I'd ever thought anything could. She didn't kiss me; she turned her head away and said, "Leave go of me."

I let go at once.

I knew what she wanted—to sit, bare-shouldered, bejew-

elled, with a fan, absolutely respectable and secure, listening
to music in the Assembly Rooms. Twenty years ahead I might
be able to give it to her. With Father dead and the business run
properly there was no reason why I couldn't be a second Mr.
Propert—he'd been the one who'd sold to Father and retired
with a house in the Avenue, a carriage and pair, a sable coat
for his wife.

Twenty years. What I wanted was here and now.

What I wanted—and it shows that however much you break
away, something of your childhood training sticks—was pure
Old Testament. I wanted Lily the way Ahasuerus had had
Esther, and all the other chosen virgins, the way Solomon had
had his many concubines. I pictured a hotel in London, bigger and finer than the Station Hotel, into which I often stared
as I passed, all plush and velvet, and lace curtains with bows,
and marble floors and stairs; I'd lie on a bed with a lot of soft
pillows and watch her take off one garment after another until she stood there stark naked. Then I'd say, "Let your hair
down," and she would. And then I'd say, "Come here," and
she'd come. I'd push my hands through the veil of hair and
take hold of her body. There was another side to this dream
too; Lily dressed in magnificent clothes and holding her head
high, in some public place, with me—also smartly dressed—
beside her and being envied by every man who saw us.

I was eighteen, and I had led a very simple life, but I wasn't
soft enough to get my dreams and my real life muddled up.
I knew quite well that long before I could give Lily any of
the things she wanted she'd have found someone who could.
Nor did I kid myself that I was "in love" with her; if I'd been
in love I *shouldn't* have thought that one day her face would
be like Punch's, and I *should* have been making poor silly
little plans to get her to love me and marry me and set up
house in two rooms, like Mike. I'd known for weeks exactly
how I wanted Lily; and until the day when I took old Miss

Walker home I knew I hadn't got a snowflake's chance in Hell of ever getting it. Now I meant to have a try.

On this April evening she'd got a new dress, prim and close-necked and long-sleeved like all her dresses, but a summer colour, pale pink. She was polishing glasses, and looked up and said:

"Hullo, David. You're early. Where's Mike?"

"At home, fretting. Miss Walker's given them notice to quit."

"And no wonder. Who'd have that messy Millie about the place if they didn't have to."

I asked her what would she drink and she said nothing, it was too early.

I said, "Oh, come on, Lily, stretch a point just for once. It isn't every night we can have a drink together just by ourselves. Tell you what, I'll have one of your ports, too, to keep you company."

So she poured two and I gave her the half sovereign.

"My word. You are in the money," she said.

"Not yet. One day I might be, though. It's not a thing I like to speak of and I'd rather you didn't mention it, but I've got expectations. An old great-aunt, a widow, left very well off in Brixton."

That was true, as far as it went. Father did have an aunt, but her husband had kept a pub, and she disapproved of Father and all his works and ways; and, her husband having been a Freemason, she meant to leave all she had to the Freemasons.

"That'll be nice for you," Lily said.

"When it happens. Might not be so far ahead either. She's over eighty." I drank some port, which I liked, and added, "It's not a thing to talk about, though. Waiting for dead men's shoes. Still, it keeps me going, thinking of myself in London."

"It would me too. Is Mike very upset? Has he found another place?"

"Millie is talking of going back to live at the Forge."

"My God! That 'on't suit Mike, will it?"

The first of the evening's customers came blundering in and she served him and then turned back to me, carrying on the conversation, as was her way, as though it had never been interrupted. "I can't think how he ever could be such a fool. Round at the *One Bull*, time I was there, Millie Fickling was a joke. That baby could have been *anybody's.*"

"Maybe that's what ails it now—crying for its real father."

Lily laughed. She had very white teeth, the dog ones sharp and long.

"You'd make a joke about anything, wouldn't you?"

"If I could. Anyway, there's no point in weeping over Mike's plight. He's stuck with Millie and the baby, whether we laugh or cry."

"That's true enough," she said.

I stayed there, drinking port and treating her, and getting a word in occasionally, and then I went home, not sorry to go to bed early and have a chance to think. I went through the whole thing again, and barring some absolutely unforeseen accident, the kind nobody, however clever, could guard against, I couldn't see that anything could go wrong. But, although I was sure, there was in me, but in much greater measure, the same kind of fear, half pleasant, half painful, that there had been every time I took money from the till, every time I went into the *Pot of Flowers*. Get it over and done with, I thought.

So next morning I said to Mother:

"Mike Saunders was telling me last night about a poor woman he knows who could get a job if she had a decent dress and hat to go in. I suppose you haven't anything you could spare."

I could see Mother struggle with herself. And she won.

"There's my grey alpaca. It's gone under the arms. I was

meaning to cut it down for Marty, but if it means the difference between getting a job and not getting a job, I could spare it. I'll try to find time to mend it up a bit."

I felt then the only pang of shame I felt over the whole business. Mother, like me, was the victim of Father's saintliness, and I just couldn't have her stitching away and contriving.

"Don't you bother about that. The woman can mend it. People mustn't look gift dresses under the arms."

It was the kind of thing which in our family passed for humour, and everybody, even Father, laughed. Marty, glad to be shut of the grey alpaca, looked at me with adoration. One day soon she'd get a new dress because Mother could say, "Samuel, the grey alpaca I meant for Marty's summer wear I gave away, you remember."

Much the same kind of thought was passing through my sister Sarah's head, for she up and said:

"The poor woman could have my brown leghorn that got so wet the day I was caught in the rain and couldn't hurry." Sarah never missed an opportunity of mentioning her infirmity and in one sentence had scored a double. Poor little lame Sarah. Sarah would need a new hat.

"Mike's mother knows the woman," I said. "I could take the things along this evening and leave them with her."

That was Friday, a busy day in the grocery trade, so it was nine o'clock before I was free to run, as everyone supposed, on my charitable errand. Down in the shop I turned the tap of the vinegar barrel and soaked the grey dress, squeezing it and turning it about until it was a kind of dirty brown colour. Then I wrapped it and Sarah's hat in the parcel again and went off.

In winter Baildon was, for its size, a well-lighted town, with oil lamps put into brackets every here and there, but in April the lamps were all collected and stored away until October. Tonight, under the bit of arch that still marked where once in olden days the South Gate of the town had been, it was as dark as pitch. And there I hurriedly pulled on the wet, brownish dress and buttoned it. I bent the leghorn hat, which was shapeless anyway, into a kind of bonnet and tied it down with a wide blue ribbon which, years ago, I'd worn across my chest when the Bridewell Lane Board School had some competition team races against St. Mary's. There was no prize in the team races, just the honour of running for your school, and the winning team was allowed to keep its ribbons.

I always wore heavy hobnailed boots, they saved shoe-mending bills. I took them off and hid them in the darkest place under the arch where some stones were missing. Without them I wasn't all that much taller than Mother, so the dress fitted me better; and I could move silently.

Walking very quickly, like a woman out after dark and anxious to get home, I went on to the Market Square and stood, not on Miss Walker's side, but opposite. I looked about, and listened. There didn't seem to be a soul about. Decent people were all at home, either in bed or getting ready. People who went to pubs were only just getting into their stride. At Number 4 there was no light in Mike's living room, which meant that he and Millie had turned in. In the room above, Miss Walker's, there was a faint light, one candle.

I knew about the front door. It was never locked. The people who had lived on the lower floor before Mike had lost the key and it had never been replaced. The door of their sitting room had a lock and a key, which they could use if they wanted to, but never did; and I supposed that Miss Walker's rooms upstairs would be locked, probably bolted too.

I went quietly up the stairs and tapped on the door of the room where the light was. Nothing happened. I tapped a little louder, not much, because I had realised from the beginning that I mustn't disturb Mike or Millie or their blasted baby.

After the second tap there was a shuffling sound and then

Miss Walker, from the other side of the door, called in her loud upper-class voice:

"Who's there? What do you want?"

I put my mouth to the keyhole and hissed, willing my voice to carry, and speaking as much like Millie as I could.

"Sssh. You'll wake the baby! I want to borrow a candle."

I heard her say, quite distinctly, "The handless slut!"

Then the key turned, a bolt screeched back, and I thought —It's done. I've done it!

So I had. The door opened and as it did so I pushed. Miss Walker just had time to say:

"But you're not M . . ." and then I had my hand clapped over her mouth, and my other hand pulling a big handkerchief out of the bodice of my dress. She was wearing her old scarf, and I bundled up the end of it and pushed it into her mouth and then tied it into place with the handkerchief. Then I half pushed, half carried her into the room and shoved her into one of the big fancy chairs which took up so much too much space, and whipped out some lengths of strong string that I'd taken.

In half a minute she was tied down, gagged and helpless; and I'd started my search. I was as calm as though I'd been cutting bacon on our provision counter. I was covered every way. Tomorrow, sometime, she'd call attention to herself, and go round to the police. She'd say a woman in a buffish-coloured dress and a bonnet with a blue ribbon had robbed her of four thousand pounds. Most people, like my father, would think that the four thousand pounds had existed only in her crazy mind; and a few, those who *believed* that she had been robbed, would think a woman did it. Women, on the whole, didn't go in for this kind of stealing, so the majority would think that the woman was as much a thing of the imagination as the four thousand pounds.

I tried the obvious place first, under the bed. Nothing but a lot of fluff and a chamber pot. There was a cupboard built into the wall by the hearth; full of rubbish. A wardrobe with one or two sad drooping garments hanging. A trunk, filled with linen and lace, tablecloths and napkins. A cabinet, a big thing, made not of wood but some very shiny red stuff with figures of birds and people raised up on it and painted with gold. Empty except for some books.

I thought—Bugger it! She's hidden it under the floor or in a hole in the wall, or in her kitchen, where if I walk about and make a board creak, it'll be bang over Mike's head. So I swung round from the red cabinet and looked at her, meditating twisting her arm or something to *make* her tell the hiding place. But there was no need. Just looking at her told me. The organ-grinder's monkey's eyes that looked out over the scarf and handkerchief gave her away. She looked relieved. I turned back to the cabinet, purposefully, and then quickly looked at her again. She looked anxious. I was, in fact, like in the game of Hunt the Thimble, "hot." I took a step back and looked at the cabinet wondering what I'd missed. Nothing that I could see. It was a plain box-shaped thing, set up on four longish legs. It had only one door which opened in straightforward fashion onto the space which held the books. I looked round at the sides; it had two gilt handles which would make it easy to lift—easy, that is, for two men. But they'd also make it easy to pull the cabinet out a little way. She'd probably got her hoard in a hole in the wall behind the thing. So I laid hold of the handle and gave a good tug. I could hear her throwing herself about in the chair as well as she could with her arms and legs tied, so I knew I was on the right track. Hot and getting hotter. The cabinet didn't budge though. And if I couldn't move it, how could she? Then I gave up pulling at the handle and twisted it instead and there was a sharp sound, not exactly a crack, the sound a drawer makes when it's opened. And there, in the front of the cabinet, there was a drawer open. Shot out of its own accord from the base of the cabinet, under the place where the books lay. One of the cunningest hiding places in the world. You'd never have guessed. . . .

The drawer was crammed with little bags, made of different stuff and sewn with great clumsy stitches, but all the same size and shape. I picked one up and weighed it in my hand. It was money all right. I thought I should choke, my heart beat so hard and fast; but I thought—Keep your head, now! and began to put the bags, one after the other, into the flour sack I'd brought with me. I was intent on this, doing it as quickly and quietly as I could, when I heard a shuffle and then a great bump, and I turned. The old bitch had somehow managed to turn the chair clean over, just by throwing her body violently to one side. And not content with that, she was still heaving, unable to move the chair more than an inch or two, but managing to make it knock the floor every time.

I dropped the bag I was holding and stepped across to where she lay and put my hands on her neck and squeaked, "Stop that, or I'll strangle you." Even then she did another heave and the chair came down smack! I tightened my hands and pressed. Her whole body gave a violent spasm, which moved the chair on the floor once more, and for the last time. Then she lay still. I stood over her for a minute to make sure. Then I went back to putting the bags into the sack. I was nearly done when there was a tap on the door and Mike Saunders' voice, asking:

"You all right, Miss Walker?"

I moved close to her, ready to squeeze the breath out of her again, if she'd got it back already and attempted to move. Then the doorknob turned, and my stomach gave a great sickening heave. I'd made one bad, bad mistake. I'd neglected to lock or bolt the door behind me. So it opened; and there was Mike, holding a candlestick. He wore just his shirt, and his hair was all ruffled, his face thick with sleep. He looked at me, and then down at Miss Walker, and back at me. His ordinarily stupid face was idiotic with astonishment.

"What the hell . . ." he began.

I'd been doing some quick thinking. Even if there'd been a chance of rushing past him—and he looked almost stupefied enough to make that possible—he would be a witness to the fact that there had *been* a robbery. The only thing to do was to involve him as much as I could.

I daren't talk; the old woman might come round and hear our voices. So I put one finger to my lips, and with my other hand whipped the hat off my head. His eyes popped, his mouth fell open, but he didn't make a sound. I pointed to the landing outside and padded across, pulling the door almost closed behind me.

I whispered, "Don't speak loud, Mike. Is Millie awake?"

"What you doing, Dave?"

"Answer me. Is Millie awake?"

"No."

"You sure?"

"She got some stuff to make the baby sleep and took a dose herself. What you doing, Dave?"

"I'm robbing the old woman. I've got a thousand pounds."

"Christ! And she towd me herself she was hard up and had to sell the house."

That was the note to play on.

"Just the sort of mean old bitch she is. All the better for a little robbing, eh, Mike?"

"Hev you kilt her?"

"Of course not. She was banging about and I didn't want to wake Millie or the baby, so I squeezed the breath out of her."

"She looked a bit funny to me. Think we should chuck water on her or something?"

"Do that," I said, "and we'll both go to gaol till we're old, old men."

"*Me?* I ain't done nothing. Just come up in a neighbourly

way to know what she was knocking for. She been nervous lately and fixed I should come if she ever knocked."

"That wouldn't help you much. You live in the house, you're always hard up."

"But I never done nothing. You did, Dave."

"And you and I have been seen about together. You're in it, Mike, for good or bad. You can go and chuck water over her if you want to and tell her I robbed her. I shall tell a different tale. And we'll see who is believed."

He looked at me, bewildered and helpless. Just as Father could always bear me down, so I could Mike. He came to the end of his resistance and muttered:

"What you want I *should* do, then, Dave?"

"Just nothing. You go back and cuddle down alongside Millie and go to sleep. You didn't hear anything, you didn't see anything. You stick to that and I'll split with you, half and half. I meant to anyway, but I didn't say anything because I wasn't sure she had it."

"You mean you'll give me five hundred quid?"

"That's a fair half."

"For doing nowt?"

"Just for doing nothing at all. Everything must go on exactly as usual. She'll say a tall woman came in and robbed her. I don't think anybody'll believe *that*. And I've got a hiding place for the money, Mike, so safe that even if they did suspct *us* they could search for years and never find it. So long as you go on as usual, and if asked say you never heard or saw anything at all, we're safe—and we have the money. You'll have to wait a bit, then you can rent a house."

"Or go to London and be shut of Millie."

"You can do that as soon as you like. If you keep your mouth shut."

He said, and in the circumstances it struck me as being an odd thing to say:

"God bless you, Dave."

He started off down the stairs, paused, looked back, and asked:

"When'll I see you?"

"Thursday. At the Institute, as usual. Everything's got to be just as usual." I felt that I couldn't impress that upon him strongly enough; so I went a few stairs down and said, "Look, Mike. If the Sunday joint was missing and the dog was digging a great hole you'd guess he'd got it. If he was lying on the hearth, with his head on his paws, nobody'd suspect him. See? That's how we must act."

"I get you. Good night, Dave." He padded off back to bed.

Well, I'd been careless and my carelessness had cost me five hundred pounds. Still there was plenty left. I felt I'd dealt with the situation cleverly. I turned back into the room and hastily put the last of the bags into the sack, tied its mouth with twine, and carried it to the door. Then I gave my attention to the old woman.

In my plan I'd intended to gag and tie her and then at the end give her a bunny-punch just hard enough to knock her unconscious while I untied her and got away. Now, as I righted the chair and her bony old body sagged against its bonds, I saw that no punch would be necessary. Her eyes weren't shut, but they were set in a senseless stare.

I'd never seen anybody dead before, but I knew.

Except for an urgent desire to get away I didn't feel anything much. I hadn't intended to kill her; she'd brought that on herself, banging about and trying to attract Mike's attention. And nobody was going to grieve over the death of a mean, dirty, mad old woman.

I untied the string and put it back in my pocket. Then I loosened the gag. The scarf was wet, and smelt sour, as though she'd been sick. I left it hanging loosely round her neck, and pocketed the handkerchief.

One last careful look round. Nothing, absolutely nothing,

except the dead woman in the chair, to show that I had ever been there.

Before I left the house I looked out cautiously. Nobody about. Over at the *Rose and Crown* some men were singing, very tunelessly. From Market Square to the arch I walked holding the sack to my middle, like a woman carrying a bundle of washing. Under the arch, now darker than before, I stripped off the dress, pushed it and the hat into the sack, and put on my boots. After that I slung the bag over my shoulder and walked like a man.

Before I got to the Old Vine I turned sharp left along a little path which ran between our road, Abbot's Walk, and the turnpike, some distance away; it was a short cut which decent people used in daylight but never after dark because it was a great place for fornication. A few yards along it had a side turning, always called "the Alley," which went along the back of our shops until it was cut across by Robins the chemist's garden. He was the only one to have a garden; the rest of us just had back yards, piled with boxes and crates. His garden was long and narrow, made up of lawn and a few rose trees and a flower border which Mrs. Robins was very proud of, and right at the end there was a stone seat and a sundial. All round and behind the seat there were thick dark green bushes, the sort which should be kept clipped. I'd settled on that spot as my hiding place. Right behind the seat, lift the great down-sweeping boughs, and push the sack well home. Easy to get at when I wanted it, no digging, no mess.

I went upstairs and into our kitchen. Father was preaching out the next Sunday and was busy with his sermon. I hoped I looked ordinary; I hoped I didn't smell of the vinegar from the dress. Father's first words gave me a mild shock.

"Who went last to the vinegar cask?"

"You did. One of the young Arbers. Don't you remember? Twopennorth, and there was a crack in the jug. . . ."

"Bless me! And I've been blaming you. A proper puddle I found when I went down for some candles. I can smell it still."

"So can I. Well, good night, Father, good night, Mother. I'm off to bed."

I went to sleep as soon as I lay down, but towards morning I had a dream that turned into a nightmare. I dreamed I was with Lily, not in the London hotel, but in a freshly cut hayfield, the hay cocked up and very sweet-smelling. She began to strip, and it was better than ever. When she'd got down to her chemise she went behind another haycock, and I thought —She's teasing me, and waited. Then she came, and it wasn't Lily at all; it was Miss Walker, just as I'd seen her last.

I woke up, sweating like a pig, and couldn't get easy again, so I got out of bed and went and stood by my window, the window from which I could see Robins' garden. Dawn was just breaking, the sky was the colour of a rose, and everything looked fresh and beautiful. I looked at the bushes, which in that light seemed as solid as a wall, and thought of what they hid. And it was the most beautiful, wonderful morning I'd ever known.

Saturday was always a very busy day in the shop; it was a market day, like Wednesday, and men were paid; and then Father liked everything tidied away for Sunday. It was after ten when we sat down for our "tea." Mother said:

"You know, in a nice little village store with a post office, you wouldn't have to work nearly so hard. And you could give more time to the chapel."

Father did look a bit grey and worn, but he managed to laugh.

"Same old tale. 'The woman tempted me . . .' And I confess, I am tempted. Robins was saying he'll sell out for five thousand; Grigg says the same. And so would I, could I be sure it wasn't the U.P.R."

"But people wouldn't be *obliged* to buy from the U.P.R. if they didn't get good value."

"People are like sheep. They huddle together. And if they think they can save a penny they'll do it even if they waste threepence doing it. I couldn't sell to the U.P.R. with a good conscience. But short of them, then I will."

And that, I thought to myself, will be my chance. In a little village shop he wouldn't really want me. The whole way of life which now enclosed us, like the glass dome over those piles of wax fruit, would be shattered. In the general upheaval it would be easy for me to break away.

So then it was Sunday. Chapel in the morning. Cold roast mutton and jam tart for dinner. Sunday school in the afternoon. Marty and I were both teachers now, where formerly we'd been pupils. Sarah, because of her lame leg, was excused the extra walk. Marty liked the Sunday school because Mr. Phipps was the superintendent and she was sweet on him. For me it was the most tedious part of the whole week. Deal out the texts and have them read, one after the other. "Thou God seest me." "Swear not at all." "When my father and my mother forsake me, then the Lord shall take me up." (Once when I was about ten there'd been a kind of joke, everybody reading the same text, no matter what it said on his card, and one afternoon when the sixth boy running said that, forsaken by his father and mother, he would be taken up by the Lord, Mr. Phipps leaned over, took him by his collar, and lifted him clean over the back of the bench. I never forgot his face; he really thought the Lord had got him!)

And the long, long prayers; the wailing singing.

But it was over at last. Marty, Mr. Phipps, and I stepped out into the sunshine. And there was Mike Saunders leaning against the wall, waiting for me.

I said, "You go ahead. Tell Mother not to wait tea. I shan't be long."

Sunday tea was Sunday tea; half past four; Granny's flow-ered teapot; two sorts of cake, and, lately, Mr. Phipps.

Marty and Mr. Phipps went off and Mike said:

"Dave, I hadta tell you . . ."

"But I told you. Everything as usual. Is *this* usual?"

"No. But listen. All day yesterday, not a sound . . . Mostly, five o'clock, down for the rent. Not yesterday. So today Millie say, 'What about the rent?' Well, you say act like you would ordinary, so I did. I took it up. Dave, she was dead in her chair. I towd you I reckoned she looked funny, din't I?"

"Yes, you did. You said she looked funny, and now she's dead. What do you want to do about it?"

"*Me?*"

"Well, who else? Who else knows?"

"You do, Dave."

"Yes. You met me out of Sunday school and told me that when you went to pay your rent you found your landlady dead in her chair. What am *I* supposed to do about it?"

"Tell me what to do."

"I've told you once what to do. Nothing. If you must be a busybody you can go and tell the coroner."

"Then there'd be an inquest. Lot of questions."

"Sure to be."

He looked at me, completely confused, miserable.

"I never towd Millie," he said.

"Oh? Why not? Surely that would be the natural thing to do. When you do break the news, that will look rather odd, don't you think?"

He said, "Whass got into you, Dave? I on'y come to *tell* you. I suppose next thing you'll be saying you never promised me the five hundred quid."

"I keep my bargains. You've broken yours. I told you to do nothing. Just behave as you ordinarily would." I looked him straight in the eye. "Any other week if she hadn't come for the rent what would you have said. 'If the owd bitch don't want it, all the better for us!' Wouldn't you?"

"I reckon I would. Specially after we had notice. But I was worried. Her being so quiet."

"You worry too easily, Mike. First you worry because she's noisy, then you worry because she's quiet."

I wanted her left there as long as possible; till the flesh rotted from her bones if that could be. I didn't know much about the police, or how they handled crime, partly because Father would only take a weekly paper which gave a summing up of the more important happenings in the world and for the rest was devoted to Methodist doings. But I'd heard talk. The police were very clever these days; they might find marks on the old girl's throat, or wonder about the sick-smelling scarf. I was sure that except for Mike—and I'd fixed him as well as I could— there was nothing to connect me with the crime; nonetheless, the longer the discovery was put off the better I should like it. And the less this stupid lout was concerned, the better I should like it too.

"You ain't being much help, Dave," he said, reproachfully.

"I've told you what to do. What more do you expect?"

He had no answer to that. We walked a little way; then he said:

"That ain't very nice, you know, living there and knowing whass just overhead. I din't sleep much last night. Nor I don't fancy my grub."

"Why not do what Millie wants and go and live at the Forge? You'll have to do it in the end, anyway."

"—— Millie, and her dad, and the Forge. I gotta better idea. Dave, could you let me hev my share right away? Wouldn't make no difference to you, would it? I could just take my lot and go off to London. What you say?"

I thought it over and considered it an excellent plan. Millie'd run straight home to her father. And Millie wasn't the girl to go climbing stairs to say good-bye, or proffer a week's rent for what she hadn't had.

"You see," Mike said, "soon she'll stink, and that I just couldn't stand."

How soon would she stink? In the Bible Lazarus did, after three days. But that was a hot country. And at Number 4 it'd be a real good stink that made itself known over Millie's baby's smell. But sooner or later, if they stayed, Millie *would* notice.

"I think you're right. Look, I have to go home to tea now. This evening there's chapel. Dark at eight. You know the Alley, back of our shops. I'll meet you there as soon after eight as I can."

"You're my savation, Dave. I can get off first thing in the morning. No more Millie; no more Platt. . . ."

I was lucky. Father was still away on his day's preaching and Mother was easier to handle. I told her it had been stuffy in chapel—which it was—and that I had a bit of a headache and meant to take a walk. "I shan't go far, or be long," I promised. She and the girls set off for home. I turned the other way, walked briskly as far as the Cattle Market, to give them time to get home, then turned and went that way myself, going into the Alley, where I climbed the wall and dropped into Robins' garden. I could see Robins' parlour window lighted, and now and again heard some laughter; I guessed they'd got friends in, having a game of cards. I could see our kitchen window too; not so brightly lit. I knew exactly what was going on inside. The cocoa was mixed in the cups, the kettle was about to boil, one of the two cakes we had had for tea was being brought out. Mother would be saying, "We'll wait for your father, and David. . . ."

My treasure was safe. I counted out five hundred pounds for Mike, took one for my pocket, hid the sack again, and went back over the wall. Mike was waiting. He almost cried when I gave him the money.

"I never really thought it was true. Bless you, Dave . . . best pal anybody ever had."

"Now don't do anything silly; and get away as fast as you can."

"I will that. I'm on'y sorry I shan't be seeing you no more."

"I may get to London one day myself." But his London and mine would be poles apart. We shook hands and said good-bye. I was home in the kitchen about five minutes before Father.

Next day I broke my own rule about everything going as usual. I was slicing bacon when I heard the first London train —the eight-thirty—pull out. I thought of Mike being on it, and I envied him. Maybe that thought started up a restlessness in me. I felt a bit like I had when I was running in the team races for my school, standing on my line, waiting for the boy before me to hand me the stick; as though an engine was inside me, building up more and more speed, and I could hardly wait for the time when I could start. By teatime, which, it being Monday, was early, I knew that I couldn't go through with the usual Monday evening procedure; Temperance Meeting at half past seven—"My drink is water bright, water bright . . ." and when that was over a talk with Mr. Phipps about whether readings from the New Testament or the Old were more suitable for the old folks in the workhouse. He believed—rightly— that the Old Testament had the more entertaining stories and held their attention better, "But you have to be so careful to avoid the coarse expressions," he said.

For the first time since they had been started, except on a rare Monday when I'd had a heavy cold, I decided to skip the Temperance Meeting. I'd skip it and go to the *Pot of Flowers*. And if Father found out and said, "You're no son of mine; never darken my doors again," they'd be the most welcome words I'd ever heard in my life.

To get to the *Pot of Flowers* I had to go over Market

Square. I glanced at Number 4. Millie had a light on, and her curtains drawn all crooked.

There were three men in the pub, all standing together and talking to Bill Cobbold. I didn't want him to serve me; I wanted Lily to see my sovereign, and I wanted to buy her a port and have the same myself and stand and drink it with her. If you could forget the counter it was almost like being out *with* her.

I heard Bill Cobbold say:

"I shoulda *known*, I s'pose." And one of the men said:

"You just get took advantage of, thass what I always say."

I had taken my stand at Lily's end of the bar and did nothing to call attention to myself.

After a minute Bill Cobbold half turned to me and asked what I wanted.

"No hurry," I said. "I'll wait for Lily."

"Then you'll wait the hell of a long time!"

One of the men laughed.

"Why? What's happened?" Try as I might, my voice sounded thin and squeaky, as though it had gone back to one of the two alternatives it had had when it was breaking.

"She's gone."

"Gone where?" That time, determined not to squeak, I growled.

"I neither know nor care," Bill Cobbold said. He added a few very uncomplimentary things about Lily. "Spring in the air, no doubt, and maybe she had a fancy to go back to Strawless and have a nice bite of roast hedgehog!"

"There never was a Cattermole pupped that you could rely on. I wonder you put up with her, Bill. Often wondered that, so I did. No doubt you had good reason, though."

There was some sniggering.

"You can stow that, Jonas," Bill Cobbold said, quite angrily. "My missus is good enough for me. And I never did have no fancy for them black-a-vised sort. Bad as foreigners, they are to me."

"What happened?" I asked again.

"Nothing. Went off last night. 'Clear up here in the morning,' she say. 'Smorning she didn't come and didn't come, so about twelve I sent the boy round to her place. Packed up and gone, bag and baggage."

I felt my face go stiff. My ears rang and Bill and all the bottles and casks went spinning off down a sort of funnel, dark at the end. I'd never fainted in my life, but I recognised the symptoms; and I knew the cure. People sometimes came over funny in chapel in warm weather. "Get your head down, and breathe deep," they'd be told. So I bent and busied myself with my bootlace and breathed deep. When I straightened up there was Bill Cobbold still waiting to serve me.

"I'll have a . . . rum," I said.

Mike, when he lived at home with his mother and hardly paid anything for his keep, had been a rum drinker. He once said that it put heart into you. He was right too. I took too big a gulp at first and nearly quackled myself, had to stop and cough and splutter, but after that I had the knack; it wasn't stuff to swill down, like beer. It went down, warm and comforting, and when I'd had two I felt myself again, and hopeful. Lily was a funny one, I thought to myself; probably something had upset her blessed pride, something a lout like Bill Cobbold wouldn't even have noticed, so she'd made up her mind to quit and told old Mrs. Pagney, her landlady, what to say if Bill sent down for her. That was about it. And me, breaking out all of a sweat and nearly chucking a faint. Daft!

I left the four of them talking, and, once outside, hurried to Baker Street. It was no distance. I was so sure that she was there that when Mrs. Pagney came to the door I asked could I see Miss Cattermole.

"But she ain't here. She come in last night and said she was off in the morning."

"Where to?"

"She didn't say. And I had no cause to ask. She paid Saturday, and last night she give me a week's money instead of notice. Thass all I know."

"But think . . . think . . . She must have said something. How'd she go? How'd she get her stuff away? Did a cart come for her?"

"She went in the train. Half past eight. And somebody came and helped with her bags to the station."

"Who?"

"Well, I don't know his name, though I seen him about. Did a job here once. Nice-looking young fellow. Carpenter. Work for Platt . . ."

IV

There's a little old pub we never go in, the *Hawk in Hand*, tucked away behind the Assembly Rooms. I go in there, but I don't stay. Not because somebody might see me. Father, Mother, Christ, and the Twelve Apostles could all walk in and see me drinking and I wouldn't care tonight. But I've got to be alone. Somewhere quiet where I can think. So I buy a bottle of rum and I go off into the Abbey Gardens.

"Gardens" is more a name of hope than truth. The council are always hoping to make this place into what the Baildon *Free Press* calls "a place of refreshment and recreation for the citizens of this borough who, with every passing month, find themselves more and more cut off from the country lanes they walked in childhood." But the citizens aren't interested in places of recreation and refreshment; they only want their rates kept down. So just inside the big gateway there's a little tended piece, a bit of lawn and some beds full of whatever flower is in season; and behind that there's a wilderness. This is another fornicating place and people like Father think it should be railed in where the wall is down, and have a gate put in the gateway. But that would cost money too; and as Mr. Robins said, the fornicators would only go somewhere else.

Tonight there's nobody about. And it's dark. So I don't go far in, just to where there's a bit of ruin the right height to sit on. I sit there and drink rum. I need heartening.

I'm like Bill Cobbold. I should have known, I suppose. The way Lily spoke about Millie; the way she was concerned as to whether Mike was upset about getting notice. Little things. But they showed. Lot of other little things too, that I overlooked at the time, no doubt.

She fooled me. So did Mike. And he's the one I'm going to get my own back on. Somehow. Just sit here quietly, don't get excited, and something will come to you. As old Miss Walker said, "There *must* be something."

There's St. Mary's; eight o'clock. Only eight. But people together for the first time go to bed early—I know I would. Right now she may be undressing for *him*. *He's* the one will lie on the bed and watch her take her clothes off, and let down her hair, and then feel it, slippery against the warm flesh. . . .

Steady now. That's the kind of thought that gives you the feeling you might burst; your brain swelling against your skull bones, your heart trying to break out of your chest. Mustn't think like that . . . Just keep calm and think, and *plan* something.

Start with the facts. Miss Walker is upstairs, dead in her chair, and Mike who lived just below is gone off with five hundred pounds in gold.

But you can't do anything about that—not without showing you know more than you should. And he'd turn straight round and say you'd done it and gave him the money. They might think he was lying, or they might not. And he's so bloody stupid, whereas you're known to be bright; after all, you did win a Webster, though you never went to the Grammar. No, it must be . . . you must think . . . tie Mike up either with something stupid, or . . . wait, wait . . . or something only *he* would have done. If he left his tools, and you went in and sawed the old girl's head off. Or gashed her neck with a chisel. But you don't like mess . . . and to get the tools . . . remember Millie's still there.

Now Millie. Over and over again Mike's said to you he'd like to wring her neck; he'd swing for her, he said.

Go easy, that bursting, ready-to-fly-to-pieces feeling is coming on again. Be calm. Take a swig of the heartener. Once Mr. Robins, defending his way of life to Father, said something about wine making glad the heart of man. Is rum wine? Port is, I know. I meant to buy Lily port by the bottleful, and the dress she should always have had, crimson velvet, bunched up behind, and earrings to match. . . .

Carry on like that and you'll never get anywhere. Go back to Millie. There's the old woman, choked to death upstairs; suppose Millie *and* the baby were choked downstairs. Wouldn't that look like the work of the same hand? And for *three* surely they'd track him down, get the London police busy. His tale about me would sound pretty thin, then, wouldn't it? Why would I choke Millie and the baby? And am I a penny the better off? Whereas Mike had enough to go rushing off to London with his fancy piece.

There's another thing too. About how the body is discovered. Make it three, and Strongarm Fickling would. In his rough way he's fond of Millie and if she didn't go round to the Forge. . . .

So that just shows. You can't think things out carefully enough. Mike went off this morning. Lily, Mrs. Pagney, the man in the ticket office . . . If anybody's *seen* Millie today this is just a burst bubble. If nobody has, well, that's different. Things like this have to be taken one step at a time. And the first step is to go and see Millie. There's still some rum left.

Shove the bottle down out of sight behind the bit of ruin. No need to waste. And you might need it again. It all depends. . . .

V

Millie said, "Hullo, Dave. Mike ain't home yet. He never said he'd be late, but I reckon I know what he's up to."

"Working late?"

"No. Hunting some place to go. I want to go back and live with my dad, but that don't suit Mike. Well, whatever he find, I shan't go. Why pay rent, I say, when Dad'd be happy to have us. I was just making myself a cuppa cocoa. You like one?"

"No, thank you. Too warm. It's been a nice day, Millie. Did you get out?"

"No. 'Smatter of fact I slept late. Weeks and weeks we had bad nights with the baby. Now I got this stuff. I give her hers and then myself a dose. I been making up for the sleep I lost."

"You miss the milkman?"

"No. Lately I been putting the jug out overnight. I only went to take it in just now, for my cocoa. I had just enough of yesterday's for the baby."

(Once I'd said to Mother, just for something to say, that Mike's baby cried a lot, and she'd said she wondered if it was fed properly. None of us ever cried, except with wind.)

"The baby's quiet," I said.

"Thass the stuff. We've had a bit of peace since I got that. Wish I'd thought of it before. Her, up there, she been quiet too. She used to lump about something awful." She stirred sugar into her cocoa. "I never known Mike be so late. He know I don't *like* being alone. Thass one reason why I shall be glad to be back at the Forge. Always somebody about there."

"Yes. I always think women like you have lonely lives. Or do you have a lot of visitors, Millie?"

"Visitors! Last person, except you or Miss Walker, ever come to see me, was at Christmas, begging for the Christmas Parcels. They can find you when they want anything!"

"You mean I'm the first person you've seen today?"

"I mean just that. And between you and me, that suit Mike. Thass why he's against the Forge; he's jealous, see?"

"I don't wonder. You're a very pretty girl, Millie."

"I was all right, once. But making the best of yourself is wasted, when all you see is your dad, and your husband, and a grizzly baby."

"And me, Millie. You have very pretty hair."

"It's soft too," she said, in a coy, dreamy voice. "Soft and fine. Some girls have hair like a horse's tail. Mine's like the fringe on a silk shawl. Feel. . . ."

She actually put her silly head forward for me to feel.

For all she was young and strong she died a lot easier than old Miss Walker had. Not even a jerk. The old woman had known me for an enemy and fought to the end; Millie gave herself to me like a lover. And the baby didn't take a minute.

I looked into the milk jug. Millie'd taken just enough for her one cup of cocoa. Nobody'd notice that. I set it on the top of the steps, in the right place. Then I looked right, left, right, left. Nobody in sight; more important, in the darkness, nobody within hearing.

I shut the door behind me.

I felt light and free. And why not? I had all that money hidden. I'd got my own back on Mike. There was Lily, of course. But Solomon had had three hundred of them, and Ahasuerus who knew how many? I should find another, just as good, and another and another. One day . . . very soon . . .

INTERLUDE

Mike Saunders, protesting his innocence to the end, was hanged. The trial was sensational, but not one person in a thousand believed the theory proffered by the defence and cried by the accused from the dock. "I never did it. It was Dave Armstrong!"

A customer in the grocer's shop, activated less by positive malice than by mischief, did say to Samuel:

"Funny, his picking your boy to put the blame on, weren't it?" and waited to see the flinch that such a barb should cause.

"It was all he could think of, poor wicked boy," Samuel said, his hands steady on the blue sugar bag he was making with the practised twist and turn that looked so easy. "My David was a friend of his, went in and out of his house."

"In and outa the *Pot of Flowers*, too, if what I hear is right."

"It can't be. David signed the pledge as soon as he could write. Besides, there's never been an hour, scarcely even a minute, when I didn't know where David was. When would he have time to go to pubs and murder people?"

But later on in that day Samuel Armstrong took counsel with himself. One fact stood out very clearly; David had been Mike's friend. Friend to a murderer, an adulterer, and drunkard—who else would run off with a barmaid?

There was Marty too. Losing her heart to Mr. Phipps. Week by week that became plainer to see. And he'd never marry her. Samuel knew that. He'd known Mr. Phipps for a long time; he was a good man, active in well-doing, but he wasn't a marrying man. He was, in fact, like one of those old tomcats, kept as pets, tame and good, fat and sleek, but no longer properly male. He'd walked out for two years with one of the ministers' daughters, he'd been on very friendly terms with a succession of young women Sunday-school teachers; and he was now going on for fifty. At that age people didn't suddenly *change*.

The boy getting into bad company; one daughter wasting her time and natural affection, one lame and ailing; and a wife who wanted to live in the country, and, hardly to be considered, but none the less true, his own increasing weariness at the end of a busy day. Everything pointing in the one direction. God made the country; man made town. He'd often thought, on his way to or from a preaching appointment, that the hand of the Almighty showed nowhere more plainly than in a wind-ruffled cornfield, or a spray of wild roses sprawling over a hedge.

That week's Baildon *Free Press*, though largely devoted to an account of Mike Saunders' trial, had kept its advertisement space for the proper purpose, and under the heading "For Sale" there was a small general store, with post office, at Minsham All Saints. And under "Wanted" somebody was advertising for premises, "one room minimum size 30 feet by 24" with living accommodation and preferably a garden. "Near town centre or station." It did not say that a garden was essential. And pacing his shop from the stairs to the door, and then crosswise, Samuel discovered that it exceeded the minimum required by three feet in one direction and four in the other.

He hadn't lived all these years without recognising the hand of God when it reached down and pointed.

Alfredo Crispi, who had framed and posted off the advertisement, was not a believer in divine guidance, for there is no less credulous creature than your lapsed cradle Catholic. Alfredo believed in Alfredo Crispi's nose, which had seldom led him wrong. He had left his native Naples twenty years earlier and come to London where he had worked as a chef, lived very hard, and saved a little money. He had bought a small share in an eating house near Liverpool Street Station and eventually married his partner's younger daughter, Elsie. There was another daughter, Dora, to whom, with her husband, Alfredo's partner (when he died in 1888) had left his share of the business. There had been nothing but rows ever since. That the English were a phlegmatic, unexcitable race was disproved by Dora and Elsie twenty times a day, and Alfredo, a peace-loving man, had begun to dream of a place of his own, in the country. He dreamed in terms of the cafés of his native land, of awnings, of tree-shaded open places.

He picked on Baildon because once, long ago, before he and Elsie were married, they had made a day trip to a place called Bywater and had been obliged to change trains at Baildon and to spend forty minutes there. Alfredo remembered the wide street that led from the station, and a great open space called Market Square. He'd always remembered it, and one evening, when Elsie and Dora had quarrelled with a vigour few Neapolitans could have matched, Alfredo had written his advertisement, bought a postal order for five shillings, and addressed an envelope "To the Local Paper, Baildon, Suffolk."

And the nose had been right. He'd had two answers. Neither place was ideal, of course, though both were in the positions that he favoured. The one on Market Square, Number 4, had no large room; the one in Abbot's Walk, one minute from the station, had no garden. But in this life you cannot have everything.

He took a day off and came to Baildon. He looked carefully at the grocer's shop at Number 3, the Old Vine. It was, by far, the more expensive of the two properties; the business was a going concern and there was goodwill to be considered. So he passed on and looked at Number 4, Market Square. It was shabby, but it could be made pretty, and the open space was an attraction, but it was far too small. Only two bedrooms, and Alfredo had four daughters. The downstairs room was small, too, and there was no possibility of carrying out his plan for knocking down a wall and enlarging it.

Slightly dashed, he went across to the *Rose and Crown* and, not wishing to seem foreign and eccentric, did not drink wine, which he liked, but beer, which he detested.

Somebody standing near him said:

"Just see you come outa Number 4, din't I?"

"That iss so."

Elsie, though she loved Alfredo, detested any reminder of his origin, and she had, over the years, taken him up so sharply and so often that except for a sibilance about the letter "s," and a slight formality of phrase which even Elsie could not pin down—though she once said that he talked like the Bible—Alfredo could have passed for English almost anywhere except in Baildon, where even people from Bury St. Edmunds were reckoned foreigners.

"You a foreigner?" Alfredo's neighbour asked.

"I am Italian—but I have lived in England more than twenty years now."

"You thinking of buying that place?"

"No. It lacks space."

"You ain't missed much. It ain't a place I'd want any doings with. Three people murdered there, little while back, *and* laid ten days afore they was found."

"Indeed!"

The man by Alfredo's side, helped out here and there by the publican, told the whole dramatic story with especial emphasis on the blameworthy behaviour of the milkman, who, finding poor Mrs. Saunders' Monday milk still on the step on Tuesday morning, had simply taken it for granted that she had gone home to her dad, "as she was always threatening to do." And wasn't it peculiar that her dad, Strongarm Fickling, who ordinarily would have been worried by Millie's not going round to the Forge, wasn't worried that week because she'd been round and said she was coming home to live and had a lot of clearing up to do. So it was ten days before he went round to see how the clearing up was going, and so discovered the tragedy. "Never been the same man since, Strongarm ain't."

Alfredo was heartily glad that the little house hadn't been suitable for his purpose. He finished his beer and turned back to the Old Vine. When he and Samuel met, honest man recognised honest man, different as they might be in all inessentials. Their business was transacted with the minimum of fuss and the maximum of expediency and goodwill.

Elsie said, "And in the new place we're going to call ourselves Crisp, which is a good English name. Alfred Crisp you'll be, from now on."

She would have denied with vehemence that marriage to Alfredo had changed her almost as much as she had changed him, and that she had acquired, together with some of his formality of speech, much of the matriarchal dignity of the Italian peasant woman who is so often the mental and physical superior of her husband. She was always known as "Mamma"; in every place except the kitchen, where Alfredo ruled, her word was law. Her girls were all given English names—Rose, Edith, Mary, Dorothy. It was her intention that they should all marry Englishmen. She was so English that it never occurred to her that her scorn of all things foreign—except, of course, cooking—could ever hurt Alfredo's feelings; or that it showed a marked ingratitude to a nation which had provided her with a singularly kind, industrious, and indulgent husband.

Life was preparing a rather ironic and subtle revenge. In her youth she had been very fair with hair the colour, as Alfredo put it, "of honey"; and her cheeks had been pink. As she aged her hair darkened and then greyed, her face grew sallow. Her dignity, her devotion to the business, her always being called "Mamma" set her apart a little. Crisp's Eating House specialised in Italian dishes, and the new owner had once, somewhere, to someone, said something about Italy. But Crisp was a good old English name; so in Baildon it was always believed that Alfredo was Cockney and Elsie Italian.

Samuel Armstrong bought the stores at Minsham and moved there with his wife and two daughters. Not his son. Ever since the trial of Mike Saunders David had been awkward, and who could wonder? He refused to go out and complained that people were talking about him.

"It'll be different at Minsham. And why should you fret about talk? You know your conscience is clear."

"It'll be worse at Minsham. They'll all have read the papers. They all know what Mike *said*. The only place where I'd ever feel comfortable again is London. . . ."

The big, bad city; the biggest of them all; riddled with vice, temptations at every street corner. Samuel was dubious. But the boy was a good boy, well brought-up, he could be trusted. Besides, a Methodist had a family everywhere. One of the ministers from Baildon had gone to Shoreditch; he'd find the boy a job, and a lodging with decent people, and keep an eye on him. So David went to Shoreditch, where he stayed a remarkably short time; he had found, he wrote, a far better job in Kensington; nice lodgings too. That he was working well and being careful with his money, and had not forgotten his family, was proved by the fact that from time to time he sent presents, things which, by the look of them, must have cost quite a bit. . . .

In Baildon no more was heard of Mr. Turnbull's mysterious client. The inquiry had come from a multiple firm of clothiers who had had their spies out, looking for suitable properties cheap in every town in England with a population of twelve thousand and over, *and* a market. They'd found just what they wanted in Colchester, and that was enough for that area at the moment.

Crisp's Eating House prospered; but it was never popular with its immediate neighbours. Clean as it undoubtedly was, there was too much cooking in oil, too much of something called garlic, which was something like onion but more penetrating and lingering. When the wind blew one way Ashworth's ribbons and laces, sheets and tablecloths absorbed the odour; when it blew the other way Robins' orrisroot was affected.

The clientele, too, came in for some criticism. Wild young men, driving wild-eyed young horses in gigs, eager to assert that they were men of the world by eating foreign kickshaws at nine o'clock at night. Commercial travellers, scorning the sound table d'hôte of the Station Hotel and walking on to eat fish fried in oil, potatoes cooked in some heathenish fashion, and ice cream, which to the average good Baildon citizen was something clean against nature.

No doubt about it, the neighbourhood was going down. Equally without doubt was the fact that a great many customers went to the Eating House on account of the girls. Three of them were fair-haired, pink-cheeked, plump and merry, and—behind Mamma's back—very come-hitherish. The fourth was quite different, tall, dark-haired, stuck-up. Give her an order and she'd look down her nose as if she wondered whether you could pay for it; crack a joke and she'd act like she was stone deaf. She could put a plateful of food down on the table as though she were doing you a favour; and whereas all the others, until they were married, were called by their Christian names, she was always "Miss Crisp." And Miss Crisp she would remain. . . .

MARY CRISP'S TALE

It was November again, the month I hate most in all the year
—at least, in the town. When I was younger and had more free
time I used to walk in the country, and there, even in November, there'd be a charm. The grey weather saying "hush, hush"
and everywhere so still; the red berries shining damply in the
black hedges. But in a town, particularly when you live near a
station, where the smoke from the trains hangs in the foggy
air, November is a dirty, depressing month, and the spring
seems a long way off.

I was feeling low-spirited, too, because I'd just had my
birthday. Thirty. A landmark in any woman's life. It seemed
to me that for years I'd gone on, clinging to little hopes, some
that could be openly acknowledged, for instance that some
new stuff called Curlmore would put a wave into my hair,
some so secret and private and outrageous that I hardly dared
acknowledge them to myself. Then the bell rings. Thirty.
What is there left to hope for? You may not be dead for another forty years, but life is over.

Everybody always said, "Mary is so sensible," "Mary has
her head screwed on the right way," "What a comfort it is to
think that Mary is still at home," "What would we do without
Mary?" I admit that I *looked* sensible; I'd inherited Mamma's
tall, spare figure and rather hard face, and Papa's dark colouring. I was always well dressed in a plain way; ribbons and
laces and feathers didn't suit me, and I knew it; the only
trimmings I ever wore were my garnet earrings, and my fob

watch on its garnet pin, and bands of velvet set into my skirts and sleeves. I never wore an apron, even in the café, none of us ever did, Mamma did not approve.

On this particular November afternoon in 1913, I'd put on my new winter dress, a dark crimson wool, with velvet insets. I wore it to cheer myself, not for anyone else's benefit. Quite apart from my being thirty, plain—and as proud as Lucifer— there was never anybody in our place in those days worth impressing. All three of my sisters had married customers and married well, prosperous young farmers or dealers in a big way; but they'd worked in the café when Crisp's was the fashion, new and different and exciting. Father was an Italian —his real name, and so I suppose ours too, was Crispi—and he had been a wonderful cook, "chef," perhaps I should say. Before whatever it was that happened to him, happened, and he lost interest, he would take endless trouble to make dishes that were specialities, and that looked as good as they were. Things were different now. We still served minestrone instead of the Brown Windsor soup that was dished up four or five times a week at the Station Hotel; and we offered spaghetti with cheese, or tomato, or meat sauce—all three if anybody fancied them: and we still offered several different kinds of cheese, supplied by a place in Soho. But our clientele had narrowed down to commercial travellers—of whom there were more every week that passed—and a few regulars who knew that we gave good value for money, interspersed, now and again, by people from trains, people too poor or too shy to face the dining room at the Station Hotel.

The man who came in at about half past seven on this November evening was one of these casual customers. He chose a table by the door, and had his back to me when I first saw him. He was tall and thin and wore what was called a "Norfolk" jacket, made of good tweed, but shabby. Lately the commercial travellers had taken to wearing country clothes. I could remember when they all dressed like bank clerks, but in the country, as one had explained to me, it was better for business to look like a countryman. So, from the back, as this man seated himself rather slowly and cautiously in his chair, I reckoned that he was a commercial, probably cattle food or fertiliser, and had had a long journey and not yet walked off the train cramp in the short distance between the station and our place.

When I had moved round to the opposite side of the table to take his order, I wasn't so sure. He had the face of a gentleman. My sister Dora once called me "a howling snob," and about that I wouldn't argue; her husband made five hundred a year, but he dropped his aitches and I wouldn't, for that one reason, have married him if he had been making fifteen hundred a year. So maybe what she said was true. And it is, I admit, hard to define how a gentleman looks, because no two are alike. And it's nothing to do with manners . . . no, I'm wrong there; it has nothing to do with politeness. Sir Albert Fennel, who once came to our place at five o'clock in the afternoon, because he'd missed his lunch and the Station Hotel had only offered him their set tea, was one of the rudest old men I ever waited upon, but rude in a gentlemanly way. And though he was dressed like a tramp who had recently robbed a scarecrow he looked like a gentleman too.

So did this man.

His voice confirmed my opinion. It wasn't the fake, "Ay'd laike the minnestonee," which to me was as bad as dropped aitches. And he didn't look me over, summing up the chances and then obviously discarding hope because I was thirty, hard-featured and sensible-looking. He just looked at me, observing that I was there, waiting to take his order, and said, "Good evening," before ordering spaghetti with cheese sauce. It was the least you could order, and with anyone else I should have taken no trouble at all. But I could tell. He was used to better things, he'd come down in the world. So I said:

"We sell Chianti by the glass."

That was Papa's idea; he was very fond of Chianti himself, and even Mamma, observant as she was, couldn't know exactly how many glasses made up one of the big, wicker-cased flasks.

"Do you indeed?" He seemed to take counsel with himself and then said, yes, he'd like a glass. I was careful to see that his spaghetti went onto one of the few pretty flowered plates still in use, and I gave him one of the old wineglasses.

Then the evening rush was on. Every time the door opened to let somebody in or out a drift of smoke-scented fog came in and made a halo round the gas globes. In the kitchen Papa worked halfheartedly, helped or hindered by the boy who was supposed to be learning to be a cook, but hadn't the brains to learn anything: Mamma, with a rug over her knees and her sticks propped by her side, sat in the little glass cash desk by the door: I did all the serving. An ordinary, nasty November night. . . .

It seemed to me that more people than usual chose fish-and-chips, and the reek that followed me every time I came out of the kitchen added itself to the smell of the station in November. I could remember the time when Papa would use only the very best olive oil for his frying, Lucca oil, and every evening one of the last things he did was to pour what he had used through a fine muslin to strain out any little pieces which, left in and fried again the next day, turned black and smelt of burning. Nowadays he no longer bothered with things like that; he bought cheap, unnamed oil and used it again and again.

I often wondered what exactly had happened to Papa. The funny thing was that I thought I knew the very day, the very moment when it happened. Just when he'd got the very thing he'd wanted and waited for—half of Robins' ground floor, and the garden. Robins the chemist had never been a very pleasant neighbour to us, complaining of the cooking smells—which in those days were negligible compared with now—and ordering his daughters not to be friendly with us. We were all glad when he sold out to a man who made boots and saddles and gloves. As it turned out, he didn't want to live at the Old Vine, he already had a house and garden on the outskirts of the town; so he sold Papa the back rooms and the kitchen and the garden, and leased the upper rooms as a "flat," which was then a new idea in Baildon.

The garden was the only one within sight of us and Papa had always envied it; he'd stand at a back window and say what he would do with it if ever he could get hold of it. He'd build a greenhouse against the south wall and grow things out of season; he'd have a herb garden; he'd grow his own vegetables.

He took possession of it on Lady Day, March the twenty-fifth, in the year 1896. I was thirteen, and Edith, my young sister, was eleven. It was a pleasant fine afternoon; Mamma and Rose and Dorothy were busy indoors, so we, and Papa, went to "take possession" of our new property. Papa was so pleased, if he'd been a dog he'd have been wagging his tail. He went through all his plans again and finally, at the very end of the garden, sat down on a stone seat which was all surrounded by dark bushes and which faced a sundial. Edith hit me on the shoulder and said, "You're It," and ran away. I chased her and hit her and made her "It" so that she had to chase me. We dodged round the rose trees, and the seat and the sundial; it was fine to have a place of our own to play in. We lost count of time, which didn't matter because what help we gave in the business wasn't yet enough to count; but Papa lost count, too, and Rose came to call him, saying that the London train was almost due.

It may sound fanciful and fantastic to say so, but he got off that seat a different man. He'd sat down fulfilled, happy, full of plans, and he rose . . . what?

He paused by us and said, "Enjoy yourselves while you can, my children." There was sadness in his voice, and the liveliness had gone out of his eyes, the spring from his step. I noticed, without understanding; and it is true to say that it was a long time, years, in fact, before the change in him showed enough for anyone else to see. I saw because, at the age of thirteen, my head was stuffed with the wildest fancies; I still had a fondness for any story with magic in it. I told myself that there was something about that stone seat, or the sundial; I made up a whole story to myself, that whoever sat there and looked at the sundial would be changed. . . .

One day, towards the end of that term, almost shuddering with excitement and the sense of my own daring, I tried it myself. I'd had a hateful day at school. I always thought I did very good essays and more often than not my teacher thought so too; mine were generally chosen to be read aloud. That week mine had been marked six out of ten and given the remark, in red ink, "Too fanciful," and a girl named Fanny Smith had had hers read out. So, if the seat changed you, I could do with it very well.

It didn't change me; but the odd thing was that as I sat there the thought came, and grew and wrapped itself around me, that really I was worrying about a very trivial matter. Fanny Smith's precious essay would be forgotten next week, would one day be just some faded writing in an old exercise book. And Fanny Smith would be a fat dull woman, with a fat dull husband and a lot of children, while I, Mary Crisp, would be another Marie Corelli. That was my secret dream. Marie Corelli stood for something that I could never explain; it was important to me that our initials were the same.

So, in a backhanded kind of way, I was right about the stone seat. I'd sat down feeling low in my mind, and got up strengthened and confident. Another thing that Miss Morley's red ink would condemn as "Too fanciful."

But from that day, Papa was changed. Little by little, an inch at a time, he seemed to retreat. Once—and I must then have been fifteen—I went into a room and heard Mamma say:

"Well, if that's the way you feel the best thing you can do is find a priest and get yourself taken back into the fold." She didn't say it unkindly; just in her downright, practical way, as though she were advising somebody with toothache to go and visit the dentist.

There again I was mixed in my feelings; I wasn't, truth to tell, very fond of my Mamma, but I did *admire* her. When we were small she'd slap us about left and right, but let anyone else so much as throw a rude word at us and she'd put on her hat and go out and raise Cain. "Put on your hat" in our family became a joke; it was a battle cry. She knew nothing about my secret ambitions, the agony of work and hope I'd put into my essays, but if I'd ever told her that Miss Morley had written "Too fanciful" on an essay of mine, she'd have put on her hat and gone round to the school and given my teacher a piece of her mind. I could just imagine it. "Fanciful, and what else do you expect a child to write when you give it such a damn silly subject as 'The World in Twenty Years' Time'? What can it be but fancy?"

And then there was the way she dealt with her affliction. That didn't happen until I was twenty-five. She'd had twinges of rheumatism ever since we'd come to Baildon; the east wind blew there very often and almost everybody at some time or another had a stiff neck, or knee or elbow. Mamma was very lame on Edith's wedding day, but she wouldn't use a stick, she held Papa's arm and managed. But the next day she had a stick and said it was very helpful. Six months later she had two and gave up using the stairs. "I'm all right on the level," she said, and had a little room fitted out for her use on the ground floor. She never made her disability an excuse for taking things easy. When it got so that it took her a full hour to dress, she wouldn't be helped, she just rose earlier. And there is no doubt about it, it was because of her, and the kind of awe in which he held her, that Papa hadn't gone completely to pieces long ago.

I thought of all these things, as I generally did, walking to and fro, doing my work. Once you're used to it, waiting becomes almost automatic. One part of my mind made a note to get that frying oil strained before tomorrow; and to get a new globe for the gas light nearest the door, which the draught had broken.

The place emptied. I tidied each table as it was vacated. Presently there was only the thin well-spoken man still at his table.

When, some long time earlier, I'd removed the flowered plate he'd asked me for coffee. I hadn't inquired whether he wanted a cup or a pot, I'd taken him a pot without asking. He'd either drunk it all, or it was cold by now.

I did the old trick. Cleared up the tables on both sides of him, removing a tablecloth where a dirty eater had splashed tomato sauce, brushing crumbs from another.

Mamma, in the cash desk, gave her irritable little cough. I think he heard it and understood. He said:

"I'm very sorry; the truth is I can't stand up."

I'd been helping about the place, little or much, since I was twelve, and I knew, like you know the alphabet or your tables, every stage of drunkenness. He'd been sober when he came in, and he'd had one glass of Chianti, with a good plateful of spaghetti and a pot of coffee. One thing I did know was that he was sober. So I said:

"Oh. Why not?"

He said, "They call it lumbago. Isn't that a filthy ugly word? Just add a 'p' and it's a beautiful flowering shrub. But it's lumbago has me in its grip. So if you don't mind I'll just sit here for a bit."

Mamma said, "Mary!" and I went to the desk.

"What's the matter? Drunk?"

"No. He says he has lumbago."

"I have rheumatism," Mamma said, "but I don't give way to it."

She reached for her sticks and began to heave herself to her feet. "Are you sure he isn't drunk?"

"Quite sure."

"Crazy?"

"Oh no."

She hauled herself across to the table and said:

"Well, young man? You can't sit here all night, you know."

In actual fact he was not a young man; there were a good many grey hairs amongst the ginger-fair ones, and his weathered face was sharply lined.

He said, "Madam, short of a miracle, that is, I'm afraid, exactly what I shall be forced to do."

"My daughter mentioned lumbago. It's painful, I know, but if you make a big enough effort . . ."

He said, impatiently, "Oh good my God! Don't you think I have? I'm already late for an appointment of some importance."

Mamma said, "Sometimes a little help. Mary, fetch your Papa, and Jack."

They came and, directed by Mamma, took their place, one on each side, put their hands under his arms, and heaved. The man said:

"Nothing less than a crane and t . . ." and then made a sound, half scream, half grunt, quickly bitten off. All the red colour ran out of his face, leaving it as white as paper, and the sweat stood on his forehead like water.

Even Mamma was convinced.

"Fetch a black dose," she said.

I sped to the little room on the ground floor which she now used, and among the multitudinous bottles, pillboxes, and liniment jars on the chiffonier there, found the bottle of powerful black pain killer which Mamma used sparingly, before one of my sisters made a visit, or before exceptionally busy evenings, such as the Cattle Show or the Horticultural Exhibition. I tipped a carefully measured dose into a small glass and carried it back to the table.

"Get that down," Mamma said, "and in ten minutes you'll be as spry as a kitten."

"Thank you very much." He looked past her at me. "Thank you. Well, here's hoping."

"Sit there till it works," Mamma said. "Now, Jack, what about the gas? Leave that one, donkey. And what about supper?"

Father, in all this time, hadn't uttered a word, or shown any curiosity or interest; but we were used to that, now. Sometimes he'd go for days without speaking at all. Once—it was after one of the weddings, and he'd been drinking rather freely —he had mentioned his malady of spirit to me; he said he'd realised suddenly one day a long time ago that nothing mattered. You set your heart on something and worked and strove, then you got it and knew that it didn't matter because nothing mattered. So I had been right about this thing setting in on the day he took possession of the garden, though my idea about the seat had been, of course, just girlish fancy. On that wedding day I'd thought that if I could once get what I wanted —either one of the two things I'd set my heart on—I'd risk the realisation that nothing mattered. But when I was thirty I had more notion of what he meant, and I'd thought to myself, in my recent melancholy moments, that I must look out or I might go the same way as Papa. He was certainly more pitiable than Mamma, for all the physical pain she suffered.

We all took supper together at one end of the big kitchen table. I finished first and Mamma said:

"Go see how he is. If he can stand up, get him out and lock up." Then she suddenly banged her hand flat on the table. "You'll find him gone, all right. He didn't pay! You see? It was all a trick."

"He wouldn't do that," I said. "He's a gentleman."

"Born, maybe. But he's lived by his wits for twenty years. I know the look! Fool that I am . . ."

I hurried into the café. He was there where we'd left him.

"How is it, now?"

"As some infant prodigy is supposed to have said at the age of three, 'Thank you, madam, the agony is abating.' But I'm still not mobile. Are you by any chance on the telephone?"

"No."

"Where is the nearest?"

"In the Station Hotel."

"I wonder then if your young brother, suitably bribed . . ."

"He's *not* my brother; he's an apprentice cook."

He looked at me quickly, "I'm sorry. Do you think he'd go to the hotel and telephone a message for me?"

"He would, but he'd get it wrong or put the telephone out of order. I'll go."

"Oh no. Why should you bother?"

"I should welcome some air. I'll just get my things."

Incredible as it may sound now, in 1913 no respectable woman would go into the street on however short an errand without a hat on her head and gloves on her hands. Even women of the working class wore something on their heads, generally a cast-off cap of their husband's. I hurried upstairs and put on my jacket with the fur collar, new, and matching the dress, and my best hat, also crimson and with a real feather bird across the front. I went and looked in at the kitchen.

"It's all right. He's better, but he can't yet move. I'm just going over to the hotel to make a telephone call for him."

I smoothed my gloves as I went towards his table.

"The number is Ockley 2. If you'd just say that Mr. Robert Fennel is quite unable to make the journey this evening. Say he's sorry. If my uncle should answer the telephone himself— he's rather fond of it, a new toy—and is rude, hang up."

"Shall I mention the lumbago?"

"Don't waste your breath. He wouldn't believe it. Then, if you wouldn't mind, book me a room at the hotel. Oh my Lord, and there's my wretched cabby. I bespoke him. He'll be waiting. Could you *possibly* pay him off for me? Tell him I'm sorry too. Give him this." He eased himself cautiously in his seat and took some money from his pocket. One half sovereign, a shilling, a few coppers. He gave me the half sovereign. "That's for Old Whiskers," and the shilling, "For the telephone. And I am infinitely, infinitely obliged to you."

Walking the short distance between our door and that of the hotel I amused myself by making my own special definition of a snob. "A snob is somebody who would rather run errands for a gentleman than have errands run for her by an aitch-dropper." And it was absolutely true.

Sir Albert did answer the ring of the bell himself.

"Hullo. What do you want?"

"I have a message for you. Mr. Robert Fennel asked me to say that he was unable to make the journey this evening and is very sorry."

"Now you listen to me, young woman. Unless he's listening over your shoulder, tell him I stretched a point agreeing to having him here at all. I give him . . . I give him three quarters of an hour. If he isn't here at the end of that time, I'm done, finished, I wipe my hands . . ." The loud angry voice rose to a bellow that almost cracked my eardrums. "You there, Robert? You can hear me. I know you. Got yourself tied up with one of those station vampires. Can't make the journey, balls, man, balls! Give her half a sovereign and come straight out here. You hear me?"

I said, "Sir Albert, Mr. Fennel isn't here. I'm speaking from the Station Hotel. He is sitting in our café, struck with lumbago."

"Tell that to the Marines!"

"But it's true. He can't move. Papa and the boy tried to lift him and he almost fainted from pain. Mamma gave him a dose, but he still can't walk, so I came out to give you the message."

There was a long silence at the other end of the line. Then the rich fruity voice said, in a ha!-caught-you-out way:

"If you're speaking from the Station Hotel, Miss Formby is within hailing distance. Ask her to come and have a word with me."

Miss Formby was there, yawning behind the reception desk. I asked her would she mind coming to the telephone. She came.

She said, "Yes, Sir Albert. No, Sir Albert. Crisp, Sir Albert, Miss Crisp from the café along the Walk. Well, no, I didn't see him, not actually. But a cabman, Joe Wilson, did come in about an hour ago and asked was he ready and I said, of course I didn't know, because I hadn't seen him. But you can't see everything, so I sent to the dining room and he wasn't there. Yes, Sir Albert. Thank you, Sir Albert. Good evening, Sir Albert." She turned, all flushed and excited, and handed me back the earpiece, whispering, "He wants to speak to you."

The old man's manner had changed entirely.

"I'm sorry, Miss Crisp. Would you be so very kind as to give my nephew a message from me? Tell him he can come some other time. I'm off to Bungay in the morning. Can't say when I shall be back. And tell him it's waste of his time anyway. Good evening to you."

I then went and found and paid off the cabby, who, though delighted to be paid for nothing, had a conscience about it and asked:

"Don't he want me to drive him nowhere? Nowhere at all?"

I said, "No, thank you." I'd already made up my mind where, if he were willing, and able to reach it, Robert Fennel would spend the night. In Jack's little room, next to Mamma's. I'd give it a quick clean out. Jack could go upstairs.

I come now smack up against what I might call a technical problem. All my life, since I could read at all, I'd been a book-worm, and since my teens romantic fiction had been my secret bread. Reading it and hoping that one day I should write it, be another Marie Corelli, in fact. And in all the books I ever read there always came a moment when the hero took the heroine's hand and looked deep in her eyes and said, "I love you," and then proposed marriage to her. I never questioned the truth of it in books; in fact I'd wait for the moment and when it came wallow in it like a cat rolling in catmint. But somehow, in the one book that I worked on, on and off in my spare time for five years—between the time when I was twenty-two and twenty-seven—when it came to the "I love you" point, I couldn't do it. Mainly, I suppose, because no-body had ever taken me by the hand and looked deep into my eyes and said, "I love you."

And now, here I am, writing my true life story, and I have the same difficulty. The truth is that Robert never did take me by the hand, etc., etc. Up to the point where I went back on that November night, and made my suggestion with an I'm-not-taking-no-from-anybody air which even Mamma wouldn't argue with, and cleaned Jack's beastly little room, spread the bed with clean sheets and fresh blankets, and put a hot water bottle in it, everything is perfectly clear. After that it's blurred. I can only remember a few facts, such as how next day, with the effect of the black dose worn off, he was in screaming agony again and I fetched Dr. Cornwell from across the road. So then Robert had a bottle of the black dose for his own, and pills to take, and liniment to be rubbed in.

"Not," old Dr. Cornwell said, "that such palliatives will do him much good. It isn't ordinary lumbago, you know."

"Then what is it?"

"An old wound. I should hesitate to give a positive opinion on this, but I should doubt if the bullet was ever properly extracted."

"You mean somebody *shot* him?"

"Men do get shot in wars. And around the turn of the century there were a few wars that you're too young to remember."

I suppose that to him anybody of thirty seemed a child: but I remembered the Boer War; the excitement the night a place called Mafeking was relieved; and the Yeomanry coming back at the end of the war.

Next time I went into the room—no more than a cupboard with a window, really—I said:

"Did you fight in the Boer War?"

He said, "Shh! It's a thing we don't mention nowadays! I was a deluded, anti-Liberal chap and I got what I deserved. A bullet from Brother Boer. But in these enlightened times lumbago sounds so much more respectable. As some soured old Roman said, 'The defeated enemy . . .' No, I have it wrong. 'Yesterday's enemy, defeated, is today's best friend. . . .' Something like that, anyway. What have you there, horse liniment?"

"Liniment. I'm going to rub you."

"You are not. I've been brought low, but not so low as that. If you think I'd expose my Gothic nakedness . . ."

I said, "Don't be silly."

"Oh, please, let me be silly! It's almost the only thing left to me. . . ."

That was the way he talked. Odd, offhand . . . but I liked it. His very voice did something to me.

I did something to him too. More than once, in the four or five days when he lay in that horrid little room, I'd say something that would make him laugh and he'd say, "Please. When I laugh it hurts!"

And all the time—this is what makes it so difficult to report exactly—the ordinary life went on all round me. Mamma had said, on the first night, "If you think that you can take the responsibility, on your head be it. The customers mustn't suffer; you understand that?"

No customer had suffered. And if you try to do three or four things at once, you do get into a bit of a daze. I was so eager to look after him properly, and yet give no one cause for complaint, that often I turned from one direction to another so fast that I made my head spin.

After two days he began to be better and managed to get, unaided, to the privy which, with the garden and the ground-floor rooms, we'd taken over from Robins. On the third day he reported with pride that he'd only taken two black doses; on the fourth he got up, still hunched and limping, and dressed himself. And in the evening he spoke to me about money.

"I'm deeply in debt to *you* for all your kindness and attention, but I owe your parents hard cash. To tell you the truth I was on my way to touch Uncle Albert when I was struck down. Act of God, he's probably thinking, but he won't get away with that! In the meantime it's a bit awkward. Would it be very inconvenient for them to wait a day or two?"

I remembered Mamma saying that he had lived by his wits.

"I'll lend you some money. That would be better."

"I don't see why you should."

"Nor do I. That's the whole point. When I come to think of it I only enjoy doing things that I can see no reason for."

"You are a funny girl. I'd pay you back in a day or two. . . . I feel a bit badly about this. Up to date the only women I've sponged on have been aunts. And with every loan, a lecture. . . . Well, if you really would, I'd be infinitely obliged. How much would you say I owed the house?"

I did a rapid sum, aimed at impressing Mamma rather than at making any accurate charge.

"Three pounds."

"And I must have a cab out to Ockley, there's no other

means of getting there. Say four. Are you well heeled enough, as they say, to lend me such a sum?"

"I could lend you two hundred pounds if you needed it. I'm well paid and I don't spend much."

He gave me what I called his "funny" look; puzzled and yet, in an odd way, understanding.

"Would you? Yes, I know. You said 'could,' but would you? I'd be interested to know."

"I could. I would. If you like I will."

"But in the name of all things wonderful, *why?*"

"Because you stand for something . . ."

He roared with laughter.

"Stand? You've never yet seen me properly on my feet."

"All right," I said. "Go ahead, make a joke of it if you want to. I'll lend you four pounds or two hundred, whichever you say, for no other reason than it would please me to do it."

He said, "I think you're the most arrogant person I ever met. Not over this . . . I thought so the first evening, before I was struck down. I remember thinking that it took something quite special to enable anyone to serve a dish of spaghetti as though she were conferring an accolade."

I said, "What rubbish!" And that was about as near as we ever came to intimacy then. I went up to my room and opened the tortoise-shell box which held my savings and took out five pounds.

Next day he asked Mamma what he owed her and she said:

"Two pounds." He gave her three, but that didn't change her opinion.

"Easy come, easy go," she said.

And then, off he went to Ockley, though I'd told him that Sir Albert had said he didn't know when he would be back.

"No matter. Mrs. Marjoram is my friend."

Then a fortnight went by; November deepening, darker, more foggy. Five pounds and an illusion lost. But then, what else had I expected? What was there *to* expect? I'd pleased myself—and the most powerful, important person in the whole world couldn't drop into his grave with a more comprehensibly satisfactory thought. I pleased myself.

One morning, early, the postman banged on our door and handed in a parcel. It was for me. There was a box, with a letter folded small to fit, not into it, on top. I read the letter before I looked into the box. It said:

"Dear Miss Crisp . . ." And that was like a smack in the face.

"I had intended to call in on my way from Ockley, but Uncle Albert's grudging largesse carried a condition, so here I am in wildest Wiltshire, peddling cattle cake, or trying to, to farmers whose mouths are as tight as their purse strings. I noticed that you had a fondness for garnets—and they become you. Seeing this the other day, I thought you might like it as a token, no more, of gratitude for kindness that the Koh-i-noor couldn't adequately repay. . . ."

Inside the box there was a screw of paper containing my five pounds, and below a bracelet made of gold and set with five garnets, each as large as a split pea, and slightly different from mine; different in colour and with more depth and glow.

At least he had thought of me; and he had sent me something pretty, not useful or sensible.

I showed the bracelet to Mamma and she said:

"They're not garnets. They're rubies, or I'm a Dutchman."

"He said garnets. Look, read the letter."

I was anxious that she shouldn't get any wrong ideas.

When she'd read it she said an unkind thing. "He's in the wrong job. Women don't buy cattle cake! And I still say they're rubies. Look how they're set, little diamonds round each one. People don't waste diamonds on garnets. And it isn't new, either. You can see where the safety chain has been mended."

I said, "Well, new or secondhand, garnets or rubies, it's pretty and I am pleased with it."

She gave me a long, considering look which I met with a calm pleased-with-an-unexpected-present expression. I wasn't going to have her, or anybody else, being sorry for me. I wasn't even going to be sorry for myself. What was there to be sorry about?

The year moved downhill to Christmas and then, slowly but surely, uphill towards spring. I had, all to myself and unsuspected by anyone, some bad moments; the first daffodils breaking; the day the lilac was in full flower; a warm evening when all the air was drenched with the heavy sweetness of the mock orange. There'd been a time, when I was young and silly, and didn't know the difference between being pretty and plain, or anything about social differences, when things like that, a hawthorn bush in bloom, one pink hedge rose, spoke to me with the seductive voice of promise. It sounds an absurd thing to say, but it's true none the less; once I put some red ramblers in a grey jar and looked at them and *knew* beyond all doubt that two things were going to happen to me. I was going to be a second Marie Corelli; and a man of the only kind I could possibly care about would fall in love with me.

For the last six, seven years I'd known it was nothing but a dream. I'd never even completed my book. And I was plain Mary Crisp, daughter of a café owner. Even my prettiest and most fastidious sister hadn't attracted the kind of man I could marry. So after that a daffodil was just a daffodil, and a rose was a rose. . . .

Now everything spoke his name. Hopelessly, insistently . . . "Dear Miss Crisp . . . Sincerely yours."

And then, suddenly, all the talk was about war. There was the usual split in general opinion. We'd never fight the Germans; dash it all, the Kaiser was one of Queen Victoria's grandchildren. Of course we should fight the Germans; it had been boiling up ever since Agadir.

Mamma was one of those who thought that war would come. We should win, naturally, but there'd be hard times ahead. The German Navy was very cocky. And England was an island. She laid in stores of whatever would keep well, rice, sugar, tea, macaroni, vermicelli, spaghetti, coffee beans, condensed milk, corned beef, tomato puree, sultanas, raisins, currants, curry powder. Papa, who once would have thrown himself into the provisioning of the café as though he were preparing for siege, watched apathetically. Jack Plant, who had never really wanted to be a cook, said openly that he hoped a war would come; the minute it did he'd go for a soldier. . . . As for me, well, I couldn't prepare for it, Mamma was already doing that; and I couldn't prevent it, that, if it could be done, was a job for the government; I could only *hope* that it wouldn't happen. I did hope that, because, amongst all the things I'd read—and I was willing to admit that in my time I'd read a lot of silly rubbish—I'd read about wars . . . Napoleon's retreat from Moscow; Sherman's march through Georgia; the siege of Paris in 1870 . . . blood and mangled flesh, hunger, homeless people. . . . I just wanted it not to *be*.

But there it was. Early in August. War. Mamma somewhat —there is no other word for it—*complacent*. "What did I tell you, Alfred?"

The war was sixteen days old when, one warm evening, I stood at the table which in winter was popular, in summer avoided, the one nearest the kitchen door, and almost under the staircase, taking an order for cold meat and beetroot, and the street door opened, and *he* walked in. He was in uniform and he looked marvellous. I thought about a dozen things all at once. I thought how marvellous and *right* he looked, so right that the uniform might have been designed for him, and him alone. And I thought—He's come back. And I thought— He's in already, he'll be one of the first to be killed. I thought . . . I thought . . . and all the time my heart was thudding like the biggest drum there ever was. And when I set out to walk to where he was—with the customer whose order I'd been taking still bleating about rolls and butter—my legs felt as though they'd give way under me.

I said, "Hullo." And he said:

"I can't stop now. I've some men to see settled . . . you can hear them pawing the ground. Could you come out, later? Say ten. Quarter past?"

"Any time."

"Good. I'll pick you up."

He went away briskly, into the street that seemed full of a sunset haze of dust, and of khaki-clad men.

I wanted to drop everything, run up to my room, throw myself on my bed, laugh, cry, and then get up and make a long, most careful toilet. But I had to go on, just as usual, until the last customer was satisfied. I was aware of Mamma's eye.

When I had set down the last dish—or what would have to be the last dish—I stopped by her cage and said:

"I'm going out. I don't want any supper."

She said, "Now don't you go making a silly of yourself."

"Not me," I said; and ran upstairs, washed, did my hair again, put on my voile dress and white straw toque, and clipped the bracelet outside my glove.

It was nine months, but it might have been minutes.

He said, "It's grand to see you. You look very handsome. Let's go to the hotel. I want to get off my feet. So must you. Well, and how are things?"

"Just as usual. How have they been with you?"

"Indifferent. Until lately. That's what I want to talk to you about. . . ."

I said, "I'm surprised to see you back in the army. How about the plumbago?" That was our old joke.

"Thank God they're not in a position to be choosy just at the moment. And I struck lucky with the M.O. He was an old-timer too, in fact as much responsible for my state as anyone else. I told him so. I said, 'If you turn me down as unfit, you're condemning your own handiwork, old boy.' So here I am. And here we are . . ." He pushed the glass door and we went into the hotel, across the entrance and into the lounge which was fairly full of officers. One said, "Hi, Bob," and another said cryptically, "Everywhere the same." He led me over to a table in the corner, under a palm that needed a good dusting. He asked what would I drink and I said sherry. He ordered whisky for himself. Then he offered me a cigarette.

"I can't here, in the open." I had two or three times smoked one with him in the little back room.

"Nonsense! All that old twaddle is going by the board. You'll see. Be a pioneer."

I thought about the war and how I might never have a chance to share anything with him again. I was probably the first respectable female to smoke a cigarette in the lounge of Baildon Station Hotel.

We exchanged remarks about trivial things in the old easy way and then his manner changed. He began a sentence or two and didn't finish; he seemed to avoid looking at me; he gulped down his drink, looked into my glass, ordered himself another, laughed, in a curious, shamefaced kind of way.

"Believe it or not, I'm nervous. I don't know how you're going to take this. . . . You can guess what I'm going to say, can't you?"

Good-bye, I supposed. He'd always spoken of being so grateful to me, and then, finding himself in Baildon, and actuated by the kind of sentiment for past things which grows so easily during wartime, he'd thought he'd ask me out and make a formal business of the leave-taking.

"You see—for the first time in nearly twenty years, I can see some sort of a future. It may not be very long, or very golden, but at least as long as I'm alive I shall be drawing pay, and if I'm killed there'd be a pension of sorts. So I'm asking— will you marry me?"

I said, "Of course. If you're sure you want me to."

"I don't make a habit of proposing to ladies in the hope that they'll refuse me! Are *you* sure? Mind you . . ." And he went on to say that I mustn't think he was any great catch; that if the war was over, as most people said, by Christmas, and he was still alive, he'd be back where he had been, a waster living on vague expectations. . . .

"Why are you making so much of that side of it?" I asked.

"Because that is why I didn't ask you back in November. I wanted to, but I was living hand to mouth. It didn't seem fair. . . ."

"I wanted you to; but I never dreamed that you would. As for the hand and mouth, I'd sooner live that way with you, than any other way with anybody else."

"Bless you, darling. I'll set about getting a special licence tomorrow."

So you see why I'm at a loss whenever it comes to love talk in a story. We hadn't used the word. And even when, later on, he kissed me by our door, and the whole universe rocked because this was one of the moments for which we had been begotten and our mothers had reared us. . . . No, even then we didn't say, "I love you, I love you." Partly because there was no need, and partly because we had no breath for saying anything.

Mamma was waiting up, sitting in the kitchen with the door open.

She said, "Well?"

I said, "We're going to be married, at once, by special licence."

She gave a heavy sigh.

"I only hope you know what you're doing, Mary."

"I know," I said.

I almost added that I'd always known. . . .

III

In the middle of my great happiness I had some pangs of conscience about Papa and Mamma and the business. Papa, in his dead-alive way, no longer seeing the point in anything, was yet still able and willing to do a certain amount of cooking; but he needed organising. Jack Plant had gone, and hard as I tried, I could not find a boy to replace him, nor a girl to do my job. Baildon, a junction, near to the port of Bywater, was humming like a beehive that has had a stick thrust into it; there were more people than ever about, but none of them wanted steady work. What was wanted, and wanted badly, was what was beginning to be called, even by civilians, "a billet." Before Robert came back we had already been asked several times whether we let rooms, took lodgers, had billets. And that had put an idea into Mamma's head. Upstairs we had four rooms, and one of them had been used by the family from whom Papa had bought the café as a kitchen. We'd never used it as such because of the inconvenience. Papa, when we moved in, had made a kitchen of what had been the grocer's stock room. Mamma now said that if she could once make—and she was sure that she could—the immense effort to get herself upstairs, she and Papa could live there. He was able-bodied; he could go up and down and do the necessary shopping. They'd use the kitchen and one other room, let two; let her little room on the ground floor, and the other which had been Jack's; put beds in the café. With screens perhaps, or match-board partitions. And the "camp followers," as she called the women who came, poor creatures, to spend a last hour or two with their men, could all use the big kitchen downstairs. They'd need no waiting on.

"We shall manage," Mamma said. "And Papa will be glad to have done with the cooking. Myself and the cash desk I will not mention, you can guess my feelings. So perhaps this is best for us all."

I was about to become one of the "camp followers" and I was glad to agree. I didn't, at the time, give her words "We shall manage" their full due. But later on I did. It was a humble battle cry. . . .

I followed camp to Yorkshire, to Wiltshire, to Hampshire, to a place in the wilds of Norfolk, to a place on Salisbury Plain. They all had names; they're written in the diary I kept over that period and have never been able to look at since. I had billets; clean, dirty, luxurious, squalid; I had landladies kind and unkind, generous and grasping, honest and crooked. Twice, because I simply refused to wait until some kind of accommodation could be found, I was literally without a roof over my head; one night I spent in a stackyard, one in a station waiting room. I didn't intend to waste one minute; even if the best thing happened and the war ended and found us both still alive, the time was all too short. I was thirty, he was almost forty; there wasn't time for all the loving we had to do before we were old, infirm, dead. . . . So where he went, I followed. Even once, when his destination was a secret.

I said, "You would tell me, if you knew, wouldn't you?"

"I swear I would. I've asked some cunning questions, but it's a secret, closely kept."

"That means France."

"I'm afraid so."

We were in Yorkshire then, and all we knew was that they were to "entrain" at eleven o'clock in the morning. That meant that if they were to embark from any channel port it wouldn't be likely to be until next day; if they were to make the longer crossing, say from Newcastle or Hull, it might be that afternoon.

Next morning there was the usual crowd of women at the

barrier, either crying openly, or doing what was even more heartbreaking, smiling those deliberate, strained smiles. I neither cried nor smiled. When I'd said good-bye to Robert I watched which way the train went—not an easy thing to do in a big station where many lines meet, and where you can't go beyond the barrier. But I got the rough idea, and before the train had got into its stride I'd got hold of an ancient porter and asked him, not "Where did that train go?" because the spy scare was on and he'd have taken me for a German agent; I asked him a lot of quite silly questions about railway lines; he thought I was wrong in the head, asking questions which as a rule only little train-crazy boys asked. But I had what little boys seldom have, a half crown ready to pay for two minutes' silly talk, and a mind set on one thing, and a memory like a steel trap.

When the troop train, which had been diverted and had to wait at March, pulled into Harwich at six o'clock, I was again at the barrier, this time waiting. And I had a room at the Station Hotel there, five minutes' walk from the line of grim, barracky huts where so many thousands of men had spent their last night in England. We thought that this would be Robert's last night in England, but at the last moment he was ordered not to sail, but to report at Amesbury. There was, as he explained to me, a shortage of men who knew a rifle from a shotgun, and a few of them must be retained to teach others. I hoped we'd get through the whole war that way. . . .

I camp-followed for fifteen months; and during that time he had two attacks of the thing we called plumbago. Each of them disabled him for about four days, and neither attracted much attention, chiefly because so many of the officers left behind to train recruits were oldish men, with little ailments. When the third one struck—we were then in Wiltshire—the M.O. chanced to be a young, very conscientious man who refused to accept the "lumbago" tale and insisted upon sending Robert to a local mansion which had been turned into a hospital. Before he had been there twenty-four hours I was there, too, in the humble capacity of dishwasher.

The busybody doctor insisted upon an operation; he'd drawn the same conclusion as old Dr. Cornwell had done, just about a year earlier. I didn't then think of the young man as a busybody; he seemed to be a friend; we thought of sick leave; *I* thought, I must confess, in terms of a week or two's freedom from anxiety, and even a possibility of discharge on medical grounds. Moving about so much, and the way we had lived, had eaten into my savings and I had under a hundred pounds left, but how we should live, and where, and what on never gave me an instant's worry. Being together was all that mattered.

I was allowed to see Robert for about three minutes before they wheeled him into the operating theatre. He'd already had a preliminary dose of some sedative, and was drowsy; but he knew me. He said, in a faraway voice:

"It was good while it lasted, wasn't it?"

I was frightened. Why say something that sounded so like an epitaph? Did he know something, had he been told something, more than I knew? And then I thought of something that I knew, which he did not. Something I'd known for six weeks and debated with myself whether to mention, afraid really that he'd say, "No more banging round the countryside for you, my girl," or something of that kind.

And if I bent down now, and murmured what I knew into his ear, and the words penetrated the drug haze, would it wake an anxiety? Rouse him? Disturb?

Before I could decide they came bustling in.

"Now, Mrs. Fennel . . ."

I kissed him, then went back to my dishwashing.

He died without regaining consciousness.

It was good while it lasted, wasn't it?

IV

I went home. Mamma turned out some billetees and I had my old room back. Papa shook off his apathy and exercised all his cooking cunning to make me tasty little dishes. I couldn't eat, or sleep, or think about anything, except Robert, dead. When I look back and think of that time I can think one of two things—either Nature is so set on the business of survival that a pregnant woman is the toughest thing alive, or I am naturally one of the toughest things alive. Once, a bit grudgingly, old Dr. Cornwell gave me some sleeping pills. Don't make them a habit, he warned me; use them cautiously, as a last resort. I took the lot, with a glass of hot milk, and went to bed, almost happy. Now I'd done it. I shouldn't wake up in the morning.

I spent some little time in Hell. I've never been able to speak, or write, of some of the things I heard, saw, and took part in for the space between lying down and waking to find myself making a horrible noise and being violently sick.

It was after that that Mamma gave me a talking-to. She'd always been a forthright woman and that day she did not mince her words. She said that I didn't love Robert or I would not be behaving so as to injure his child. My grief, she said, like all grief, was more than half selfish self-pity.

"You lose this baby," she said, "and Robert has gone from the world forever. Bear it and you may see him live again. And unless you eat you may have a baby with no bone to its nose."

I stared.

"I can't explain. I'm not clever. But I do know that the babies of ill-fed mothers have those flat boneless noses, what I always call a *poor* face."

Somehow or other the days passed and in July my baby was born. It was a boy. Robert Fennel.

Instantly my life left its old orbit and began to move on a new one. I suppose every woman who is normal looks down on her baby and plans it a life better and fuller than her own has been. I looked at mine and determined that he should have, first, all the so-called "advantages" that his father had enjoyed, and something more, something to back them up with, training, a profession, something that would be of use in this real, down-to-earth, modern world.

I faced the question of ways and means. I had already been informed that I was not to receive a pension—the Medical Board having taken the view that Robert's death was in no way attributable to his having been on active service.

I was not averse to earning a living for myself and my child; I'd worked ever since I left school and was by nature energetic and independent; but there were other factors to be taken into consideration. I wasn't in a position to command a very high wage in the labour market—unless I went to make munitions, which meant leaving Bobbie with Mamma. I could, of course, revive the eating-house trade; bully Papa into the kitchen, cajole Mamma back into the cash desk; do the waiting myself. I should then be able to live with my child—and my parents— but I should not have much time to bring the boy up as I wanted to bring him up. And—call me a snob if you like—it wasn't the *background* that I wanted for Robert's child. Robert had never been one to dwell upon or to be sentimental over the past, and I daresay that, knowing my background, he had been careful in what he said, but it is impossible to spend fifteen months in close companionship with anyone and not pick up echoes here and there. Green grassy places to play in, trees to climb, ponies to fall off, dogs to love—all these were part of Robert's past, and if I could contrive it they should be part of his son's future.

By the time I was about again I had made up my mind to appeal to Sir Albert Fennel.

It was rather a delicate situation. The last time Robert had seen his uncle had been in the November of 1913 when he'd given him a cheque for ten pounds, said that that was positively the last penny he'd be milked of, and sent him off to the head office of the cattle-food firm with a letter to the managing director. When we were married I had asked Robert whether he ought not to let his uncle know, and he'd said:

"Why should I? If he got married he wouldn't tell *me*. Our last interview was positively the end of an association."

Then, when Robert died, I'd felt that perhaps I ought to let the family know—besides Sir Albert out at Ockley, there were two aunts, one in Bath, one in Dorchester. But writing to them meant explaining who I was and I'd felt unequal to the effort. (Robert had told me the history of the bracelet. Mamma had been right; the stones were rubies; the aunt at Bath had told Robert, when he appealed to her for a loan, that she had no money to spare, but she gave him the bracelet and told him to sell it for what he could get. He sent it to me, which I found extremely touching.)

I had absolutely no reason to think that Sir Albert would do anything for me or my child, but a successful confinement brings its own peculiar form of *hubris*. As soon as I could sit up I wrote to him.

Three weeks passed.

Mamma, who disliked letting billets—we had at that moment fifteen soldiers accommodated in the café, and eight wives in the spare rooms—had begun to make tentative suggestions about going back into what she called "our proper business." Her hoard of dry goods was still practically intact, and there would be plenty of customers now. I was perfectly frank with her, and she'd been frank with me.

"For an able-bodied woman who could have her own business to look to be *kept*, even by her husband's family, is wrong. When I married your father, did I sit down and expect him or his family to put bread in my mouth? No, I worked. And I'm ready to work again."

"It isn't that I mind work. But I want things right for Bobbie."

"And you think that starting off as a parasite will make things right for him?"

"It isn't that. It's hard to explain."

"There's no need. Your husband, Mary, was a good example of what happens to those who have things done for them. I saw that from the beginning. It took this dreadful war to put him in a position to marry you; and now, poor man, he is dead. Do you want your child to live like that?"

"Not entirely. I want him to have everything. . . . And some kind of training too. That was Robert's real trouble, he'd never been trained, he'd never expected to have to earn a living."

"Isn't that what I'm saying? If we get back into our proper business the boy will be brought up to work. He will see his mother and his grandparents working, he will learn to work himself. He can go to school and work for a scholarship, and at week-ends and holidays help about the place, as you all did, and see that money is something to be earned." She shifted in her chair and winced. "We could do well," she said. "I'm no worse than I was, and your father, since he took my advice and started going to St. Egbert's, is a new man. You're strong again."

What she said about Papa was true. He was like a man who had had a long, mysterious illness and then found the cure. It had happened in March, when a German zeppelin had come over and dropped some bombs. Papa had hustled me down and then carried Mamma, and stood over us, his arms spread, and with every thump said, "Oh God! Oh God!" He'd sounded like a badly frightened man, but the moment it was known that one of the bombs—intended, it was thought, for the station—had fallen on the thatched roof of some stables where the milk-cart horses were, Papa had rushed out, despite Mamma's protests, and behaved heroically. Next day he'd gone off to the Catholic Church in Westgate Street. He had a lot of leeway to make up. He'd married a Protestant, he'd reared his children as agnostics . . . he was, so to speak, stood in the corner, but at least he was back, a member of the class. And happy. It interested me, because I had seen his malaise begin and grow gradually; his happiness didn't grow, it simply happened. I envied him passionately. I wished that I could believe that Robert was alive somewhere, and that my prayers could do him good. . . .

I said to Mamma, "If I don't hear during next week . . . all right, we'll start again."

And it got to Friday. Everybody was going to have notice to quit next day. But Friday's post brought me a letter. Abrupt, unpromising. The old man had been away from home and found my letter when he returned. He was sorry about Robert. He thought we should meet. Could I go to luncheon at Ockley on Saturday or Sunday? On Monday he'd be away again.

I went to the station—it was the first time I'd been outside the door since Bobbie was born—and rang the number I remembered. I said I'd go on Saturday.

It was all so horrible that I still can't think of it without being ashamed. Everything so beautiful too; despite the war the lawns smoothly shaven, the edges trimmed, the herbaceous borders blazing with delphiniums and poppies and flowers I didn't know the names of. Indoors everything absolutely beautiful; a table for two set out as though for a wedding. A butler and a black-and-white parlourmaid on duty.

The old man began by beating me into the ground. What, he asked bluntly, did I think he should do for me? I said that I'd *hoped* for a little help to enable me to bring up Robert's

son in a fitting way. He said he had his own son to think
about; he'd helped Robert again and again; so had Veronica
and Laura. Things were changing, there were rough times
ahead. Look at the income tax!

That kind of talk went on and on. I could see that Mamma
had been right, so in the end, when I had a chance to speak, I
said:

"There's no need to explain any more. I'm capable of earning a living for myself and my child."

He said, "Now if you speak of earning, that's different. Did
you . . . did Robert ever mention Mrs. Marjoram?"

"Once."

("Mrs. Marjoram is my friend.")

"She kept house for me for twenty-five years, was a mother
to Stephen. . . . Stephen's my boy; he's in the trenches at this
moment. You knew that?"

"Yes. You mentioned it earlier."

"Everything falling away, you see. Robert gone. Stephen in
the trenches, Mrs. Marjoram dying. . . . A wrench; quite a
wrench. Now you strike me as being a competent, sensible
gel. How about taking over Mrs. Marjoram's job?"

I thought—I'll be honest—about those applications you
must make for getting a boy into a prep and then a public
school. A good address; and the name right. What more natural than that Sir Albert Fennel's great-nephew should live at
Ockley? Who, outside a few intimate friends, would know that
Mrs. Robert Fennel was housekeeper at Ockley? And there'd
be room for the pony, the dogs. . . .

I said, "I should be very willing to consider that."

I had a sense of triumph. I'd got what I wanted for Bobbie,
almost; and I wouldn't be a parasite.

Sir Albert said, "Splendid . . ." And then I knew.

I'm not, I never was in any sense, pretty; maybe in moments of excitement and joy I qualify for the word Robert used
to use, "handsome"; but in 1915 widows still wore long filmy

black veils, and there was an almost perverse attraction about
them. My figure had always been good, and my black coat
and skirt fitted well. I saw the old man's eye assessing my
"points" as though I were a horse. I saw the lecherous gleam.

Quite apart from my own disgust, my near-horror (after all,
I had not yet been widowed for a year), I had another thought.
This *would* be something for Bobbie to be ashamed of. The
eating house might not be the ideal, or even the proper, background, but kept by hard-working, decent-living people, it was
nothing to be ashamed of. . . .

I thought that; and then I knew a moment of doubt. Could
I be mistaken? Had I fallen into that tiresome old female way
of thought which takes hold of almost all women whom one
man has found attractive? Was I deceiving myself?

No. He'd put out his hand and closed it over mine which lay
on the table. He gave it a little squeeze.

"That's right. You consider it, my dear."

I had no wish to anger, or to alienate him, so I edged my
hand away and said that I would consider it. Then I went
home and after two days wrote him a letter and said that I
had, and that my parents were thinking of reopening their
business and needed me.

(Sometimes in the morning, early, when I was sweeping
down the front I would see the Ockley car taking the new
housekeeper to catch the one good train to London. One winter her coat was beaver lamb, the next it was dyed ermine.
She had two poodles, one black, one white. It was said that
she went to London regularly in order to have her hair dyed
that particularly attractive rose-grey colour. . . .)

Whittled down to "The Old Vine, Baildon," it wasn't such
a bad address; and I deliberately chose schools where the name
Fennel meant something. Before Bobbie was a year old I had
him safely entered, as they call it, at Cumberland House,
Broadstairs, and at Marlborough. I used to wake in the night,

sometimes, and know that I'd bitten off rather an outsized bite; but every morning I rose with the determination to chew it.

During those last years of the war, and immediately following, I worked as I'd never even dreamed of working. There was no help of any kind to be had; I swept and scrubbed and washed up as well as waiting. I shopped, I stood in queues. I should think that I am one of the very few women who never pushed her child in a pram for the sake of the airing. We always had some definite goal, we were always in a hurry. Luckily for us all, Bobbie was healthy and a "good child," content to lie in his pram in the garden or in Mamma's little room without attention; content, later on, to spend hours in a home-made play pen in the corner of the kitchen.

Until the end of the war—and for about a year afterwards—we were prosperous; trade was brisk. For all my work—which included washing for the family, no small item with Papa's shirts and aprons—I claimed four pounds a week, as well as my keep, which in those days was big money. It was a rare week when I spent more than five shillings, and that almost entirely on Bobbie.

Every penny Papa had, after expenses were paid, went to St. Egbert's. The priest in charge there, Father Minsham, had got hold of Papa by the most sensitive part of all—his conscience. Papa had lapsed when he was nineteen, he was now almost seventy; more than half a century's wickedness to make up for. . . . But it was money well spent; he was busy and cheerful again, and honestly, throughout this period his main concern all through the week was to get and save up any kind of food that could be used for Saturday evening's "cold table." He always went to Confession on Saturday evening, and didn't cook.

I'd written to both Robert's aunts, tracing them down through Telephone Inquiries since he had never given me their exact addresses. I didn't *ask* them for anything; just told them that Robert was dead and his child born, and that I was sorry not to have written to give them the first piece of information sooner.

The one who lived in Bath, Veronica, wrote back, after a long time, and said that she was now in a nursing home, "an ante-room to the cemetery."

"I was always fond of Robert, he was a scamp, but likeable." [She was the one who had given him the bracelet to sell.] "I'd like to send the baby a present, but in this place I have literally 'fallen among thieves,' like the man in the parable. But perhaps you could buy the baby a rattle. . . ." A five-pound note, folded small, was enclosed.

From Laura, the one in Dorchester, I heard nothing at all.

Work went on. Nineteen-sixteen, 1917, 1918. The Armistice. Nineteen-nineteen, and the heroes coming back to the land which they had made a place fit for heroes to dwell in. When Bobbie was four, and of an age to be "walked out," I could have hired, for five shillings a week and a mid-day meal, thirty girls to do the job. For ten shillings a week and one good meal we could have had a man to sweep the front, scrub floors, and clean windows. We could have put all our dirty linen into a bag and had it done for two shillings. We could have hired a kitchen boy for fifteen shillings a week, a waitress for seventeen and sixpence.

But we couldn't afford to hire anybody. There'd been a wild spending spree for a month or two after the war ended, and then there was nothing. . . .

I suppose there had been signs and portents, but the truth is, when you're over-worked, you don't have much time to notice such things. It's like when you're running to snatch a saucepan that is boiling over on the stove, and catch your foot in the ragged edge of a mat. Damn, you say, and make for the stove.

Anyway, the change seemed to me sudden, unheralded. And

I daresay a good deal of my attention had been diverted by getting Bobbie's things ready to start him out at Miss Brook's Kindergarten and fixing my day so that I could walk him there in the morning and fetch him at three o'clock. (Four pounds a term, and the little blazer and cap, and a shilling a day for a mid-day meal, and a fixed charge of thirty shillings a term for books and stationery.)

Everything seemed to happen at once. It was a January evening. January 1920. Bobbie was snug in bed. He'd had his bath, in the old brown hip bath, and I'd talked to him, as usual, forcing myself to be leisurely while he had it, and I changed and got myself ready for the evening's work. Then I went downstairs and through the kitchen, where Papa was busy, into Mamma's little room. Lately she'd had trouble doing her hair. Raising her arms hurt. I'd suggested that she should follow my example; I'd had mine bobbed soon after we reopened, it saved time. But Mamma wouldn't hear of that. So twice a day I did her hair for her, a thorough do in the morning and then a tidy-up in the evening.

This evening I did it, as usual, fixing in the tortoise-shell combs which had once upon a time exactly matched the colour of her hair and nowadays looked very red against the grey. And just as usual she reached out and took her sticks, both in her right hand, while she pressed against the edge of the chiffonier which also served as a dressing table. Ordinarily she got herself up and very nimbly transferred one of the sticks to her left hand. She very much objected to being helped.

Tonight she bungled it, dropped one stick with a clatter, let go of the edge of the chiffonier, and dropped back onto the stool.

"That's done it," she said, in the most matter-of-fact way. "I think it's my collarbone." She put her right hand to her shoulder. "I'd yell," she said, "but I'd wake the boy. Run across for Dr. Cornwell. I can't stand this very long. . . ."

Dr. Cornwell was the young one; he'd been out of the Army a few months and his father had retired.

Two people were already at the tables, waiting to be fed. I said:

"I shan't be a minute," and ran past them and across the road. Dr. Cornwell had just finished his evening surgery, and came back with me. When we hurried through there were six or eight people, all looking impatient. Papa had wondered why Mamma hadn't come through the kitchen, so he'd looked into her room and seen her sitting there, white-faced and wrenched with pain, and when we arrived he was on his knees by her side, holding her right hand and saying, "It'll be all right, Elsie. It'll be all right. . . ."

The fish and the French-fried potatoes, the spaghetti and the cheese sauce and the meat sauce were all there, ready to serve; so I ran out hurriedly and took orders, served them, and said, "Leave the money on the table, will you?" and then went back.

To Mamma Dr. Cornwell gave a very plausible explanation. Her arms and shoulders, he said, had for a long time been doing all the work, taking all the weight off her legs. To me he told a very different tale. It was a "spontaneous fracture" and it had serious implications. She died three weeks later. She'd known she was going to die, and while I was fetching the doctor she'd made Papa promise that she should die in her own bed, with her own people and her own things about her. Papa hardly left her for a moment, and I had the nursing to do, so we closed the restaurant, and that lost us what custom we had. Not that it mattered much, for Papa was in such a state, so heartbroken and guilt-stricken as to be on the verge of a mental breakdown. Even during his melancholy days, when the futility of all human effort and ambition troubled him so much and sapped his energies and darkened his spirit, he'd been kind and indulgent to his family, and had stayed at work:

so it was pitiable to hear him now accusing himself of lack of duty towards us all. Oh, the wasted years, when he should have been trying to convert Mamma to the true faith, and seeing that his children were reared in it.

It was impossible to get him to give his mind to the discussion of mundane matters—such as what steps we could take to get the place going again. Restlessness and change were in the air; there was a depression, and a great deal of unemployment, but there was still some money about, in the hands of the young who wanted something gay and new. Crisp's Eating House, old-fashioned and sombre, had no appeal.

I found myself, for the first time, with leisure to sit on Bobbie's bed and read him a story before he went to sleep.

One evening I was doing that. Two old-time customers had come in, been served with fish and fried potatoes, and paid me, as people did now, when I set down the plates. If another customer entered I should hear the jangling bell, for I sat in Bobbie's room with the door open. Presently I heard the bell; so I put down the book, kissed Bobbie, and hurried down to find Father Minsham. I thought he'd come to see Papa, but he said no, he wanted to talk to me; he'd waited until he'd seen Papa go into church. (That was typical of Papa these days; cook for two people and then go off to pray!)

I led him into Mamma's room and offered him a cup of the coffee which Papa had left ready on the stove. He accepted it and I poured one for myself. Then he began. He was, he said, very much concerned about Papa. I said that I was too.

"We'll not be blinking the truth; he has been in error, grievously in error, for many years."

I felt my neck go hot, as it does when I am angry, but I didn't intend to be drawn into an argument. To my mind Papa had been in error twice, neither time deliberately. He'd erred in being born in a backward and superstitious community, and he'd erred when he took the notion—on the stone seat at the bottom of our garden—that because man was not immortal it didn't matter whether he achieved anything or not. I was no philosopher, but it seemed to me that I could see straight; simply because this life was the only one we had, it should be as good as we could make it. All my time with Robert had been spent on that premise.

Father Minsham said, "I have a suggestion to make. I believe that, put into operation, it would result in considerable happiness for your father; but since I am a practical man, and since you are intimately concerned, I felt it right to consult with you before I mentioned it to him."

"Anything that made him happier would please me."

"I hoped you would say that. It would entail changes. Giving up the business . . ."

"Which has already given us up," I said.

"Then that makes it much easier. . . ." He proceeded to tell me about a little community of monks who had settled in a place called Abbas, about twenty-five miles away. It had been a small Abbey, so small and poor that it had been done away with long before the general dissolution of the monasteries under Henry VIII. (The name was a corruption.) The ruins had stood in a meadow. Some five years earlier eight monks—Benedictines, I think he said—had gone there and begun to rebuild the place with their own hands. They'd already got a church, and some living quarters. They kept cows and made some special kind of cheese; they had beehives and sold honey; they grew herbs and all kinds of medicinal plants for which, with the new back-to-nature movement, and health stores springing up everywhere, there was now a brisk demand. Their project had attracted a lot of publicity—monks, even hampered by their habits doing three times the amount of wall-building in one day that the average trade-union member would do, that kind of thing. So now they had a lot of visitors, both from England and overseas. And visitors needed refreshments. So they were going to open a public refectory.

Father Minsham's idea was that Papa could go there and cook. He'd be what they called a lay brother, but he'd be part of it and he'd feel that his labours were dedicated. . . .

"If it would make him happy. . . ." I said. "I'm all in favour of people doing what makes them happy, so long as it doesn't hurt anyone else."

"Or themselves?"

I could have said that unless there was something very wrong with a person, doing what made him happy couldn't hurt him much, but my mind was too busy, leaping forward, planning. Fresh paint inside and out, glass-topped tables and gay wicker chairs in place of our old heavy furniture; a piano— there were plenty of people about just then who'd play for a whole evening for a shilling and a meal; food that could be got ready beforehand, sandwiches, salads, snacks. Make the whole thing lighter and gayer and different, more in keeping with the twenties. I could manage.

But I reckoned without . . . shall I say without Holy Church, or without Papa's sturdy peasant independence?

He was entranced by Father Minsham's suggestion and threw himself into it in the wholehearted way in which—I realised—he had always done everything; his break away from his cradle religion had been complete; his despair had been complete; his reacceptance had been complete, and so had his penitence. And now he did not intend to go to Abbas with nothing in his hand.

Once, frantic with anxiety, I found myself speaking to him in Mamma's forthright way.

"If you sell this place, what about Bobbie and me? I've worked here; worked damned hard. And if you throw me to the wolves now, next time you have a change of heart, you'll have me on your conscience."

He gave me a look I shall never forget. He had enormous dark eyes which had defied all the changes of the years; they were as frank, as innocent-looking, as Bobbie's—though his were blue.

"Mary, when you heard the call of your heart, I put no obstacles in your way."

That was true, and unanswerable.

"And when the business is sold, half will be yours."

It was a bad time for selling anything: and Crisp's could no longer be called a going concern. Lots of people came to *look* and, having looked, went away again. Then one morning two men arrived and I felt, from the first moment, that they meant business. One was a man who had for the last two years been a fairly regular customer; he was one of a firm of accountants who had their offices a little way up the road on the other side. His name was Swallow. The other was a man whom I also recognised because I'd seen his photograph in the Baildon *Free Press* under a headline "At Last—A Taxi Service." And there was an article, all about how Mr. Corby had come to Baildon and found no means of transport at the station and had said to himself—here is a chance for an enterprising man, and was now operating a taxi service, something that Baildon had lacked for years.

To me they were two nasty, bad-mannered little men, with horrible ties and even more horrible voices—but then, I was a snob. To Papa they were St. Michael and one of his angels. Because, having stamped all over the place and looked grave and shaken their heads, they made a firm offer of two thousand pounds—a third what Papa had paid for the place without the two extra rooms on the ground floor or the garden which he had acquired when Robins the chemist retired.

But, as they pointed out—not that that was necessary—when Papa bought the place, the Old Vine had been in the centre of a thriving part of the town. Things were different now. More and more farmers were buying cars and driving straight to the town's centre. Train travel was going out. . . .

I heard it all, but to me, nearly as I was concerned, it was like a conversation overheard in the street. Maybe in more than the colour of hair and eyes I was truly Papa's child. For, for at least three weeks before Mr. Swallow and Mr. Corby came, I'd gone whole-hogging down a road of my own. . . .

It had all started when, immediately after Father Minsham put his proposition to Papa, I'd begun to clear out a bit. One day, at the bottom of a drawer, I'd come across my old school report. It was in a hard-covered book—not the flimsy things you get nowadays—it was meant to last. I turned over page after page, the record of my teachers' opinion of me for four years. "English . . . very good." "English . . . excellent." "English . . . outstanding." "English . . . distinguished." I stood there with the thing in my hand, and remembered how often my essays had been read aloud; and how I had always, in those days, been certain that I should be another Marie Corelli.

Where had it all gone? Into waiting at table; into waiting for Robert; into loving Robert; into rearing Bobbie; into the slavery of the last years. . . .

We'd been brought up without any particular religion, but at school there'd been prayers every morning and a subject called "Divinity," and I knew the Bible, which, if you can read it dispassionately, has some very shrewd and true things to say. Standing there, I thought of the Parable of the Talents. I'd had a talent, and I'd wrapped it in a table napkin, literally, and laid it aside.

I stopped my clearing out there and then—let it wait. I found an old exercise book which had lain just under the report book, and in which only the two first pages had been used, and I sat down and began to write.

It was, plain and simple, a love story, though I avoided the actual word. It was my story, though nobody would have recognised it. Mamma had contributed. In my story the girl's husband was killed in action and she was desperate until she realised that she was pregnant. Then she had said to herself what Mamma had said to me, and the last line was her, saying to herself, "When my child is born, Alan will live again."

Put like that, perhaps it sounds slick and glib, but there was more to it, of course, and most of the feelings I had felt, most of the thoughts I had thought. . . . And writing it, though in part it made me unhappy, made me happy too. I enjoyed fitting it together and finding some lighthearted piece to put in just when it might seem too gloomy, and I loved picking on the exact word. It took me a week to write and two evenings to copy out without corrections. When it was done it was a long-short story, suitable, I thought, for a magazine.

I'd never been a magazine reader, partly perhaps because I'd done most of my reading, since I left school, in bed, and a hard-cover book which you can prop up on one corner is so much easier to read that way. So I went scouting round the bookstall at the station. Mine was a serious story, so I picked a serious-looking magazine, which contained articles as well as one long-short story. The magazine was called *Thursday*, and I sent my story to the editor—using the name Mary Crisp because of Marie Corelli. I could no longer read her books because they no longer seemed to me to be about real people or real things, but I was still sentimental about her.

After three days—that is a little time before Mr. Swallow and Mr. Corby came to look over the place—I had a letter. The editor of *Thursday* said that usually they returned any uncommissioned article or story unread, and that usually they never even looked at anything that wasn't typewritten. But he'd happened to have a spare moment and had glanced at my story and read it to the end. He said he was puzzled to understand why I should have sent such a story to him. Had I ever read the stories in *Thursday*? (I never had!) My story was completely unsuitable for his publication, but it was so charming and full of human interest that he had taken the liberty of passing it on to a friend of his, the editor of *To-*

day's Woman, for which he thought it might be suitable.

Then, on the very day when Mr. Swallow and Mr. Corby came, I had a letter from *Today's Woman.* They'd pay me fifteen pounds on publication, and would like to see any other stories I had to offer, but please, they must insist that they be typewritten.

Like all the unenlightened, I thought—Fifteen pounds for a few odd hours' work, never thinking that what had gone into that story was a great slice of my life. Never thinking that I had, in a sense, *told* my story and might never have another. No, I thought that if I could get fifteen pounds for nine evenings' work done after hours, I could earn as much in three days if I stuck at it all day.

So, when the figure of two thousand pounds was mentioned, I wasn't horrified; I didn't see my half as all that would stand between me and Bobbie and penury; I saw it as a bridge. It would serve me while I wrote a few more stories and mastered the typewriter I intended to buy. . . .

And when Bobbie, in January 1924, went to Cumberland House, if the other boys asked that inevitable question, "What does your father do?" he'd be able to say, "My father died in the war and my mother writes stories." A respectable . . . no, that is wrong, it is respectable to run an eating house so long as you run it properly . . . a *good-sounding* occupation.

Papa had two hundred and fifty pounds saved; and he was lucky enough to sell the chairs and tables to the newly formed British Legion Club. We were lucky, too, when it came to selling what furniture I didn't want. I had no idea, when I began looking for a place for me and Bobbie to live in, that I was behaving in the conventional manner—"a little place in the country," the writer's, the would-be writer's dream. I wanted somewhere where I could live cheaply while I wrote my stories, and somewhere which had a good-sounding address, and somewhere near a station. A place called Little

Court, at Steeple Strawless, sounded just right to me. It was small, one large room and a kitchen, two bedrooms, and wonder of wonders, a bathroom. Its price was five hundred pounds.

Papa never asked what I meant to do there, how I proposed to make a living, and for some reason that I never really was clear about even to myself, I never told him. Shyness perhaps. I told him that I had found a place to live and he said that I could, of course, have any furniture I wanted. The rest we'd sell. And one thing I certainly did *not* want was the thing we'd always called the chiffonier in Mamma's room. Her grandmother had given it to her for a wedding present; it was ornate, inlaid with several kinds of wood, and decorated with gilt work. But it was French, eighteenth century, and made two hundred and fifty pounds, that kind of thing being in great demand in America at the moment.

Both Papa and I were anxious to get out of the Old Vine as soon as we could; but first we must have a farewell family party. A sad mistake that was. For one thing the last time we had all been together was at Mamma's funeral, and being all together again was a reminder; and the children were all of wrong ages, Dora's teen-age daughter and Edith's teen-age son, scorning everything and bored, not enough of the middle-age group to play any game properly, and Bobbie merely wanting to romp. There was a lot of ill-feeling about too. Nothing was said directly, but hints were dropped. None of my sisters could see why I should have half Papa's money and they nothing at all except "souvenirs," Mamma's silver tea set, and best china service, a pair of silver candlesticks—things of that kind. They overlooked the fact that each of them had had a grand, expensive wedding, and that I had been, for years, the mainstay of the place.

So, despite the fact that we got out all the decorations which normally we put up just before Christmas, and that Papa excelled himself in the making of party food, and provided plenty of wine for the adults, the party was not a success. A typical shred of conversation was Edith saying, "But what do you propose to do out at Steeple Strawless?"

Dora said, "Why should she do anything? She'll be in the money."

Rose's husband said, "Capital is expendable. Times are bad and they're going to be worse. I know I've got my work cut out to weather the next year or two."

In other words—Don't look to me!

I said, "I'm not going to live on my capital, as you call it. There isn't enough. I'm going to work."

"What at, out at Strawless?"

"I haven't yet decided."

Dora said, "I think you're daft."

And they all told me, at various times, that I was spoiling Bobbie disgracefully and laying up trouble for myself. And that didn't disturb me one whit. Bobbie was the only one—the grand teen-agers included—whose table manners passed muster, and whose voice didn't grate on the ear.

Bad as the party was, however, it provided me with what I was looking for—a new story. "Happy Families," it was called—or was to be called. It was all about a family squabble going on in one room while the children played the game of Happy Families in another.

(When it was written, and then—most painfully—typed, I sent it to *Today's Woman* and they sent it back; it lacked, they said, the charm and naïveté of the former story. So, very much discouraged, I put it away, and five years later—through the agent I'd acquired—sold it to an American magazine for sixteen thousand dollars—then worth about two thousand pounds. I smiled to myself over that. . . .)

So Papa and I left the Old Vine. He took nothing with him but his clothes, so he went by bus in the morning, while the furniture removers were still packing what I was taking with me. Bobbie and I were going by taxi in order to get to Steeple Strawless ahead of the van. The last thing I had to do in Baildon was to drop the keys in at the place Mr. Corby called his office. It was in a newish building not far from the Saltgate market place. And the plate on the door didn't mention either Mr. Swallow or Mr. Corby. It simply said, "Baildon Property Company, Ltd. Registered Office."

INTERLUDE

Steadily, inexorably, the decline of the Old Vine as a shopping area went on. Fewer people on fewer trains, and those few disinclined to walk from the station to the town centre; they boarded a bus and rode past the row of shops which—with one exception—grew shabbier every day, and changed hands with a sinister frequency, always, it seemed, for the worse. Only the café in the centre ever received a fresh coat of paint, such decoration always coinciding with the optimistic notice, "Under New Management." It changed its name several times. Painted blue and white it was "Pet's Pantry," decked with scarlet and orange it was "The Sunshine Café," green it was "Joe's," done over in a particularly revolting shade of mauve it tried again as "The Lilac Tea Shop," and then, re-dressed in the scarlet associated with Woolworth's, and with a good deal of chromium, it was reborn as a Coffee Bar. As such it was mildly prosperous, catering for two very different kinds of customer; clerks and typists from the offices around lunched there parsimoniously on sandwiches, beans on toast, or sausage rolls, all accompanied by cups of frothy coffee; then in the evening it was the haunt of young people, male and female and all intermediate grades; a place upon which the police were keeping an eye, rather a blind one, some people thought, when one evening a row broke out and windows were smashed, a girl trodden on and a boy knifed—not seriously.

In 1955 a young man named Jonathan Roper alighted

from the train and set out to walk—he believed in exercise and was careful even of his pence, and was, moreover in good time for his interview—towards the Borough Offices. The Coffee Bar, though the scarlet was fading and the chromium peeling, still stood out brightly, flanked on one side by a shoe-mending place—"Repairs while you wait," "Shoes reheeled"—and upon the other side a news agent-and-tobacconist's. The end shop nearest the station sold second-, third-, or fourth-hand a number of things without which life in the sixth decade of the twentieth century would be considered intolerable, dolls' prams, children's trikes and bikes, wirelesses, TV sets, sewing machines, crash helmets. The other end shop was empty and the dusty window was plastered with several notices, futuristically arranged at odd angles, all saying "To Let" in large letters, and in smaller ones announcing the name and address of agents who were willing to sell it and thus to assist any fool on his road to ruin.

Mr. Roper gave the place an indifferent and yet professional glance. He didn't smoke; his shoes were in good repair; he had no wife or child nagging at him for a tricycle or a sewing machine, and he hadn't come to Baildon to rent a shop; nor did the Coffee Bar attract him. So like the Pharisee in the parable, "he passed by on the other side," never dreaming that this particular building with its five varying faces was going to be his testing ground. He went on to his interview, and two hours later, in the mayor's own car, he was driven back to the station. He'd got the job. He was Public Health Inspector for Baildon.

There had been three applicants for the post; both older than he was, both more confident of manner and—he admitted, being an honest man—better-looking.

Mr. Roper knew exactly how he looked—like a white rabbit. He was small and thin, and had almost no chin. And he'd been myopic from childhood and wore spectacles which from one angle made his eyes mere pin points and from another magnified them so much that they gave him a soulful look. He'd been aware of the drawbacks in his appearance, things nothing anyone could do about, ever since he was twelve; whatever counter measures were possible he had taken. His accent was impeccable, pure unaffected Oxford; it had cost him fifteen pounds, five sessions, at three pounds a time, paid to a "retired actress" who had advertised in the personal column of *The Times*. Most of the people who came to her to have their voices improved went away, after twenty, thirty lessons, very little better because they had no grasp of principles. Mr. Roper absorbed basic principles as he breathed air, effortlessly. And he was well dressed—he'd realised some time ago that a simple starched collar was the secret; spend thirty pounds on a new suit and then wear it with a soft, non-starch, non-iron collar and you'd wasted your money; don a stiff white collar and nobody looked at your suit. . . .

It would not have perturbed him, or shaken him in his convictions, to have been told that the reason why the mayor of the moment had so staunchly spoken in his favour was that he "looked harmless." Naturally he looked harmless; he'd never deliberately hurt anyone . . . well, unless you counted Sam Baldman, who'd asked for it, who was a menace to society, who had been fairly warned, and who was—never forget that—twice his size and three times his weight. . . .

Oh, harmless enough, with those great eyes and that chinless face—a sign of a weak character, as everyone knew.

His Worship the Mayor of Baildon, Alderman Mr. Stubthorn, did not, of course, *say* that Mr. Roper looked harmless. He said that he was young and young men should have their chance; and he said that he wasn't married, so he wouldn't immediately start clamouring for a council house. (Housing the officials was a hellish problem; if you didn't house them they'd move off to some authority which did, and if you did house them the Baildon *Free Press* was full of sour comments about queue-jumping.)

So Mr. Roper was appointed, and shaken hands with, and sent to the station in the mayor's own car.

And maybe the mayor and Corporation of Baildon were not the first people to be deceived by the fact that a lion cub does bear a superficial resemblance to the domestic pussy.

They hired what they thought was a harmless, well-spoken, well-dressed, well-mannered little man, likely to be amenable and easily influenced. And what they got was a man of steel. A crusader. A fanatic. Or as Mr. Stubthorn said, at the end of it all, "Simply daft."

JONATHAN ROPER'S TALE

People are often stupidly sentimental and romantic about what they call "the country," by which they mean anything outside London and a dozen big towns. When I made public the fact that I was taking a post in Baildon, a town with a population of twenty thousand, they said, "Oh, how lucky you are to be going to live in the country," or, "Do you think you'll really like living in the country?" according to their own particular tastes and dispositions, but one and all hinted that in the country I should have a cushy job. No slums in the country, you see. No over-crowding. Roses round the door and now and then a little bit of bother with the Clean Food Act. . . .

Baildon is a pretty little town, full of Georgian houses with handsome, fanlighted doorways, with wistaria on red brick walls, Virginia creeper on grey; it has many older houses, too, good examples of half-timbering, some pargetting. It has never been industrialised, so it has singularly few of those long rows of workmen's dwellings, hastily erected in the early part of the nineteenth century, which most people think of when they think of slums. You could very well make a visit to the town, or even reside there if you were unobservant and unimaginative, and think that here the public health inspector, whatever else he might find to busy himself about, wouldn't be over-worked with problems concerning slum property.

Actually this pretty, picturesque little town had some of the worst slums you could ever wish *not* to see.

There is—and I'm grateful for it—a specific definition of what makes a house unfit for human habitation. Applying the act which deals with such things is rather like applying the liniment which Mum used to use for stiff necks and backache. You can just apply it in a lackadaisical kind of way, or you can rub it in till it stings. I am one of the rubbers-in. Personally I don't think the law either as regards over-crowding or necessary amenities goes far enough. I have my own experience to draw upon. I was born in a slum; I lived in it; I got out.

To me it seems intolerable that any family should be obliged to share any necessary amenity. . . .

In Shoreditch we shared a lavatory with the Baldmans. Four of us, two of them, a proper flush lavatory; not too bad on the face of it. But who knew or cared how many times my mother cleaned that lavatory and put Harpic in it, and how many times Sam Baldman came home drunk and was sick and piddled on the floor? Or how often Shirley Baldman put something that she shouldn't into the pan?

It also seems to me intolerable that any kid should live in a place where he can't do his homework undisturbed.

Mum, apologetic, "Jon, shift over a bit. I want to lay Dad's tea."

Carol, angry, "Mum, tell Jon to give over, I want to iron my blouse."

Dad, point-blank, "Out of that, boy. I want to do my Pools."

How did I ever do all the homework that was necessary to get that scholarship, and then all the homework which came after, and then all the studying later on?

I did it. I "shifted over," I "gave over," I got "out of that, boy." But then, I'm tough and determined. Hundreds and thousands aren't. They're halfway cases to start with, things go hard and they say, "Oh, what the hell!" and give up. They take to the Amusement Arcades, the street corners, and the pubs and they're lost forever. I'm not one of those sentimental, there-but-for-the-grace-of-God-go-I fellows, but I often look at a crowd of louts and think that there's probably one who wouldn't be there if only he'd had some quiet place to do his homework.

I'm not a Commy either; and I know little about Russia. They say the over-crowding there is worse than it is here. If it is, and if they get the results they do from conditions worse than ours, then they're tough; better men than I am, Gunga Din.

You see what I mean about the acts stopping short; nobody yet has ever put a word into any rule or circular about there being a place, isolated from family activities, and in winter warm, where studies may be pursued.

Feeling so strongly as I do, on this and twenty other points, I am, all the time, like a man set to do a job which he knows calls for a steam shovel and all he is armed with is a teaspoon. If he's honest, and tough and determined, he plies that teaspoon with all his might. And that is what I did in Baildon.

The whole thing has worked itself up into such a drama that sometimes even I have some difficulty in believing that it can really have happened, here in a pretty little market town, in England, in the second half of the twentieth century: but I know it did. I'm the last man to imagine things, but I've had two very near escapes from what could have been nasty accidents in the last ten days; there may be a third, and I may not be so lucky. That's why I'm going to jot down a few things which no official record would show. . . .

II

I like to think that I began my work in Baildon in a sensible fashion. It was the first job I'd had on my own. The place where I'd been trained was a very up-to-date, go-ahead place and naturally I didn't expect exactly the same conditions. My predecessor at Baildon had been an old man, waiting to retire, and he'd been easygoing; that was plain both from the state of the department, and from the way people spoke of him. "Mr. Padmore," they said, "he was never one to make trouble." Or, "Mr. Padmore didn't go out of his way to upset folks." I had no wish to make trouble; I had no wish to upset folks; and I knew what people always said about new brooms. All the same, the rules are laid down, and to a good public health officer they should be what King's Regulations are to the Army.

In Baildon everything was so *personal*. Where I came from a baker with a dirty bakehouse was a baker with a dirty bake-house, a potential danger to the public, who must be warned and then, if he persisted in his insanitary ways, prosecuted. In Baildon he was "poor old Jim Hobbs. You know, Jim Hobbs, Yeomanry sergeant major one time. Been having a rough time, missus gone a bit wrong in the head, and then all that bother with his boy. So even if his pans don't suit Mr. Roper. . . . Well, overlook it this time, eh?"

It *sounded* all right; but in fact it was wrong. It was on a par with Seddon the poisoner giving the judge the sign that he was a fellow Mason. By Baildon Borough Council standards the judge should have said to Seddon, "That was just a bit careless, old boy. Easy on the arsenic next time." The judge didn't say that; it is on record that he wept as he sentenced the murderer, but he applied the law, and he sentenced him.

One way and another my first few months in Baildon were months of frustration. Practical as I am, I am not insensitive. I was aware of a decline in my stock, of a growing unpopularity. Wistful references to Mr. Padmore. A plain hint from one of the aldermen, administered jovially, "Go-ahead young fellow like you, wonder you want to waste your time in a little place like this. I see there's a vacancy in Barwich. Nice slums there, you could condemn houses there, left and right. . . ."

I didn't take the hint, for three very good reasons. The first was that I could see that Baildon really needed somebody like me. It had had Mr. Padmore, or his like, for too long. I think the council picked me because I was young, out on my own for the first time, and they thought I'd be manageable. What Baildon, as a community, needed was a public health officer who wasn't manageable. I was he. The second reason was that I'd found a very good place to live in. It was on Market Square, Number 4, and was supposed to be haunted. Back in the eighties it had been the scene of a triple murder; there hadn't been a murder—or perhaps I should say an exposed murder—in the town since then and people still talked about it. My landlady was a dear little old lady whose father had bought the house, very cheap because of its bad reputation, and she felt obliged, when I answered her advertisement, to say, "Perhaps I should warn you, this house is supposed to be haunted. I've lived here all my life and never seen anything worse than myself, but then I'm not psychic."

"I've no reason to think that I am either."

She said, "All the same, I don't discount it. That is why, since circumstances obliged me to have a paying guest, I think it only fair to warn people. I had one very shattering experience. Before I began to warn people, that was."

"Indeed?" I said.

"I believe it was genuine too. A young lady. She said nobody had told her anything, and actually there couldn't have been time. . . . But her first night in that room—the room you will have, Mr. Roper, she woke screaming from a nightmare; a young man had taken her by the throat and tried to strangle her, she said. . . . She left next day. So since then I've thought it only fair. . . . You see, they were strangled. Three people, in this house."

"I'll risk it," I said. And I was glad that I did. She cooked superbly; she wasn't out to make money, just to have a little help with living expenses, and she was lavish with things like hot-water bottles in the bed, sandwiches and a flask of coffee if I missed a meal. And it was, I think, because I lived in a haunted house that first made Katie notice me as a person.

Katie was the third reason why I wanted to stay in Baildon.

Well, I'm writing down what may never be read by anybody, so I can let myself go.

For a long time I'd felt that somewhere, sometime I'd find somebody like Katie, somebody who wouldn't judge on appearances. I know that I'm a long, long way from being any girl's dream man. I'm short, even in the built-up-inner-shoes that I always wear; no amount of food will fatten me, my chin slopes, and without my glasses I'm almost blind. But I'm normal; apart from having my tonsils out and one bout of pneumonia I've never had a day's illness, and what there is of me is all bone and muscle. When I hit Sam Baldman that time he cheeked my mother for the last time, I knocked him flat out.

Katie was, very nearly, as much a botched job of Nature as I was. She had a most beautiful figure, so exaggeratedly long and thin that it was like a window dresser's dummy. Clothes always looked wonderful on her. But her face was plain, far too wide and flat, a Mongolian face (and it was a fact that for three generations her people had been missionaries in China). She worked in the Treasurer's Department, but socially she was streets ahead of any of the other clerks and typists. She lived in the country and drove a vintage Morris Minor which one evening, just as I was coming out of the Borough Offices, was refusing to start. I went to help, not that I knew anything about cars. The Borough Offices are on Market Square, on the site of a big old house that was burned down years ago, and by the time I'd shoved the car downhill and she'd slammed the gear in, failed to start, and we'd done it all over again, and finally got it going, she looked out and said, "Thank you so much. I'm afraid I've brought you out of your way."

"No. Practically to my own doorstep."

She revved up the engine, listened, eased it off.

"You mean you live with Miss Burr?"

"Yes. Don't you think I'm lucky?"

"It's supposed to be haunted," she said, looking over my shoulder towards the house.

"I know. But I've lived there for almost six months, and as Miss Burr says, 'I've never seen anything worse than msyelf.'"

"I shouldn't care to live in it, all the same. I'm afraid I shouldn't wait to *see* something. I should begin to imagine. . . ."

Straightway we were embarked upon one of the few subjects which make for immediate intimacy, a short cut, as it were; like religion. Once you've said, even in argument, "I believe . . ." "I feel . . ." to anyone, and had them say the same things back to you, mere acquaintanceship is done with. A week or two later when there was a concert in the Assembly Rooms it was easy enough to ask Katie to go to it with me, and to have dinner at the *Abbot's Head* beforehand. In the next week-end she made a return gesture of asking me to spend Sunday at Minsham All Saints where she lived with her aunt and a slightly dotty male cousin who bred pigs and grew Cox's Orange Pippins in a commercial way. They were plainly poor, and just as plainly upper middle class. Everything in the house was old and worn, but elegant. One day, if things went as I had begun to hope, I should tell Katie that my father was a docker; to say it then would have been both premature and presumptuous.

III

I first went to the block—the American term, though incongruous in a story about Baildon, is the only possible one—known as the Old Vine, on a windy October morning. It

stood in a street which in any other town in England would
have been called Station Road, but in Baildon, always looking
over its shoulder to the past, was known as Abbot's Walk. It
was a street which had plainly boomed with the railway, and
then declined with it, and then known a revival when the demand for office space and living accommodation became acute.
Almost all the other buildings on both sides had been turned
into flats, or offices, and were well kept. The dilapidated Old
Vine, very early Tudor by the look of it, stood out like a sore
thumb. It consisted of four shops and a café, or Coffee Bar,
known as Cliff's. I'd passed the place on my way to my interview and thought the roof had some suspicious-looking dips
and humps, but the truth is that some of these very ancient
places were very solidly built and even now much sounder
than they look. On that day one of the shops had been to let
and I remember thinking that anyone who took it must be
either very optimistic or mad, when the other places nearby
were so unprosperous-looking. It was let now and cleaned up,
but not painted. It displayed secondhand clothes; not quite
in the huddled squalid way common to such businesses, but
rather nicely; a great jar of Michaelmas daisies in one corner
of the window and no more than two dresses on show. A dis-
creet little notice said, "Model dresses at reduced prices."

My concern was with Cliff's Café; part of the routine
check on such places.

The proprietor, a man named Cliff Fickling, very fat,
middle-aged, had a truculent and unco-operative manner, but
his premises and equipment were reasonably clean. So were
his toilets. They both worked on the penny-in-the-slot method
and it was that which made me ask the apparently innocent
question, did he have separate toilet accommodation for himself and his staff.

"In the yard."

That was satisfactory too; and there was nothing to com-
plain about in the small space that was his yard; but just

beyond it, separated by a broken-down fence, there was a wilderness of desolation. One of those stinking dumps containing everything from a soiled and rotting mattress from a baby's cot, to the rusty ruins of a bicycle. A pen in which six fowls, bare-necked as vultures, scratched in their own heaped-up dung. A scarecrow dog, tethered to the trunk of an old pear tree. The whole thing stank.

Cliff Fickling had come as far as his own back door and stood watching me with a sardonic eye. Before I could say that this yard made, to say the very least, an unsuitable neighbour for a food-selling establishment, he said:

"No good looking at me. 'Tain't mine. I just hire the ground floor."

Out of the café, at the back of the spacious room, a staircase ran up to a landing and turned. On the landing there was a screen, one of those imitation Japanese jobs, badly tattered. I'd taken it for granted that the staircase led up to the living accommodation belonging to the café and that the screen had been placed there in the interests of privacy.

"You don't live here?"

"Not me," he said.

"Who does?"

He shrugged his fat shoulders.

"How should I know? All I hev to do with it is chuck the dog a bit of grub from time to time. Case for the R.S.P.C.A., that is. *And* the hens."

"I agree. And that"—I pointed to the dump—"constitutes a public nuisance. To whom do they belong?"

"That you'll hev to find out for yourself. You got power to come nosing round my kitchen. Nose round *that!*"

"There are people living over your café? How do they gain access? Do they use your stairs?"

"No fear. Up there." He jerked his thumb and I turned and saw an iron staircase, the kind used for fire escapes, running at an angle across the back of the café. It led to a door in the wall. And above and around it there was the green look that spoke of perpetual dampness, so I looked higher, cricking my neck, and saw one of those great lead gutter headings, as big as a bucket, with a date on it, which from that distance was indecipherable; but the point was that four inches below the heading, the pipe which should have carried the water down, ended, broken off. The fuzz of mossy growth on the bricks, the little ferns sprouting from each crevice, were pleasing to an eye that did not look beyond them. Mine did.

"I think I'll go up and have a look round," I said.

"Bear in mind that's nothing to do with *me*. Mr. Padmore, he never bothered about that part of it; he'd come in, congratterlate me on having the cleanest place in town, and leave it there."

I said, "I congratulate you on having a place which compares very favourably with any I have yet seen in Baildon, Mr. Fickling."

I then mounted the iron stairs and rapped on the flimsy warped door.

A slattern, with a dressing gown clutched around her and a lot of yesterday's smudged make-up on her face, came to the door, gave me a suspicious glance, and said:

"Well?"

I told her who I was, and she said:

"So what?"

"I'd like to come in and have a look round."

"Who's stopping you?"

Another unco-operative type.

I said, "You live here, Mrs. . . ."

"Miss. Miss Cattermole. What d'you think I'm doing here in this get up? Making a morning call?"

I ignored that.

"Do you occupy the whole of this floor, Miss Cattermole?"

"Who'd you think I am? Rothschild? I got a room. That one." She indicated a door. We were standing in a long, nar-

row passage, the inner side of which was made of cheap board-
ing, the outer one almost entirely taken up by a great window
with many broken panes.

"Who else lives here?"

"How should I know? I told you where I live."

"Then I'll start with you."

"I always thought you had to have a warrant before you
could go into anybody's home."

"In a sense I have. Will you lead the way, please?"

She had a room, about nine feet square. One wall was composed of sound oak panelling, three of the matchboarding; all
four, and the ceiling, bore evidence of dampness. She had no
cooking facilities at all.

"Why should I have? I get my meals down in Cliff's caff.
If I want a cuppa tea any odd time when he's shut, Ma
Woody'll always boil me a kettle. I give her a bob now and
again."

"And what do you do for a water supply, and sanitary arrangements?"

"There's a lav halfway down the stairs."

"Which you share with other people?"

"How else?"

"And what rent do you pay?"

For the first time she showed a glimmer of interest, almost
friendliness.

"You aiming to bring it down? I said so. I said so from the
first."

"What did you say, Miss Cattermole?"

"That two quid was a lot to pay for this hole. Believe it or
not, when that rain good and hard, the water pour down there,
you'd think it was a waterfall." She pointed to a corner of the
ceiling.

"Two pounds a week, or a month?"

"Don't make me laugh! A week. Shocking, ain't it?"

"It's shocking all right."

"You aim to do anything about it?"

"I shall hope to," I said cautiously, knowing as I spoke that when it came to doing the one thing within my power to do, she'd be one who'd scream the loudest. She was now, for a moment, my ally, and when I left her, said, "You wanta give a good bang next door. The old girl's as deaf as a beetle."

In Miss Cattermole's apartment I had confined my attention to essentials, ignoring the filth and the clutter; but I had been aware of them, so the next room I entered was a pleasant surprise. A bright little fire burned in an old-fashioned range; there was a scent of cooking. Under the window was an ancient slate sink, served by one cold tap. On the window sill several geraniums bloomed in pots. It was all clean and tidy, and so was Mrs. Woody, a little woman of about sixty, with shining white hair and that particularly attentive look often seen on the faces of deaf people who have not yet lost their wish to remain in contact with their fellows.

I told her who I was, and she said:

"Look round by all means, sir. The inner room is mine too. D'you mind if I get on? I've promised this job for this afternoon."

She indicated the table where a sewing machine stood, surrounded by an expanse of flowered chintz, humped into waves and hollows like a roughish sea.

The damp had entered here too. The inner room was divided from the kitchen by a wall made of canvas, papered over; pink rosebuds and blue forget-me-nots showed where the paper had escaped the damp; elsewhere they'd run together and blurred into a greenish, bluish-grey. The inner room had no window at all; a little light came through a pane of glass let into the ceiling; the pane was permanently fixed and admitted no air. The narrow bed was neatly made; a man's suit hung on a chair; the top of a chest of drawers—the only other furniture there was room for—bore a razor, a man's hairbrush, a jar of hair cream.

When I re-entered the kitchen the whirring of the sewing machine ceased. Mrs. Woody looked at me inquiringly and then asked:

"Everything all right, sir, I hope?"

"You don't live here alone?"

"No. I'm lucky. My youngest boy is still with me. I had three, but two are married now."

"How long have you lived here?"

"Ever since my husband died. That'd be . . . nearly eighteen years." With three boys, I was thinking; but the past was *not* my concern.

"I know what you're thinking. How did we sleep. Eh? Well, I had a full-size bed in there; two at the top, one at the bottom, till Jim went in the Navy. Then, when Toby got married, last Easter, I swopped and got a small bed, so Joe could have a chest of drawers. Fussy about his clothes, Joe is."

Good for him, I thought. He must be a tough boy, too, to have kept vanity alive in such conditions.

"And where do you sleep, Mrs. Woody?"

She pointed to a big wooden armchair with worn velveteen cushions.

"Pull out, that does. It'd be a bit short for some people, but it's just the right size for me."

"Have you never contemplated moving into another place? A council house, for instance."

"Thought about it, you mean, sir? Well, I have and I haven't, if you understand me. I been here so long, I don't think I should settle in a new place. And here I'm near the town. And, most important of all, my ladies know where to find me. Loose covers and curtains, you know."

"Yes, of course," I said, wondering what the ladies who came to find her made of the yard. "You share lavatory accommodation?"

Her periwinkle-blue eyes clouded.

"I do and I have done. And no complaints till lately . . ."

She lowered her voice a little. "I brought up my three here and I never let them be a nuisance to anybody. And unneighbourly as it is to say, the people next door just ain't fit to live in a decent place. She's a slut and the children are hooligans." She looked at her geraniums. "Had a nice fuchsia once, I did; one of my ladies, Mrs. Franchise, gave it to me when I admired it. 'Take it, Mrs. Woody,' she says, 'take it with pleasure.' Days when it rained nice and gentle I'd put it out on the stairs. Knocked it down, they did, the wretches. And as for their yard! I could no more eat an egg them chickens laid. . . . And why *keep* a dog, I say, if you don't treat it right? I mean either you like a dog or you don't."

I got her back to essentials. She paid thirty-seven and six-pence a week for her kitchen and cupboard.

"Catty—that's Miss Cattermole, next door—she don't reckon that's fair, but as I point out to her I been here a long time. When I first came it was seven-and-six." She laughed a little. "I thought that was a lot then, but I hadn't been used to paying rent at all. Gamekeeper, my husband was, cottage thrown in. Still, I'm lucky. Every time the rent go up I can charge more for a set of covers. I ain't like some that have to make do on a fixed income."

Because to know the name of the person who comes to the door gives one an initial advantage I asked her the name of her neighbour on the other side.

"Huddlestone." She laughed again. "Just between ourselves, we call them Muddlestone. Fits better. And bang as you like, she won't answer the door. She'll have heard your voice by now and think it's either the rent or the school attendance. They don't call him that nowadays . . . Welfare something or other. He come here a lot, but she'll never answer."

I banged, nobody came. I banged more loudly and a child began to wail and was quickly hushed. I tried the door and it opened. I found myself, with almost disconcerting suddenness, face to face with a great fat woman wearing an angry expression which quickly changed to one of sycophantic apology.

"I was just a-coming, sir. Sorry to keep you waiting . . ."

Behind her, with a dummy stuck into its mouth, was a child of about two, wearing one garment, a dirty vest which just concealed its sex, and nothing else. The apartment was typical, even down to the new nineteen-inch television set that stood dominating all the filth and clutter and evidence of poverty. I mastered my repulsion and said:

"Good morning, Mrs. Huddlestone."

"You're new," she said, looking me over. Unsure. N.S.P.C.C.? R.S.P.C.A.? School welfare officer? Rent?

I enlightened her and she looked relieved.

"Oh. Drains. They're all right, sir. No complaints at all."

I told her that I was glad to hear that, and that I was making a routine survey. She said, a little grudgingly:

"You'd best come in then. And I'll tell you this before you start. Susie don't sleep here no more. I got a arrangement with Miss Cattermole, just along there. Susie go sleep there, away from Alfie and Tom. So thass all right, ain't it?"

"I've no doubt it is an improvement." There was an echo of trouble there; not primarily my business. "I'm more concerned at the moment with your facilities, where you cook and so on. . . ."

"I gotta fireplace."

So indeed she had, an enormous fireplace, with a marble mantelpiece and surround and hearth, all badly cracked and stained. It had been enclosed with sheet iron, with just enough space left in the centre to accommodate a Victorian grate, at the moment piled high with rubbish, discarded fish-and-chip wrappings, empty cigarette cartons, cigarette ends, and, insecurely wrapped, a parcel of those objects which Shirley Baldman, whom my mother regarded as the worse sloven on earth, had been in the habit of putting into our lavatory pan.

In front of it all there was a gas ring.

"'Cept when it's cold I don't light the fire till evening."

"You use the gas ring?"

"Thass right."

"And water. Where do you obtain that?"

"All depends. Ma Woody got a tap. If she's in a good mood I go there, save me a walk. Lately she ain't been very friendly, so I go down to the lav. There's a tap there."

"I see."

Here again there was the outer and the inner room; the inner containing a double bed, unmade—it was now half past twelve in the morning—and wedged beside it a cot.

Mrs. Huddlestone seemed preoccupied by the family's sleeping arrangements.

"That there," she said, pointing to an object in the outer room, completely obscured by a pile of dirty clothing, topped by a chamber pot, "is a proper studio couch. Thass where Alfie and Tom sleep. Jerry here, he's in with us for the present. And we'll be moved afore *thass* illegal."

"You are thinking of moving?"

"One day. In the country. When my husband get the shuvver's job he's looking for. You know, cottage provided. Thass why we hung on to the fowls and the dog. . . ."

She was a heavy woman, fourteen or fifteen stone, and as she spoke she moved to slap the child's hand away from the control of the TV set. The whole room lurched. Faulty joists, I thought, and remembered a tenement, not far from where I had lived as a child, where a whole floor had collapsed in the night: no one, by a miracle, was seriously hurt, and everyone except the families who had lost, the one their floor, the other their ceiling, had regarded it as very funny indeed.

I gathered a few more details. They'd lived here for six months and paid two guineas a week rent; they hadn't bothered to put their names down for a council house because they didn't intend to stay in Baildon anyway; also they'd once lived on a housing estate and found the neighbours very stuck-up and unfriendly; Mrs. Woody wasn't exactly stuck-up, but she'd turned unfriendly after the kids had broken one of her damned plants.

"And now I'd like to see the lavatory."

"You may not find that right up to the nines," she said. "We take turns to do it and this is my week. Thass all very well for the others, one single, one with just the grown-up boy. Thass different from having a husband and four kids to do everything for, ain't it?"

I said, with truth, that I wasn't expecting to find anything very elaborate and asked her how I reached the place. She indicated the fourth door, which I opened, and almost precipitated myself down the top flight of the stairs which rose at the back of Cliff's Café. There was the door and immediately beyond it the drop of the first step.

The stairs—incidentally, very handsome, all carving and inlay—led down to the half landing where there was a door. Now I saw the purpose of the screen.

The lavatory, except that it was as large as any of the sleeping places I had seen that morning, and panelled throughout, was very much in the same state as ours at home used to be during my mother's occasional "strikes," when she'd cry and say, "Oh, what's the use?" Even my mother, with her Harpic, could not have restored this one to a sanitary condition, for the pan, inside its heavy mahogany casing, was cracked, and sewage leaked out at floor level. And unless I was out in my bearings this unsavoury apartment was immediately above the kitchen upon which Cliff Fickling had so recently demanded to be congratulated! Oddly enough, since people in my line of work would be supposed to have discarded all fastidiousness, this thought made me retract the intention I had been forming, of having lunch in the café and then proceeding to inspect the rest of the block. I intended to go all over it this day; for if the moderately clean café concealed such places, what might not lie behind the secondhand clothes, or the near-

junk shop? I went along to the station and lunched on sandwiches and a half pint. (My arrangements with my landlady
were for breakfast and an evening meal only during the working week.)

By the end of the day I was certain that the five shops and
the rooms over and behind them had once been a single
house, with one good staircase—that in Cliff's Café; one water
closet—that on the half landing; one decent larder—now at
the rear of the shop that sold secondhand bicycles, sewing
machines, and wireless sets; one good kitchen—now owned
by the news agent's family. Long ago, before anyone gave any
consideration to any factor except the making the most of
space, the place had been divided in a haphazard way, and
other kitchens, like Mrs. Woody's contrived. Five families
could have, and doubtless had, lived there in decency and the
modest standard of comfort of the Victorian shopkeeper.
Later on, still predating, or ignoring all public health and
housing acts, further divisions had been made. Additions, too.
At the rear of the shoe-mending establishment there was a
very pleasant garden, long and narrow and high-walled, and
built against one wall was an edifice called "The Maisonette,"
pretty as a picture and nicely kept. I think it had once been a
summerhouse. The walls were of wood, the sloping roof of
tarred felt, the floor concrete slapped onto the bare earth. The
indefinable yet easily recognisable smell of damp mingled
with that of Turkish cigarettes and of the potpourri which
stood in a bowl on a small gate-leg table. The plumbing had
been done, I should think, sometime in the twenties, by an
unemployed man anxious to earn a few shillings, and everything went into a "soak-away" in the garden, which was no
doubt very good for the roses and lavender. It was occupied
by a retired schoolmistress from London who had, she told
me, always wanted to live in the country. I had a moment's
fear that I was confronted with the public health officer's special bugbear—the owner-occupier, but that was not the case.

Miss Barstew paid two pounds five shillings a week for this picture-postcard place.

"With all this lovely garden too! Am I not lucky? I might be in the heart of the country, might I not?"

She at least was not pitiable. Nor was the family of the near-junk dealer, who either had some other income, or sold more old sewing machines than one would imagine. The kitchen made a good living room, its drawback, in my eyes, being that the lavatory opened off it and the door was ill-fitting; there was a parlour, too, very small but big enough to contain a sideboard heavily laden with silver cups. (Won by members of the family, I wondered, or acquired by way of trade and judged too nice to sell?) The three bedrooms above, like every other room on the upper floor in the Old Vine, showed signs of damp.

"Last time the rent went up my husband said he wouldn't pay, less something was done about the drips, and some men did come. But if you ask me, they put two tiles on and kicked five off, it was soon as bad as ever, or worse," the woman said.

The news agent had no family; behind his shop was one room which he used for all purposes, and a kitchen that had been built on. He let his two bedrooms, one to a single woman, one to a widow with a daughter. They all shared the kitchen.

"Help with the rent, you see; and we don't get in each other's way. I look to get one good meal next door mid-day, and my *young* lady eat there most nights."

There was piped water here and there in the block, but it had missed this unit, somehow; over another vintage sink—the same year as Mrs. Woody's, I should guess—there was a hand pump.

"From the main?" I asked; prepared now for almost anything.

"No, thass soft. Come off the roof, I reckon, and go into storage somewhere about. All right to drink though; after all, you boil it, don't you? And the women like it for washing, specially when they do their hair."

And where would that hidden storage place be? In close proximity to the ex-schoolmistress' soak-away. The garden did back on to this shop.

The café I had already inspected, so I passed on and went to the shoe mender's. Two men worked there, brothers; both married, one with two children, one with none. An unmarried sister and a widowed sister-in-law shared the accommodation which consisted of one large downstairs room, with a beautifully moulded ceiling, panelled walls and tall French windows, and a built-out kitchen. Above there were three bedrooms, one of them without ventilation. Statutorily they were not over-crowded; two to each room, not counting the kitchen; four rooms, eight persons; on the face of it just right. But their sleeping arrangements must have been interesting, to say the least. I noted the defects and passed on.

The woman who had just opened the "Model dresses at reduced prices" shop was a type well known to me, a refugee Jewess, wheedling, self-confident, shamelessly "on the make" and yet not without attraction.

She offered me first a cigarette and then a cup of coffee, both of which I refused. Then she said:

"I know what you've come about, so well I know. But when I took over the place, empty rooms. I advertise. They come and they come. 'But anywhere,' they say. They say, 'For one night, just to have a place to lay my head.' My heart is not stone. How could I turn them away? 'One night,' they say, and so it goes on, another and another. What can I do?"

On the ground floor she had a largish shop—the biggest of them all, except the café; it was divided into two by curtains, so that the main bulk of her stock was hidden—as in the best establishments—from customers in the shop. Also behind the curtain was a sewing machine; she was able and willing to make alterations. Abovestairs there were a kitchen and three small rooms. She had seven lodgers. She had exercised the peculiar genius of her race and her household was a community in a way that the others were not. It was just on teatime when I arrived and a young woman who did not, she explained, start work until Monday, was setting the table. The cloth was plastic, but pretty, and in the centre of the table one enormous dahlia floated in a saucer.

"Miss Morgan," the Jewess explained to me, "will have other accommodation when she starts her new work."

The girl let a teaspoon drop rather loudly into a saucer and swung round and said:

"Oh, but Mrs. Friedland, you . . ." I turned and caught the aging but still vivacious face conveying its message of reassurance.

"Oh yes," Miss Morgan agreed. "And I start Monday."

Another girl came pounding up the stairs and stood in the kitchen blinking raindrops from her eyelashes and dabbing her shoulders with her handkerchief.

"Raining again, Mrs. Friedland. I shall have to have that mackintosh, after all."

"It's still on the rail. Help yourself. I am at the moment engaged."

"No reduction, I suppose?"

"A shilling maybe; better I should lose a shilling than have you sniffling with a cold."

A pleasant little set up; but over-crowded by any standard; and housed, like all the others, between rotted joists and leaky roof.

Finally I went out into Abbot's Walk, crossed the road, and looked at the Old Vine as a whole. I'd spent almost a whole day there, taking note of the people, as well as of the conditions in which they lived: I had not, as somebody later said, accusingly, "gone about the whole business in a typically inhuman soulless way." I simply knew what it was my duty to do and proceeded to do it.

IV

This is my own personal story, so I will touch lightly on the movements of the machine which is set in motion when a public health officer finds that a house should be demolished; I'm more concerned, at the moment, to get down the things which will not be found in any report or any minutes of the Public Health Committee.

The first of these was a little talk I had with the borough housing officer, whom I met on the steps of the Borough Offices when I returned from the Old Vine. His name is Colney; he is a cheerful, foul-tongued, efficient ex-Army type with no illusions about anything or anybody.

"Hullo," he said. "Been buggering about finding more work for me, I suppose."

"I'm afraid so. I've spent most of the day at the Old Vine."

"Shops. No concern of mine, Christ be thanked."

"You'll be surprised," I said, and showed him the list of people he'd be required to rehouse.

He ignored it.

"Look. You take a tip from me. Leave the Old Vine strictly alone. Likewise Alma Court, Mafeking Terrace, Priory Close, and Goose Lane."

"Why?"

"Because otherwise you're going to make yourself bloody unpopular. You know who they belong to."

"I know to whom the Old Vine belongs. Something called the Baildon Property Company. I looked in the rent books."

"Bright boy. Go on being a bright boy and leave hornets' nests alone."

"But this property is unfit for human habitation."

"If you looked at the rent books you must have realised that it's also a gold mine. And people don't like having their gold mines closed. Be seeing you."

Undeterred, I made another visit to the Old Vine, taking my assistant with me, and uncovering a few more unsavoury details. One was that the café's kitchen ceiling had shown signs of damp until it was lined with something called Dribord. After that I sent out the routine notice to the owners, giving a list of the defects found and informing them that as, in my opinion, the place was past repair at a reasonable cost I should report to the May meeting of the Public Health Committee and ask for a demolition order.

Here again, the response was unusual. Ordinarily such a notice evokes immediate response; angry or pitiable letters; angry or pitiable visitors to the office. Once I had a man who threatened to bring a libel action against me; to suggest that he owned unfit property was, he said, a defamation of character.

The B.P.C. made no move at all. Or did they?

I usually lunched at a little place in Pound Lane, cheap and clean, run in self-service style. One morning, a week after the serving of the notice, as I was carrying my tray to my favourite table a man bumped into me and spilt my coffee. He was abjectly apologetic and insisted upon getting me another cup, which he brought, with his own tray, to my table and, having asked permission, sat down and began to talk. He talked about Baildon, what a pleasant little town it was, and how the Abbey ruins ought to attract more visitors than they did; then he mentioned the paucity of hotel accommodation in the town.

"Still, if all goes well, that's going to be put right."

He launched into an enthusiastic account of the kind of

establishment he hoped to open; a place catering for all levels of society; a gay, cheap, café-like part where a boy with a pound could take his girl out for an evening; some formal rooms that could be hired for weddings or parties.

"I've been scouting round for a long time, and today I found the ideal place. The Old Vine. Know it?"

I said I did and asked if he'd been over it.

"With a toothcomb. Horrible mess at the moment, but it's got potentialities. Atmosphere too, and that's very important —look how Trust Houses always go for old places. The Old Vine is a fine old place, and the fabric is as sound as a bell."

All I could think of was that there were two places called Old Vine. But when I voiced the doubt that we were talking about the same place he said he meant the one near the station, now a cheap café and four scruffy little shops.

I said, "Then I feel impelled to tell you that that building is very far from sound."

He smiled.

"Ah. You're looking at it with a layman's eye, if you don't mind my saying so. You think the place is in bad repair— agreed, a bit tumble-down—agreed; but in everything that matters it's sound; my God, there's enough solid oak in that place to build an old man-o'-war."

I told him that far from looking at it with a layman's eye I'd surveyed it professionally. I mentioned a few of the more glaring defects; told him who I was, and that I had recommended the demolition of the place.

He said, "You can't be serious. Well, if you are, you're crazy. Twelve hundred pounds, fifteen hundred at the outside —properly spent, mark you—would put that place in tiptop shape."

"It wouldn't pay for the reroofing; the rafters are so riddled with worm they're practically powder. And all other considerations aside, the owners have no right to offer it for sale since I've reported it as unfit."

"Nobody offered it. I've been after it for at least six months."

A little earlier he'd said that he'd found the ideal place today.

I let that pass.

"Tell me honestly. In your opinion, what's the least that it would cost to make it seaworthy—not to equip it for my purpose, that's a different pair of shoes—fit to live in?"

"That's a little hard to say offhand. Six thousand pounds perhaps. Roof, joists, complete new plumbing; there isn't an inch of L.C.C. piping in the whole place. The brickwork all needs repointing. . . . Six thousand is the very minimum."

He said, "This is the hell of a blow to me. Oh, not your estimate, because I know you're out, way out in that. Your having condemned the place, I mean. It's going to hold me up. Appeals, inquiries. They all take time."

Not unsubtle.

"If you'd take a word of advice," I said, "you'd either abandon this project entirely, or go over the place again with a surveyor."

"I don't need a surveyor. I was just about to take my qualifying exam when the war broke out. Afterwards, after three years in a Jap prison camp, I didn't feel like exams, wanted something active and lively. So you see I do know what I'm talking about."

But that, too, may have been a lie.

Nevertheless this interview had the effect of making me pay yet another visit to the Old Vine. People don't like having their gold mines closed. People might well be willing to spend a little of what came out of the gold mine to preserve the rest. Appeals. Inquiries. And, as everybody knew, you could always hire an expert to take the opposite view.

I came away even more confirmed in my opinion.

And I'd had a rather embarrassing meeting with Mrs. Woody.

"They're saying you're going to turn us out, sir. That ain't so, is it?"

"I'm afraid it will come to that in time, Mrs. Woody. Not immediately, but eventually. You have no need to worry. You'll be rehoused."

"Out on the Saxstead Estate?"

"Probably."

"My ladies'd never find me, and I couldn't get to them. Not easy. Oh, I'm sorry I ever said anything about the Huddlestones. Me and Mrs. H. had a talk and if you look at the lavatory now you wouldn't recognise it. She even hung up a block of Sweet-Air on a string. We're all right, here, sir. We're happy." Then she said, suddenly, vehemently, "Healthy, too. None of my boys ever ailed. . . ."

It was one of those moments when I wished that I'd chosen a different job.

Four days later I had my first accident. It happened in a little house which I had, some months previously, closed for essential repairs and improvements. The owner was a co-operative type, and on a Thursday morning telephoned me to say that he was sure I should be pleased to see how nice—his word—the new kitchen, with bathroom over, was. The message wasn't quite as disingenuous as it sounded, he had a tenant waiting to move in and wanted the all-clear sign.

In addition to building out the new kitchen and bathroom —which had a flat roof—he'd been asked to repair a chimney; and that work was still in progress, with the bricks which were to be used for the purpose already carried up the ladder and stacked on the flat roof, ready to the bricklayer's hand. The owner of the house was waiting for me; he displayed with pride, and I surveyed with approval, the neat modern kitchen, the bathroom above. Then he said:

"If you'd step out at the back you'd see how the chimney

work is going." So we stepped out and he looked up and called:
"Bill!" There was no answer, and he said:

"Funny. He was there a minute ago. Lazy sod. Gone round
the other side, gabbing to the nurses as they come off duty.
I'll give *him* a surprise!" He went nimbly up the ladder which
led to the flat roof, stepped briskly off, and then stumbled or
something. Anyway an avalanche of bricks showered down.
It all happened so quickly—as such things do—that the first six
or seven had hit me before I had time to jump for the only
shelter available, which wasn't much, merely the angle between the kitchen wall and the ladder. But the ladder did
break the fall of the bricks, which rattled down with comparative harmlessness. The first ones had struck me, knocked off
my hat, split my head, cut an eyebrow, broken my nose; and
had I been one second later in jumping behind the ladder, I
might well have been seriously hurt. As it was, I was bleeding
like a pig and a bit dazed. The hospital was next door, and in
the Casualty Department they gave me an anti-tetanus injec-
tion and put seven stitches in my head and three in my nose,
gave me a cup of strong, sweet, but tepid tea, and sent me
home. The little man who had caused the accident hovered
about and finally drove me to Miss Burr's; he kept saying, "I
can't tell you how sorry I am, Mr. Roper. I really am most
terribly sorry."

At that point, not knowing what I was up against, I took it
that he was sorry to have caused me injury and pain. . . .

Actually my mishap acted as a catalyst. Miss Burr insisted
upon putting me to bed; anyone with stitches should be in
bed. . . . And at five o'clock, when the Borough Offices
closed, Katie came to see me. She'd been to the house before
and to Miss Burr she'd always been "Miss Glass-Drury," but
this afternoon, because she came to visit the afflicted, bearing a
bunch of pallid forced lilies of the valley, Miss Burr relented
and announced her as "your young lady, Mr. Roper."

To be honest, I was rather grateful for my accident. The

situation between Katie and me had become somewhat static. We were both inexperienced and physically unsure. It was easy enough, when a film which had been well reviewed in the Sunday papers came at last to the Regal Cinema, for me to say, "Such and such is on at the Regal, would you like to see it? And how about dinner at the *Abbot's Head* first?" It was the same with any musical thing, or any performance of the local Amateur Dramatic Society. Then, in return, she asked me out for a Sunday. We talked about everything under the sun; Katie was a girl with very decided views on every subject and sometimes we discussed, sometimes we argued, but we made no progress because we were both shy. The truth is that shy people like other shy people and up to a certain point get on very well together; and *past* a certain point they get on well together too. But there is the hurdle over which unshy people jump without a thought; or the unshy one of a pair will take it, saying, "Look, follow me, it's easy." But given two shy people, both realising that physically their attraction is low-rated, and you have an impasse.

So I didn't grudge the accident which brought Katie into my bedroom saying, "You poor, poor thing." And it seemed natural enough that she should sit down on my bed and take my hand. I could say:

"I know I look awful," and she could reply:

"You look all right to *me*."

We made more real headway that afternoon than at any time since our talk about psychic manifestations at our first encounter.

I was back in harness, looking only slightly battered, by the time of the May meeting of the Public Health Committee. Everything that was decided then is more or less incorporated in the minutes and here it is only necessary for me to note that the old timesaver, "site inspection," was decided upon.

Just a month's delay, shoving off the decision upon the fate of the Old Vine from May to June; that was all.

What next?

Oh, some silly little skirmishes, which in the official files seem to have no significance at all.

One afternoon when I went back to my office I found, of all people, the town clerk waiting for me. The town clerk for Baildon Borough was a walking contradiction of the theory that fat men are easygoing and non-worriers. Mr. Dysart weighed sixteen stone and rather resembled Charles Laughton, but he was fretful, peevish, and hypochondriac, one of those people who suffers from "my" diseases. "The east wind is bad for my rheumatism"; "my migraine is troubling me."

He held, with a justifiable distaste, a dampish-looking brown paper parcel and three letters pinned together. He wore his long-suffering look.

"I thought I'd better contact you direct," he said. "Why all this should be landed on me I really can't imagine. I have enough to do."

The first letter referred to the piece of liver which was in the parcel. It was properly headed with an address and the date, and firmly signed. It said:

"Dear Mr. Town Clerk, what about this liver, enclosed herewith and bought this morning; if you think it's fit for human consumption, I don't. Yours truly. R. Dearman (Mrs.)."

The second ran, "Dear Mr. Dysart, Four times lately I've complained about the smell of the drain in the middle of the paved area of St. Egbert's Yard where the little children play. Today it is quite awful. Something should be done. I live at Number 6, so I know. Yours sincerely, Bertie Pelham."

The third was anonymous.

"Yore saniterry man want to get bissy with the kitchen at Myrtle Bank pull-in for lorries enuff to give evverybody food poysoning."

All complaints until investigated must be taken as genuine;

what struck me as suspicious was that they should all have
come on the one day and all been addressed, not to me, but
to the town clerk. If the aim of the complainants were to
prove that "yore saniterry man" was falling down on his job,
they couldn't have chosen a better method. To everyone whom
he met within the next week Mr. Dysart was quite certain to
say, "It's not enough that I'm overworked in my own department, I have to deal with letters like these. . . ." And he'd
memorise them all; he had a memory like a filing cabinet.

In the current slang term, "I got the message." It read—
Instead of bothering about the Old Vine where everybody is
so happy and so healthy, the public health inspector had better
attend to his more outstanding duties.

This suspicion was confirmed when I found that the liver-
sending lady bred poodles and under pressure admitted that
she couldn't be absolutely certain that she hadn't muddled the
pet-shop liver with the butcher's. The drain in the centre of
the paved cul-de-sac known as St. Egbert's Yard stank because
the children who played there—and probably not they alone—
had been using it as a urinal for several days. The Myrtle Bank
pull-in kitchen was disgusting; the owner had twice been
warned and would now be prosecuted.

The next move—of which no trace or echo can be found in
my office—had at least the virtue of being entertaining.

I'd been to spend Sunday at Hatfield, where, since she was
widowed, my mother has lived with Carol and kept house and
looked after the children while Carol went back to her work.
Carol's husband and I are far from being kindred spirits, so I
make my visits as short as I can without hurting Mother's
feelings, and on this Sunday had left just after tea. When I
reached Baildon Miss Burr had a message for me. Mr. Michael
Hartopp had telephoned twice, once at three o'clock, once
about five minutes before I arrived. He'd asked that I should

ring back the moment I got home. The number was Ockley
48.

A pleasant, rather precious voice answered me. Mr. Hartopp
realised that it was Sunday and that he was imposing, but he
was only in Suffolk for a few hours, on his way to a Book
Fair in Frankfurt, and most urgently wished to see me. If he
rushed into Baildon immediately, would I eat with him at the
Abbot's Head; or better still, since the food there on Sunday
evenings was so poor, would I make the enormous effort and
go to Ockley to share the meagre snack he had provided for
himself? I said I'd go to Ockley and he gave me directions for
finding what he called his tiny cottage.

I sensed, when I told Miss Burr that I should not, after all,
be in for supper, a kind of disapproval—not, I felt, entirely
due to the alteration of arrangements, for she was remarkably
placid about such things. As I turned to go upstairs to wash
my hands she said:

"You know who he is, don't you, Mr. Roper?"

"No. I never heard of him in my life before."

"Well, he's the one that wants to be Labour member here.
Put up against Mr. Horley last time. And nearly lost his de-
posit." She added the last sentence in a voice that only a
staunch Conservative would use.

I drove to Ockley wondering what in the world Mr. Hartopp
could want with me.

The tiny cottage proved to be a sizable house made from an
old pub and expensively furnished in very modern, Scandina-
vian style. Everything was ill-kept and Mr. Hartopp matched;
he wore a pair of filthy flannel trousers and a polo-necked
jersey that needed mending. He himself was tall and slim and
good-looking in a rather girlish way with very long eyelashes
and very long, wavy, floppy hair.

He greeted me with effusive thanks for having come and
led me to the table where his meagre repast was spread. About
a pound of smoked salmon—a taste for which I have not yet

acquired and doubt if I ever shall—and a chicken pie, highly glazed and decorated and saying "Fortnum & Mason" very clearly. There was also a bottle of wine which he called Rüdesheimer, and hoped I liked, though he himself had never fully enjoyed it in England since the day when he had drunk it in the village from which it took its name, on a vine-shaded terrace overlooking the Rhine.

I had a curious feeling that under cover of the easy, casual chat he was summing me up, and that his conclusions would be much sharper and shrewder than his manner would indicate. At last he said:

"I felt I simply must see you and *try* to explain. God knows what you've been thinking about me!"

"Why should I think anything?"

"You mean nobody told you? What's become of the Baildon gossips? I own some shares in the Baildon Property Company. You might with justice say that I'm in some measure responsible for this shocking state of affairs at the Old Vine."

I said, "Oh," and waited; and he rushed on to explain and exculpate himself. Some twenty years earlier a man named Corby had got into financial difficulties and sold his shares in the company.

"Daddy bought them—to help out. He was like that, very kindhearted and a bit vague. I'm afraid I've been a bit vague too. About four years ago, just when I began to nurse this constituency, I remember opening a model house, the first of a number the B.P.C. were planning to build. I'm afraid I thought all their property was of that type. This has been quite a shock to me."

"The company owns a number of tolerable places, but the bulk of its property is definitely sub-standard."

"That is what I wanted to see you about. I was afraid you might be cherishing hard thoughts. And in my position . . . Anyway, this is what I have decided to do. You've been in

Baildon long enough to know about the Reed Charity. Alms-houses. Goodies for old folks at Christmas."

"I know the almshouses."

"Well, I've decided to make over my holdings in the B.P.C. to the Reed Charity."

Did he expect me to fall flat on my face?

"I had planned," he said, a little plaintively, "to go from Bywater to the Hook tomorrow morning; but I shall put that off and fly over in the evening. I shall go to see Steward, my solicitor, and make a deed of gift or whatever the legal term is."

So what? I thought. And I couldn't think of a thing to say; in my eyes he was about to give a beggar an apple rotten to the core. So what?

"Don't you think it's a good idea?"

"I can see that for you it is a way out of an embarrassing situation. For the Reed Charity it will be a welcome, if temporary, increase of income. From my point of view it's just another complication. But that I don't mind. I'm used to that kind of thing now."

"I don't quite follow."

I said, "Sentiment will rear its sacred head, Mr. Hartopp. There are those who don't want the Old Vine—because that is what we are really talking about this moment, isn't it?— to be demolished. Your action will immensely strengthen their hands; they can say that by demolishing the Old Vine the Reed Charity will be robbed of X pounds a year. Not that that will affect the issue. I hold a public office and I go by the book. Who owns the property or profits from the rent makes no difference to me at all."

"Rightly so. And of course, should anyone suggest that by taking this attitude towards the Old Vine you rob the Reed Charity of certain small sums, you have the perfect answer. The whole of my almost negligible share is not in the one property. Call what I give the Reed Charity X and that part of it derived from the Old Vine Y, and the Charity still benefits by X minus Y. You tell them that!"

"Whom should I tell?" I asked, and laughed. "I'm not allowed to debate in committee meetings."

"Then someone else must say it. Mrs. Franchise, perhaps. I'll ring her tomorrow and explain."

Mrs. Franchise—the only woman member of the council—was the very person whom I had imagined pleading for the preservation of the Old Vine on the grounds that the old folks would now benefit. She was a professional sentimentalist and in her world there were no ordinary *people*, only old people and little people, by which she meant children.

"Anyway," Mr. Hartopp said, "I promise you that my act of expiation shan't complicate things for you. So that's settled. Now let's have coffee and a wee drain of brandy and change the subject. You must be bored to death . . . on Sunday, too.

It was Sunday again, a week later, when I had my second accident. The weather was fine and warm, and Katie and I had decided to spend a whole day by the sea, using my car. Human nature is very strange. I looked forward immensely to having a whole day alone with Katie, but I dreaded the moment when I must stand up beside her with bare feet. In my built-up shoes I was an inch and a half shorter than she, without them. . . . But that was ridiculous, and I chided myself as I went to fetch my car. Miss Burr had no garage, and I had been lucky enough to find one in a yard a few minutes' walk away. The yard was in the middle of a lane called "The Twist" which zigzagged along between the high brick walls of gardens. The Twist was so narrow that it had been made a one-way street; one entered at the comparatively straight end and emerged via two almost right-angle turns.

My garage was one of six lockups on the far side of the yard. I drove out, across the yard and into The Twist, and, still in bottom gear, negotiated the first sharp turn. An instant later, just as I was approaching the second bend, my car lurched, went down on the left-hand side, and began to wobble, with a horrible grating sound, from side to side in the narrow road. I actually hit the left-hand wall, ricochetted off, wrenched unavailingly at the steering wheel, and then, as the turn loomed ahead, braked, too late. It all happened with an appalling suddenness, but to me it seemed slow, like something shown in slow motion on a cinema screen. The wall came at me, the bonnet of my car concertina-ed, and there I was, sitting pinned between the steering wheel and the back of the driving seat. I thought, with astonishment and relief— I'm not hurt! And then I saw a car wheel, spinning along, taking the corner, all on its own, very cleverly.

Fright, relief at finding myself unhurt, and the sight of the wheel careering away combined to throw me into a state not far from hysteria. I laughed, and went on laughing until a stab of pain in my ribs reminded me that I was in no position to draw the breath needed for laughter. I tried the mechanism for fixing the driving seat to accommodate a driver with longer legs than mine, and it worked. Released, I found that neither front door would open, so I climbed over and got out by one of those at the back.

The garage that I habitually used stood only a few yards from the corner where The Twist joined Southgate Street. I walked there, passing my wheel which had come to rest against the wall. Farley, the man who owned the garage and worked all the hours there were, was just adjusting the sign which announced that he was open.

"Thass funny," he said, when I had described my mishap. "You had the wheel changed since you brought her in for servicing?"

"No."

"Been trying a do-it-yourself job?"

"I know better than that."

"Thass funny," he said again. He added that he was sure that the last time he'd done anything to the wheels—which was changing front to back, a matter of two months previously —they'd all been replaced securely.

"Did it with my own two hands. Thass a thing I'm very particular about." He readjusted his sign so that it read "Closed" and came with me into The Twist, where we surveyed the wreck and the deep-scored marks in the road where the axle had scraped; and he said he was afraid the car would have to be "wrote off" and I certainly was a lucky man.

"You look a bit pale and shook up, though. Are you all right?"

"I think I bruised my chest a bit; but I'm all right."

He then set to work to hunt for nuts, and could find only one.

"And she musta been hanging by a thread. Well, all I can say is, thass funny. Very funny." He also said something about boys and how the Devil seemed to be in them these days. "Look how they'll try to derail trains. You been round the Saxstead Estate lately, Mr. Roper, leaving the car any length of time?"

I said truly that I had been in many places.

"Thass all I can think of, boys. There's nothing they 'on't do."

He promised to have the wreck removed and I went back to Miss Burr's to telephone Katie.

Her concern and agitation were, to say the least, flattering. I assured her that I was quite unhurt, fully willing and capable to carry out the day's programme as arranged, if we could use her car.

I remembered with pleasure that I had left my bathing trunks and towel in my car; so the sunny day shimmered ahead of me unmarred.

Katie said, "Well, if you are *sure*, I'll come at once and pick you up. Actually I was very anxious to go today because I've promised to make a call on somebody you'll adore. . . ."

So she came, looking very elegant and summery in a yellow and white dress; and Miss Burr, seeing us off, said:

"Now you drive carefully, Miss Glass-Drury. Accidents always go in threes and Mr. Roper has had two."

Katie promised to be very careful.

We drove along the Bywater road and at some crossroads turned off.

"We shan't lose any time, really," Katie said, "because after we've seen Miss Hatton we take a short cut where there's no traffic at all."

Miss Hatton lived in a doll's house set in a miniature, most carefully tended garden. She was of the same generation and class as Katie's aunt and all the friends of hers whom I had met from time to time. But she had what they hadn't, a slightly ingratiating manner, an obvious desire to please. And she was more obviously poor; nothing in her house would have fetched more than a few shillings at an auction.

She was expecting us and had coffee and some stale biscuits all ready. For a minute or two I was inclined to regard the detour and the visit as a waste of time, and to wonder why Katie should think that I should "adore" Miss Hatton. I soon learned. She was the most incredibly witty old woman I'd ever met. What she actually said is too allusive and evanescent to bear repeating, but it was all very funny without once being ill-natured. I was sorry to have encountered her just at a moment when it *hurt* me to laugh. The intermittent stabbing in some ill-defined area behind my ribs had turned into a continual sensation, as though someone were probing there with a sharp and fairly thick knitting needle.

At last Katie said, "Hattie, we must go." We thanked her for the coffee and the entertaining hour, and unloaded the basket of strawberries which cousin Charles had sent, and drove on.

"Isn't she a sweetie?" Katie said. "You'd never believe what a hell of a life she has had."

It was almost the traditional story; one unmarried daughter —fiancé killed in the First World War—nursing both old parents, left penniless, spending years in drudgery as companion, companion-housekeeper, nurse, to various old, ailing, crotchety people.

We lunched at some place that Katie knew, a little outside Bywater, and then drove on to a lonely piece of beach, where I discovered, with false regret, that I had left my trunks in my car. Katie went behind some bushes halfway up the chalky cliff and changed and went into the sea and swam—very expertly, so expertly that I was glad for a different reason that I was unable to join her. Then she came and lay on her towel in the sun. Charles had kindly provided us with a basket of strawberries, too, and we ate them, slowly, gloatingly. We talked, or were silent. Sea gulls cried overhead: the air smelt of the sea, of the thyme that grew on the cliffs, and of the sun-warmed strawberries.

I made up my mind that this evening I would ask Katie to marry me. The time was plainly ripe now. This was being such a *happy* day—easy, intimate, and undemanding. I intended to set the scene properly, too. I said:

"Katie. You remember that roadhouse on the Minsham road, the one with the tables under the trees?"

"Ugh-hugh," she said sleepily.

"Let's have dinner there. It's going to be a warm evening, warm enough to eat out."

A table under the pollarded lime trees; a large gin-and martini apiece—I knew Katie's preferences now; a bottle of Rudes . . . Rüdesheimer . . . It wasn't, I told myself, that I needed Dutch courage; I merely wanted to do the thing properly.

I said, "I've got something I want to talk to you about. . . ."

She rolled over and sat up.

"And that reminds me, I've got something I want to talk to you about, Jon."

"Go ahead," I said.

"You're not . . . you're not going to close the Old Vine, as they're saying, are you?"

The needle gave an extra sharp jab.

I said, "Darling, you know that that's not the way to put it. It's nothing to do with me, personally."

"You can't *say* that. Be reasonable. The Old Vine has been there a long time; and it hasn't *suddenly* deteriorated. Mr. Padmore never found fault with it. The first time you go in you condemn it. So it must be to do with you personally. *You* began the trouble."

I said, "All right, let's get this clear. I admit responsibility insofar as I discovered its condition, looked closely into the matter, applied the rules. I am, if you like, the instrument."

She began to pile sand over my hand, burying it.

"Then you can be the instrument in getting the demolition order revoked, can't you?"

"Tell me how?"

"Oh, there are ways of doing everything—if you want to. You could say, for instance, that you'd over-estimated the dilapidations. . . ."

"But, Katie, I didn't. If you like I'll take you over the place and you can see for yourself. Anyway, why are you concerned about the Old Vine?"

"You saw Hattie this morning; I told you her story. Well, one of her wretched old bullying employers left her a little share in the Baildon Property Company. Jon, her only steady income, a poor little forty pounds a year. You wouldn't do that to her, would you?"

I said, "But closing the Old Vine isn't going to *ruin* the B.P.C."

"It's going to make a difference to their income, so they'll pay less dividend. Even a pound less would really hurt Hattie. And it'll be more than a pound less. Those shops bring in a lot of rent, shabby as they are, and then there are all the other parts let off. What's more, you know very well they'll have to pay for the demolition. Blast it, poor old Hattie's money could be cut by half next year or whenever this is done. Doesn't she matter? Just as much as some shiftless feckless people who'd live anywhere so long as it was cheap."

"They're not living cheaply. The rents there are high by any standard and for what they get in exchange they're extortionate. Your friend Miss Hatton may not draw much income, but somebody does and it's money made out of other people's misery."

Katie stopped piling sand on my hand.

"You know what's the matter with you, don't you? You're a Socialist!" She said the word as though it were some particularly foul disease or form of perversion. "All you think is that Hattie's forty pounds are unearned income. My God. She earned every penny of it a thousand times over. The old woman who left her those shares was ill for two years with the most disgusting complaint and poor Hattie did everything. Now she has that miserable pittance and you think it's immoral or something."

"I think nothing of the sort. I'm sorry for Miss Hatton. Come to that, I'm sorry for some of the people who live in the Old Vine and contrive to live decently in impossible circumstances. But what I think and what I feel have absolutely nothing to do with the case. The Old Vine is fit for nothing but demolition and that's all there is to it."

She then changed her manner and tried cajolery, and that was a mistake. There are women upon whom cajolery sits well, but Katie isn't one of them, and I think that she knew it, and when she failed was all the more virulent because of a secret self-scorn. And there are men upon whom cajolery works, however clumsily applied, because fundamentally it flatters their vanity and appeals to their sense of power. I am not one of them.

She said, "Darling, just as a favour to me, say the place can go on for five years. Hattie's seventy-two and her heart isn't good. Five years will probably see her out. Please, to please me, Jon, schedule the thing or whatever you call it for 1961 or 1962."

I said, rather weakly, "What with the rehousing and the shops demanding compensation it may very well *be* five years before the place is finally closed."

Her manner changed abruptly.

"That has nothing to do with it. I've asked you a favour and you've refused. Well, now we know where we stand. Thank God I found out in time."

She jumped up, lifted the towel, and put it round her like a cloak. I got to my feet, too, and reached out and took her by the elbow.

I said, "Katie, don't be like that about it. I'm very fond . . . I'm in love with you. Anything I could do that I *could* do to please you, you know I would, whatever it cost me."

"This would cost you nothing; but you won't do it. *Why* not?"

"Because in the final count a man has to be able to live with himself, Katie."

She said, "Spoken like a true, smug, work-to-rule little Civil Servant. Aunt Bee was too damned right. When I first spoke of taking you home and told her what you were she said you were funny company for me to keep. Fool that I was, I said you were different and she said petty officials were all the same."

She would have tugged free, but I held on.

I said, "Katie, it can't end like this. . . ." I tried to find words, to pluck up courage to tell her how much she meant to me, and what I'd meant to ask her that evening. But she looked straight into my eyes and I realised for the first time that hers, so oddly set, were very beautiful, not brown as I'd always thought, but bright tawny, with almost greenish flecks. And her face with its high cheekbones and flat planes was beautiful too, unique, incomparable.

She said, "What can't end like this? A day at the seaside?" and she jerked her arm free and walked, tall and beautiful, towards the place where she had left her clothes.

I waited and presently she emerged, carrying the bundled-up towel which she pushed into the empty strawberry basket.

I said, "Katie . . ."

She said, "I'm going home now. I'll give you a lift if you like. The buses are liable to be crowded."

I said, "I must talk to you. . . ."

"About the Old Vine?"

"Good God, no! About us."

She said, "I amend my offer. I'll give you a lift if you will either talk about the Old Vine or remain silent."

"You mean that?"

"Just that."

At heart, by choice and conviction, I am an egalitarian; but I am also observant and, as far as is possible, honest; and there is no doubt about it, when it comes to a showdown people of Katie's kind always have something to fall back upon. (There was a well-worn story current in Shoreditch. A neighbour of ours used to go to clean house for a woman who lived in a more residential district a short bus ride away. During the bombing the charwoman's windows had been broken and some ornaments on a table just inside the window smashed. She went to work as usual and told her employer what an awful night they'd had and what damage was done. The woman listened and sympathised and said, "If you'd like to take anything from my china cabinet, Mrs. Stokes, to replace what you have lost, please do. I have no use for my things any more. Both my boys were killed yesterday." And that is an absolutely true story.) Katie fell back on that quality, whatever you may call it. And I fell back upon what I have inherited and said:

"If we can't talk I think I'd better go back by bus."

The bus didn't start until half past six, and by making detours to take in various villages managed to make the journey last for two hours and twenty minutes. By that time the weather had changed and monstrous purple-black clouds piled up in the sky, bringing an early twilight. The pain in my ribs had worsened; it now hurt me to draw a full breath, so I made do with small shallow ones, like a dog panting. Most of the time of the wretched journey in the crowded bus, full of tired women and noisy, damp, sand-roughened children, I spent brooding over the break with Katie. I could see her point. For love men will commit murder. . . . I claimed to love her, and wasn't willing even to tell a few lies. She was right to be angry, hurt, spiteful. I knew I had only to ring up when I got home and say I'd thought it over and changed my mind, and all would be well—on the surface. And then what would happen? I should end up one of those pitiable, wife-dominated little men whom everyone finds so comic. Once you give in on a moral issue you're done. Also, in a very few words, she had betrayed something, a class-consciousness as inborn as my own. "Funny company"; "I said you were different"; "smug little Civil Servant." Because I was moderately presentable, prepared to devote myself to her, and tolerable company, she had been prepared—being lonely herself—to consort with me. She'd even seemed fond of me. But a fondness which could so easily turn to virulence wasn't much to build on. My common sense, which, oddly enough, always seems to speak to me in my mother's true Cockney voice, told me that I'd had a lucky escape. Another, less robust part of my mind knew that I had sustained a mortal blow. My self-respect might have escaped but my vanity had succumbed; for, secretly, I, too, had thought that I was "different."

The bus turned in at the station yard and stopped. Every-one prepared to alight; it was obviously the end of the stage. I stood up too and the change of position alleviated my pain a little. A short walk, I thought, would do me no harm; so I ignored the other bus which announced that it was bound for the Saxstead Estate, and for which most of my fellow passengers were hurrying.

Within a few minutes I realised that I had made a mistake. Almost as soon as I began to walk the pain was there, worse than ever. A man must breathe, and every time I drew breath it wasn't a knitting needle, it was a two-edged knife that pierced me.

It was like the time when I was twelve and had pneumonia. Pneumonia, I thought. And you could get pneumonia from shock. Crashing my car this morning, that was a shock, wasn't it? Hadn't Farley said I was a lucky man, meaning that I was lucky to be alive? And then I'd had another shock . . . from Katie. Walking slowly along and breathing as slightly as I could and still live, I thought of Katie from another angle. She'd been loyal to her kind. . . . It was that attitude—my people right or wrong, hang together, and damn the consequences—that had kept them where they were, all this time.

But I'd been loyal, too, I thought cloudily. I'd been attacked on all sides. Two attacks made on my life.

Oh, nonsense, nonsense. The pneumonia-delirium. But it wouldn't be dismissed like that. That avalanche of bricks. The one nut left on my car wheel . . .

Now I was opposite the Old Vine. There it stood, a dark bulk against the only-just-less-dark screen of the sky, humped, threatening.

In all the old folk tales, even in the Bible story of Eden, there is the thing that is tabu, don't touch *this* door—Bluebeard; don't open *this* box—Pandora; don't eat *this* apple. In Baildon the tabu thing was the Old Vine.

Gasping, because even the smallest breath now made the

knife turn, I leaned against the fence of the house opposite the Old Vine and I used, in my mind, the language of the streets of my childhood.

"—— you and —— you!" I said. "And all connected with you. Think you'll get me down. Never! You've done your worst. You've lost me my girl; you've given me pneumonia. But I'll survive. I'm one of the professional survivors. I'll see you levelled yet. . . ."

INTERLUDE

Mr. Roper was not suffering, as he imagined, from pneumonia. A passing motorist, seeing him leaning in an attitude of distress against a wall in Abbot's Walk, stopped, took him into his car, and drove him to the hospital where he was X-rayed and found to be suffering from two broken ribs. His mishap was treated with what he considered inappropriate lightness and several jokes were made about his being "accident prone."

Mended and returned to the workaday world once more, he suffered some embarrassment at the thought of meeting Katie on stairs, in corridors, on the forecourt where cars were parked; he had thoughts, too, hopes almost, about a reconciliation, thinking that perhaps he had been hasty on account of his pain, too quick to accept dismissal. When, at their first accidental meeting, Katie made it perfectly plain that for her he was invisible, non-existent, he toyed with the idea of resigning his post. The thought of the Old Vine deterred him. He'd vowed to see it pulled down, and see it pulled down he would.

Slowly, and with a seeming inevitability, the business went on; the shopkeepers put in their claims for compensation, some of staggering size which had to be disputed; promises of rehousing were made to all the tenants. Miss Barstew, learning that she was to be turned out of her small Paradise, primed herself with a half bottle of gin and then swallowed all her digitalis pills at one go, and Dr. Cornwell, who knew the state of her heart and had prescribed the pills, signed the death certificate without a second's hesitation. There was, on the subject of the Old Vine, a sharp division of opinion and some fiery debates in the Council Chamber, and a spate of very partisan and often incoherent letters in the Baildon *Free Press*, whose circulation, during what was called "The Battle of the Old Vine," rose by thirty per cent.

Mrs. Franchise also benefited from the dispute.

Mr. Roper knew that Mrs. Franchise was going to be vociferous at that particular quarterly meeting of the Borough Council because she was wearing a hat. Ordinarily she was a casual dresser, inclined to hairy tweeds and camel hair, all of the best quality but dowdy. She had other, London outfits, sleek and black, and some noticeably frivolous hats. On this evening she wore a complicated turban of black chiffon topped by a large, very pink rose. Mr. Roper, going to the table in the corner where the town's officials sat, deduced that Mrs. Franchise was going to speak about the iniquity of closing the Old Vine and thus robbing the old people of the Reed Charity of X pounds a year. (Had she been going to oblige Mr. Hartopp and make the X minus Y speech, she would not have made the effort to look seductive.)

When Mrs. Franchise rose she did not mention money at all. She spoke very feelingly about human interests and the heartlessness of the rules. "The rules, as we all know, are made in London. The Jacks-in-Office there can't be expected to understand conditions in our little town. But the Jacks-in-Office here," she paused and looked at Mr. Roper, "can't plead ignorance. Here we have a property which may not measure up to the standards laid down by some theorists in London, but *we* know that it is home to a number of humble and harmless people, and with all its faults it is as dear to them as our homes are to us. From the very first I, at least, have been aware of the potential heartbreak and tragedy here, and tonight I am sorry to tell you that your heartless policy has claimed its first victim. Mrs. Woody, who has lived, and made a home, and been happy in a small portion of the Old Vine has been so worried by rumours that she has had a stroke and been taken to St. Egbert's Infirmary. I hope you're all pleased with yourselves." She sat down.

There was an awkward hush; then the mayor, from the chair, said:

"I'm sure we're all sorry to hear that."

Without rising Mrs. Franchise said:

"Mr. Roper isn't sorry. Mr. Roper is glad!"

The mayor said, "I must ask you, Councillor Mrs. Franchise . . ."

A councillor who disliked her and was a stickler for the rules murmured, "Speak to the minute." Another said, "Out of order."

Mrs. Franchise stood up, said, "Heartless vandals!" broke into tears, and hurried from the Council Chamber.

The young reporter from the Baildon *Free Press*, which would not appear until Friday, scribbled like mad; the older man, representing the *Eastern Daily News*, which was printed in Barwich, made a few cryptic symbols on his pad, looked at his watch, and crept out to the nearest telephone. The *Eastern Daily* circulated throughout the whole of Suffolk and Norfolk, a portion of Essex and Cambridgeshire, and Baildon was not of sufficient general importance to rate much mention. But "Scene in Council Chamber: Woman Councillor Weeps" was a headline for any paper.

Before eleven o'clock next morning Viking Television, that part of the Independent Television Network which operated from Barwich and specialised in East Anglian topics, had telephoned and invited Mrs. Franchise to appear that evening on a programme called "Eastern Events." She put on another remarkable hat and went, and spoke so feelingly, so unguardedly, and with such apparent sincerity about the wickedness of officialdom generally that she made quite a sensation. The English, who from 1066 onwards have accepted officialdom more meekly than any other people on the face of the earth, like to think that they do not. Mrs. Franchise, for ten minutes, confirmed them in their misapprehension, and they loved her. The young man who interviewed her, who was having his own private feud with the Barwich Town Planning Authority, managed to squeeze in one last question:

"And how do you feel about the Town Planners, Mrs. Franchise?"

Mrs. Franchise said, "I can't go into that now. It would take too long. Ask me another time."

Two hundred supposedly phlegmatic East Anglians sat straight down and wrote letters to Viking Television, demanding that Mrs. Franchise be asked to appear again. "The sooner the better," they said, and "It can't be too soon for me."

The thing snowballed. Within three months Mrs. Franchise was a Television Personality. And she was at least a personality, for to the end, surrounded by familiar young men and women who on the slightest provocation would have called the Monarch by her Christian name, Mrs. Franchise remained Mrs. Franchise. Quite early in her television career she had fulminated against the over-lavish use of Christian names and said:

"My own name is Augusta, but if you or anybody else presumes to address me by it, I shall simply rise and walk out."

They knew that she would too.

Mrs. Franchise always strongly denied that it was she who drew the attention of the County Council Town and Country Planning Authority to the fact that the house called the Old Vine was at least five hundred years old and thus entitled to be placed on the list of scheduled buildings which must be protected and preserved.

Everybody else denied it too; but the fact remained that

somebody must have done so. The architectural merits of the building were recognised by the Ministry of Housing and Local Government, and the demolition order was rescinded. The closing order remained valid.

So there for a year the old house stood, empty, derelict. The Baildon Property Company, very busy with other schemes, didn't intend to spend the money necessary to put the place into repair; the council didn't intend to saddle itself with a white elephant; the ministry wouldn't let the place be pulled down.

It looked as though the Old Vine might stand there until it rotted away.

"Unless," as old Mr. Swallow said, greatly hampered by his ill-fitting dentures, "we could find some daft body with money to spend on it. Offer it in a Sunday paper for a thousand. There're a lot of suckers about. . . ."

II

Frances and Larry Benyon arrived in Baildon on a bright spring morning. They travelled by bus because their very old car had broken down again, and Frances' brother with whom they were staying, informed of this fact, had maintained a very positive and significant silence. He owned two vehicles, a car and a landrover, and he would willingly have lent, or given, either to his sister but he knew that Larry would insist upon driving, and that Frances would let him. Where Larry was concerned, Frances had no sense at all. When the silence had lasted long enough he had remarked that the bus service to Baildon was very good.

Knowing Larry's feelings about any form of public transport, Frances had offered to make the journey alone. Larry had said:

"Presumably I've got to live in the damned place, surely I have a right to look at it. I know what you are."

That speech was typical of the way in which he had spoken to her lately, even in front of Peter, in front of the children. Paul, almost seven and very observant, had asked, "What have you done to make Daddy angry with you?" There'd been some sympathy in the question, but some reproach, too, and it had started a new uneasiness in her. How long before the children must know that there was something wrong? Then she'd thought—But that's over; he's cured; this surly irritability is just a sign of convalescence.

The bus set them down on an immense open space. There were some pleasant Georgian houses, large and small; the *Abbot's Head* hotel, the Borough Offices, with a billboard full of posters about drinking a pinta milka day, and polio killing adults too, a large white edifice called the Assembly Rooms, painted white and shining in the sun, and alone on the fourth side, opposite the hotel, the Great Gate of the Abbey which was one of the finest examples of early English architecture in the country. Five hundred years ago, when it was already of respectable age, the man who had built the house which they were about to inspect, had helped to save it from destruction, acting to serve his own ends and with no regard for posterity.

"Well," Larry said, keeping up the pretence that this outing was some self-indulgent scheme of her own to which he was merely giving countenance, "which way do we go now?"

He knew where he'd go, left to himself; straight into the bar at the *Abbot's Head*. For a moment the longing, the need for a drink took him like an orgasm. There was nothing, he was nothing, but a walking desire for whisky. Six months and a fortnight since he'd had a drink. They said every day passed without one lessened the craving; they'd discharged him as cured. They knew nothing. How could they? They dealt with poor simple little fellows who wanted to be cured, because they were getting stomach ulcers, or d.t.'s, or hardened arteries, or their wives had threatened to leave them, their employers threatened to sack them, their uncles threatened to disinherit them. Poor little bastards, they went to the place full of hope and good intentions and they came out cured. He'd gone through the mill with the others, in at one end, out at the other. He'd gone because, frankly, there was nothing else to do; he had no job, no money, and the rotten little bungalow was full of squalling brats; and there was a possibility, more than a possibility, that if he didn't make for, let's say, a clinical refuge, he'd go to clink, which would be worse. And Fran had just got her hands on old Aunt Bucktooth's cash. . . .

Six months and a fortnight of sheer slow torture. That's what none of them thought about. Like hanging a man up by the thumbs—it's all for your own good, dear. Well, somehow today, somehow, sooner or later, no matter how, he'd . . .

Frances said, "I'll ask the bus driver; they always know everything." She was back in a minute, touching him lightly on the elbow. "He knew. It's this way, and not far."

Larry said, "Come on then. This wind cuts through me."

She thought—That's because he is so thin. Sometimes she wondered whether, apart from his obvious trouble, there wasn't something wrong with him. In their one happy year, the first after their marriage, when he'd hardly drunk at all, and she'd tried to show all her love and gratitude and devotion by exercising her domestic arts, had, to tell the truth, delighted in being able to buy good food in plenty, Larry had never gained an ounce. And at his worst, when he was drinking Heaven only knew how much a day, and whisky, everybody said, was full of calories, he'd still stayed thin as a bone. And another peculiar thing about him was that he never had a hang-over. Put him to bed, speechless, insensible, and he'd wake with never so much as a headache, able to eat breakfast.

She said, "It's a pleasant-looking little town, don't you think?"

"If you like Dickens. I don't."

Honestly, you could understand Paul's question, "What have you done?" What *have* I done? Gone plodding on, doing the best I could, holding on. Peter said the other evening that I was mad to put up with . . . But Peter doesn't know what I owe Larry. I was young, full of dreams, full of hopelessness, that great tangled garden, that great awkward Rectory, the Parish Magazines, the Mothers' Meetings, the Girl Guides, the Youth Club, the Red Cross, the Civil Defence. Peter brought Larry home for a week-end, and it was like a bomb exploding. He was the knight in shining armour coming to rescue me from a dungeon. I'm grateful for that. I'm grateful for my two children. And for that one year of shining happiness.

This awkward mood will pass. Peter will persuade Tom Eliot into giving him a job; against his will he'll do it, but he'll do it. And we'll find a house. Maybe this one.

Anyway, I have Aunt Madge's legacy.

She knew that it was dreadful to be so mercenary, to attach such importance to money; but after such a long period of insecurity, of struggling to make ends meet, it was wonderful to wake in the night, heart pounding in the same old frantic way, the dread waiting to pounce with the first glimmer of consciousness. What is going to become of us all? And then to think of four thousand five hundred pounds, safe and solid in the bank. Turn over, go back to sleep, all is well.

They had reached another, smaller open space, one side occupied by a large church, with a clock tower, and a graveyard full of ancient tombstones, lopsided under dark yews and twisted hawthorns just speckled with vivid green. Quiet at last, under the rough turf, lay Reeds and Rancons, Kentwoodes, Hattons, Walkers who had all in former days walked this road between Baildon market place and their home at Old Vine.

Frances tried again.

"Those trees are almost in leaf. Spring is on the way."

"It doesn't feel like it. How far is this place?"

"The man said just through an old archway. This is it, I should say."

They passed under the archway under whose shadow a young murderer, on his way back to the Old Vine, had stopped to divest himself of his disguise.

"This is it. Abbot's Walk," Frances said.

It was no longer a residential district. Brass plates announced the premises of doctors, dentists, solicitors, architects, accountants. Here and there rows of bell pushes and name cards identified flats.

Larry said, "Space is obviously at a premium in Baildon. God alone knows what you expect for . . . what was it?"

"A thousand, or near offer. I intend to offer eight hundred."

That crisp, bossy way of speaking. How he hated it. What happened to people, for God's sake. She'd been so sweet, so downtrodden, so anxious to please; and then, with the slightest encouragement, so anxious to be pleased, delighted with everything, like an ill-used puppy, let off the chain that is all it has ever known, and treated kindly. He remembered the first time he'd ever taken her out for a meal. How shy she'd been, and how, having solemnly read through the whole menu she'd chosen the cheapest thing, and he'd said, "You can have that any day; have the lobster," and she'd said, "Oh, but that's ten and six!" in a voice of such awe that he'd almost kissed her, there and then, across the table. Now here she was, his gaoler no less, stepping out to buy him a new gaol. And saying, as though she were making a take-over bid to Onassis or somebody, "I intend to offer eight hundred." Amazing. And the money—let's be fair—had nothing to do with it. The change had been coming on for years, ever since, if you wanted to pinpoint it, she'd become pregnant with Paul. He hadn't wanted the baby, that was the truth of it, and she had, and the gay carefree days were over, she'd started on about economising, saving for the baby, she called it, no more parties. His gambolling puppy-off-the-chain had turned, overnight almost, into a haggard, bone-hoarding bitch. . . .

Frances, who had been setting the pace, walked slowly and more slowly, peering at every place on both sides of the road.

"The bus driver said you couldn't miss it, standing all by itself about halfway between the arch and the station. There's the station. Larry . . . this, this couldn't . . . You don't think this is *it?*"

A row of empty, derelict shops; a good deal of the wall space occupied with those old-fashioned enamelled advertisements which little boys throw stones at and in time render quite senseless; dirty, sun-browned, fly-speckled notices saying "Must close down, everything half price," saying "End of lease sale," saying "Reopening at 10 St. Martin Street."

Larry said with quiet malice, "I think it must be. I don't see any other place for sale."

"The man I wrote to and spoke to on the telephone said he'd meet us here at twelve. It's now striking." She delved into her handbag and took out a clipping. " 'Early Tudor house, scheduled as historic building, in pleasant market town. All main services. Needs repair. £1,000 o n o.' Of all the fraudulent, wicked . . . If this . . ."

As she spoke a small car stopped and a large man extricated himself, smoothed his jacket, prepared a professional smile.

"Mr. and Mrs. Benyon? My name's Simpkin. I hope I haven't kept you waiting."

The last booming stroke from St. Mary's clock tower fell on the air.

Larry stepped back with his now-you-deal-with-this look.

Frances said sharply, "You haven't kept us waiting, but

you've wasted our time, and yours. We're looking for a house, not a row of empty shops."

"The shops," he said, "are what you might call incidental. Inside, you'd be surprised. Beautiful panelling and fireplaces and a superb staircase—the staircase alone is worth far more than the price asked. *If* the owners were allowed to pull it down," he said, answering the unasked question. "There's the snag, you see. The site, for building on, is worth three thousand; the garden at the back is worth a thousand, but there is no other means of access. The panelling is practically priceless. But there you are, it's a scheduled building. Strictly speaking, it should be National Trust. . . ."

She'd mentioned the word "station" but she hadn't caught the implication; where there was a station there was usually a hotel, or at least a refreshment room. Now, if she'd only go in. . . .

Larry said, "If you waste time looking over that dump, you're crazy, my dear." That should provoke her. "I'm having no part in this. I shall stay in the sun."

It worked.

FRANCES BENYON'S TALE

If you have been brought up in a religious atmosphere, and trained early to be conscientious, you are forevermore inclined, when anything disastrous happens, to ask yourself, "Was I to blame?" "What could I have done differently?"

I've asked myself these questions endlessly with regard to the major disaster in our lives and never yet reached any answer. I ask myself the same questions with regard to what happened on that Thursday in last March, and here I can give myself a positive answer. If when Larry refused to enter the Old Vine I had agreed with him that the advertisement was a hoax and stayed outside myself things would have been different. Better? Worse? That I don't know. Different, certainly.

As a matter of fact I was inclined to agree with him. I actually stepped back, intending to give the place a look of withering scorn and then turn to Mr. Simpkin and say that so far from apologising for wasting his time I thought he should apologise to us. And I looked up, and saw, above the marred and cluttered façade of the dreadful little shops, the old red bricks, warm in the sun, the grave beauty of an oriel window.

I said, "I'll just look inside. It won't take long. Are you sure you won't come, Larry? At least you'd be out of the wind."

He said the wind wasn't so bad just there; besides, I knew how cold empty houses could be.

The house agent opened a door in the centre of the building. Everybody—and especially Larry's cronies—looks upon me as a dull, matter-of-fact woman. I'm the kind to whom the neighbours run if they scald or cut themselves or little Billy pushes a pebble into his ear or little Mary falls out of a swing and is stunned. They're less likely to run and ask me to join a party. Nobody would believe that the sight of blood or any other physical abnormality makes me feel absolutely sick and that my calm, grown-up Girl Guide manner is simply a front. Nobody would call me a fanciful or an imaginative woman. So when I say that the moment I stepped into the Old Vine something happened to me it may sound a bit out of character.

I immediately wished that I were there alone. Mr. Simpkin must have known that he had a well-nigh unsaleable property on his hands; and in any case, even if he sold it, the commission on a thousand pounds would be very little. But he was a professional and almost automatically he began on the slick, professional patter, drawing my attention to this thing, praising the other, and slurring over the manifold faults. And all the time I wanted to be by myself; to savour this curious feeling—not of belonging exactly, though there was an element of that, too; almost of excitement, of being on the verge of some most overwhelming experience. . . .

The house—I'll call it that, though it was really a collection of dwellings—was in a shocking state of neglect and disrepair; but there were things in it of great beauty, things which, when you came upon them suddenly in the midst of so much ugliness and desolation, seemed to strike at the heart. I wanted to linger over them. But Mr. Simpkin was busy, leading the way, upstairs, downstairs, out of doors and in again, and talking all the time. Damp marks on the walls and ceilings? A simple matter of a slipped tile or two. People were inclined to misjudge old places, they were frequently more solid than they seemed; for his part he'd sooner give a thousand pounds for a place like this, fundamentally sound, than three for some new houses he could mention, run up in five minutes from shoddy materials.

All the time I kept trying to take notice of the doors which had been blocked up, and the walls which had been made when the house was divided and sub-divided and sub-sub-divided. The panelling on the original walls gave a clue, so did, at one end of the house, the beautifully moulded ceilings: a cherub's head would be in one little cubicle, his body in another. Finally, when we had been all over, I said:

"As I make it, in the original house there were three rooms and the hall and the kitchen quarters downstairs and upstairs six or seven bedrooms. Am I right?"

He said "yes" but I could see by his face that he had never given the matter any thought. "That's right," he said. "A good family house. Just the right size." He didn't say the right size for what. It'd be a bit large for a family with one child, and a bit small for the Barretts of Wimpole Street. That was the kind of thing which in the really old days I could say to Larry and count on a laugh. Not any more though.

That reminded me of Larry, and as Mr. Simpkin and I were now downstairs again, just about to go into the garden, I said:

"Excuse me a moment. Perhaps my husband could bear to look at the garden."

I ran through the hall and looked out into the street. There was no sign of Larry anywhere.

If you live with a dread long enough you can find evidence of what you dread everywhere. I reproached myself for thinking, instantly, he's sloped off to get a drink; but that is what I *did* think. And that, I told myself, going back into the house, was unfair of me. He was supposed to be cured. In the whole fortnight since he'd been out of Compter he'd been very good; but then Peter's farm was four miles from the nearest pub, and I'd always been around, and Peter had been very helpful, taking Larry about with him and trying to interest him in the farm, especially in the mechanisation part.

Still I was disturbed. I didn't feel that I could spend any time looking at the garden until I knew where Larry was. So

I told Mr. Simpkin that I wanted to go over the house again, at my leisure, and see the garden, and he said he'd leave me the keys and I could drop them in at his office when I'd done.

"You have the address?"

"I have the advertisement. Oh, and it says 'or near offer.' My near offer would be eight hundred pounds. Do you think they'd consider that?"

"That's hardly for me to say. They might. The point is that standing empty doesn't do a place any good."

I then said, as casually as I could manage:

"And where is the nearest place where one could get a drink?"

He said at the Station Hotel, a minute's walk along the road.

Then he went off to show somebody—I hope—a more sale-able property and I went scurrying to the station, thinking of all the things the psychiatrist at Compter Hall had said to *me* in an interview that Larry knew nothing about. Like all psychiatrists, he seemed anxious to land the blame on somebody, and he seemed to have settled on me. He said that I was a dominant character and part of the trouble was that I evoked feelings of inferiority in Larry, and therefore he drank to compensate. That was rather like blaming a woman who had been murdered for the thirty shillings in her handbag for carrying a bag with thirty shillings in it; for the truth was that Larry had been a drinker before ever he met me. However, that wasn't important; what was, was the advice the psychiatrist had given me, all about unobtrusive supervision, never letting Larry suspect that I suspected that he might take to drinking again; and no reproaches . . . all that kind of thing. Personally I think he was all wrong about Larry, who, so far as I can see, more often feels *superior* to other people, thinking they're fools and often saying so, with most calami-tous results. However, I'm ignorant about psychology, which always seems topsy-turvy to me, so I was willing to be advised, and I ran along to the Station Hotel prepared to exercise, if possible, some "unobtrusive supervision."

Larry was in the bar; I knew that before I pushed the door open. I heard him laughing. Other people were laughing too. That was always the way. In any bar, or at a party where the drinks were any good, Larry could quickly become the centre of a gay, admiring circle. The psychiatrist had mentioned that too. He told me that Larry had strong gregarious instincts but couldn't give them rein except under the influence of alcohol. I looked up "gregarious" in the dictionary afterwards and it said "associating or living in flocks or herds," which didn't help much. What I *thought* the word meant—fond of people —didn't apply either, for Larry didn't really like people at all. He'd gather them round and make them laugh, make them think he was charming and wonderful, and then afterwards he'd say the most unkind and cutting things about them. When I first knew him I was silly enough to take this as a kind of backhanded flattery; Larry is so critical, I'd think, yet he loves me; therefore I must be something quite special!

There were three men, all standing in a tight little knot around Larry and laughing at something he was saying. When he saw me he broke off and said, gaily and pleasantly, "Here *is* my wife," as though he'd just been whiling away the time until I came. He didn't look caught out, or ashamed—but then he never did. Never once, through all the years of recurring crises, of lost jobs and worse things, had he ever once said to me that he was sorry. I'd devised my own theory about this. In laboratories, preserved in alcohol, there are things which once were human, or part of humans; they are now preserved, immutable, but no longer human. The alcohol seemed to have had the same effect upon Larry's human feelings; he felt no shame, no remorse, no love. Not even for his children, who completely adored him. Paul, our eldest, was just six when Larry went to Compter Hall, and he cried himself sick when Daddy had to go into hospital—that was the explanation I gave. He went to a little nursery school in Salisbury at that time, and one day came home, scowling and looking at me with hatred, and refused to kiss or be kissed good night. When I probed the trouble to the root Paul said:

"I hate you. You put Daddy away. Ian Stamper said so."

I said, "But Daddy is ill. He's gone to be cured."

Paul said, "You could have cured him here. You cured me with mumps."

Larry made room for me in the group and said:

"Darling, what will you drink?"

The honest answer would have been "strychnine," I felt so absolutely despairing for a moment. Six months at Compter Hall, supposedly the very best place for alcoholics (let me *not* think, oh God please, let me not think about the cost, over seven hundred pounds of poor Aunt Madge's legacy!), and a fortnight out in the world. Now here we were again.

I said, "Tomato juice, please," trying to make it sound as though that really were my choice; dieting or Puritanic.

Larry said, "A wise choice. One of us must stay sober in this town of ravening wolves." He turned and said, "A tomato juice, and the same all round." He turned back. "I've just been hearing the inside story about that place, darling."

One of the men—he looked rather like Peter so I judged him to be a farmer and the owner of the red setter which lay just behind him—said, rather shyly:

"Too bad really, advertising like that. On the other hand they were in a spot. Told to pull it down by one ministry, told to keep it up by another. I guess you found it pretty grim inside, Mrs. Benyon."

(Completely true to pattern. "My name's Benyon, Larry Benyon." Never mind about theirs. What did their names matter?

And so, off we go again. "Met an absolutely charming fellow in the bar at the Station Hotel. Name of Benyon." "Chap named Benyon in the bar this morning. New to the place. Wasn't half sloshed, too."

And any one of these three might have some connection with the firm of Curwen and Eliot, makers of agricultural machinery, where Peter was trying his hardest to persuade Tom Eliot, whom he knew, to give Larry a job.)

I said, "Actually it's far better inside than out. That's why I came looking for you, Larry. I really do want you to see it. It has great possibilities."

Larry said, "That's my wife all over! Once somebody offered us our choice out of a litter of puppies. Dachshunds, impeccable pedigree. Three were show specimens, the fourth had his legs on back to front or something. She chose him!"

So I did, and nobody ever had a better dog, faithful, intelligent, and brave as a lion. I'd have him still if we hadn't had to move to that beastly little bungalow, open to the road. So he was run down. And may he rest well, with his insufficiently bowed legs and loyal heart, under the rosemary bush that I planted for remembrance. My God, I'm now going to cry in a public place . . . over a dog, eighteen months dead. After all I've been through. . . .

The one I thought was a farmer said:

"Oh, I can well understand that. In a dog looks don't mean much. But with a house . . ." He was drinking beer, and he picked up his mug and drained it, said something about collecting some chicks, and went off. Larry looked anxiously into everyone's glass. The only other man drinking whisky said:

"No, no, old man. This is mine." There is one of him in every bar in England, just waiting for Larry to come along.

I said, "Larry, I think we should have lunch and then go and look . . ." He interrupted by thrusting under my nose a smudgy, handwritten menu.

"You go and stoke up, darling. All kinds of goodies await you just through there." He nodded towards a door. "Brown

Windsor soup well thickened with glue; plaice fried in train oil; boiled mutton with caper sauce—the caper in memory of what the sheep cut twenty years ago."

Whether he had memorised the menu at a glance, or had studied it beforehand, or merely guessed, I don't know; but that was exactly what was on offer, and it all sounded good to me. I have a hearty appetite, and in the not-too-distant past I hadn't always been able to satisfy it.

I looked quickly at the man behind the bar to see whether he had taken offence at Larry's words. Apparently not. The man who was drinking beer drained his glass and set it down.

"Talking about lunch. I must be off. Be seeing you around, I expect."

That left the two whisky drinkers and me. I made another effort.

"I don't think I could face boiled mutton alone, Larry. Come and support me."

He shot me one of his venomous glances and for a moment I was afraid he was going to speak rudely and try to work up a scene. However, he only said:

"I'm not nearly fortified enough yet. You go ahead and leave me here with my friend, who is, like me, more for the bucket than the manger."

"How right you are," the man said. He raised his fresh glass and said, "Incredible luck! And don't go buying any Old Vines. White elephant. Absolute white elephant. Know the definition of a white elephant? Gift that gives the recipient more trouble than it's worth. I looked it up, once. Kings of Siam, if they wanted to ruin anybody, sent him a white elephant. Interesting, eh? The Old Vine, case in point. Is a gift really. Anything these days with a roof and four walls is a gift at a thousand. But it'd ruin you. Unless, of course you're Rothschild . . ."

He looked us over with eyes which, though whisky-reddened, were shrewd enough. We obviously weren't Rothschild. My camel-hair coat was seven years old and, to put it mildly, had had a hard life. Larry's clothes were newer but not of such quality. About two years before, at the end of our sojourn in London, he'd disappeared one day and stayed away for a week. I'd gone almost mad with anxiety; the police were no help. It wasn't a crime, they told me, for a man to leave home—unless his family became chargeable to the rates —and unless I had reason to think some crime had been committed there was nothing they could do. When he did come back, without apology or explanation, he had on a pair of trousers, filthy and past repair, and a shirt, that was all. So he had had to have a new outfit.

Remembering this as Larry's new friend assessed our financial position, and seeing Larry drinking again, I had suddenly such a feeling of weariness and failure that my legs went weak and my sight blurred. I just managed to get to a chair near a table in the corner and sit down. There was an ash tray on the table and the sight of it set me off. I have my weakness, my addiction, too, and I suppose that it has made me at once more, and less, tolerant of Larry than I should otherwise be. I daresay that my smoking has some deep psychological significance; Father thought it was definitely immoral for a female to smoke, but Peter didn't, so whenever Peter came home for holidays or week-ends I used to smoke with him on the sly— never at any other time, for one thing I couldn't have afforded it; and thus smoking became associated, for me, with the happy times when Peter was home and the atmosphere was more cheerful, and we had roasting beef instead of stewing steak. Then, when Larry and I were first married, we were comparatively well off, by my previous standards rich indeed; he was earning a thousand a year then, with good prospects. So I smoked. Later on, when things went wrong, I'd had to give it up, but I never mastered the craving, and in Salisbury, when I began to earn a little money, I'd occasionally buy myself a packet of cigarettes for a treat, and then make up for it by washing all the sheets instead of sending them to the laundry. (I had seven beds on the go most of the time, so that was quite a job.) Now I had Aunt Madge's legacy, and Peter was always tossing me his packet and saying, "Fill your case," but I was determined not to become enslaved again, so I rationed myself to three a day. Sometimes I felt that if I could do that about cigarettes Larry might do the same about his whisky; but of course that wasn't fair. His was a disease.

I took out a cigarette, lit it and smoked it slowly. I wondered whether I should have risked a scene and insisted that Larry come away from the bar. That was the hell of it; whatever I did seemed wrong. Worse than wrong, useless. There'd been a time when I'd cried; I'd cried myself silly; I'd nagged, protested, argued, cajoled. "Why do you do it?" I'd asked a hundred times. "There must be *some* reason."

He never attempted to explain. Mostly he wouldn't even answer; he'd either walk away or sit there, looking ill-used. Other times he'd say, "Oh, for God's sake!" or, "Shut up!" Sometimes I used to think that he was a little mad—on this one point. When I got my hands on my legacy and said, as tactfully and pleasantly as possible, "Larry, will you now, to please me, go to Compter Hall and try this wonderful cure?" he'd said, "Oh yes. I don't mind going and joining the other bottle boys." He behaved, he always had, as though his complaint was no more serious than, say, nail-biting, and all the rest of us were making a great fuss about nothing. And all the time he had only to look round and *see*. In the eight years we'd been married he'd had six different jobs, each worse paid than the one before, and finally no job at all. Twice he'd done things which were definitely dishonest, things he could very well have been prosecuted for. He once said, in one of his gay, drunken, communicative moments, "It's a good thing I'm not a lawyer or a medical man, they'd have defrocked me, wouldn't they?" He was an engineer, quite brilliant; but engineering is in its way a closed circle too; if one firm of repute employs a man for nine months and then lets him go, even if no specific reason is given, other firms *know*.

I couldn't, at that distance, hear every word; but I saw two more double whiskies served. I thought, suddenly—Where does all this money come from? That income-tax rebate?

Income tax is something I have never properly understood. You seem to pay it on what you earn, but actually you pay it in advance or something. While Larry was in Compter, because in his last job he'd been on the pay-as-you-earn level, and paid, and then become unemployed, there was a voucher for a rebate, quite a lot, which would have been very useful to me; but I couldn't cash the voucher; only Larry could do that. By the time he got it he was in that state of rehabilitation where he was allowed to go into the little town, Compter-under-Lynn, by himself. So he went in, drew his money, and went straight into the local where the first person he saw was one of the staff. They drank a beer together and walked home. The doctor in charge was quite jubilant about that little incident; it was proof, he said, that Larry had learned to handle his problem. And I was ashamed because I immediately thought—I bet if he hadn't run into somebody he knew, he'd have drunk whisky until he was senseless. And that was just the sort of thing I shouldn't think, and mustn't think . . . and did.

I finished my cigarette and ground it out. Then I stood up. Tact, consideration for the patient's feelings, unobtrusive supervision be hanged. I couldn't sit here in a corner and wait until Larry, after another couple of drinks, turned incoherent and incapable. I'd have to do what I had on certain other shudderingly memorable occasions done, just take him by the arm and walk him away. (Once I'd done it in a pub in Chelsea where there was a cadaverous, long-haired young man with a guitar, and he began to strum and improvise a song; "Momma, come fetch me home" was all I heard then; but afterwards I heard it on the wireless and everywhere. . . .)

On this day I was spared the worst. Just as I crossed to the bar the other whisky drinker set down his glass and said:

"Joe, take a look out the window. My car waiting?"

Without glancing at the window the barman said:

"It's been there fifteen minutes, Mr. Summerville."

"Got myself dis-disqualified at Christmas," Mr. Summerville explained. "Road like glass. Anybody else they'd say, 'Poor chap!' Being me, 'Bad boy. Doghouse for six months.' Bloody unjust. Nice seeing you, see you again if you settle here, but no Old Vines, mind, no Old Vines. Altogether too slippery."

Weaving slightly, he made for the door.

I said, "Larry, are you sure you couldn't eat something?"

There was one theory about alcoholism being allied to a protein deficiency.

"That is one of the few things I am sure of. I told you to go ahead and eat."

"I'm not hungry. Let's go and take a proper look at this house."

"Oh, all right; if we must." Resentment and unwillingness sounded in his voice, showed in his face, in his very walk; but at least I'd got him away and he wasn't too far gone.

Neither of us spoke during the short walk, but as we stood on the pavement opposite the house, waiting to cross the road, he said:

"Just take a look at it. Just take a look. You've had some daft ideas in your time, but this is the daftest. I'm not going in."

"Please, Larry. Honestly it's much better inside. Some parts of it are fascinating."

So I got him in, and felt a mild triumph until he started, with another unpredictable switch of mood, one of the most

irritating tricks he was inclined to when about three-quarters
drunk.

"Absolutely fascinating. How right you were, Fran, I
wouldn't have missed this fascinating experience for anything.
What a fascinating way to treat a wall, seven different colours.
Excuse me while I patronise this fascinating jakes. . . ."

Nobody who hasn't been subjected to it can imagine how
nerve-racking that kind of thing can be. I wanted to scream.
It was futile to try and direct his attention to what was good
about the place, he ignored all that, sought out the horrid and
squalid things and called them fascinating.

We came to the ugly, but quite sound, iron staircase which
led to one section of the upper floor.

Larry stared at it with mock appreciation.

"Complete with fire escape too. How absolutely fascinating."

Something gave way in me.

"There's no point in going on with this," I said.

His manner changed again.

"I'm glad you realise it, at last. I said so, didn't I, the minute you showed me the advertisement."

That helpless, hopeless, baffled feeling came over me again,
with, again, the urgent need to sit down. I thought of sitting
on one of the steps of the iron staircase, but they were all
filthy; and then I remembered seeing, from one of the upper
rooms, into the long narrow garden, at the far end of which
there was a seat. There was a door in the wall which divided
the garden from the back yard in which we stood; I opened it,
walked quickly through, and along the path, not seeing anything, just willing my shaking legs to hold up until I reached
the seat. I did it, and sank down. The shakiness had spread,
I could feel my head wagging as though I were a victim of
paralysis agitans, and only by biting my teeth together hard
could I keep them from chattering. I drew some deep breaths

through my nose; deep breathing was supposed to have a steadying effect. . . .

Larry had followed me into the garden and came strolling towards me.

"What's the matter *now?*" he asked, as though this were the culminating act in a long series of curious happenings.

I unclipped my teeth and said in a voice which shook so much that it sounded as though I were about to cry, though I was as far from the relief of tears as I had ever been in my life.

"Everything. You won't look, or listen, or take anything seriously."

"You mean you expect me to take this broken-down barn seriously?"

"It's a place I could buy at a price I could afford; and a place where I could earn a living. . . ."

"Oh," he said, with the kind of desperate patience one uses at the end of a long day with a troublesome child, "we're back on that, are we?"

Thousands, literally thousands of times, when he had adopted that attitude, so utterly stupid and irresponsible, I'd formed scathing angry sentences in my mind. Sometimes for whole days I'd go about my work, mentally berating him, going into every detail of his ruinous behaviour, reeling off sermons that would have done my father no discredit. But for the last five years—ever since the doctor who'd looked after me when I had Sally, and who was one of the first people I'd ever really talked to about Larry had said that alcoholism was a disease and just as involuntary and pitiable as cancer—I had never said any of the things that came into my mind. Before that I had. And my silence was made easier by the reflection that in the past nothing I had said, however angry, however logical, however pleading had had the slightest effect.

Now, sitting there, I was honestly surprised to hear my own

voice saying some of the things which ordinarily would have been a silent monologue.

"We're back on that," my shaking voice said. "Somebody has to think about what this family is going to live on. I can't go out to work; for one thing I'm untrained, for another I can't leave Paul and Sally. So all I can do is what I did in Salisbury in that beastly cramped little bungalow, take in other children whose parents for some reason or another can't make a home for them. I could buy this place for eight hundred pounds, and do the most essential repairs for a thousand, or twelve hundred. And that would still leave a little in the bank for an emergency. . . . You know what Peter said the other evening, even if Tom Eliot does give you a job it won't be more than seven hundred and fifty a year. This"—I waved my wobbling hand in a gesture that included the house, the back yards, the iron staircase, and the garden—"would help out. I must have something firm and settled. I can't go on as we have been, never knowing from day to day. . . ."

In my silent monologues I always spoke in a firm, clear, controlled voice, but now I sounded like a very worn gramophone record played on a machine with a loose needle. By contrast, when Larry spoke, he sounded cool and reasonable; anybody listening behind the overgrown yew hedge around the stone seat would have thought he was the sober one, reasoning with a hysteric drunk.

"I haven't the slightest intention of staying in Baildon and working for Peter's good friend for a pittance. Or of living in a mended-up barn with a lot of squalling brats. I can read advertisements too, you know. Yes, I can still manage to read advertisements."

I was so used to him, so accustomed to all the stages of his retreat from reality that I merely thought that he had substituted the word "advertisement" for the word "fascinating." I had a little secret pang of shame because I, cold sober, had tried to argue with him, three parts drunk. But he fumbled in his pocket and produced a letter and a crumpled, worn piece of newspaper which from the print I recognised as being from *The Times*.

"The postman came while you were telling Mrs. Hooley what to give the children to eat mid-day. I put the letter in my pocket and didn't read it until I was by myself in that squalid little bar. Like to look?"

I thought to myself with amazement—*How* could anyone keep a letter, presumably of importance, for two and a half hours without opening it?

Once again the feeling I had that I was dealing with something not quite human assailed me, and my bones shook, my sight blurred. I saw "Government of Nigeria" and a list of engineering qualifications "or equivalent," and some sums of money, £2,100 the lowest, and "first-class passage." That was all in the advertisement. The letter was simple, a date and place for an interview.

"These countries," Larry said, "are emerging. There's some future there. Baildon always was a one-horse town, and now even the horse is dead."

I was never very good at geography and most of what I knew about foreign countries came from reading novels. Nigeria was in Africa; tropical. Out of a vague vision of steamy heat, great markets run by black "mammies," and a horrible rite known as horse-tithing, three things stood out and clamoured for my attention. One, in the tropics even ordinary men tended to drink more than they should; two, hot countries were unsuitable for white children after the age of six; three, Africa was a long way from Peter. All three mattered to me, but I mentioned only the one least likely to give offence to Larry.

"I don't think Nigeria would be very suitable for the children."

"Does that matter? Other people leave their children. Peter'd have them for holidays. There's your choice, Fran; park or be parked upon."

I didn't know what to say for a moment. I had honestly tried to be motherly to the children left with me, tried to treat them as individuals, not just a means of making ends meet . . . and I had no *reason* for thinking that I was any more honest or kind than any other woman, no reason at all, yet the idea of leaving Paul and Sally and just sailing away appalled me. I turned to take a look at Larry, who could so lightly suggest such a thing; and I saw that he was regarding me with a peculiar fixity. There was a slyness too. . . .

"Or," he said, "if you don't like that idea, you could stay with Peter and go on stuffing them with all that healthy farm produce. I'd send you money, of course."

The full truth was like a smack in the face. The very marrow of my bones shook. I had the insane idea that I might be on the verge of a stroke. Twenty-eight was surely very young, but strain and stress. . . .

I groped in my bag and took out another cigarette and lit it very carefully. Then I said, not looking at him:

"It's me you want to get away from, isn't it?"

It seemed a long time before he said:

"Not you. I want to get away from Paul and Sally's devoted Mum, and Peter's ill-done-by little sister, and Dr. Weiss's deputy head-shrinker."

He spoke very quietly, and very bitterly.

I thought—and it was far from the first time—of our wedding. It was in June, and because of all my links with Girl Guides, Youth Clubs, Mothers' Meetings, Civil Defence, and the Red Cross, to mention only a few, it was a much showier affair than anyone would have expected. It was June and the church was full of roses, so full that the air was almost swooning with the sweetness. And a double choir, mustered from both Father's parishes. The Voice that breathed o'er Eden.

To have and to hold, for better, for worse, for richer, for poorer, in sickness, in health, *till death do us part*. . . .

Choking with love and wonder, rigid with good intentions, I'd meant every word.

People laugh about religion and its old-fashioned ceremonies, but I swear that often, often, often, when I was full of anger and rebellion, or cold despair, I'd thought of that, and thought that it was a vow, and however much everything became confused one thing was clear, to keep a vow *must* be right.

Now, between one heartbeat and another, I realised that there are other sorts of death than the one that calls for a funeral.

Larry said, "Well, it's up to you."

It was like standing on the edge of a wide, turbulent sea and being offered two ships. One the Nigeria, manned by Larry, into which I must step alone, knowing that it was bound to go down; the other my own, the Old Vine, where I should be captain and crew, where I could have my children and in which, if I tried hard enough, I had some hope of staying afloat.

I said, "I'm sorry, Larry. I can't leave the children."

"And I can't live in Baildon." He didn't say he was sorry. "So that's all there is to it." He was glad.

Despite that, I had some half-baked idea of saying couldn't we compromise, go somewhere else in England, start again. But we'd done that so many times. And where else would I find a place so spacious, so beautiful and so cheap? So exactly suited for my purpose?

"There's really no point in sitting here any longer, is there?" Larry said, and looked at his watch. I looked at mine. It was two o'clock. The bar at the Station Hotel would be open for another hour. He'd go straight there and get absolutely sozzled. I knew it. He knew it. And we both knew that there was absolutely nothing we could do about it.

"I'll make my own way home," he said. "And tomorrow I'll go to London."

He stood up and walked along the path. From the back he looked boyish and vulnerable, and the old weakness in me made me long to run after him and protect him. But I knew, with a clarity that I had never known before, that to do so would be useless and merely make him hate me more than ever. We were dead to one another. I thought of that silly old song:

> When I am dead, don't bury me at all,
> Just pickle my bones in alcohol.

I sat there for quite a long time, thinking this and that. How long it would take for Paul and Sally to resign themselves to a permanently fatherless state. How glad, really, Peter would be. He did so blame himself. Once he'd said to me, "I do curse myself for ever bringing this about. I'd have shot the bugger first, had I known." And I'd said, "Peter, Larry is my husband, you mustn't talk that way."

I looked about the garden with half-noticing eyes and saw that though it had been neglected lately, it had once been well cared for. Daffodils and polyanthus were in bloom, tulips like green lances were thrusting through; the rose bushes were russet-coloured with new growth. There was a very surprisingly well-built summerhouse, just the place for children who loved to play houses.

The sun went in and a chilly little wind sprang up. I knew a moment of complete desolation, but I braced myself; I thought—I wanted to go over the house alone, and here I am, alone with the house.

So I went in. And despite the fact that so much of it was awful and dismaying, I felt again the feeling I'd had when I'd first entered, a homecoming feeling, a sense of belonging and acceptance, something I believe the Americans have a word for—togetherness.

By the time I had walked all over it again, I had a feeling of ownership. I should make my near offer of eight hundred, but if they stood out I'd give the full thousand, so it was almost as good as mine already. I locked every lockable door, and eventually stood in the hall, with its floor of worn oak planks, each fifteen inches wide, and the beautiful staircase.

I thought some of my regrettably down-to-earth thoughts. The truth is that most people, when they hand over their children to somebody else's care, have some guilty feelings; and when they leave them in a nasty, cramped little bungalow those guilty feelings are inflamed. I could make the Old Vine the kind of place where people who felt like that would be comforted, thinking that their children were being left in *privileged* circumstances. Which is how, if I had ever decided to leave Paul and Sally, I would wish to feel.

Out at the farm there was a great old Welsh dresser and a tallboys which another aunt had left me and which I had never, in my peripatetic life, been able to house. Peter had kept them for me, and once, when I was on the rocks, I'd written and asked him to sell them for me. Ten pounds would have been very welcome. He had just installed his milking parlour and was very hard up, but he scratched together fifty pounds and sent it to me with an elaborate, homemade pawn ticket. Sugaring the pill of charity. The dresser on one side, the tallboys on the other, and the place would look furnished. And fifty pounds, carefully expended on good old secondhand stuff. . . .

God, I'm going all mercenary again. Consider the lilies of the field . . . Take no thought for the morrow. And yet you must set alongside those dictates the parable of the unjust steward, and the one about the unused talents. And even the little boy who had thought to provide himself with a few loaves and fishes and thus enabled Christ to feed five thousand.

I just do not know. I've done the best I could. I'm prepared to do the best I can.

God, I've failed with Larry, let me not fail with the children. . . .

I leaned against a strong old carved pillar which ended the rails of the banisters and I prayed to something I didn't understand and which I could hardly hope would understand me. It was all such a muddle. God, don't let Larry suffer too much humiliation, God let me get this place for eight hundred, God forgive me for not managing better, God help me. . . .

All around me the dusk thickened; the old boards, having been trodden on, creaked. The old house seemed to gather strength and purpose. Battered, both of us, but not yet completely defeated. Shaken, abandoned . . . but ready to go on again, together. . . .